DIVERTED

HOUSTON NEAL GRAY

This is a work of fiction and is presented as such. All names, characters, places, events, and incidents are solely the product of the author's imagination, or are used strictly to advance the story and are used fictitiously. Any resemblance to actual persons, living or dead, is strictly coincidental and unintentional. Historical events are used in promoting the fictitious story.

Published by Lower Coast Media, LLC

Text formatting by Lisa DeSpain of Ebookconverting.com
Cover design by Deborah Bradseth of Tugboat Design

ISBN: 978-0-9904653-0-0

www.houstonnealgray.com

For Jo Ann

With whom the journey began

ACKNOWLEDGEMENTS

Most things don't just happen and so it was with this novel. My thanks to all those who read, reread, commented, persevered and never told me to leave them alone. I must thank Jo Ann first and foremost because she encouraged me day after day and never stopped believing the story was worth writing. It simply would not have happened without you. I also thank my daughters, Savannah, Ciera, and Angelis because they never complained and never tired of hearing about it.

Andy Lang, a true friend who saw enough in the story to get the opinion of several others to further encourage me, and for the many articles and links on writing which helped beyond measure.

To all my friends, especially Ed Moise, Rick Conway, Kathy McBride and Dania LaSpada, who took the time to read the early draft and encouraged me to proceed. I am humbly grateful for your unselfish time devoted to my effort.

CHAPTER ONE

Rainey came to, dazed and in pain. He lay on his back and couldn't move. His mind was blank and he struggled for any remembrance, like a drowning man struggling for air. He clenched his eyes closed and begged for some thought or memory. Fear and panic had Rainey in its grip and tightened around him. A state of falling into a dark void washed over him, and though he tried to cry out nothing came. He quit fighting, and the plummeting stopped.

A disorienting feeling had fogged his mind and as Rainey again opened his eyes it was gone. All he could see was a vast, cloudless blue sky. Nothing came to him, no inkling of where he was, or how he had come to be there. He tried to lift his head and a throbbing pain transcended throughout his body. Even his minimalist attempt to move produced a pounding ache. He lay still, holding his breath in an effort to gain control.

Again he tried to relax. He questioned where he was and how he had gotten...

"SHIT!" he yelled as he reached with his left arm to prop himself up. An acute, hot pain close above his left wrist shot up his arm straight to his head, intensifying the already severe headache. He collapsed and fell back grabbing his left arm, holding it against his stomach. His loud scream had been inaudible, and he heard no sounds around him.

Rainey concentrated and still nothing came to him. His right arm relaxed its grip on his left, his eyes closed, and exhausted, he drifted off. Awakening with a start, his eyes flashed open. The headache and body pains were still present, but less intense as when he had regained consciousness. Rainey's breathing slowed and his body no longer trembled. His right hand fell to the ground and he clenched soft, pliable sand. A faint wheeze, far off in the distance, rhythmically sounded. His breathing was starting to register as sound and he was encouraged his hearing loss might be temporary.

"HEY! ...HEY! ...hey..." He yelled loudly but heard a faint, distant echo of his voice. Again he lay still, and far off in the distance he thought he heard the sound of gentle surf.

The heat of the sun engulfed him and small beads of sweat blistered from his forehead. A slight breeze, similar to an early summer morning wind, swirled from all directions but did not cool him. His memory had been slow to cooperate but now ridiculous thoughts started to invade him. This is a bad dream, he thought, or maybe some sort of a practical joke. Perhaps he had been drugged or kidnapped. Ridiculous, but he could not stop them.

Rainey again sat up, but this time without using his arms, a sit up of sorts and a struggle for a guy in his early forties who had given up serious exercise years ago. He crossed his legs Indian style, bent completely forward, bowing his back, while again holding his arm. He grimaced as a dull pain needled his lower back, with the stretching of the muscles. As he straightened upright his eyes followed the white, sandy beach stretching out in front of him. Beyond the sand, clear water soon turned a pristine blue, appearing endless as it reached to the horizon and married into the sky.

Rainey turned to his left and saw tall, thin palm trees amidst a line of dense bushes, grass, and a thicket of trees, all set back from the beach at least thirty yards. He swiveled to his right and saw more of the same. He wanted to collapse back onto the sand, hoping the next time he sat up this would all be gone. But he knew better.

"WHERE AM I?" he cried out. His head lifted after the spontaneous outburst. His voice had sounded more normal. He nodded, thankful for the sound, and gazed out at the vast, empty sea.

The air was dense on Rainey's skin and he tasted salt as he licked his lips. The thick humidity covered him. A street scene flashed through his mind. His back straightened and he strained his neck, as if to see more, but the image disappeared. His shoulders drooped as he relaxed and concentrated. More thoughts. The French Quarter. New Orleans. A quizzical expression registered for a moment and he remembered he had grown up in south Louisiana, where the days of summer were often so humid everything moved slowly, as if fighting against an invisible tide. The familiar feeling had swept over him, helping him to remember.

His head throbbed while random images popped into his mind like exploding flash bulbs. As he sat a particularly pungent odor emanated up from him. However long he had been unconscious was enough for him to have soiled himself. A flush of embarrassment consumed him and he was reminded of an accident in grade school when the teacher refused to excuse him to the bathroom. The embarrassment waned and was soon gone, replaced by anger.

"Now what the hell am I supposed to do?" he yelled.

Taking a deep breath, he struggled, almost clown like, to get up. A simple act of rising from a sitting position took on a new challenge without the use of his left arm. Favoring the injured arm he was careful not to push off with it. His legs were weak and dizziness engulfed him but a moment later subsided. Grimacing, Rainey rose to his feet and though he swayed and wobbled like an aging alcoholic on a three day binge, he managed to stand erect.

The water's edge was less than fifty feet from where he stood. He looked down at his feet. His shoes were missing but his socks were still on. He decided against removing them knowing he would never get them off without falling. He cautiously turned and started walking toward the water. His pace was slow and his body still ached, but he felt better as he walked.

Entering the tepid, salt water he waded out and stopped when it was waist deep. Never before had he seen water this clear and he watched his sock-covered toes wiggle on the sandy bottom.

The flashbacks started again. He had a job. There was a big warehouse. He was standing at a bar eating raw oysters. His mother's face smiled at him. Big O...who the hell is Big O? He tried connecting the images but then went blank. Relax, and let it come, he thought.

Rainey was able to remove his pants while standing in the water. He swished the pants back and forth and watched the soiled underwear descend, wavering to the sandy bottom, abandoned. He hooked a belt loop of his pants on a finger of his injured arm. The arm was swollen but did not ache as much as before. Maybe it's a sprain he thought, or a mild fracture, but certainly not completely broken. As he held onto his pants, he proceeded to clean himself with his right hand. Reaching down, he grabbed a handful of sand and gently rubbed it against the cheeks of his butt sure this would aid in the cleaning process. He repeated scrubbing himself, gently working the sand between his legs several times. It helped to clean, but he stopped before rubbing his skin raw especially while standing in salt water.

The water was calm and he was buoyant but Rainey still struggled to put his pants on. A sudden chill ran down his spine and his head jerked up. He stared into the trees. Was he being watched? Were there others? Rainey walked out of the water scanning the trees, seeing nothing, but not releasing his stare. Water dripped into the sand as he stood in the tropical heat, his eyes flicking back and forth.

Rainey looked down the beach and caught the glimmer of the sun reflecting off a large object partially obscured in the trees and foliage. He started walking toward it and the glint of the sun disappeared. At the edge of the thicket small vines with leaves snaked across the ground, intertwined, and changed direction. An unfamiliar grass about six inches long grew among the vines and covered most of the sand. The roughness of it all intimidated Rainey, especially without shoes on. He cautiously stepped, prepared for a briar or thorn to jab his foot. Instead, the ground cover was softer than expected and reminded him of the St. Augustine-grass lawns in the neighborhood where he had grown up. He took large steps, his eyes focused on the ground, moving toward the partially hidden object. Rainey stopped, steadied himself, took a deep breath and raised his eyes. The tail section of a private jet loomed over him. Rainey recognized the plane, and a flood of memories came rushing back and jolted him.

CHAPTER TWO

Rainey stared, his heart racing while he struggled to understand what had happened. He moved to his right several feet, keeping his distance as he surveyed the wreckage. The plane was badly damaged and beyond repair. The right wing was still attached although dented and bent, the tip dug into the sand, keeping the plane upright with a slight list. The two jet engines were still attached to the rear of the fuselage. The engine on the right side was packed with sand and the opening was completely obscured. Behind the plane was a furrow so precisely cut it appeared as if it had been intentionally excavated. The jet must have slammed into the shallow water and bounced, he thought. The momentum obviously pushed it through the sand, into the trees and brush. He remembered being on the plane, but he did not remember the crash.

Rainey sat at the edge of the thicket. With his legs crossed, he rocked back and forth while staring at the plane. The sun and the heat intensified his incredible thirst. His tongue was swollen, and cotton mouth did not describe the dryness. It was like having spit out a mouthful of desert sand. Water and supplies, including food, were on the plane but Rainey struggled, apprehensive to get up and enter the plane. He was afraid of what he might see. The tropical sun beat down on him and compounded his discomfort.

Desperate for water he stood up, but this time with less difficulty. Rainey walked around the tail section to the left side of the jet and stopped. The pounding of his heart vibrated in his head. The door was hanging open and he had no memory of the crash, opening the door or leaving the plane.

"Quit being such a coward and look inside the damn plane. For God's sake," he said. "HELLO?" he yelled.

Sweat ran down his face and his breathing was labored. He stood outside the door and stuck his head through the opening. The floor and seats were strewn with bottles of water, cans of food, bags of chips, magazines, clothes, papers and all one might expect to find on a private plane. Reaching into the plane he picked up a bottle of water, unscrewed the cap, and downed it in large gulps. He squeezed the bottle tightly, collapsing it in his hand. He picked up another bottle, ignored the dizzy feeling and drank. His stomach cramped and he was nauseous. He leaned back against the door frame and breathed deeply. He should have drunk slowly, but his thirst was beyond anything he had ever experienced. Thoughts of old movies he had watched with his mother came to him. Never give a man dying of thirst lots of water, but instead start with small sips. His face flushed with anger.

"First of all, I'm not dying, and secondly, who the hell can believe those old black and white movies anyway." He spoke with anger, overwhelmed with questions but no answers.

The queasy feeling passed, helped by his anger. Rainey tried to remember what had happened, how he had survived. Moving into the plane might help, he thought.

Rainey turned and faced the open door. It was difficult but he raised his left leg two feet and propped his foot against the bottom of the opening. He grabbed a handle on the inside of the plane and his face contorted from the pain and effort. He lunged and simultaneously pulled himself up. His momentum propelled him into the plane and across the floor, stopping when he fell against the wall.

"God, what's next," he said through clenched teeth, his left arm pounding with more pain. Rainey stared but didn't move, as if his feet were shackled to the floor. The small cockpit door hung open. Eeriness pervaded the cabin. Taking a deep breath he cautiously stepped toward the open door, preparing for the worst. Rainey agonized with each of the four short steps. He stopped, stood in the cockpit door and looked at the pilot's seat. It was empty. Creston, his best friend for more than twenty years, was gone. Rainey's eyes focused on a large area of dried blood.

CHAPTER THREE

Panic gripped Rainey as he remembered. Creston had been flying the plane. Standing between the pilot and co-pilot seats, he bent at the waist and closed his eyes in an effort to slow the thoughts rushing in.

"Stop!" he yelled. The outburst cleared his mind and his concern turned to Creston. Where the hell was he and what had happened to him? A rush of adrenaline coursed through Rainey and he set to work.

The first aid kit was located in the locker mounted on the bulkhead behind the pilot's seat. Inside were syringes, a stethoscope, several vials of drugs, bottles of pills, and other items foreign to him. Rainey was intimidated, looking at more medical supplies than expected. He remembered taking CPR and first aid classes, and wished he had paid more attention. His left arm throbbed and Rainey wanted to immobilize it with a splint before setting out to find Creston.

Rainey took two flat sticks about an inch wide and twelve inches long from the kit and placed one on the top of his left arm. He wrapped adhesive tape around his wrist, placed the second stick on the under side and finished wrapping. His arm still throbbed but the pain subsided.

"Good enough for now," he said moving back to the door of the plane and climbing down. It was late in the afternoon and long shadows were stretching out from the trees, creeping toward the water's edge. Rainey looked toward the sun and guessed there were several hours of daylight left.

Rainey concentrated on the many footprints around the plane and questioned whether he had made them all. The ground cover leading away from the plane was thick but he noticed several footprints in the sand, obviously made by bare feet. Had Creston lost his shoes, too, he wondered.

To the rear of the plane the beach sloped to the water. A hundred feet or so to the right, an exposed coral reef was visible for at least several miles. The vastness of the sea and the reflection of the sun on the water were deceiving, and he was unsure of the distance. Perhaps this was an atoll with other islands connected by the reef, and if this were the case then the calm water was a lagoon.

Rainey walked to the water's edge looking for signs of activity other than the ones he had made. There were none. He looked into the trees, calmed his fear and started the search.

The change in elevation from the beach to the tree line was slightly less than five feet. Rainey labored in the loose sand as he ascended toward the dense tropical growth. The thick grass and foliage tangled around his feet as he entered the island forest and he stopped after passing the first trees. Uncomfortable, like walking into a dark alley, his breathing quickened and he watched the shadows move as the wind rustled the trees.

The evening was fast approaching and anxiety consumed Rainey. Was Creston alive? Had he gone looking for help? Rainey wondered if he should return to the plane and wait. He was emotionally crashing and his indecision was overpowering, pummeling him like a boxer. Two bits of advice from years ago came back to him. Should he become lost in the vast, uninhabited marsh of south Louisiana or anywhere, rule number one was always stay where you were. A person had a better chance of being found if they would not move around. Rule number two was to climb a tree or structure to get your bearings. Both rules seemed useless to Rainey. He had been in the same spot for hours and nothing had changed. And, with his bad arm climbing anything would be a challenge. Rainey stood still for several minutes and then shook his head. Some decisions are made for you, he thought as he marched into the jungle.

"Creston!" he yelled and then held his breath. Again he shouted Creston's name, waited for a reply, and again was disappointed. He traveled several hundred yards and came upon a tree with limbs low enough to climb and tall enough for a better view if he could manage to get high enough.

Rainey grasped a sturdy limb but his peripheral vision caught movement to his right. He turned his head quickly, but there was nothing. He stared, sure he had seen something move. His breathing quickened and he decided against climbing the tree.

Darkness was on him. Rainey had gone off without water or provisions and his stomach ached from lack of food.

"Damn, DAMN!"

The trek back to the plane was faster than the journey out and Rainey had nothing to show for his effort but a sweat stained shirt and a ravenous appetite. How could he think of food when his best friend was probably in dire need of help?

Rainey paced back and forth by the plane, his right arm flailing. "It's senseless to go looking in the dark. I wouldn't see him if he was ten feet away." Rainey stopped and stared into the blackness of the trees. "Admit it you coward, you don't know what's out there and you're scared." He took a deep breath. "And stop talking to yourself."

Rainey sat crossed legged on the floor of the plane in darkness. The minimal ambient light outside did not intrude through the open door and the absence of light intensified his unrest. He patted the floor with his hand, moving it back and forth in an arc as he crawled toward the rear of the cabin. The plastic wrapping of a honey bun crinkled and he felt the pastry squish as his knee smashed it into the floor. He ate as he considered his situation.

The plane was equipped with large seats good for use as beds when reclined. Although it was hot and stuffy, Rainey decided to sleep inside. Handling the heat would be easier than trying to get comfortable outside on the sand, even if he could convince himself there was no threat, that he was alone on the island. He argued back and forth, stay and rest or search for Creston. His eyes closed, and though his body ached and his shirt was wet with perspiration, sleep overtook him.

The morning sun illuminated the cabin and woke Rainey. He stared at the ceiling, disoriented until he remembered where he was. His exhaustion had put him into a long sleep.

"Creston," he said. His body ached more this day than before but the pain in his arm had subsided. He rolled over and fell off the make shift bed.

"Damn it." Hearing his voice gave him comfort and he managed to get his feet planted and stand. He searched the plane and found a bag large enough to carry water and food, and with a strap long enough to wear over his shoulder. He hurried to throw enough into the bag to last most of the day, placed the strap over his right shoulder, and climbed down from the plane. His awareness this morning was much keener. He inhaled deeply and studied the area in all directions. The sound of the surf was loud and closer than he had realized. Because the plane had crashed near the end of the island he had one direction to travel. He headed back into the thick of the trees.

Rainey drank a bottle of water as he trudged along over thick grass, vines, fallen leaves and branches, working his way through the trees and bushes. He traveled a quarter of a mile or so in about an hour, taking his time, carefully looking for any indication Creston had come this way. Frustrated with his slow progress, Rainey decided to get a better feel for where he was and the size of the island. Reluctantly, he admitted he had to climb one of the taller trees. He looked upward and out trying to spot the tallest and most climbable tree and noticed one about twenty yards away. It was tall enough and had low limbs easier for climbing. He took a step toward it.

"Where ya goin, pal?"

Rainey stopped short.

"Hey…Rainsford," came a raspy voice. Rainey turned and spotted Creston twenty yards away, sitting on the ground with his back against a tall palm tree, and partially obscured by the island flora. Running hard and too fast, he was half way to Creston when his busy feet tangled in the thick foliage and he fell. The ground was soft but it still slammed against him and a searing pain screamed up his left arm. Before he was able to speak he heard Creston's labored voice.

"Not too… graceful."

"Where the hell have you been?" Rainey said, holding his arm as he rose to his knees.

Creston's head turned to the side and Rainey saw a large gash across the right side of his face.

"Jesus, Creston!" he said.

"I…I haven't moved …in over a day. What … took you …so long?"

"What took me so long? What **took** so long? Yesterday I didn't even know who I was, and you ask what took so long.

"What the hell are you doing out here so far from the plane? And how did you get here? And why did you leave me?"

Creston stared at him and Rainey blushed with shame at his outburst.

"Stay still and let me think for a minute," Rainey said. "I don't suppose you can walk?"

Creston shook his head. "I was trying to find help…this is as far as I got. I couldn't go anymore."

"I was unconscious on the beach," Rainey said. "When I came to I didn't know who I was or where…never mind," Rainey noticed the confusion in Creston's eyes. "I can go back to the plane and get a blanket to rig up a way to drag you back. You know, like a travois the old plains Indians used," Rainey spoke trying to sound positive and in control.

"Don't leave …me. I've been here …too long."

It took great effort for Creston to speak. Rainey stood up and took his pants off.

Creston took a deep breath, wincing in pain, "What… the hell…are you…doing?"

"Look, I need to get you back to the plane. I'm going to tie the pants legs around your waist, then put my right arm through the unzipped fly and then out through the waist of the pants. I think I fractured my left arm or at least bruised or sprained it pretty bad. It'll be slow going and hard, but I think I can pull you back to the plane. Do you think you can be moved?"

"Not sure…but… let's… Water…"

Rainey held a water bottle to Creston's lips, spilling as much as he drank. Creston leaned his head back as Rainey tied the pants legs around his waist. A large amount of dried blood covered Creston's lower torso and upper thighs.

It proved much harder pulling Creston back to the plane than he expected. His right arm tired and he repeatedly stopped to catch his breath. Rainey envisioned a sled fully loaded, without wheels, and trying to pull it through a field. This was just as slow and difficult. It took over two hours of pulling, stopping, giving Creston water and then continuing. He was exhausted by the time he got Creston to the door of the plane. It was mid morning and the sun was already blanketing the island with a tropical heat unfamiliar to Rainey. The plane's wing provided shade. They sat on the ground, depleted of energy. Rainey took a minute to look closer at Creston. The gash in the side of his head had quit bleeding some time ago, and dried blood had crusted in Creston's scalp and on his face. The deep red stain on his pants was concerning. He had lost more blood than Rainey first thought.

"It's hotter inside the plane but the large seats are comfortable and you'll be out of the sun. I need to get you inside but you're going to have to help."

"Let's stay here for now. I'm tired… and I hurt. I think …I might have…" Creston stopped, too tired to go on. He reclined onto the sandy ground and moaned with discomfort.

Rainey paced to the door of the plane, then back toward Creston.

"Rainey…you need …to relax. Get me some water…a little food. I'll rest a little … then we can talk."

"Do you think it is a good idea to eat, with your injuries and all?"

"Look, I'd rather die …with food than without it."

"Ain't nobody dying, not today," Rainey said.

Creston's speech was slowing and his words slurred. He was slipping in and out of consciousness and Rainey struggled to understand him. Inside the plane, he found a blanket, a large seat cushion, a can of chicken and rice soup, and more water. Rainey sat patiently, taking a full hour to feed Creston who rested between each bite.

The air was still, and warm like a sauna. Rainey moved the cushion close to Creston and then eased his friend against it providing a modicum of comfort. As hot as it was at mid-day, he still covered Creston with the blanket and got no objection. Rainey took a bottle of water from the plane and a towel from the lavatory to clean the gash on Creston's face. He was careful to keep the added pain from the cleaning to a minimum. The crusted blood softened with the water and Rainey gently wiped the towel over the wound several times, removing most of the dried blood. The cleaned wound gaped and looked worse than before Rainey had started. Fresh blood oozed from the large cut. Rainey sat patiently at his friend's side, remained quiet, and fought back tears of frustration. Creston was in pain, and Rainey sat helpless. He remembered the syringes and bottles of medicine in the first aid kit but had no idea of how to administer the medicine or what most of it was for. Creston's breathing softened, and he slept.

Several hours passed before Creston stirred. He opened his eyes but did not move. Rainey managed a smile but said nothing.

"Water?" Creston said. "How long…was I out this time?"

"About two hours. You rested and barely moved. How are you feeling?"

Creston was slow to respond. "Not too good…I think…"

"You need to rest and take it easy. I'll get you more food and water. We have enough on the plane to last us for a while, maybe two weeks or so if we take it easy."

"Rainey, we…need to talk…"

"No, we don't need to talk. You need to rest. We can figure out what happened later. And, what we're going to do about it," Rainey said with force, but comforting at the same time.

"I'm pretty sure about what happened." Creston said before slipping into unconsciousness again.

CHAPTER FOUR

Creston stirred, his face winced, and his eyes opened. Rainey was staring at him as he woke up. "You were out for an hour this time. So, where the hell are we and what happened?"

"You ain't gonna like this." Creston shifted and groaned with pain. "Look, planes are mechanical. Things can go wrong. No matter how much you do to prevent problems... well, I think we had a cabin pressure leak. We both suffered... oxygen deprivation. But it must have been a slow leak. For some reason... the alarm didn't go off. You went to the back and fell asleep.

"Stop," Rainey said. He took a deep breath. "Let's relax and take it slow. You're wearing me out watching you try to talk."

Creston closed his eyes and his body slumped. Rainey knew Creston was fighting the fatigue. He watched Creston and his mind raced, as his thoughts drifted into a void removed from Creston's explanation of what had happened. He was feeling anxious and overwhelmed with no idea of what to do or how to begin to try and figure out his next step.

"Hey! Pay attention. This is hard enough. I don't need to repeat myself."

Creston's words closed the void and Rainey again focused on his friend.

"I thought I was tired, fighting sleep, but it wasn't sleep. I passed out. The auto pilot wasn't on which probably saved us. We were in a slow decline. I must have relaxed the controls when I passed out. We started dropping in altitude. I think the drop in altitude stopped the oxygen level from depleting completely. I woke up when we were a couple hundred feet above the ocean. We were diving almost straight at the water. I panicked, but then recovered enough to get my hands on the controls. I managed to get the nose of the plane up right before it slammed into the water. We bounced hard. I hit my head and that's the last thing I remember. When I woke up the plane was where you see it. I got up, went to the back looking for you. You were gone. I got scared and left the plane to find you but didn't realize how badly I was hurt. I couldn't go any more." His head drooped and without looking up he said, "Then you found me."

Creston stopped, exhausted from describing the accident. Beads of sweat had formed on his forehead and several rivulets ran down his face. His breathing was labored, and though the pain was evident, he did not complain.

"I'm sure there's more to this than either of us realizes but you need to rest. I'll organize what's in the plane and figure out what we have. Thankfully we have a medicine kit. When you wake up I'll clean the wound on your head and patch you up as best as possible. My first aid knowledge is pretty limited but I'm the best you've got."

"Is that supposed to make me feel better?" Creston said.

Rainey nodded, encouraged with Creston's sarcasm.

"I need some sleep," Creston said. "We'll try to figure this out later."

Rainey watched as Creston drifted off to sleep. The more he thought about their situation the angrier he became. And he didn't fight the anger. He looked at Creston and tried to imagine him gone, dead, having to bury him, and with those thoughts his anger vanished, replaced by fear and insecurity, as he collapsed against the fuselage of the plane. Tears welled up, and he prayed. He drifted off into a dreamless sleep and his body gave way to the exhaustion.

The tropics can produce daily rainfalls predictable almost to the minute, much like catching a bus on a busy city street. The patterns are consistent from one day to the next, sometimes for weeks at a time. It was early evening and clouds moved in from over the lagoon and darkened the sky. The temperature dropped, feeling like a northern cool front pushing through on an early fall day. Large raindrops fell heavily onto the island.

"Hey, wake up," Creston yelled.

Rainey stirred, opened his eyes but then closed them as the large raindrops hit his face, each drop stinging like a mosquito bite. The rain fell with a fierce intensity as the storm rolled over the island, covering it like a large canopy. He turned, ducked his head and got up on his knees, his face toward the ground. The rain was cold and he shivered from the contrast in temperature of a few minutes earlier. His left arm still ached but supported him better as he used both arms to prop his body up enough to see Creston. Unlike Rainey, he made no effort to move or protect himself. Creston's large grin consumed his face. Rainey smiled, as he watched him.

"I didn't expect I'd be happy to see your obnoxious grin," Rainey said as he stood up, soaked from the rain. "But I am, even though you look like hell."

Rainey considered refuge from the storm inside the plane. He looked up at the rain while shielding his face with his hands, and then dropped his arms to his side and shook his head. His first impulse had been to get out of the rain but this was different, and he realized nothing was similar to what he had known. The rain was fresh and stimulating as it washed over him and he enjoyed the downpour. With his head held back and eyes closed, he opened his mouth like a child trying to catch a snow flake, and tasted the fresh water. It was cool and refreshing, sweet, and washed away the dried salt deposited by the misty winds. Rainey began hopping up and down, going in circles while his arms flailed wildly.

Creston's smile disappeared as he watched Rainey perform his adolescent dance in the sand. Seeing Rainey like this was new to him. Creston knew they had both been through a lot in the last twenty-four or forty-eight hours, but had no idea what was prompting this strange transformation.

Rainey stopped, looked at Creston and said, "What?"

Creston calmly asked "Are you ok? You're starting to scare me a little."

"Kiss my ass! I have the right to go a little crazy."

Rainey looked out through the storm and watched the heavy curtain of rain move across the lagoon. He had enjoyed the experience of summer rains in the swamps and marshes of Louisiana. The storms, with a sharply defined leading edge, moved fast and would bear down on the landscape as they rushed ashore from the gulf, pummeling everything in their paths. And then an abrupt finish as the equally distinct trailing edge of the storm passed. Rainey watched the end of the tropic storm move toward him. The rain would be over in a matter of minutes and the island would glisten in the setting sun.

Rainey climbed into the plane, still wet from the intense rain. The hot air inside was humid, heavy and still. His wetness would soon change from rain to sweat. He went to work gathering all the food items and stacking them neatly between the seats, making mental notes of the supplies. Several cases of water had broken open during the crash and the plastic bottles were scattered throughout like toys in a child's room. He tediously picked up the bottles and placed them in the larger seat and was surprised to find large boxes of candy bars and several cases of soft drinks.

He moved to the door of the plane, stood motionless for a minute and then jumped down onto the sand. Creston had fallen asleep and the evening sun was burning into the lagoon as it set. Rainey decided to take a closer look around the plane. The fuselage had burrowed several feet into the sand, causing the plane to appear smaller than when on the tarmac. At the airport the plane had loomed much larger. He walked around the plane, assessing the damage. He stopped when he got back to the port side of the plane. The cargo door was almost completely buried below the sand and unable to be opened. All our clothes and gear are in there, he thought, but they might as well be back in Louisiana. The realization of what he had overlooked caused him to stop and walk back to the front of the plane. The cockpit glass was intact. The plane was weather tight and would provide shelter from any serious storms which would undoubtedly blow up and cover the island.

"Hey, tell me next time when you're taking off," Creston said.

"Yeah, and where do you think I'm running off to?" Rainey said. "Sorry, I was right here looking at the plane and trying to figure things out. How ya feeling?"

"Maybe better. Still hurt, got a headache but the rain felt good."

"We have to get you comfortable."

"Why, so I can die in peace?"

"Is that what you think? That you're going to die?"

"Yeah, maybe I am," Creston said. "I'm scared."

Rainey did not remember being truly afraid he might die. Even after the crash, waking and disoriented, he didn't fear imminent death. He didn't fear it now, but Creston's words shook him to his depths.

"Creston, I'll do all I can to keep you alive. Let's focus on what we need to do and not on what happened or how we got here."

Creston nodded and a tear rolled down his cheek. Rainey turned away and busied himself in the door of the plane, hiding the concern and anguish evident on his face. Rainey climbed back into the plane, removed the first aid kit from the bulkhead, and went back outside to help Creston.

"The first thing I need to do is patch you up the best I can. I've got some water to clean the blood from the gash on your head. There are bandages and antiseptic ointment in the kit. It'll be dark soon and all we have are a couple of flashlights and a handheld beacon. I don't want to build a fire this close to the plane. I sometimes catch a whiff of fuel, depending on the direction of the wind, and I don't want to take a chance with an open flame."

"Always the boy scout," Creston said.

"Too bad for you I was never a boy scout. Maybe you'd be in better hands if I had been."

"Yeah? Well, you'll do."

Rainey took gauze from the first aid kit and placed it under the gash to absorb the water as he irrigated the large cut. The dried blood was thick and heavily crusted, resembling dark clay in a field where it had not rained in weeks. He knew he would have to use more pressure to remove all the old blood, and was sure it would be painful. Under different circumstances, he would have teased Creston and given him a hard time about the cut.

"This is going to hurt, but I have to put more pressure on the cut to clean it properly. You might want to bite down on something to help deal with the pain."

"Yeah, and what would you suggest Doc?"

"Well, start with your tongue," Rainey said. "Sorry, guess that was insensitive of me."

"Rainey, I'm not dead yet so quit being so damn careful. Be yourself and let's get on with this."

As he swabbed the cut with the wet gauze, the dried blood softened and flaked off. Rainey realized it was larger and deeper than he had thought. The cut started a quarter inch inside the hair line, moved downward close to the right temple and ended below his right eye. It was almost three inches long, deep, and had opened up more than a quarter inch. The skin was thin and not fleshy. Rainey was sure the skull had taken a hard blow and it was probable Creston had sustained a concussion. He irrigated the cut and as more of the dried blood washed away the wound seeped fresh blood. He pressed the gauze onto the wound in an attempt to stop the bleeding.

"Damn it, Rainey, ease up a little. You're killing me."

"The cut is bigger than I thought, and it's starting to bleed again. I've got to stop the bleeding so I have to press on it. There's some hydrogen peroxide in the first aid kit. I think I should pour some on the cut. It'll clean it better, and then we can use the antiseptic for infection. But I still have to stop the bleeding."

"There are sutures in the kit. Finish cleaning it and then try to sew it closed. The stitches should help stop the bleeding. And one more thing, you better not be enjoying this."

"Come on, allow me a little pleasure. I've sewn a tear in my pants, and maybe a shirt or two, so don't blame me if you wind up looking like Frankenstein's monster when we get rescued. And WE WILL get rescued. Me AND you," Rainey said.

"I hope you're right."

Rainey poured the peroxide onto the cut and Creston winced but managed to stay quiet. He placed fresh gauze over the cut and then opened the first aid kit, removed the sutures and tried to imagine how he was supposed to use the curved needle and thread. The paper envelope containing the sutures had a basic diagram illustrating the procedure for tying the knot on each stitch.

"This might take a little longer than sewing up a pair of pants," Rainey said.

He studied the diagram over and over, still less than confident in what he was about to attempt.

He removed his belt. "I'm ready to start. Put the belt in your mouth and bite down on it when it gets too painful."

Creston never made more than a low growl as Rainey pushed the needle into the skin on one side of the cut and out through the skin on the other side, drawing the suture tight. Each penetration of the needle produced a sharp pain and Creston grimaced. As each suture was pulled through his skin Creston emitted a low, grating sound and felt vibration from his forehead into his ear. He bit down harder and harder. Rainey finished dressing the wound with antiseptic ointment, gauze, and tape. He had used twelve stitches with no idea if twelve were too many or too few, but the wound was closed. Creston had marred the leather belt with his teeth, almost biting completely through it. It was dark by the time Rainey finished. Anything else would have to wait until morning.

"Hey Rainey, I have to go to the bathroom."

"Great, that's just great." Rainey stood, spotted an area with some bushes about fifty feet from the plane. "I'll dig a hole in the sand over there, help you to it, and undo your pants. But I am not wiping your ass."

"Some friend you are."

Rainey woke with a start. He looked over at Creston and watched him closely. The gentle repetitive expansion and deflation of Creston's chest reassured him and he relaxed. He was peacefully asleep and Rainey was encouraged with the progress. The morning breeze was cool, gently blowing from the opposite direction than the storm the previous day. It had a different smell to it, saltier, and it penetrated deep into his sinuses as he inhaled, causing his eyes to water. First light. The sun was low on the horizon and obscured by the trees. A faint orange hue faded into the softening blue above the rising sun. The sky was mostly clear, with a few scattered, non-threatening and motionless clouds high above the island. It was still dark toward the west.

Creston's wound had bled through the bandage during the night and colored the gauze a deep, dark red reminding Rainey of the Alabama Crimson Tide. He wondered why the hell that came to mind and why he was having repetitive and nonsensical flashbacks. Many random thoughts had invaded him and he had begun to suspect it was his subconscious survival mode sustaining him. There was comfort in familiar thoughts, especially when contrasted to such unfamiliar and foreign surroundings.

Rainey was anxious to explore the island, to find out what they had crashed onto, but he was reluctant to wander off until Creston was awake and fed. His hunger caused a deep growl. A cup of coffee, he thought, how the hell am I going to make a cup of coffee?

"What are you thinking about? I've been awake for five minutes and you haven't budged an inch."

Rainey turned toward Creston. "I'm thinking about all of this. Where we are, how long we've been here, is anyone looking for us, how long can we survive? And thinking I'm gonna head out around the island after breakfast. But mostly right this minute, I was thinking how much I'd like a cup of coffee."

"Coffee would be good."

"This whole thing's a little overwhelming. I was concerned about you because there was lots of blood on your lower body when I found you. I thought it might have been from another large cut and maybe you had some internal injuries. But after helping you go to the bathroom, and thank you for that lovely experience, it looked more like a large, severe bruise. The blood must have come from the gash in your head, and there was plenty so you need to take it easy.

I think it's a good sign you're feeling better, but let's not take any chances."

"I still hurt…but not as badly as yesterday. I don't think I can do much of anything. God, I can't believe how sore I am and my head is killing me."

"We sewed up a large gash so it should be sore. I'm sure it's going to be painful for a while. It bled through the bandage so I think we have to clean it." Rainey stood up.

"Look, I'm sore and hungry. Can't we take it easy for a few minutes and…maybe think through a few things over some food? Then you can butcher me up some more."

"Yeah, I guess we can eat and discuss all this. It's not like we have anywhere to go. But I don't want the cut getting infected. It's too close to your brain and as much as I hate to admit it, your brain is the one thing I need working."

Creston watched Rainey get up and move toward the plane. As he waited for Rainey to return with food he looked around the area and could not remember ever feeling this helpless. Their bleak situation registered and thoughts rushed at him too fast to comprehend while his head beat with the rhythm of a pile driver. He shut his eyes tightly trying to stop the incursion, took a deep breath, and when he opened his eyes it had all slowed down. He lifted his left arm up enough to check his watch. The time was of no importance to him but the date shown on the dial was. If his mind was working correctly, and he questioned this, they were two days out of Hawaii, and thus two days overdue on the flight plan. Their scheduled arrival in New Guinea was long passed and word of them missing should be spreading through the system and reaching New Orleans. It bothered him so many people would be worried about them.

CHAPTER FIVE

Rainey had managed to feed Creston and himself a breakfast of crackers, peanut butter, strawberry preserve and water. They were both hungry for more but realized they must conserve their food. Rainey made note of the coffee on board the plane. He would figure out a way to brew a cup soon.

"Did you see anything suspicious while you were waiting for me to find you?" Rainey said.

"We're alone if that's what you're asking me. If not, they'd have already found us, or killed us."

"Killed us?"

"If there were hostile natives here we'd be dead. There are parts of the world still uncivilized," Creston said. "Did you see anything?"

"My mind playing tricks on me, that's all. Hey, what's with all the soft drinks and candy? I've never seen you eat or drink much of that stuff," Rainey said.

"Well, I knew we'd be traveling through some undeveloped areas. Some third world type places, so I brought it for some of the kids we were bound to meet."

"Third world? Well, this is about as third world as it gets. Hell, this is no world."

"We might be glad we have it. No telling how long it'll take them to find us," Creston said.

They had finished breakfast and Rainey rose to his feet, stretched, feeling better and more energetic. Looking down at Creston, he considered changing the bandage but decided it would be better to save the bandages and use them sparingly. He had already decided to do the same with the food and water.

"Do you have any ideas of where we are?" Rainey asked.

"Everything was happening too fast and I got groggy right before the plane crashed. But, for a few seconds I had an overview of the island. It appeared flat and oblong, as much as I could see anyway. I think it might be about two or three miles long, maybe half a mile or so wide. I'm not real sure. Pretty much covered with trees and all. I'm sure this is a coral atoll. They have hundreds of them in the Pacific Ocean, and I'm sure we're in the Pacific. What I'm not sure of is whether we are north or south of the equator. Guess it doesn't matter much either way."

"Well, if it is a coral atoll, then there are other small islands attached by the coral reef, right?" Rainey asked.

"Yeah, and it means there's a lagoon side and an ocean side to the island," Creston said. "The real problem with no natives is it probably means there's no source of fresh water. It's a dry island."

"You're certainly thinking better. And your speech is good. Hell, you might make it through this," Rainey said. "All right, I guess I'll get started. I suppose this will take several hours assuming I can make it all the way around the island and back in one trip. Are you okay with me being gone for a while?"

"Yeah, I think so. But look, you still need to be careful out there. Ya never know. Got it?"

Rainey scowled as he contemplated Creston's warning. "Great. All your talk of being alone and you send me off with a threatening comment."

His gut feeling told him there was a whole bunch of nothing out there. He guessed it to be about eight o'clock. The morning sun was visible above the trees and the tropical air was heating up with each minute. As he turned toward the sun he squinted like a new baby being brought outside into the daylight for the first time. Where had his sunglasses wound up? He tried to make a mental check list of what he thought he might need to venture out but he was apprehensive, his mind clouded and his thoughts had no logical sequence.

Rainey was able to care for Creston because he concentrated on one thing at a time, and it did not require much thought. Caring for Creston was spontaneous and obvious. Thinking for himself was a bigger challenge.

"This standing around is driving me crazy, so I'm going. Do you need anything before I head out?" Rainey asked.

"I'm good and I feel much better, so get out of here. I'm dying... I mean curious to know what you find. Take some water and maybe some candy bars. Neither of us is accustomed to this kind of heat and it will zap your energy faster than you think, especially since we're not a hundred percent."

"You sound like my mother," Rainey said walking away.

The inside of the plane was starting to smell musky. Rainey moved into the cockpit hoping to find his sunglasses. He looked at the lifeless instrument panel and then toward the pilot seat. Creston's dried blood was conspicuous and trailed to the floor. He relaxed. The tension drained from his neck and shoulders, out through his feet and gave him peace. They were lucky to be alive and he offered thanks.

Looking around the cabin, he found his left shoe up against the bulkhead behind the cockpit and covered by a blanket dislodged from an overhead bin. His right shoe required more searching. He made several passes through the cabin, moving bags, boxes, and whatever was not secured in place. When he had given up hope of finding the shoe, he noticed a bulge in a window curtain. He reached inside the curtain and grasped his shoe. He was reminded of how violent the crash must have been.

Rainey donned his shoes, and even without socks he enjoyed a much needed sense of confidence as he left the plane. He had grabbed his bag, put two bottles of water into it as well as two Hershey chocolate bars, and slung it over his shoulder. His plan was to circle the island by traversing the water's edge and not venturing into the interior where the trees and brush were so thick they would slow him down. He was feeling apprehension in leaving. The first trip needed to be as quick as possible. Creston should not be left alone for an extended period of time. He was getting stronger but Rainey was not yet comfortable the worst was over.

Rainey made Creston as comfortable as possible by arranging the seat cushions to resemble a large lawn chair. He positioned them so they would remain in the shade of the fuselage and wing. Several bottles of water were close to Creston.

"I'll be back in time to fix some lunch. If your description of the island is accurate, this should be a breeze," Rainey said.

"Take your time but, uh, hurry up."

"When I get back I think we should go to the lagoon. We'll start slow but a swim would do us both some good. The salt water will help heal the gash on your head. It'll hurt like hell, but anything to keep it from getting infected is worth it. We should try to swim everyday. You need a little exercise to keep up your strength."

Creston watched as Rainey disappeared through the trees. He thought about the first time he and Rainey had met.

The Oyster House in the French Quarter was where Rainey and Creston had met twenty years earlier. Merely by chance, they were standing next to each other at the oyster bar trying to get the attention of the bar tender with Big O embroidered on his shirt. It was carnival season and the restaurant was packed with Mardi Gras revelers impatiently waiting for food and drink.

Creston took the initiative and yelled "Hey, how about a couple of dozen for me and my friend?"

Rainey gave the stranger an inquisitive quick glance but said nothing, figuring what the hell. After all, he was there for oysters.

Big O did not reply but soon placed two dozen raw oysters in front of them. He turned and walked away, continuing to work the rowdy customers.

"Damn, look at the size of his hands. I'll bet that's not why they call him Big O," Creston said flashing a toothy grin at Rainey and laughing.

Rainey nodded. This guy's a jerk, he thought. He looked down at the oysters on the half shell. They were sitting in ice, surrounding containers of catsup, horseradish, and lemon. He looked up to get the attention of Big O but heard Creston bellow again.

"How about some extra horseradish and a beer? I'll have a Heineken. What about you, stranger?" he asked, looking at Rainey.

"Dixie, in a bottle," Rainey said.

"Dixie?" Creston asked. "Dixie?"

"I like Dixie beer. It's local and it's cheaper than Heineken."

Creston changed immediately. He melted into humbleness, realizing his brashness was not amusing, and in fact was annoying and offensive.

"Two Dixies, please," he said to Big O. He put his thumb to his chest and said "Creston."

Rainey looked at him, nodded but said nothing. The beers came and they ate and drank together. They finished the first two dozen and then ordered two dozen more. This was the perfect way to start a Friday night. It was Mardi Gras weekend and the French Quarter was packed with people. Sardines in a tin had more room than the people on Bourbon Street. The restaurant was getting more crowded and noisier while they stood at the oyster bar and tried to talk.

"Hey, I'm headed to Savvy's Bar on Toulouse Street," Creston said. "Come on, let's get out of this tourist crap and go listen to some music."

"Why not," Rainey said and chugged the last of his beer. He reached for some money, but Creston was quicker and put too much cash on the bar.

"Got it," he said and made for the door.

Rainey followed Creston out onto Iberville Street. He had nothing else to do and did not think he would get into trouble with this guy.

The five block walk up Bourbon Street and over onto Toulouse took almost an hour. The thick crowd moved slowly and stalled many times. The French Quarter of the mid-seventies during Mardi Gras was all about people and drinking. The female tourists in the streets had not begun to flash their breasts for cheap beads as openly as they would in the years to come. Most of the nudity was confined to a few hotel balconies on Bourbon Street, but this would cause the crowds below to completely stop, like too many cows being crammed onto the ramps of the slaughter house. A person would get stuck in the same spot for ten or twenty minutes hoping for someone to break out and start the flow again. Since almost everyone had a drink of some type in their hand, the lack of movement didn't bother them.

Rainey and Creston stumbled out of the crowd at Toulouse Street, and walked half a block to Savvy's Bar. The blues, being performed by a no name quartet, was wailing and carried through the large open windows out onto the street.

"It almost never matters who's playing, love the blues," Creston said not caring if Rainey heard him. "New Orleans has great blues, and these guys know more about blues than you or me," he said.

Rainey was ready to tell Creston he was arrogant and presumptuous but two guys approached and interrupted him.

"Man, the quarter is crazy tonight," the taller of the two said to Creston.

"Hey, Earl, Sonny. How's it going tonight?" Creston said.

"Too early to tell," Earl said. "But the music's good and the beer's cold. How bad can it be? Who's your friend?"

Creston turned toward Rainey. He had not responded when Creston introduced himself at the oyster bar. "Well," he said over the noise and music, "I'm not sure." The moment was awkward as he waited for Rainey to respond.

"Rainey," he said as he looked at them.

"You look a little cloudy, maybe, but not rainy," Earl said. The three of them laughed loudly enough to distract several guys drinking close by. Rainey's head drooped as he thought of how many times he had heard the same stupid joke about his name. And each time the offending person acted as if Rainey had never heard it before.

While Rainey considered a response, Creston grabbed four cold beers from the large wash tub full of ice at the end of the bar and held them up for the bartender to see. He waved back indicating he would put them on Creston's tab. Creston called for them to follow him outside into the street where there was more room, less chaos, and the cool February air. This was Creston's first big mistake of the evening.

Earl was the last of the four leaving the bar when a partially sober patron purposely got in his way, acting too chummy while pushing against Earl. Earl pushed right past him stepping hard on the guy's foot, and moved into the street.

Rainey and his new friends were doing the more formal introductions and drinking their beers. A loud "HEY" from the doorway of the bar interrupted them. Rainey looked up to see the partially sober patron pointing at Earl and speaking to a very large, red headed guy who glared at them. The big guy's large right arm was draped around the smaller man's shoulder. He nodded his head, removed his arm, and stepped into the street.

"You stepped on my friend's foot. Why don't you watch where you're going, and while you're at it, tell my buddy you're sorry?" The talking behemoth spoke with an unmistakable Mississippi twang.

"Uh oh," Creston said.

"What?" Rainey said.

"Earl is a great friend. He'd do anything for ya. But, he's got a short temper. He saved my ass more than once when we were growing up. You probably didn't notice but I can be a little arrogant sometimes."

"Uh huh," Rainey said.

"He'll fight at the drop of a hat," Creston said. "His old man used to punch him all the time. Told him it would make him tough. And, he's one of the toughest guys I've ever seen. My mom helped him out through one of those social programs. That's how we met. My mom…"

"HEY! You hear me talking to you?" the big guy shouted.

"Why don't you kiss my ass?" Earl shot back.

Rainey's head jerked to the side as he stared open mouthed at Earl. When he turned back there were six or eight guys standing behind the red headed giant. Rainey wanted desperately to talk his way out of this but Earl was too quick. The big guy put his hand on

Earl's shoulder and it was too late for talking. Rainey never saw the first punch Earl threw, but he saw the head of the large man snap back hard.

The big guy reeled from Earl's punch and stumbled backward toward his friends. "Take his head off, Charlie," one of the big guy's friends yelled as several of them pushed him back at Earl in time for the second punch to land hard in the midsection of the dazed aggressor. Charlie started flailing his arms trying to land a blow to Earl's head, but Earl was quick. Creston, Sonny, and Rainey stood there and watched, but not for long. Charlie's friends started moving to form a circle around all of them and Rainey knew he had to act. He crouched low and took aim, charged Charlie hard and shoved him back into his friends, breaking up the crowd. Bodies tumbled onto the street and Rainey, half dazed by the effort to move the large man, stepped back to Creston and Sonny. He readied himself. Earl moved and knocked Charlie to the ground with another hard right to the side of the head as the big red haired giant had half managed to stand up. He was down but not out, and his temper was erupting like the shaken beer bottles they had dropped with the start of the fight. He let out a scream so loud the crowd stopped and froze, as if they had never heard anything as blood curdling. Charlie managed to get to his feet and stare down Earl. Creston made his second big mistake of the evening.

As Earl was about to move forward and again engage with Charlie, Creston wrapped both arms around Earl from behind and said "Earl, that's enough. Let's get out of here before this thing gets too far out of control."

Creston did not see Charlie winding up to throw a large fist at Earl's head, but Earl did and bent forward to duck the punch. Creston had not released Earl from the bear hug and was pulled forward right into the flying fist of the big red headed man. Creston crumpled to the street and let out a low moan. The big fist had rendered him unconscious.

"Holy shit!" Rainey exclaimed, as he watched Creston fall. He rushed to Creston and knelt at his side. Sonny did likewise. Creston lay motionless. The crowd backed up as they must have thought Creston was dead.

Earl and Charlie were alone in the street and Earl wasn't finished. The big man was no match for Earl's speed of punches and body quickness. His hands moved with control. Anyone watching knew Earl had spent many rounds in the ring. His left jabs were precise and came in pairs. His right hand followed the jabs with crosses to the head and uppercuts to the chin. In less than a minute, Earl had left Charlie's face resembling his hair, red and a total mess. Several cuts oozed blood, the big man's nose looked broken, and swelling had both eyes partially closed. He held up his arms in front of his face signaling he'd had enough. Earl backed off, shaking his hands which were starting to swell from the constant hammering against Charlie's face.

Police sirens wailed in the cool night air. The crowd dispersed with most of them heading back into Savvy's bar as if nothing had happened. Another typical Mardi Gras weekend night. Fights start, fights end, and everyone goes back to drinking and listening to music. Creston lay still but was conscious. Rainey, Earl, and Sonny lifted him to his feet.

"How's my teeth?" he asked.

"Well," Rainey said, "they're still in your head, but I don't know how."

Earl looked at Rainey. "Thanks for staying with us. If you hadn't charged the big guy and broken up the crowd it would have gotten ugly. And they had more friends in the bar. I think they were all with a fraternity from Ole Miss. I heard some of them talking before you and Creston showed up." Rainey nodded.

"Hey, let's go over to the 500 club," Earl said. "They got a young guy, Jimmy somebody, from Alabama playing tonight. Plays the guitar, sings ok and doesn't do the blues. I think Creston has had enough blues for one night."

Sonny spoke up, "Earl, don't you think we should call it a night?"

"My uncle Anthony is working the door," Earl replied. "We'll get in for free and the bar maid likes me. She'll slip us free beers when no one is looking. That's a good deal during Mardi Gras."

Creston was silent but went willingly as they all headed back toward Bourbon Street.

Rainey looked back toward Savvy's bar. He wasn't sure what all had happened, but he was sure the last five minutes to Charlie seemed like hours. They were walking down Toulouse Street as the police cars turned the corner.

"Just keep walking," Creston said as they passed the police.

I hadn't planned on stopping to chat, Rainey thought.

Rainey sensed Creston watching as he walked away and disappeared into the trees. The heat of the sun was intense and he enjoyed the warmth on his face while the sounds of the island became deafening.

The most discernable sound was the ocean waves and Rainey moved toward it without intent, as if pulled by a quiet force. The venture started with calm but anxiety was building inside him like a pressure cooker and his breathing was quick and shallow. Indecision to continue, driven by fear of what he might find, overcame him. He knelt down and bowed his head. The disappointment of finding nothing vied with his fear of finding evil, and he wasn't sure which one was the lesser threat. He wrestled with his emotions until a semblance of calm returned and then he continued.

Rainey became impatient to see what the island had to offer. His other trek into the dense foliage was a blur, and there was little remembrance of anything except finding Creston and struggling to return him to the plane. The loud sounds of cresting waves crashing onto the reef emanated from his left. He turned and walked toward the sound of the waves, focused and concentrating, and soon emerged from the trees onto a narrow stretch of sand. He stopped in the shade of the trees and his feet settled an inch deep into the soft sand. The intense brightness of the mid-morning sun and tropic heat did not distract from the beauty of the reef and the vast ocean, but added to it. The image was as if captured on movie film, shot from the perfect angle, and played for Rainey until he shook his head and started down the narrow beach.

It took several hundred yards of walking for Rainey to relax. The line of trees curved in and out along a beach five yards at its widest, and narrow to as little as three feet. Rainey stood at the water's edge, his shoes again sinking into the firm, moist sand as he gazed into the water covering the reef. It was no more than twelve inches deep. The hollows of the reef's craggy surface had a moon-like appearance of swirls and pockmarks, contrasting shades of gray and green, and random patches of thick green algae and seaweed. The texture of the reef was a stark contrast to the sandy bottom of the lagoon. It captured his stare as he raised his head. His eyes followed the reef twenty feet out from shore before the reflection of the sky, and the brightness of the sun caused the water to turn mirror-like and obscure his view below the surface. Thirty yards out shallow waves broke rhythmically over the edge of the reef in sets of three. Water sprayed into the air like small geysers as each wave toppled, producing foam which dissipated before the next breaking wave. He had experienced a similar serenity many times watching the Mississippi River from randomly picked spots on the levee in old Algiers.

Rainey's feet tired from continually sinking into the sand, and his muscles fatigued from working much harder than when strolling around the French Quarter. He struggled through the first mile, his lower body ached and he perspired profusely. The scenery had been unchanging.

Rainey settled into a rhythm as he walked with his head down, concentrating on the sand with each step. He was lost in thoughts of survival. The effort of walking in the sand coupled with the intensifying heat of the day was exhausting Rainey. He stopped to wipe his brow. Less than ten steps in front of him the beach ended. A cove, at least two hundred feet across, lay before him.

He approached the cove and looked into the water, expecting to see the bottom. But the water was too dark, and he presumed, very deep. He looked to his left and his eyes followed the dark blue water out beyond the reef. It was not a cove but an inlet and Rainey wondered why the reef was split.

Rainey skirted the narrow edge of the inlet, the tree line two feet from the water, and stopped on the opposite side. The water level over the reef was dropping and his head jerked when he saw a four foot shark dart across the reef and disappear into the deeper water of the inlet. Low tide was minutes away.

The beauty of the reef, water, sand, and island flora abandoned Rainey, as anxiety again took hold of him. He worried about Creston and about being gone too long, but moved onward. An outcropping appeared in the distance, another island but smaller, and excitement replaced his concern. His spirits lifted and he hoped maybe there was more to the situation he and Creston had fallen into. The reflection of the sun on the water was blinding and he squinted as he stared at the other island. Creston had been correct. The islands were connected by the reef and formed an atoll.

The end of the island was coming into view and Rainey approached it eagerly. The trees to his right were thinning and he peered through them to the lagoon. He had been walking for almost two hours and had covered what he guessed to be three miles. The sun had risen to his left so he knew he was approaching the southern end. The island in the distance was becoming more visible but was farther than he first thought.

Rainey stopped at the last tree. Unspoiled, white coral sand lay before him and gradually sloped thirty feet to the water. Rainey imagined this must all be virgin, never touched by a human. The beach was a hundred yards wide, spanning from the ocean to the lagoon. Low tide was nigh and exposed the craggy surface of the reef which stretched for miles to the other islands. The beach was wider along the lagoon, varying from twenty to thirty feet, and continued to the end of the island where Creston waited. The scenery was postcard beautiful.

Rainey walked to the water, knelt and rinsed his face. Too salty, he thought, as he wiped away the water with his shirt sleeve. He needed to rest and walked back to the palm trees, searching for a shady spot of sand. A few minutes more before heading back to Creston shouldn't make a difference, and resting would help. The shaded spots were sparse and changing, interrupted by rays of light filtering through fronds moving with the gentle breeze. Rainey selected the largest patch of shade at the base of a palm tree and sat with his back against the long, thin tree trunk. It was undisturbed beauty and Rainey thought of the irony in his situation. Other people would spend thousands of dollars to experience an island so natural and pristine, and he would give anything to be somewhere else.

The lagoon was still and quiet. The wind had calmed and the stillness engulfed him. The surf breaking over the reef had diminished with low tide and was barely audible. It was impossible to get comfortable, the palm tree hard and rough against his back. And yet his eyes closed, his mind wandered, and an image of a tranquil New Orleans filled with familiar faces and favorite restaurants appeared. He worried what his mother must be feeling.

CHAPTER SIX

A strange and faint clicking sound coupled with a distant scratchy noise caused Rainey to wake with a start. He tilted his head back and looked up the trunk of the palm tree he had fallen asleep upon. A large, purplish, crab-like crustacean was moving about the top of the tree by the coconuts. It had a body almost the size of a football and legs stretching out at least two feet. A large claw reached out and worked feverishly on the stem of the fruit until it was cut free and fell toward the ground like a dislodged boulder going off a cliff. Rainey jumped up and moved out of the way as it came to rest inches from where he had reposed. The large crab scampered down the tree and lit on the ground almost before the falling coconut. It grasped the large coconut in its claw, dragged it into the thick foliage and disappeared while Rainey stood with his mouth agape like a young boy at the circus. What the hell is that he wondered as he watched the creature disappear?

He opened the last bottle of water, tilted his head back and pressed it to his lips. A vision of his ex-wife, Leslie, ran through his mind. The water rushed into his mouth and for an instant he imagined the taste of cold beer. He looked at the candy bar in his hand and shook his head. It was time to move on and return to Creston. The satchel lay on the ground by the palm tree and he bent down to pick it up. Movement caught his eye and he looked up. Nothing. He stared into the trees, and still nothing.

The lagoon side of the island was tranquil, reverent like with a beach wider than the narrow strip of sand on the ocean side. Rainey moved toward the upper edge of the beach as he made his way back.

The sun was approaching straight up and there was no shade on the beach to protect him. He considered moving to the interior of the island but dismissed the idea as he realized the foliage was much too dense and would slow him down.

Almost four hours had passed since Rainey had set out from the make shift camp, and he was slightly more than halfway back to the northern end of the island. He was confident Creston was fine and resting, but he had urgency to get back. The beach in front of him held his attention and he quickened his pace as much as the sand would allow.

A pod of palm trees distracted him as he approached. One palm tree had grown out over the beach in an upward sweeping arc. It was picturesque, but more importantly provided a small patch of shade Rainey was thankful for. The sun and heat had become as intense as a steamy August day in New Orleans. The shade was welcome and reminded Rainey of a refreshing and unexpected burst of cool air gushing through a door held open a minute too long. He had, on occasion, experienced the cool blast of air escaping from one of the office buildings as he walked the downtown streets. How soft we become, he thought.

While he cooled off in the shade, he glanced toward the interior of the island. He stared for several seconds. It struck him as curious how much thicker and denser this area of the island appeared. The foliage was much more overgrown and the trees closer together than in the area near the plane. His gaze traveled up the taller trees and fixed on a forest canopy higher than the other areas he had seen. He dismissed it all as nothing, turned back toward the beach and again started his return to the plane. After about five hundred yards, the jungle thinned out and remained consistently so for the rest of his journey.

Creston lay motionless. Rainey stopped fifty feet from the plane and watched him.

Creston Labouef was the only son of an only son. His grandfather, Charles Labouef, had made the family fortune working the oil fields of south Louisiana in the 1930's. He was in the right place at the right time. His first venture on his own, after an accelerated apprenticeship with several steel fabricators, was building drilling platforms to be used in the marshes of Plaquemines parish. The oil companies spent money freely but were demanding. Charles Labouef made sure they got what they wanted. He hired the right engineers and the right geologists and his company grew, expanding into the oil exploration business as the industry moved toward offshore drilling in the Gulf of Mexico. Charles dragged Paris, his only son, into the business. Paris was honest and hard working but he seldom pleased his father. Charles was incapable of relinquishing any control to his son even though he continually promised "one day this will all be yours." Paris's one saving grace was when Creston was born. Charles, as do many grandfathers, tried to make up for his many shortcomings with his own son by spoiling Creston practically from the day he was born. Ironically, this was the one thing Paris admired and approved of with his father.

The Labouef family business had been sold to a major oil company several years after Charles Labouef had died. Creston's parents spent most of their time in the south of France even though they maintained several homes in the United States. Their main residence was an old mansion on St. Charles Avenue in the uptown garden district of New Orleans. They would visit Creston several times a year but preferred the European lifestyle. Creston had gotten his share of the family money to do with as he pleased because his parents knew Creston would be responsible enough to manage his finances. All the money, extravagance, and upper crust living had never gone to his head and he seldom spent money foolishly, but Creston had inherited some of the "wildcat" energy of his grandfather. He preferred living in New Orleans. There was always something happening in the French Quarter and Creston was often right in the middle of it.

Rainey approached the camp and knew it would be as he had left it. He and Creston were alone, and he struggled with the reality. A choppy snore escaped from Creston and his eyes opened.

"It's pretty bad when you wake your own self up from snoring," Rainey said.

Creston winced as he struggled to make himself comfortable by attempting to sit up. He looked at his watch and said, "You've been gone over four hours and you come back here with a smart ass remark. The island must be bigger than I thought. I figured you'd have been back over an hour ago."

"I think the island's about three miles long, give or take. And it's not wide, but it's hard to tell. I'd guess maybe a little less than half a mile. It narrows at both ends and the reef continues from the other end like it does here. There's another island off in the distance, but I don't know how far away it is, maybe three, four miles, maybe less. It's too hard to tell."

"It doesn't sound like you found anything interesting," Creston said.

"Well, nothing of interest. The rest of the island pretty much looks the same as here. The reef side is the same for the entire length of the island with one exception. There's an inlet through the reef right up to the edge of the sand. It's like an opening. The water there is darker so it must be deep. The other thing is the thickness of the trees. There's a section toward the middle of the island much denser and thicker than here. And of all the palm trees only one leans out over the lagoon, but otherwise, nothing special."

"So, no Hilton or Hyatt hotel tucked away on the other end?" Creston asked.

"Nothing," Rainey said. "We're it. Well, except for some strange, tree climbing, coconut loving crab."

"There are hundreds of islands in the Pacific like this one," Creston said. "Many are dry islands, meaning they have no source of fresh water, and thus are uninhabited. It might be years, hell, maybe never before someone stumbles upon this island."

Rainey turned toward the lagoon and stared out at the vastness of the water and thought maybe this is it. It all ends here. His mind went blank and the emptiness sent him back to his first waking moment on the island. His mental void persisted and he stood almost motionless for five minutes, his mind locked. Anger built inside him and he didn't try to fight it or understand it, but it brought him back to a conscious state.

"You want to talk about it?" Creston asked.

"Talk about what?"

"Where you went for the last ten minutes. You were zoned out so far you didn't even hear me trying to talk to you."

"No, I don't want to talk about it. But I do need to look at the cut on your head and clean it," Rainey said. "How's it feel?" Creston remained silent. "Look, I'm sorry. I didn't mean to sound harsh."

Rainey entered the plane to retrieve the first aid kit. The inside was hotter than before, uncomfortable and stifling, like going into a New Orleans attic in the middle of summer. He stood in the doorway awash in the sudden realization his loathing, self pity was because of the unfamiliar feeling of defeat. He had given up without realizing it.

"The wound is healing, but I'm a little concerned about the darkness of the skin. I don't like the color around the cut," Rainey said.

"As long as there aren't any red lines streaking across my forehead I think I'll be fine. It's badly bruised is all. I hit my head hard against the plane."

"Hold still while I clean this again. I know it hurts and I'm sorry, but we have to keep it clean." Rainey applied an antiseptic ointment to the jagged stitches. "Take these. They're antibiotics. I found them in the medicine kit. There's enough for two a day for about a week."

"Thanks," Creston said. "We go way back but…"

"You'd do the same for me?"

"Yeah, I guess I would."

"How about a late lunch?" Rainey asked

"What do you suggest?"

"Cold soup, take it or leave it," Rainey said.

They ate in silence. Rainey's anger at having resigned to defeat stirred purpose in him and he vowed to get off the island. Creston's guilt caused him to think about how they had come to be here.

CHAPTER SEVEN

"Hey, Rainsford!" Rainey did not have to turn around. He knew the loud, obnoxious voice instantly.

"You're a real pain in the ass, Creston," Rainey said as he turned to greet his friend. "I've asked you a thousand times to call me Rainey and not Rainsford."

"Yeah, yeah, Rainsford. Your mom was clever," Creston said. "Unlike you." His toothy smile beamed and he would continue to ignore his best friend's request.

"RAINEY!" Creston barked. "I've got a new plan and it includes you, *if* you're willing to be part of it."

Rainey stopped short and looked at Creston. He tried to be firm but knew he'd give in and listen. "What is it this time?" Rainey asked. "You should be the poster child for the proverbial 'more money than sense' person people make fun of."

"Yeah, like I care. Come on, let's go inside and get some oysters. I'll explain it all. You'll love this," Creston said. He walked toward the door knowing Rainey would follow whether he wanted raw oysters or not.

"Creston, it's Friday evening. I might have important plans for the night," Rainey said as they approached the oyster bar.

"You haven't had anything important to do on Fridays since your wife left, and you and I both know it."

Rainey shot Creston a hard look. "You'd make somebody a good friend one day." They entered the restaurant and walked to the oyster bar.

"What is it this time?" Rainey asked.

"First things first," Creston said. He turned and looked at Big O who was working the oyster bar as he did every Friday night. And before Creston could order Big O put a tray of fresh shucked oysters on the bar in front of Creston.

"A dozen on the half shell Mister C?"

Creston looked at the oysters. "Yes, Big O, a dozen. And when are you going to drop the Mister C stuff? We've been coming here for twenty years. It's Creston, got it. And extra horseradish, ok?"

"Yes sir, Mister C," Big O said, and went to shuck more oysters.

Rainey recalled his mother's teaching. In New Orleans, you called your elders, and people with money, mister before their first name. Creston had money and most people knew it. His net worth was well over five hundred million but he downplayed his wealth.

Two parking attendants from the garage next door were seated along side Rainey enjoying their raw oysters and beer. No where else but in New Orleans, he thought. You stand next to a blue collar worker on one side and a millionaire on the other and eat oysters as if everyone had come from the same shell.

"Ok, what is it this time?" Rainey asked while he and Creston drank their beers and considered more oysters.

"Ok," Creston responded ignoring the skepticism in Rainey's voice. "This is a good idea and you're going to like it. I promise. We're gonna take another little trip."

Creston stopped and took a sip of beer. Rainey shook his head.

"Big O, I'm gonna need another Dixie down here," Rainey yelled as he turned back toward Creston.

"Look, you can't still be upset about our last trip. It wasn't so bad. I thought you'd like Napa Valley. You certainly like the wine. Besides, I told you I needed to fly the jet and log some more hours. And my reserve in the cellar was running low. I needed to restock it."

Big O placed two Dixies on the bar and looked at Rainey. "What is it this time?"

"I'm not sure, but I'm about to find out."

"Who's your next of kin?" Big O asked.

"You guys ain't one damn bit funny at all," Creston said glancing back and forth at Rainey and Big O.

"Hey, not so loud, and stop with the language already," Rainey said. "They have real ladies in here." He looked at Big O. "Not like the one in Napa."

"I didn't know she was a guy!" Creston said loudly. "I was trying to do a friend a favor. You needed some company. You'd been divorced from Leslie a couple of months and honestly, you were starting to piss me off with all your moping around. You were turning into a real drag."

Rainey gave him a suspicious look.

"Sorry, bad choice of words. Forget I said drag, ok?"

Big O laughed loudly and moved down the bar to wait on two middle aged women, tourists who had no idea as to how to attack their boiled crawfish.

Rainey recalled the trip to Napa Valley. He had appreciated the offer from Creston to fly out to California, tour a couple of vineyards, and pick up a few cases of wine. He had acted nonchalant; aware of the real reason Creston wanted him on the trip.

Creston was quick to pick up and go when the urge hit him and he had enough money to go and do whatever he wanted, and take a friend. Rainey was still feeling the pain of the failure from the divorce and was sure the trip would do him good. He enjoyed red wine but usually with Leslie, his wife. Sampling wine with Creston would be interesting, and a special experience since Creston purchased good wine.

Creston had picked Rainey up early on a Friday morning and drove to the lakefront airport where he maintained his small private jet in a hanger. It was more convenient to come and go from the smaller airport than the large commercial one on the outskirts of New Orleans. On the way to the lakefront, Rainey told Creston he would be ready to date when he was ready, and not before. Creston suggested he still wanted to go out at night when they got to California. Maybe meet a few local Napa *Valley* girls. Creston laughed, but the humor was lost with Rainey.

"Sometimes I wish you were as funny as you are rich," Rainey told him.

The flight took almost five hours as they bucked the jet stream. As big a kid and screw off as Creston strived to be, he was nothing but serious when it came to flying. Rainey admired and respected Creston for this, but would never tell him so. It would go straight to Creston's head, and his head was already too big.

It was in the bar of their hotel where the "Napa" incident occurred. The early evening crowd had not yet started showing up and Rainey practically had the bar to himself. He was sitting in an overstuffed black leather chair at a small mahogany colored table, nursing a cold beer, when Creston showed up.

"Rainey, this is Liz," Creston said. "Liz, this is Rainey."

Rainey stood and waited for Liz to offer her hand. "Please, let's sit," Liz said, without offering to shake Rainey's hand.

Creston was half way to the door before Rainey and Liz sat down. Liz was attractive, tall and thin, with auburn hair, but wore too much makeup. Her cocktail dress was sleeveless, shimmering black with a high neckline and cut right above the knees. He suspected she might be older than she appeared. The lighting in the bar was dim and the background music was a distraction so it was hard to tell. But Rainey considered for a moment he might be ready. Leslie had certainly been ready. He didn't want to get even, but he did want to get well.

"I'd love a beer," Liz said.

Rainey motioned to the waitress to bring another beer. "I thought you'd prefer a different type of drink," Rainey said.

"High metabolism, I can drink anything I want. Lucky I guess."

"You're attractive," Rainey said. "I take it you know Creston from his other trips to Napa."

"No, we just met. I come here to relax. We met outside and he said you needed some company. He's nice, and concerned about you."

The conversation was good but Rainey thought things were a little too easy and convenient. He hoped Liz was not a "working girl" Creston had hired to cheer him up. He was starting to enjoy being with her. It was early evening and quiet in the bar. Rainey and Liz had the waitress practically to themselves and she was overly attentive.

When they ordered their second round of drinks, he detected a peculiar mannerism in Liz. He was unable to put his finger on it but she was definitely different than other women he had met.

"I have to visit the men's room," Rainey said, and excused himself. Maybe he was more nervous than he thought, and some cool water on his face would help settle him down. As he passed by the waitress he noticed an obvious smirk on her face as her eyes followed him. He was sure the smirk was at his expense.

"What?" he said.

The waitress looked at Rainey and said nothing, but did not turn away from him.

"I'm sure you have lots of regulars here. Is she a working girl, you know, a professional?"

"No. It's not…Okay, it's none of my business, but my gut tells me you're a good guy, but maybe a little naïve."

Rainey stared at her.

"Liz is really…Leo," she said. "I thought *she* might not be the kind of surprise you wanted back in your room. And, well, you look like you would want to know. Personally, I don't care. We have some guys who come out here looking for dates like Liz."

Thank God for the kind hearted waitress, Rainey thought. He looked over at Leo then looked back at the waitress, shook his head, looked at Leo again and exhaled deeply.

"Thank you very much. You saved me," Rainey said and returned to his table.

"So Leo, we're going Dutch treat on the drinks, right?" Rainey said.

Leo glanced over at the waitress and said, "I hate her," in a voice half an octave lower than before, and rife with sarcasm. He turned toward Rainey and said, "What about your friend that introduced us?" as his voice went back up in pitch.

"Not a chance," Rainey said.

The awkward moment with the drag queen had become humorous, although Rainey never revealed this to Creston. They had finished their drinks and laughed about the entire misunderstanding. Leo assured Rainey he would be surprised at how successful he, Liz, had been with tourists. Rainey was learning not much surprised him anymore. He wasn't ready after all.

Creston showed up in the bar several hours later, surprised to find Rainey alone and talking with the waitress.

"Where's Liz?" he asked.

"Leo went home."

Creston sank low in his chair. Rainey and the waitress looked at him, each wearing a curious smile. His confusion was replaced by an eyebrow lifting, jaw dropping understanding. He sank even lower.

The flight home to New Orleans was too silent. The harder he tried to have conversation with Rainey the quieter Rainey became. Eventually, Creston gave up and concentrated on flying the jet. Rainey knew his silence was driving Creston crazy but Rainey also knew Creston deserved it. Even with the best of friends, there are some things definitely off limits.

"It's been over a year since the Napa incident, right?" Creston said. "And, I bought a new jet; it's a Gulf Stream model GIII built in 1986. I got it from an old family friend in the oil business. Anyway, it is much better than the last one. It's a twin engine model with a range of over four thousand nautical miles and a special customized cabin with seating for eight plus the pilot, me, and the co-pilot, which would be you."

Creston tried to breeze by the co-pilot comment hoping to avoid a response from Rainey.

"Whoa!" Rainey said. "Whoa, whoa, WHOA!"

Creston stopped, let out an exasperated sigh and looked hard at Rainey.

"Co-pilot?" Rainey asked. "I don't know the first thing about being a co-pilot. I'm no more than a steward, at best, who helps carry the luggage. How the hell did I make it to co-pilot?"

"Well," Creston said. "It looks a whole lot better on the flight plan when you have a co-pilot. Especially," Creston lowered his voice and looked directly at Rainey, "when you are circumnavigating the globe."

Rainey stared hard into Creston's eyes looking for a telltale flinch, or any slight movement which would belie Creston's seriousness. Rainey nodded. "For a moment I thought you were serious. Nice try." He reached for his beer.

Creston looked at Rainey and then turned toward Big O who was walking back from the other end of the bar. "Big O, tell this big dim wit I have this whole thing planned out and to keep an open mind."

Big O looked at Rainey. "You're right," he said, "this sounds crazy to me. I think yo boy here had too much horseradish."

Rainey enjoyed the cat and mouse game he and Creston played, but he knew Creston always had a well thought out and solid plan. And he knew he'd eventually give in to his friend's wishes. Creston was careful and smart, and Rainey was loyal to his friend. He was certainly free to go.

CHAPTER EIGHT

"The good news is we're overdue," Creston said.

"That's your idea of good news," Rainey said without looking up. He twirled a stick in the sand as if drawing but created nothing more than squiggly lines. He and Creston rested in the shade of the plane's wing.

"Rainey, let's assume we lost one day after we crashed. You found me on the second day, patched me up, got us comfortable and settled here by the plane. Yesterday was day three and you explored the perimeter of the island. If this is all correct, then we're on day four. The point is we should have landed at Papua, New Guinea four days ago. We're overdue, and all the authorities have surely been notified we never showed up. They're looking for us. I'm sure of it," Creston said.

"We don't have any idea where we are and neither does the search and rescue team. They have no idea of where to look. Like you told me, it's a big ocean. Planes get lost all the time and are never found. Hale Boggs, remember him, U.S representative from New Orleans, disappeared in Alaska in 1972, and was *never* found. And Alaska is much smaller than the Pacific Ocean."

"Yes, but this is 1995. They have better equipment and more efficient ways of searching for us than when Mr. Hale disappeared. We're overdue. They are looking for us, I'm sure of it," Creston said. "My father will contact as many people as necessary to get help. And I gave Leslie power of attorney before leaving. No one is more determined and tenacious than she is. She won't give up."

Rainey looked at Creston but said nothing. She gave up once he thought.

"I know what you're thinking."

"I doubt it," Rainey said.

"Look, something's been bothering me for a while, and I need to ask," Creston said. "Do you resent me for introducing you to Leslie? The divorce was hard and took a lot out of you so I guess I'd understand. I've avoided the question because I didn't want to hear the answer."

"Don't be ridiculous," Rainey said. He stood, turned toward the lagoon and looked out over the water. "I owe you. My life was better because of Leslie, even if it didn't last."

Leslie Annette Fremin met Creston while working in the commercial loan department of the bank handling the majority of his financial needs. He was the exception to her typical clientele, far younger than most of the people she dealt with, rich, aloof, carefree, and single. They clicked almost immediately. He was eight years older than she and it impressed her immensely he was so rich at such a young age. And because he was wealthy and young, and she knew she was vulnerable, she remained professional, even though some of the older ladies at the bank continually made a point of telling her "he's single, and rich."

She found the entire situation ironic because she had a degree in finance, worked at a large private bank, was focused on money, and yet getting close to Creston was probably wrong largely because of his money. Or maybe it was because she abhorred the stereotypical idea of the woman latching onto the rich man and having it easy, of not earning anything and not appreciating what she had. Leslie knew she had to earn her way, to work for a feeling of accomplishment. She was too driven in this respect. Leslie knew she would make money, but she also knew family life was what she truly wanted.

Her casual dating had virtually come to an end. She rarely found the weekly or, as it more often worked out, monthly dates of any interest. The boys, of which there were far too many, tried much too hard to impress her and didn't try hard enough to be themselves. At twenty six she was more mature than the men she dated, until she met Rainey.

Creston was the one who introduced them to each other. And even with all of his philandering, Creston had become infatuated with Leslie. But Creston was smart enough to realize he was not ready to give Leslie what she wanted and needed. Rainey knew Creston liked Leslie but their relationship was none of his business. He respected his friend's privacy and expected the same from him so it surprised him when Creston said he wanted Rainey to meet Leslie.

"Creston, I'd be happy to meet Leslie but you don't need my approval, and I'm not comfortable discussing someone like her with you when I don't know her," Rainey said.

"Look, pal, I was merely infatuated with her. I mean, I like Leslie but I'm not ready to give up my lifestyle and settle down. You, on the other hand, have shown signs of needing more in your life. I think you'd like to get serious with someone and make a go of it." Creston paused thinking Rainey was not listening. "You're like a bad cousin I need to get rid of."

Rainey looked up, stared at Creston and said, "Yes, I heard you. I listen with my ears, not my eyes. So stop trying to be cute."

"Well it sounds kind of mushy to say you're like a brother to me and I want you to be happy and settle down and go forward with your life and not waste it all away and before you realize you'll be too old and time waits for no man..."

"Stop and breathe," Rainey said. "I get it, ok? You've made your point. I'd be honored to meet a lady who can see right through your bullshit and not be head over heals in love with you...or money."

"Yeah, now who's trying to be cute?"

Rainey understood the intrigue when Creston introduced him to Leslie. She was attractive but conservatively dressed. She did not arrive trying to impress him or anyone else. Her confidence was obvious, and so was the challenge. She was not a typical blind date dying to meet some guy she had been given to understand was a good catch.

After the somewhat formal but relaxed introductions Creston ordered drinks, a scotch and water for Rainey and a sloe gin fizz for Leslie, nothing for himself.

"I'm sure you'll like the fizz. It's refreshing this time of the evening," he said. "I have a dinner meeting; some guys want me to invest in a new software company. You two have a nice evening." He headed for the door. They look good together he thought.

"Creston has told me how helpful you have been to him with his banking needs." Sounds lame, Rainey thought as soon as he had said it. "It's impressive you're so involved in the banking community," he said trying to recover.

"You mean at my age?" she asked.

"No, not what I meant at all," he said. "It's apparent you've worked hard, you're smart, qualified, and must do an excellent job. That's all I meant. You look good for 35." Rainey avoided eye contact with her but Leslie was quick.

"Well, an old man like you can't keep up with me," she said. "Even if I was 35, which I am not."

Rainey looked at her, a slight upturn of his closed lips appeared. Leslie leaned back in her chair, returned the smile and looked Rainey in the eyes. Rainey passed on the next exchange of wits.

"A sense of humor, and up for a challenge," he said.

"At the right time and the right circumstances I can be quite the adversary."

"Then I look forward to the right time and place," Rainey said. He hoped there would be many chances to trade wits with her. He liked the possibilities.

"What is it you do, I mean, to earn a living?" she asked.

"Well let's see, I uh, I'm an account executive with one of the larger oil field supply companies," he answered.

"I would guess, you're a salesman," she said. "It's an admirable profession if you're honest and ethical," she said.

Rainey picked up his drink and took a slow swallow wondering if she was testing him on his character or simply conversing. He liked his profession, had been working in the oilfield business for five years and knew he was honest and ethical, although it was difficult at times to remain so. The commission only basis for income was intimidating when he first converted from base salary with incentives, but he had adjusted and liked being able to earn as much as possible with no limit on salary. Business had started to be lucrative and he knew it would get better as he persevered. It was a relaxed environment in which to work and he was free to come and go as he pleased. He also liked being able to take time off without having to answer to anyone provided his sales were good and he didn't abuse the privilege. In a sense, he was his own boss. This had grown on him.

"Being honest and ethical would be a minimum requirement," he told Leslie.

Their meeting was anything but love at first sight. Still, it was pleasant. Rainey was comfortable with Leslie and knew he wanted to see her again.

Leslie was committed to her banking career. She had graduated from Spring Hill College in Mobile, Alabama with a degree in finance. Leslie had an obsession with being precise. Attention to detail was a compulsion she seldom ignored. Banking had been a logical choice for her. The long hours and entry level salary stimulated Leslie. She was driven and enjoyed the sacrifice of the training period the bank insisted she complete. Somehow, she never expected to be a teller after graduating from college, but after several months she had a new appreciation for the position. The responsibility and pressure was much greater than she ever imagined. On more than one occasion, she spent many hours looking for five cents to balance her cash drawer. She learned to appreciate the rigors of being nice and friendly to the customers while paying close attention to each transaction, and did not enjoy looking for five cents at the end of a busy day. Leslie worked hard and graduated from her training period into the commercial loan department. She met many important, successful, and rich clients while working in this area of banking. She was young, vibrant, fresh, and full of energy. The older and more sophisticated clients enjoyed her youth and enthusiasm as much as they were amused by her naiveté.

Rainey would sometimes meet her for lunch and often thought how professional she appeared. He enjoyed seeing her in business attire. And on weekends, when they would attend a movie or a casual dinner somewhere uptown, or in the outskirts, she was usually dressed down. They had been dating for about a month and their relationship had become comfortable. Rainey was proving to be polite and unassuming. He opened doors for Leslie, pulled out her chair, waited for her to make her menu decisions first and then ordered for her. Perhaps he had been influenced by all the old movies he had enjoyed watching with his mother. He was much more like Jimmy Stewart in "It's a Wonderful Life" than Clark Gable in "Gone with the Wind".

There was touching without being rude or offensive, hand holding, some stimulating kissing of more than the first date type of kiss, and they both would look at each other suggestively. The tension was building, yet neither had made the right move or the right response at the right time to advance the relationship to a more intimate level. But it changed when they attended the Krewe of Bacchus Mardi Gras ball. She had been given a special invitation by a client who was wealthy and moved in the old circles of New Orleans. Leslie had received the invitation for help she had given him on a delicate deal requiring help from the bank.

Rainey borrowed Creston's Mercedes and called on Leslie at her apartment. When she opened the door, Rainey was awe struck. He was sure he must have resembled the cartoon wolf character whose eyes popped out of his head and tongue hit the floor. And Rainey knew, even in his rented tuxedo holding a fifty dollar corsage, he was outmatched. Leslie was breathtaking. Her hair was exquisite, her makeup perfect as a new day, her gown impeccable and appearing painted on as if by Rembrandt. He had never imagined her so beautiful. He handed her the corsage. Had the evening ended right there at her door he would have been content. But it got better. The extravaganza of the Bacchus Ball was painstakingly coordinated and it all occurred without a hitch. Rainey and Leslie danced to the music but never heard it. They drank and never tasted the liquor. After, as they drank café au lait and ate beignets at two in the morning, Rainey wondered where the night had gone.

Rainey knew there are, on rare occasion, those few moments throughout a man's life when he can do no wrong. Everything he touches turns to gold and even the gods are in awe of him. It was three in the morning and the magic of the night lingered in the air much like a favorite fragrance stimulates the senses. Rainey parked the Mercedes in front of Leslie's apartment, got out and moved around to her side, opened the door, and helped her out of the shining red car. Taking her hand, he escorted her to the door. The winter air was cold on his face and he was content, realizing what had been missing from his life. He waited at the door for Leslie to turn and allow him the kiss to complete his evening, a kiss telling him she knew how lucky she was to have been with him this night.

Rainey was vulnerable to the moment. His heart sank as he watched Leslie reach for her keys, insert them into the lock and open the door without turning toward him. As he stood there with a look of doubt, she took his hand and pulled him inside her apartment. The look of doubt was gone.

Rainey bent down and tasted her open lips as he had done before, but this time with an appetite not satisfied with simply a kiss. Leslie pressed her body to his. Even after the liquor, café-au-lait, the beignets, and the long night her breath was sweet and intoxicating. His pulse raced, his heart pounded and he lost himself to her. He carefully and skillfully maneuvered the zipper to the small of her back and her gown drifted to the floor. Her underwear was silk, of the barest essentials and undetectable through her gown. His exposed chest pressed against her bare breasts and only then did he realize she had been undressing him. He ached to be one with her, giving and receiving as she lost all inhibitions and succumbed to her desires. They fell together onto the couch and she straddled Rainey. Her dampness and warmth briefly rendered him motionless as he entered her. His mind swelled with an euphoric high he had never experienced before. Their movements were perfectly timed and they exploded together in a rare and simultaneous eruption of perfection which caused them both to collapse, each happy with the other. Rainey then clenched her tightly to him, and with his body begged her not to move. Leslie lay atop him. He realized he and the moment would wilt but hoped it would not be soon.

Leslie looked at Rainey, kissed him, nibbled his lips gently, approvingly, and then excused herself to the bathroom. He lay exhausted, and as men so often do, looked at his watch. It was five in the morning. When they had arrived at her apartment the clock in the Mercedes showed three o'clock. Rainey looked at the ceiling, relaxed his arm and allowed it to fall to the floor. Leslie returned from the bathroom and stood next to him. She took his hand and pulled him to the bedroom. Their night and becoming as one was not finished.

They slept through the morning, their exhausted bodies lay next to each other, drained of energy and relaxed at a level neither had ever experienced. Rainey awoke first and chose to absorb the moment and relive the memory of the previous night. Leslie rolled over and opened her eyes to see him staring up at the ceiling, as if in a trance.

"I'm wondering what you're thinking," she said, moving closer to him, her head on his chest.

"Regardless of what I want to say it will sound like clichés, or predictable words inadequate for last night."

"It's nice. I mean you trying so hard to find the right words. I'd hate if it was too easy, or if you tried to make it humorous," she said.

Rainey placed his arm around her and brought her close to his body. "Last night was incredible. It was so intense and yet natural and effortless. We slept passed noon and missed the morning coffee hours ago."

"I usually don't drink coffee after the morning but I would love a cup of coffee with you. I'll make us some but don't let it go to your head and don't get used to it," she said, jabbing a finger into his ribs. She rose from the bed and moved toward the kitchen. Rainey watched her lithe movement, feeling like a teenager again. His excitement stirred and his face flushed with embarrassment. He closed his eyes and tilted his head back. She picked up her robe and turned back toward him.

"Hmmm," she said, looking at his display of excitement. "Are you sure you want coffee? I mean, right now?"

He was entranced with her confidence and vulnerability. "The coffee can wait but I can't."

The night turned into their first weekend together. It was similar to so many new relationships, exciting, fresh, different and exhilarating, but at the same time more intense. Neither stopped to consider the moment might be a fleeting moment. They followed their urges like children at Christmas searching for presents, and they found each other. Their early relationship was what each had been looking for.

Leslie had never given herself to a long term relationship. School and her professional ambitions were her focus. The more serious, devoted commitments remained absent from her life. Or perhaps it was a simple matter of never having met the right man as all her college friends continually complained. There had been several possible right men, but it was never the right time. Leslie believed timing was important, but she would come to realize she might need more in her life than a big career.

Rainey had come close several times, but never made the promise to a lasting relationship. He had also come close to almost having the serious talk, and even after mustering up the nerve, had always stalled. Then it came to him one evening when he was trying to push himself to make the decision to plunge into the long term commitment. What he realized was the plunge was more like going over a cliff into a canyon than diving into a refreshing pool full of clear water warmed by the sun. Rainey had come to realize the right relationship would never require the big promise. His right relationship would happen and develop naturally, and they would both understand promises were not necessary. Rainey was calmed and comforted by this revelation, but it also left him lonely.

Rainey would prove to be a balanced soul who came to Leslie at the right time in her life. She found herself waking in the morning and thinking of him before anything else. This was a new and enjoyable experience for her, a contentedness not related to work in any fashion. And Rainey found Leslie filled his needs. She was a commitment without having to make one.

Rainey and Leslie were married less than a year after meeting. The marriage lasted almost six years. The divorce was amicable but devastating to both of them.

CHAPTER NINE

Rainey got up from the couch and walked across the floor of the living room to answer the phone.

There was a short silence then a soft voice, "Rainey, is this true about you and Creston going around the world in his plane?"

He had not heard from Leslie since their last meeting six months ago. His heart was racing, his face flushed, and he had an eerie feeling she knew.

"Rainey?"

"Hello, Leslie."

"Well, is it true?"

Rainey looked across the room at Creston, who was sitting in the recliner waiting patiently for him to get off the phone and continue their discussion. Creston still had business dealings with Leslie but he had asked Creston to not discuss him with her. Rainey tried to calm his anger.

He covered up the phone with the palm of his hand. "You and I will discuss this later." Creston sat quietly.

He put the phone back to his ear. "Yes, we're going over the details now. I've told him I would go but I'm starting to have second thoughts. And why do you know about this?"

"I still do business with Creston. He literally has millions of dollars invested in our bank as well as many other ventures we are directly or indirectly involved in. We like to know as much as possible about him and what he's doing. He's on the board of directors."

"He told me. What has this got to do with me, and why are you calling?"

His curtness was unintended but he knew it went right through Leslie like a cold February wind gusting off Lake Ponchartrain. He wanted to break the tension, but the words would not come.

"I was hoping to ask you to keep an eye on him. Try to keep him out of trouble. You're the more sensible and cautious one. Creston lives a little too large at times. I want him, I mean I want you both back here in one piece."

"Ok, I…"

"And," she interrupted him "this scares me to death. Do you have any idea how many small planes go down and are never found?"

"I've discussed it with him already," he said.

"Rainey, I was hoping to see you before you leave on the trip."

"What?" Rainey blurted out. Creston sat up with a look of concern.

"What about old what's his name? How would he feel about you meeting with your ex-husband?"

"You know his name is Charles," she said. "He has nothing to say about it. He left for New York, took a position with a big Wall Street firm. I didn't want to go. And he didn't ask me."

"I'm sorry," Rainey said.

"Thanks. I'm…never mind. Today is Saturday. You have several days to get ready for the trip. I'll be at Hillery's restaurant in the quarter on Wednesday about noon. I'd like you to meet me."

"I'll see what I can do. Wednesday at Hillery's." He hung up the phone.

"Where were we?" he asked Creston.

"Look, Rainey, a trip around the world in a properly equipped private jet can be done in a few days if you push it. We, however, are going to take about ten days, maybe two weeks because we're not in a big hurry. Arnold Palmer did it years ago, and I think it took him a couple of days. He set a new record at the time."

"Yeah, and Dodge Morgan did it by himself in a sailboat and set a new record, but he was going stir crazy toward the end. I don't want to do either, set a record or go crazy. And sometimes, you drive me crazy."

"I've already filed my flight plan. We'll fly from New Orleans to San Diego. Leave early enough to be there for a late lunch and get the plane refueled. Then we'll take off for Honolulu. With the time change we should make it there right before dark, depending on the jet stream and if we get out of San Diego on time. I figure we'll spend a day or so in Hawaii, maybe check out the night life. Then we head southwest toward New Guinea. We'll cross the intercontinental date line and the equator into the southern hemisphere. We make it to Papua for fuel, a late dinner, spend the night and then off to Sidney, Australia. What do you think so far?"

"Creston, as crazy as you can be I learned a long time ago to trust you. All of this works for me if you're sure about it."

"Man, you're no fun at all," Creston said. He sat silent for a moment. "Leslie, right? On the phone?"

"Yeah, so what."

"It's been a while since you've spoken to her. She asks about you all the time but I've stayed out of it like you asked me to. It wouldn't hurt to see her. She's had a rough time of it. It might do you both some good. You two were one of the best couples I've ever…"

Rainey stared at Creston. It was seldom he caught Creston in an awkward position.

"Ok, I'll stay out of it. As I was saying…"

"Spare me the rest, save it for the plane," Rainey said. "We still leaving Friday?"

"Well, the plane has been checked and certified. All the provisions are ready to be loaded, all destinations have been notified and refueling has been arranged. We're good to leave tomorrow. But, I was thinking Wednesday morning, the 11th, day before Columbus Day. Rather appropriate, I think. And, I'm getting itchy to get going."

Rainey thought for a moment, "I've already told work I'm going. I'll pack and be ready by Wednesday," Rainey said.

"All right, that's what I wanted to hear. I was getting nervous for a minute. Get all your affairs in order over the next couple of days. Contact your bank, neighbors, post office, and things like…"

"I know what I need to do, Creston. I've already started working on it."

"Oh, yeah? Well, what about a last will. Did you make one?"

"What the hell are you talking about? Why would I need a last will?"

"Calm down, it's a formality, not a premonition. You should have one. I updated mine and have a copy of it stored in a safety deposit box. Leslie has power of attorney to open it should anything happen."

"Well, nothing is going to happen. We'll be back in a couple of weeks eating oysters, right?"

"Hey, you might meet a little hottie in Australia or South Africa and jump ship on me, never to be seen again," Creston said. But he knew it would require more than a pretty face to get Rainey to leave New Orleans.

"You're not making me feel real good about this. Make a will, jumping ship, South Africa, what's next?" Rainey stopped then said, "But I do like the little hottie idea."

It was an unusually cool October morning and Rainey inhaled the freshness of the early day. It was stimulating, like the first nectar flavored snowball of summer he would go out of his way to get at Hansen's Sno-Bliz on Tchoupitoulas Street. The air was crisp and the humidity was much lower than normal. Rainey was exhilarated with energy. A cool front had come in during the night; the sun was low and painted the sky an orange hue that softly blended into the dark blue of the fading night. The scattered clouds wafted across the sky like giant cotton balls and Rainey was at ease. Creston was waiting outside by the plane drinking a cup of coffee. The jet was shiny and clean, and Rainey's excitement grew as he grabbed his bags.

"There're coffee and beignets on board. Throw your bags in the hold with mine. The tower is waiting on us," Creston said. "Come on, let's go. Move it!"

"Then what the hell are we waiting for, mon capitan?"

"Corny, but I like it," Creston said. "Let's get on board."

Rainey strapped himself into the co-pilot seat, put on his new aviator sunglasses and stoically watched Creston as he settled into the pilot's seat and secured his harness.

"Nice touch, the glasses. You almost look like you know what you're doing," Creston said. "Almost."

"I thought you'd like them. A gift from Big O. I stopped at the restaurant yesterday for lunch and to talk with Big O about the trip."

"Aviator glasses? What the hell does Big O know about flying? And, what about me? He didn't give me anything, and I stopped at the restaurant, too."

Rainey reached down into the flight bag, pulled out a black case and handed it to Creston.

"From Big O, he said to give it to you when we got on the plane."

Creston opened the case. Inside was a small compass.

"You set me up. Why didn't you stop me before I complained about Big O not giving me anything. You like it when I put my foot in my mouth, don't you?" Creston shook his head, disappointed in himself.

"I always assumed you like the taste of leather," Rainey said. "Read the back.

Creston,
You always know your way.
Come home safe.
Big O.

"Damn, don't I feel foolish. I should have more faith in my friends."

Rainey looked straight ahead and said, "Let's fire her up and get out of here."

Rainey paid attention to everything Creston did preparing for departure. He watched how Creston's demeanor changed to total seriousness and confidence as soon as he started the check list. Rainey knew to sit quietly and not interrupt. There would be time for questions after the plane was airborne.

Creston tapped his own headset indicating he wanted Rainey to put on the co-pilot headset. "It's good to have a second pair of ears. Can't be too careful, and you can listen to the other pilots."

"I've done this before, remember?"

"I remember, but I never assume anything when I fly. "Tower, this is N9866Q requesting clearance for departure on runway 36L," Creston called into the headset.

"N9866Q, proceed to runway 36L and hold," came the reply.

"Roger , tower."

Creston maneuvered the jet into position on runway 36L and stopped. He looked at Rainey with a tight lipped grin. Take off was Creston's favorite part of flying. A small single engine Cessna came in for a landing while they sat waiting for clearance.

"N9866Q, you are cleared for take off. Creston, we'll be looking for you in a couple of weeks."

"Thanks guys. See ya soon."

Creston pushed the throttle forward and the jet started down the runway picking up speed. They lifted off and in a few seconds were climbing almost vertically into the sky above New Orleans. The force pinned Rainey against the co-pilot seat as if he was on the losing end of a wrestling match with a three hundred pound opponent with a bad attitude. The take off was flawless and thirty seconds into the flight the plane began to level off, the G force subsided, and Rainey was able to relax and get comfortable.

Creston's trademark grin was no more than a childish smile following each take off. Rainey enjoyed this humbleness so seldom seen in his friend. It was several minutes until the plane leveled off at the assigned cruising altitude of thirty eight thousand feet. The sky was clear and the air was smooth. Creston had turned the plane toward the west and the sun was behind them. It was a perfect day for flying.

"How about some coffee?" Rainey asked. "It's like an early morning sailing trip on the lake. It's better with a cup of coffee after the sails are trimmed and all is under control."

Creston shook his head. Rainey got up from the cramped quarters of the cockpit and took one step past the bulkhead to the galley. The layout of the plane was tight but efficient. Rainey was impressed with the completeness of the plane. He returned to the co-pilot's seat with a spill proof tankard and secured his harness, put his head set on and gazed out at the horizon. They both sat silently, absorbing the view from all angles.

"It never fails to amaze me," Creston said.

"You say that each time we fly."

"Yeah, and I'll say it again. So, what did you do last night?"

"I had dinner at Maspero's, by myself," Rainey said. "Then I went into Jackson Square, stopped and watched the tourists taking pictures of Andrew Jackson on his big horse." Rainey reflected on the evening. "Then I left the square and went into St. Louis Cathedral, sat in a pew in the back and said a few prayers. I asked for a safe trip and then sat. After a while I went home and finished packing. Nothing exciting."

"Still a good Catholic boy. I never told you this but I admire your faith. I've learned a thing or two from you," Creston said.

"Well, Catholic, yes. The good part's in question from time to time."

"Why you think I hang out with you so much? I'm hoping some of it rubs off on me, or at least I'm close by when you're being saved."

Rainey shook his head. "You need a lot of help, pal."

Creston set the autopilot and relaxed as he focused on the horizon touching the sky. The rest of the flight into San Diego was uneventful, the air was smooth, and there had been almost no turbulence. The sky remained cloudless and stretched endlessly. Rainey and Creston spent much of the flight admiring the changing scenery below as they jetted across the southwest of America, oblivious to the hundreds of thousands of people below, invisible and soundless as they sailed across the sky. They approached San

Diego's Lindbergh field thirty minutes ahead of schedule, received clearance and had a perfect landing.

"Nice job," Rainey said as they taxied to the private jet area and came to a stop. "You're getting pretty good at this."

"It's not all me. This new jet is great and handles much better than the smaller one," Creston said while finishing the post flight routine. "It's a long flight to Hawaii. Let's go into the grill and get a sandwich while they refuel the plane."

The San Diego air was cool, much like the morning air when they left New Orleans. There was vigor in their step as they walked across the tarmac amid dozens of private jets, and Rainey wondered where the aircraft were heading to or coming from.

"Hey, flyboy, lose the glasses."

"I like these glasses. They make me look good," he said as he entered the restaurant.

Creston shook his head and followed.

An hour later they were taxiing to the departure runway and requesting clearance for departure. Rainey knew already the trip would end too soon.

"In about six hours or so we should be in Honolulu, and with the time change we'll arrive early enough to check into a hotel, get some dinner, and check out the Hawaiian night life."

"What time are we scheduled to leave in the morning?" Rainey asked and heard the tower give them clearance as he spoke.

"Roger, tower. Thanks for the help," Creston said and accelerated down the runway. The force created by the thrust of the jet was as powerful as the previous one. But this time the wrestler was gone, Rainey was more comfortable and in control.

"Now, where were we?" Creston asked as he leveled off. "Oh yeah, we're not leaving in the morning. We'll do a little tourist stuff in Waikiki tomorrow, get some rest and leave early Friday morning. The flight from Honolulu to New Guinea is long and we're not trying to set any records, remember? And, I tried to tell you this earlier but you wouldn't let me finish."

Rainey sat quietly and stared straight ahead. Creston set the auto pilot again and leaned back in the seat. The light blue sky touched the dark blue pacific and even at over four hundred miles an hour it was as if they were motionless, hanging in the air. Rainey looked at his watch. It was 2:30 in New Orleans. He wondered what the lunch special at Hillary's had been.

"We'll be in Hawaii by five o'clock. We can catch a cab to the Hyatt on Waikiki Beach and check in. Hey, you listening?"

Rainey turned toward Creston, enjoying the calm. "Yes, I'm listening. I've never been to Hawaii. I think I'm going to like this."

"There isn't much to see on this leg of the trip. It's about twenty five hundred miles of open sky and water. There are no reports of bad weather and no reports of any significant turbulence along this flight route. The boys flying the big planes give pretty good updates to the towers. We should be good for the whole trip."

"OK, then what do you want to talk about?"

"Nothing, I don't need to discuss anything, unless you want to tell me about Leslie and what she said."

Rainey hesitated for a minute. "She wanted to meet and have lunch today. I told her I'd think about it, but then you moved the departure up from Friday so I knew I wouldn't make it. I wasn't sure how to call her and tell her."

"You left her somewhere expecting you to show up? And you didn't tell her you weren't coming? Jesus, Rainey, what the hell is wrong with you?"

"There's nothing wrong with me. I told her I would think about it. I didn't tell her I'd meet her. And, besides, I don't owe her anything at this point."

"Bull shit! You owe her consideration and respect. You got hurt but she's paid for what she did every day since she left. You might never get over it but you're hurting yourself as much if not more than you're hurting her. She made a mistake, but you might be making a bigger one."

"Creston, remember when I asked you to not discuss me with Leslie? Well, I don't want to discuss Leslie with you."

"Fair enough, but it's not like you can go anywhere, can you? Creston lowered his head and said, "Dumb ass."

"What!"

"Dumb compass, I said where'd I put the dumb compass."

"Right, that's what I thought you said."

The conversation died. They were about an hour out from Honolulu when Creston pointed straight ahead.

"Looks like we got a little thunderstorm in our way. We need to change our course and try to fly around it. It'll push our arrival back about an hour."

Rainey glanced at Creston. "Is there a problem here?"

"No, this happens all the time. It would be a problem if we tried to fly into it or over it. The storm is too big so we have to go around. Relax, this is no big deal."

Rainey had gotten a little edgy discussing Leslie and his comfort level had diminished. The storm in the distance had replaced the monotony of the flight with some marvelous cloud formations and lightning flashes, but Creston had the plane under control. It calmed him. The clouds were voluminous and covered the sky. Rainey was in awe of the natural beauty. Where young children's imagination might conjure up dogs, bears, dragons and trees, Rainey witnessed the majesty of God's creation. The lightning backlit the clouds, and the many different shades of gray were evident, but then gone as the flash died. Seconds later another jagged bolt lit up the sky like a large beacon slashing through the clouds. Creston had been correct and the storm turned out to be uneventful. Soon the weather was behind them and they were staring down on the island of Oahu as they made their approach. The islands of Hawaii contrasted with the deep blue of the massive pacific and looked like scattered green jewels. The evening sun's light danced across the ocean and large shadows leaped from the islands as the jet descended and maneuvered into the landing pattern.

Rush hour traffic from the airport was heavy and the arteries to the hotel were full and moved at a slow pace. Rainey was tired and even the excitement of the trip and being in Hawaii did not revive him.

Rainey and Creston walked into the Hyatt and approached the front desk. The check-in was quick. Rainey turned toward the openness of the lobby as a bell hop approached offering to help him and Creston with their duffle bags. Rainey waived off the bellhop then walked around the lobby.

"It's an open air lobby," Creston said. "It stays open year round. Nice breeze almost constantly."

Rainey hadn't noticed the openness but took a minute to scan the lobby. He pivoted around and thought this would never work in New Orleans.

"I'm kind of tired so maybe we can skip the big dinner and Waikiki night life. I think I'll do some room service."

"Rainey, this is your first night in Hawaii, and you want to stay in your room? Does this make any sense to you at all?"

"Okay, I get it. But dinner in the hotel, and maybe a drink in the bar. I can't go any more."

"I'll meet you in the main restaurant in thirty minutes. Don't keep me waiting. I'm starving, and I want a drink so make it quick."

Rainey and Creston turned and headed for the elevators. They got off on the eighteenth floor and went to their separate rooms. Rainey slid the electronic key into the lock, removed it, and the green LED illuminated. He shook his head as he entered the suite. Creston had overdone it again. The suite was big enough for an entire family. He threw his bag onto the king sized bed and walked to the wall of glass offering a view of Waikiki Beach. The waning sunset cast the slightest orange hue on the horizon as night was nigh. "Creston makes it hard to be humble," he said.

Rainey turned, intending to use the bathroom when he spotted the phone next to the bed. He stared at the phone, and his mind raced remembering the conversation on the plane. It was too late to call Leslie and apologize, and he wasn't sure what he wanted to do. As he reached for the phone it rang and startled him.

"Thirty minutes, pal. I'm headed downstairs for a drink."

"Shit, Creston, you're worse than my mother. I'll be there, but I need to wash my face. Hey, you think they have Dixie beer?"

"The only Dixie you'll get tonight is if we run into a redneck band in some bar on the outskirts of Waikiki."

The restaurant was not crowded. He had expected a wait but Creston was already seated. Rainey sat and stared at the colorful drink in front of him.

"The umbrella is a nice touch," he said. "What the hell is this?"

"It's a Mai Tai," Creston said. "THE island drink. I told you, they don't have Dixie Beer."

Rainey swirled the miniature umbrella and tasted his drink. It was cool and refreshing. He nodded with approval.

"I've already ordered for us. The cattle industry is big here. They have great steaks. And they serve them with island flair."

Rainey knew it was senseless to argue, closed his menu and handed it to the waiter. Lifting his glass he said, "To my good friend, and for an adventurous trip."

They finished the meal and a bottle of wine over the course of the next two hours. Rainey felt a surge of energy and was not as tired as when they had arrived.

"So, what would you like to do tomorrow? Anything specific you have in mind?" Creston asked as they got up and started for the elevators.

"Pearl Harbor monument. I promised my mother I'd visit it if I had the time. I didn't expect to be here with an entire day to kill, but since we have tomorrow open I'd like to keep my promise," Rainey said.

"Pearl Harbor?" Creston questioned. "Any particular reason you promised your mom you'd visit the monument?"

"I'll tell you tomorrow. I'm worn out and ready for bed. Let's meet in the lobby at nine o'clock."

"Nine is good. Let's get some sleep. Guess I'm more tired than I thought."

Rainey lay in bed and stared at the ceiling. What was it about a bed away from home that made it hard to sleep regardless of how tired he was? It didn't matter where or what type of bed, it was always the same. It was hard to get comfortable and thoughts came at him one after the other with no congruity. He took a deep breath, exhaled and focused on his mother and the promise he had made. He looked forward to telling her about Pearl Harbor monument. Sleep came as he thought of all he would tell her.

Rainey and Creston caught a cab to the Pearl Harbor monument. Their first day in this natural paradise was sunny and clear with a soft ocean breeze tumbling across the island. But the paradise had become more and more hidden and disguised as men rushed to build high rise buildings and shopping centers. It was still beautiful, but Rainey wondered what it must have been like thirty years ago.

"Is the promise to your mom the only reason you want to see Pearl Harbor? I don't recall you being a history buff or talking about it."

"My mother had an older brother. He enlisted in the navy and got stationed in Hawaii right out of basic training at San Diego. She was a young teenager when he left home. She never saw him again. I think she got one letter from him and then the Japanese attacked. He went down with the USS Arizona and the body was never recovered. He's still down there. It feels a little strange going to the monument. It's sort of like going to the wake of a good friend's relative, but someone you had never met. At least in this case I'm related."

"You sure you want me to go along? I mean, you might want some solitude, some time to think and all."

"I want you there. I don't know what to expect or how I'll feel. This is mostly for my mother. It's more than an obligation. It's also an honor."

Rainey shrugged his shoulders and said nothing more for the next ten minutes. The cab stopped in front of the ticket booth at the Pearl Harbor monument. They bought two tickets and walked to the dock of the water taxi for the ride to the monument. As they approached Rainey remembered the USS Arizona was a sunken battleship. He was first to step onto the platform built over the ship. A sense of reverence prevailed as he walked around and viewed the displays. The names on the wall burned into his consciousness and the pictures caused his mind to race back to the war movies he had watched, and then to news reports broadcast every year on December 7th. Those news reports and movies would never be viewed the same. He and Creston were in a sacred arena.

It was peaceful but surreal, and he had an unfamiliar feeling of loss. A loss for someone he had never known, or perhaps a loss felt vicariously through his mother. He tried to understand what she must have gone through. She had never visited Hawaii and the monument, and maybe had never completely said goodbye to her brother. Rainey found his uncle's name on the wall and knelt in prayer.

"All the men still down there in the ship all these years. We've all heard about it a hundred times but I never truly understood," Creston said. He stood trying to absorb it all but it was too much and he promised to return one day.

The water taxi ride back was much more somber than the ride to the monument. Nothing need be said. They caught a taxi back to the Hyatt and Rainey was the first to speak.

"Thanks for coming with me. It was more emotional than I anticipated. My mother and I need to have a long talk."

"Include me in the conversation. I'm not family, but this was special and I'd like to share it with your mom." Creston placed his hand on Rainey's shoulder and pushed. "Besides, she loves me more than you."

"True, but only for your money."

They entered the lobby and walked toward the elevators when Rainey noticed the gift shop beyond the registration desk.

"You go on ahead," Rainey said. "I've got to make a stop at the gift shop."

Creston gave Rainey a puzzled look and asked, "What'd you forget? You had plenty of time to pack and you still forgot something, didn't you?"

"I didn't forget anything. I mean, I didn't forget anything from home. I was caught up in the experience of Pearl Harbor and didn't get a card to send home to my mother. They must have one in the gift shop. I'll meet you in the lobby in about an hour."

"An hour it is. Tonight is Chinese food night. A friend told me of a place here in Honolulu called Wo Fat. Been around for years and supposed to be real authentic." Creston turned away and said, "Don't keep me waiting."

Rainey ignored the last comment and walked into the gift shop. The post card rack was next to the cash register. He spun the rack without looking at the cards, his thoughts returning to Pearl Harbor. The rack stopped and Rainey glanced up and down, looking for a post card of the Pearl Harbor monument. One card gave him a different perspective than anything he had seen. He removed the card from the rack and a chill coursed up his back. The picture was an aerial shot straight down on the monument. It had never occurred to Rainey, as he stood on the platform, the large battleship was still distinguishable in the water, and he and the other tourists were standing directly above it. The photograph clearly showed the ghostlike outline of the huge ship through the dark blue water. He stared at the card and wondered how close he had been to his uncle, where in the ship his uncle had been at the time of the attack, and where was his final resting place. The sales lady at the register took the card without looking at it, placed it in a white, gift shop bag stenciled with the hotel name over Hawaiian flowers, entered the sale into the cash register and asked for $2.50.

It had been almost fifty five years since the attack on Pearl Harbor. Rainey understood the sales lady's nonchalance, but he knew he would never feel the same again. The experience was vivid in his mind, and the passion of it all would remain with him forever.

Rainey stopped at the front desk and asked to borrow a pen from the evening attendant. He wrote his mother's address on the card and then proceeded to write.

Mom,

I visited the monument today. I found Uncle Larry's name listed with the others and felt as if I knew him. Thanks for telling me about my uncle. It was an honor to be there. I love you. See you soon.

Rainey

He put the pen down and motioned to the attendant. She was a young oriental woman with long black hair that reached the small of her back and glistened under the ceiling lights. Her skin was like fine alabaster; her almond shaped eyes dark and exotic. Rainey stared into them and was captured by her beauty. His trance was broken as she spoke.

"May I help you, sir?"

Rainey's face flushed deep red with embarrassment as if he had been caught ogling her.

"You wear an interesting shade of red. It looks good on you," she said. Her playfulness and confidence belied her age.

"Would you see this gets mailed for me, please?" Rainey said taking the direct approach. Before she answered he added, "Sorry I was staring. You are very attractive and…"

"Of course, sir. It would be my pleasure to handle it for you. And don't apologize. I'm flattered. Perhaps you don't see many oriental women at home."

Rainey considered what she had said, and it was true. He had not seen many oriental women, and certainly not one this attractive. His embarrassment returned.

"Thanks," he said and turned away. He stopped and turned back around. "Are you familiar with Wo Fat restaurant? My friend thinks we should go there for dinner tonight. Someone told him it was authentic and excellent."

"Wo Fat is very Chinese and worth the trip. Catch a taxi out front and you'll be fine." She reached for a small card and wrote on it in Chinese. "Give this to the host when you walk in."

Rainey took the card and looked at it as if expecting to read what she had written. He turned the card over several times, put it in his pocket and said, "I suppose your uncle is the host."

"You read Chinese?" she asked with a serious tone.

Rainey looked at her and before he mumbled a reply she smiled and said, "Got you."

His head dropped slightly. This is ridiculous he thought, and stepped toward the counter until he leaned against it, his face inches from Lilly's. "I don't read Chinese," he said, "I read people."

"So you see me as a book?"

"More like a classic novel, one to be savored and consumed," he teased.

"I think you prefer the Braille method," she taunted in reply.

The levity was appreciated after such a serious and engulfing afternoon. Her candor and playfulness lifted him and put things in perspective. He stared a moment longer and her look of question suggested she expected him to be defensive or retaliatory. He took the coward's way out.

"I'll see you again."

"You see me now," she said, refusing to abandon the jousting.

He bowed in a respectful, oriental manner, and then shook his head. Her verbal battle had him at a disadvantage. He decided to desist before he dug himself into a hole too deep to climb out of.

"Good evening, Lilly," he said reading her name tag, and then turned toward the elevators.

"And good evening to you, mister…"

"Room 1816," he said. He knew she would look up his name and he hoped he might have regained a foothold in their sprightly exchange.

He stretched out on the king size bed, the mattress firm but pliable enough to form to his tense body. He exhaled and the day's excitement drained from his body, melting into the bed. His mind imagined the image, but Lilly was too young, and he had no business entertaining thoughts of her. Maybe though, for one night with no strings attached, no games played, and no guilt…he smiled with how it might be. What a dumb ass, he thought, as he sat up and gave in to his insecurity.

He chastised himself as he rode the elevator down to the lobby. The boy in him had been doing the thinking for a forty two year old man, a recipe for disaster, he thought. He'd had enough disasters in his life as he recalled his divorce.

The elevator doors opened and Creston was waiting. Rainey stepped out but didn't stop walking. Creston turned and double stepped several times to catch up. Rainey stared at the unattended front desk as he walked.

The hard marble floor stopped his fall as he tripped over a large potted plant placed close by one of the interior columns of the lobby. The crimson red color returned to his face and he stared up at Creston.

"Shut up," was all Rainey said. Creston helped him up.

"What the hell was that about? And what were you looking for?"

"Can we go to dinner?" Rainey said. "I got distracted, okay?"

Creston managed to stay quiet even though inside he was about to explode with laughter. Rainey's embarrassment was slow to wane and he tried to hide it as he again scoured the lobby looking for Lilly, hoping she had not seen him. Convinced she had not seen his graceful departure through the lobby, Rainey relaxed. Maybe he would see her again before leaving the next day.

The cab stopped in front of Wo Fat Chinese restaurant. Rainey brushed Creston off and handed the cab driver twenty dollars for the fourteen dollar fare.

"Keep the change and thanks for taking the direct route," Rainey said.

"No problem, braah. Lilly tell me take care of you."

Rainey shot the driver a look. The cabby's comment had surprised him. He was pleased but did not show it.

"Lilly, who's Lilly?" Creston asked.

"She's the young oriental lady who works the front desk at the hotel. She was helpful in handling the mailing of a post card I wanted sent to my mother. And she has a good sense of humor, verbally sparred with me," he said. "She won."

Creston moved in front of Rainey, leaned into him and said, "She won? A young lady got the best of you? Haven't I taught you anything?"

Rainey did not back off as he stared at Creston. His confession of defeat did not warrant a reply, and Rainey was in no mood to tolerate anything snide Creston would spew at him. Creston backed up a step and gave Rainey space. He held both hands up in a mock gesture of surrender and said, "That's good. We all need to be humbled from time to time. I imagine my day is coming, but then again, probably not."

"You? Yeah, probably not," Rainey said. They turned toward the restaurant.

Wo Fat was in an old, nondescript building. One would pass it on an average day and never give it another look. But there was an aroma in the air and it captured the senses like honeysuckle or fresh baked bread. The fragrance was heavy with oriental seasonings from hot woks, and beckoned to the busy people hustling by who would lift up their heads to get a better whiff of the food as they walked. Even before they entered the building they knew they were in the right place.

The entrance was a set of double wood doors, each with a large pane of glass. The left door glass had a sign informing customers the restaurant was upstairs. The right hand door opened freely and had to be pulled shut as there was no spring or automatic door closer. A single, bare light bulb, hanging on a frayed cord, dimly illuminated the entrance. A corridor to the left of the stairs led to endless darkness. It was evident no one was supposed to venture down the ominous hall.

Rainey and Creston gave each other an inquisitive look. The noise of the busy restaurant escaped from the top of the stairs and became louder as they walked up. A heavy curtain made of strings of different colored beads hung across the entrance. They pushed through the beads into the dining room.

The aroma downstairs had been enticing, but as he pushed through the curtain it unleashed a hunger in Rainey previously dormant. He would overeat and love every bite of it. The décor was a dire contrast to the aroma. Most of the tables were large, round and seated eight to ten people. Each table had a lazy-susan in the middle where all the food was placed. The lights mounted on the ceiling were glary, hard to look at, and the room had an uninviting flatness to it. The walls were wood paneling and the room had four small windows. Most of the tables were occupied by large oriental families. The lazy-susans were spinning and each person helped themselves to whatever dish stopped in front of them, served it onto their plates and then replaced it, but not in the same spot from where it had been taken. At one table was a group of U.S. Navy sailors dressed in their whites, all young enlisted men. His thoughts immediately returned to Pearl Harbor, and Rainey took comfort in seeing them.

A small oriental hostess approached. Rainey reached into his shirt pocket and handed the card Lilly had given him to her. She read the card, turned and gestured with her hand for them to follow. She led them toward a table by the kitchen door. They seated themselves and Rainey reached out his hand for the menu, but instead the hostess bowed, turned and walked toward a waiter, still clutching the menus.

Rainey purposely avoided Creston's stare.

"Maybe we get special menus?" Creston said.

"Look, I gave her the card like Lilly said."

"Maybe they'll bring us some Dim-*wit* Sum, compliments of your new friend."

"Life's full of so many challenges, and then you on top of all of it. How did I get so lucky?"

The waiter approached and set a pitcher of hot tea in front of them with an order of pot stickers. In perfect English he said, "Lilly asked us to feed you. Please relax and enjoy your meal."

"All right dim-wit, enjoy the meal," Rainey said.

The waiter brought a bowl of fried rice, a bowl of white rice, and set both in the center of the table. He was followed by two young Chinese women, each carrying two entrees. They uncovered each dish, pronounced the name of the dish in Chinese, replaced the cover and set it on the table. After the four main dishes were introduced, the waiter and his assistants politely bowed and left the table.

"All this was on the card?" Creston asked.

"I doubt it. The more intriguing point is we had a somewhat casual conversation, fun and amusing, but certainly not warranting this kind of treatment. Especially from someone I had just met and will likely never see again."

"Well, I hope you can do as well on the rest of the trip. Wait until we get to Africa," Creston said. "That'll be a challenge."

Rainey considered what Creston said. He had not thought much about all the places they would visit and the people they would meet. "True, but we're off to a good start."

The waiter returned and placed the small tray with the bill face down in front of Rainey. Creston gestured for Rainey to hand him the bill but Rainey picked up the small tray and turned the bill over.

"Don't tell me she got them to comp the meal on top of the great food and service."

"No. It's fifty dollars even, including gratuity. I've got this," Rainey said.

He handed the waiter the tray with three twenty dollar bills and told him he didn't need change. The waiter thanked him and said a cab was waiting to take them back to the hotel. They got up, made their way to the stairs, and exited into the Hawaiian evening.

The cool night air splashed across their faces. China town was awake and starting to swell with people out for a night of dining and fun. The evening was electrified with excitement, the young couples laughing and moving hand in hand. Rainey and Creston looked at each other, both tempted to stay in China town and experience the culture of Hawaii with a Chinese influence.

"We have an early departure," Creston said. "I don't party the night before flying. Where were you last night when we had more time? Let's head back, maybe you can tell Lilly thanks for both of us."

The hotel lobby was quiet except for the faint sound of the surf far off Waikiki beach. Rainey looked through the open walls toward the beach. The lobby lighting was bright enough to make it impossible to perceive anything in the darkness beyond. The many people walking the beach were invisible in the night.

"Order room service for breakfast. You can eat while you get ready or whatever, but be in the lobby for seven. I'd like departure by eight. It's a longer flight than the leg here."

"I'll be here by seven. I'm turning in shortly but first I've got to leave a note for Lilly thanking her," Rainey said. "Get some sleep. I want you rested and awake."

Rainey stood at the front desk and watched Creston walk toward the elevators. The breeze filtering through the lobby was cool with a hint of salt. He tilted his head back slightly and took a deep breath, filling his lungs to almost bursting and held the fresh air in, waiting for the slow burn in his lungs before exhaling. A natural high teased him.

Rainey reached for a piece of guest stationery positioned on the counter, picked up a pen and wrote Lilly's name at the top of the paper. He stared at the paper while trying to conjure up the right words to thank her. His body stiffened as his brain solidified like concrete.

"How was the dinner? Did they treat you good at Wo Fat?" Lilly said, standing behind him.

Rainey pulled his shoulders back, his body stiff as he turned toward Lilly without replying to her question.

"Such a serious look, was dinner unacceptable?"

He was being ridiculous and gave up trying to impress or fool her. "Dinner was more than good, and the service was exceptional. I was about to write a witty and charming note thanking you for the extraordinary service you have provided."

"It was my pleasure. And you *are* witty and charming," Lilly said. "But your friend is intriguing."

"And you find him interesting, I presume?" Rainey asked.

"Yes."

"What about me?"

"Witty and charming, but your friend has a special allure about him. I find it...interesting."

"I'll tell him when we're forty thousand feet over the middle of the Pacific somewhere," Rainey said. "After I find a pump to fix my deflated ego."

Lilly smiled at Rainey, took one step toward him and reaching up kissed him on his cheek. It was a kiss reserved for friends, never lovers. Rainey stood still, resisting the urge to hug her. After a brief moment he returned the smile. A thought of Leslie back in New Orleans caught him off guard.

"I think my mother would find you appealing," Lilly said.

"I'm sure I am too old for her," Rainey shot back.

"Yes, witty and charming."

Rainey relaxed and enjoyed her presence, aware he should never have entertained the idea of Lilly in a romantic, lustful, way. Perhaps it was the thought of Leslie, or maybe it was maturity setting in, the maturity he had suppressed, fooling himself while enjoying his juvenile mentality. He would give it some thought, but later. There was much to do in the morning.

CHAPTER TEN

Creston received clearance from the tower and accelerated the jet down the runway, heading away from the sun, the wind aiding in their departure. The early morning take off provided boyish excitement. A new sun had cleared the horizon and bathed the islands in light while volcanic mountains cast shadows. The image etched into Rainey's mind, more breathtaking than any artists rendering. Would each new location and departure be better than the previous ones he wondered? There was so much to see.

"What are you smiling about and what is it you need to tell me?" Creston asked.

"You had an admirer at the hotel, one of life's mysteries I don't understand."

"What are you talking about?"

"Lilly. She thought you were, 'interesting' as she put it."

"Another lost opportunity I presume," Creston said.

"Yeah, and I thought the gourmet Chinese meal was because of me."

Four hours into the flight Rainey became lightheaded and tired. He shook his head briskly several times in an attempt to revive himself with new energy, but instead it made him dizzy. The drone of the engines with the monotony of the unchanging sky and endless ocean below compounded the unexpected fatigue. He unhooked the seat belt, removed his headset, rose from his seat and made his way back into the cabin, ignoring Creston as he left the cockpit. He reached for a seat back to steady himself as he stumbled along the short aisle. He fell into the larger sofa style seat and struggled to take a deep breath as he slipped into unconsciousness.

CHAPTER ELEVEN

By the fifth day Rainey had developed a routine to start each morning. Creston was responding positively, comfortable with Rainey's confidence and control. Both were relaxed as if they had been on the island for years. Rainey prayed the worst was over.

The fire pit Rainey had dug by hand, after determining to make coffee one way or another, was a three foot diameter hole in the coral sand. The fumes from the jet fuel had diminished and posed no threat as previously feared. The stainless steel carafe from the plane's coffee maker was dented but otherwise in good shape, and there were six, two pound bags of Café du Monde coffee and chicory in the plane's locker. It was curious to Rainey why Creston had brought so much coffee for what was supposed to be a two week trip. Perhaps he had brought enough extra coffee to leave a bag at various ports of call, as a gift for a local who had been more helpful than necessary. Or maybe it was because Creston enjoyed leaving his mark as he traveled and made new friends.

The coffee making process had been trial and error, but Rainey had watched enough of the old westerns with his mother to know if the old cowboys brewed coffee in a pot over an open fire then he would figure it out. He poured one bottle of water into the carafe and then added what he estimated to be two tablespoons of coffee. He placed the carafe on a metal panel he had removed from one of the large cabin seats. The metal panel had been a seat back surrounded by thick padding and then covered with plush Italian leather dyed a deep burgundy. He was reluctant at first to damage anything on the plane, but realized how ridiculous it was to preserve any part of the plane which could be better used for their comfort and survival. The coffee had become a priority, not for the taste and desire of the hearty, rich brew, but because it connected him to home and all he was missing.

Rainey had placed the metal panel over the fire pit, leaving an opening to add leaves and branches to keep the flames going. The dried leaves he had gathered were quick to ignite. Fallen branches were plentiful and he had scrounged them in abundance, stacking them in a neat pile close to the fire pit. He added the branches to the pit and they caught fire easily from the flaming leaves. The carafe was placed on the metal panel, and the four minutes it took the water to boil was agonizing as Rainey watched, eager to taste the coffee. He timed the boiling water for a minute then removed the carafe from the fire. The dark, strong brew was aromatic and intensified as the coffee steeped. Rainey was reminded of the coffee plants in New Orleans and the aroma of roasted beans carried in the air for miles. He inhaled deeply and nodded, pleased with his effort. His sense of smell was more acute, perhaps, he thought, because of the lack of the many subconscious distractions encountered in his day to day life. Rainey waited five minutes and then poured the hot brew through a tee shirt into mugs salvaged from the plane.

Rainey tasted the coffee, shook his head, and told Creston he would keep trying. For a brief moment Rainey was back in New Orleans, enjoying a lazy Sunday morning. He looked at Creston and thought how it might have been, thankful it was not worse.

Rainey handed Creston a mug of the coffee. "Here, try this. It'll get better, but I'm not wasting anything so I'm not throwing it out."

Creston's lips formed a straight line and his face tightened as he took a sip. "Hope you're right. It has to get better. Hot milk and sugar would help but not much we can do about anything at this point."

"You ever feel this helpless before?" Rainey asked.

"Helpless? Well, let me think. I'm stuck in the middle of the Pacific Ocean miles from who knows where, can't take care of myself, having to depend on you to survive, and all my millions doing me absolutely no good at all. Yeah, helpless describes it pretty well."

"You forgot feeling sorry for yourself," Rainey said.

"And what do you know about feeling sorry for yourself? Always so carefree, and moving about as if you have no problems at all, what do you know about it?"

"After Leslie left me, and then the divorce and I disappeared for weeks at a time, well, I was majoring in self pity. But fortunately I got some good advice and came to my senses. I got over it and moved on. Well, accepted it anyway, not sure you ever get over it."

"Good advice from who?" Creston said.

"Barbers and bartenders, best free advice you can get."

"You can't be serious. Besides, judging from the haircuts you've been getting for the last few years it couldn't have been your barber. I'm not sure he knows what end of the scissors to hold."

"You're right, it wasn't the barber. Big O straightened me out. I was in the restaurant one night sitting at the oyster bar, drinking a few beers and talking with him. It was late and the place was quiet so we chatted for a couple of hours. He laid it out for me. It all comes down to making choices. For instance, no one can make you unhappy. You choose to be angry and blame someone else for it, but not being angry is a choice as well. You don't have to like something, but it doesn't have to anger you. Anger is negative and drains energy. Get over it and let the experience teach you. It took a while to sink in and O had to remind me a few times, but I decided it was up to me to control myself, to control my outlook. It made sense so I worked at it," Rainey said.

"That simple, huh? If it were only so easy."

"Simple, yes, but not easy. You have to work at it."

"I'll give it some thought. O's philosophy doesn't go with my personality. But it makes sense in a different sort of way," Creston said. "I'm not much help, but I can at least keep a look out for the rescue planes."

Leslie walked into the Oyster House and sat at the counter. Big O was moving fast as he shucked oysters, waited on customers, talked with them, and yelled out drink orders to the waitress. It was a typical busy lunch crowd and the noise level was almost as deafening as a Saints game on Sunday afternoon in the Superdome. He looked up and his smile disappeared. Leslie was walking toward him and wore a somber expression. He placed his big hands on the counter as he looked at her worried face.

"I don't think you come in here for oysters. What's the matter?

"O, their plane's overdue. It never landed in New Guinea. It took off from Hawaii on schedule but it never showed up when it was supposed to. It's been five days since it left Hawaii and"

"Leslie, what you tryin to tell me?"

"O, they're missing. There was some kind of mix up in New Guinea and no one there bothered to report them missing when they didn't show up on schedule. We should have been notified at least three days ago. I was the primary contact should something go wrong, or not according to schedule. I'm scared and I feel helpless."

"We been friends for more than twenty years," Big O said. "Creston done more for me than I can tell ya. What cha need me to do?"

"O, I don't think there's anything we can do. We have to wait and be patient. Wait to see if anything is reported, or wait till they show up somewhere after whatever side-trip adventure they might have pursued. I wanted you to know, just in case."

Big O looked at Leslie, troubled with her suggesting they had deviated from the flight plan, or had not reported in. Big O stood still, looking like a large statue as he leaned on the counter, and thought hard for the right words to calm Leslie.

"You have to get back to your customers. Say a prayer for them. Rainey would like that."

She got up and walked to the door. As she grabbed the large brass handle she heard Big O call to her.

"Leslie, come back tomorrow and see me. Meet me here at six o'clock. I'll explain it to you then." Big O turned to check on the tourists from California.

CHAPTER TWELVE

It was five o'clock, too early in New Orleans for the evening crowd to fill the restaurant. But in two hours it would be full and there would be a line out the door and down Iberville Street, waiting for a table or place at the bar. Leslie had been gone for a while and O was haunted by an image of his friends missing. He shook his head at the possibility they might even be dead or lost forever.

O looked at the clock on the wall, hesitated for a moment and then yelled at Johnny Tap. "I need you to cover for me for an hour or so. I got ta go see somebody. It's real important. Take care of the customers. I'll be back soon as I can."

"I got it, O. I can cover for ya. Go do what ya gotta do." Johnny looked at O, gave him a wave then did a quick three step tap smooth and graceful, honed from years of performing on the street, and O knew Johnny had him covered.

Big O walked out onto Iberville Street. The early cool front had been pushed back to the north by the changing jet stream and the October evening was more like another hot summer night. The humidity was thick, causing beads of sweat to form on Big O's face as he stepped outside and started down Iberville toward Royal Street. Big O was in a hurry and knew the humidity would have him covered in sweat by the end of the block. He turned the corner at Royal Street and headed deeper into the quarter. Usually, he would drop fifty cents or a dollar into the hat of the trombone player on the sidewalk, but this time Big O waved and continued walking. Charlie, the street performer, never missed a note as his trombone

91

wept St. James Infirmary. Several times someone tried to stop O and engage him in conversation but each time he would gesture politely and keep moving. His purpose led him up Royal Street to Pirates Alley. O took his handkerchief from his rear pocket, left it folded and wiped his brow. He walked through the alley, made the sign of the cross as he passed the side entrance to St. Louis Cathedral, and came out at Jackson Square. He avoided the fortune tellers, tarot card readers and artists who invaded the areas all around the square. Big O turned up Decatur Street and walked several more blocks until he reached Governor Nicholls Street. He stopped for a couple of minutes, stood on the corner catching his breath, trying to slow his pace. A block ahead O could see a small section of the French Market. The stalls were busy with tourists and locals, shopping and milling around like ants on a sugar cube. O walked the last block to the market and entered the stall where Mama Mary was selling African art and clothes.

"Hello Mama," Big O said. It had been too long since his last visit.

Mama turned and relaxed O with a look of understanding, held her arms open, inviting him in and said, "Oscar, where you been child, and why you been so long in comin ta see me?"

"Mama, I been busy and"

"Hush, I don't need you explainin nothing to me. It's so good to see you, baby. But why you here when you should be working... you brought me some oysters?"

"Mama, I'm sorry but I didn't have no time for no oysters. I need to talk to ya about somethin. It's important, and nobody else but you can help."

Mary was five feet tall and fifty pounds heavier than her doctor wanted her to be. But the weight was evenly distributed and she appeared plump, but not heavy. She wore her short black hair in a neat afro, and stood taller and straighter than her seventy years should allow. Mary had skin the color of light chocolate. Her frequent smile emanated kindness and people approached Mama Mary with comfort. A traditional African Dashiki style dress, loud with color and print, draped her body.

Big O's oversized hand swallowed her much smaller hand as she reached out to him and he took it. She led him to the back of the stall where it was quiet and away from the tourists. "Oscar, you in some kind a trouble, boy?"

"No, Mama. Everything is good with me. But I got friends and they might be. I'm worried about em. Mama, you know how sometimes you get those feelings or see things. Things that ain't happened yet, or things maybe did happen but somewhere else and not here."

"Oscar. We don't talk about it where people can hear. White peoples don't understand it or believe it, and black folk gets scared and crazy about it. Besides, I told you I can't control it. It's a gift from God, and it happens when it happens, when He makes it happen."

"I know, Mama. But I need to come see ya tomorrow with a friend of mine. She can tell you more bout what's happened. Then maybe you can tell us what you think. It's important. Mama, she's a white lady. She was married to my friend, Rainey. I toll you bout him. They been divorced for a while but I can tell she still loves him. She's good mama, and she won't cause no trouble."

"Oscar, you bring dis lady round here bout six or so. I'll be shuttin down and we can all go get some coffee and talk about what's botherin you."

"Thanks, mama. We'll be here bout six or so. How bout I bring you some fresh oysters? I'll get Johnny Tap to shuck four dozen and put em in a bucket for ya. Jus remember to call me when you make your oyster stew," O said.

Big O had grown up in the sixth police district of New Orleans, close to the area known as the Irish Channel but not in the projects. He had seen too much of the bad the city had to deal with, and had been part of it at one time. Drugs and crime were out of control and O had seen too many of his friends die in the street, victims of drug deals gone bad, or simply in the wrong place at the wrong time. Most of the cops were good but the sixth district made them hard. The rookies from the academy and assigned into the sixth were full of "by the book" attitude, trying to use reasoning and understanding to resolve the numerous calls they had to handle. But after six months, they were as hard as the veterans and had little to no capacity for reasoning. They almost all developed a "sixth sense" as to how they handled their calls. For years Big O had resented the police and the way they took care of things. But Big O had changed, and it was Mama Mary who helped O see the truth.

Big O retraced his way back to the restaurant, but taking his time. He stopped along the way and talked with some of the friends he had ignored earlier. Big O was always street wise, but more importantly, he was people wise. He knew the con men, the hustlers, crack whores, pimps and prostitutes who dirtied up the quarter. But, they knew him too, and stayed away from him.

By the time Big O got back the restaurant was filling up. He moved behind the oyster bar and bumped Johnny Tap out of the way.

"Hey, I tole ya I got dis man. Why you come bump me, treat me like a common street thug?"

"Cause I ain't ready to give up my job to you no matter how good you getting to be. And you was a street thug. Don't ever forget where you come from or you be going back there, and real soon, too."

"Yeah, you right O. But I ain't never goin back to da street. I toll you befoe and I meant it," Johnny said. Big O placed his arm around Johnny's shoulder before he moved away.

"I can always count on you," Big O said. "Thanks for covering. You gettin real good at this Johnny, real good."

Johnny Tap had been a street kid growing up around the French Quarter. He made his money tap dancing on Bourbon Street and hustling tourists. Big O had saved Johnny Tap more than once from an angry tourist or other street kids. O enjoyed watching Johnny tap dance and entertain the people as they walked by. Johnny had charm and talent but no education, and O couldn't explain his need to watch out for him. He tried several times before he was able to get Johnny a job at the restaurant and take him off the street. It saved his life. Big O had insisted Johnny get enrolled in a school program and Johnny had earned his high school diploma. He worked hard and learned to shuck oysters almost as good as O. Sometimes, when business was slow Johnny would tease O into a shucking contest. O would always win but the gap was narrowing, Johnny was getting better and faster.

Leslie picked up her purse and walked to her office door, leaving for the day when her desk phone rang. She walked back and picked up the receiver on the third ring.

"Leslie, this is O. Look, this is real important. Like I told you earlier I need ya to pick me up tomorrow evening by the restaurant at six and drive us over to the French Market."

"Ok, but what is this about?"

"I'll tell ya later but don't say nothin to nobody," O said. "And bring a picture of Rainey."

"I don't understand, but I'll be there," she said.

Leslie was waiting outside the restaurant at six O'clock as Big O had requested. The streets were wet from an earlier rain and small puffs of steam rose from the hot pavement. Rainey had told her years before the puffs of steam were trapped ghosts escaping from the asphalt poured over their ancient graves. Living in New Orleans had made her second guess the fantasy of the story.

Big O came out carrying a large metal bucket full of ice. She looked at the bucket, even more confused than yesterday's conversation with O had left her. She said nothing as O gave her directions. In five minutes they were parked behind the French Market. They had not spoken. Leslie was nervous and did not ask any questions and Big O was not able to explain what he was trying to accomplish. O got out of Leslie's car, went around to the driver's side and opened the door for her and led her to the back of Mama Mary's stall where they stood together and waited.

Mama, feeling their presence, turned, walked to Big O and opened her arms to him. He hugged her while fumbling with the bucket of oysters.

"Mama, this is Leslie."

Mary turned and clasped Leslie's hands in hers. Leslie relaxed with the warmth and comfort Mama exuded. She released Leslie's hand and took the oysters from O.

"I'll put these in the ice chest and then we can go get some coffee. You do drink coffee don't you?" Mama asked.

"Yes, I'd love some coffee."

The trio left Mama Mary's stall and headed up Decatur street. The quarter smelled fresh and reborn from the rain. It was still early evening and Café Du Monde was mostly empty except for a few tourists who preferred their dessert of beignets and café au lait before going to dinner. Mama led them to a table in the far corner of the patio. A wrought iron fence protected them from the tourists and street people milling by. The waiter, who was of Asian descent, approached them and Mary ordered three coffees with hot milk.

"I suppose this is the awkward part," Mama said to Leslie. "You don't know why you're here, and I don't know why I'm here. Maybe Oscar can clear this up for us."

"Oscar?" Leslie said. "I don't think I ever knew what the O stood for. I guess I always thought it was O."

O dipped his head slightly, breaking eye contact with Mama and Leslie, thought for a minute, looked up and said, "I believe Rainey and Creston are missing because of an accident and not because they changed their plans. It's a feeling I got. Mama, you heard me talk about them two since a long time ago. Well, they my good friends. And Leslie, I toll you she and Rainey, they got divorced, but I think they is still connected somehow. I wasn't sure what to do but I couldn't stand around and wait. So I went to see Mama yesterday and well, here we are."

"O," Leslie said, "You might have to do a little better because I'm confused as to what you're saying and what this is all about."

"Oscar, even though I told you we ain't supposed to talk about certain things, you gonna have ta explain a few things to both of us." Mama said as she looked at Leslie.

"Years ago, I was a bad kid growing up near the Irish Channel, Mama Mary lived right around the corner from me. I was always in trouble. Drugs and bad people had moved into the neighborhood and it was getting real bad to live there. I was big for my age and I got in fights all the time. If not for Mama Mary, I would have ended up like them, or most probably dead.

"One day Mama stopped me on the street, right out da blue and tells me, 'Oscar, I don't think you should go over by the park tonight.' I was all set to go and meet up with my brothers over by Magazine and Napoleon streets but for some reason, what Mama said bothered me so I didn't go. Later the same night, two of my friends got shot and killed."

"Don't you think it might have been a coincidence?' Leslie asked.

"I did at first, except, I never told Mama I was going to the park. Anyway, little things kept happening. Mama would show up right before I was maybe gonna do somethin I shouldn't do. Soon, I quit believing it was always a coincidence so much."

Leslie turned to Mama Mary. "Mama, is there anything you can tell me about all this?"

"Oscar's waiting for me to tell you so I'll try to explain a few things. See, some people is born different. Not bad, but different. I ain't like dem charleytains in the quarter or dem voodoo fools with all their craziness and blasphemy. My mama told me when I was a little girl I had the gift. She said I was born with a veil. People back then used to try and steal the veil when a baby was born with one. They thought it brought good luck and would keep evil away. I still got mine because my mama saved it for me. Mama, she told me don't never do anything bad or help somebody to do bad. I was to keep to myself about things that made me different. But most of it don't mean nothin anyway cause it's little things. Sometimes, I see, well, I mean things sort of come to me. I don't go looking for nothin but sometimes they show up. Like Oscar, he showed up one day, but Oscar had a glow about him. Some people call it an aura. And it was good. I knew it was good so I always watched out for him. The day he was supposed to go to the park, it came to me he might be goin at night and there would be trouble. So I warned him not to go."

"One day," Oscar said, "a long time ago, over twenty years, I was getting out of the neighborhood. It had gotten too bad and I couldn't take it no more. I didn't have a job or no place to go but I told Mama I was leaving. She held my hand and we sat on the stoop for a while and talked. Then I asked her what she thought. She told me she wasn't sure why but she seen oysters. I told her I wasn't even hungry and she laughed. Well, later I was walking up Bourbon street like I would sometimes do and instead of going straight I turned on Iberville and right there was a oyster restaurant. Somethin made me go in. I told the man I needed a job and I'd work real hard. So, he says okay, surprised the heck out a me. Then I tell him I don't have no place to live and he looks at me real hard and then tells me to call this guy and gives me the phone number."

Oscar described several other instances where Mama had intervened with similar outcomes. Leslie was enthralled with the stories, but still reluctant, not able to buy into all O was saying. He looked at Mama Mary for help.

"Leslie, I think what Oscar is lookin for is some kind a sign or somethin, and he figures I might be able to come up with one. Did you bring a picture of Rainey or anything of his with you?"

Leslie reached into her purse and retrieved a wallet sized photograph of Rainey and her, taken in Gulfport several years before. It was a small picture but it was one of her favorites. She was reminded of a better time and place in her life when she looked at the photograph. She handed the picture to Mama Mary and watched as Mama viewed the picture.

"I told you both before, I don't ask for nothing. It comes when it comes. I ain't sure when or if I'll feel or see anything. If I do, I'll tell you what it is. If I don't, well then, I don't. It's not up to me. Now, we all need to be gettin back to what we supposed to be doin. Oscar, you got work to do and I suppose Leslie does, too."

Mama Mary held the picture in her right hand, reached across the small table with her left and placed it on Leslie's. She looked at O with approval and silently said a quick prayer for Rainey and

Creston. O placed money on the table to cover the cost of the coffee as they all moved to get up.

"Leslie," Mama said still holding Leslie's hand, "Does Rainey know about the miscarriage, and that it was his?"

Leslie's blood chilled instantly and drained from her face as she stared at Mama Mary. But the understanding look from Mama comforted her, and Leslie bowed her head.

"No, Mama; he doesn't. I was going to tell him right before he left but he stood me up. Creston moved the departure date up and I didn't see Rainey before they left. We got together about six months ago to discuss a few things, had some wine and one thing led to another and well…"

"That's enough baby. I already have a good idea of what happened and it don't matter none."

The walk back to the market was quiet. Big O and Leslie helped Mama Mary close down her stall and load the ice chest and oysters into Mama's car. Leslie drove O back to work and made him promise to call if anything changed. At two in the morning Big O's phone rang.

"Oscar, that boy is alive and somewhere in the middle of the ocean. That's all I can tell ya but I feel strongly he's alive and…"

"I knowed you'd see somethin," O said sitting up as he interrupted her.

"Oscar, there's one more thing. He ain't alone."

Big O hung up the phone and fell back in bed, his heart pounding so hard it echoed in the room. He sat back up, took a deep breath and called Leslie.

"Leslie, they're alive. Mama just called. She said she don't see nothing else but she's sure of it. I believe her. She wouldn't a called if she wasn't sure."

CHAPTER THIRTEEN

The quarter was quiet. It was mid afternoon, too late for lunch and much too early by New Orleans time for supper. Big O stood behind the oyster bar with his large boot propped up on the low stainless steel sink used for cleaning the oyster knives and trays. His mind wandered, searching for an answer or anything to give him hope. Mama Mary had told him Rainey was alive, but every once in a while she was wrong, she got a mixed signal or misunderstood a vision, and he feared this being one of those times. He tried to dismiss the thought by gazing at the lone customer sitting near the end of the bar nursing a long neck, Blackened Voodoo beer. He yelled at Johnny Tap to watch the bar as he moved toward the front door to clear his mind with some afternoon air.

O leaned against the front wall of the garage next door. He looked up and down Iberville, people watching, assessing the early evening. The streets of the French Quarter smelled of beer, oyster shells, and overflowing trash from the many waste receptacles stashed in alleys and vestibules. It would get much worse as the late afternoon changed into night and the streets would again teem with locals and tourists, most with open containers of beer, hurricanes, and daiquiris spilling over as they stumbled about. Big O shook his head as he took a deep breath. The air was too odoriferous and he scowled like a scolded school boy.

New Orleans was a grand old lady and she deserved better treatment, but she was also tough. She rebounded every morning as the garbage trucks removed the trash and the street sweepers were followed by the water trucks rinsing the good and bad memories of the night before into the gutters.

Big O's favorite time in the Quarter was Sunday morning before the first mass at St. Louis Cathedral. The clean up would have been finished, the air fresh, the streets quiet, and the presence of the grand lady commanding the respect denied her the night before. But Big O usually slept through most early Sunday mornings as the Saturday night late shift overtaxed his body and mind. Once he crashed for the night he was out until at least noon. But as he stood with his back against the brick wall he made a mental note to walk the quarter this coming Sunday before attending mass at the cathedral. He wondered if Father would let him in.

"What are you smiling about?" Leslie said. "Although, it's a refreshing change from the worry and concern you've been wearing like a theatre marquis the last few days."

Big O turned toward Leslie and focused on her eyes. "Nothin, I was thinking is all. What you doin round here this time of day? How come you ain't working?"

"For the same reason you're out here holding up a brick wall instead of inside getting ready for the evening crowd. I'm having trouble keeping my mind on my work," Leslie said. "And I'm scared."

"Yeah, I reckon so. It's only been a couple a days but it could be a month the way it feels. And sittin and waitin just makes things drag on and on." His mind drifted again. He looked back at Leslie and asked, "So, why you here?"

"I'm not sure, maybe because misery loves company, birds of a feather, whatever. Or, because they loved coming here to see you and hang out. Maybe I thought I'd feel closer to them."

"Come on inside, I'll buy you a cold drink." Big O gently took her arm and escorted her inside to the oyster bar.

Leslie sat at the bar for several hours making idle conversation with O. The Saints looked like they might have a good season and win some games. She was going to make a trip home to Alabama and spend some time with her parents and friends. The bank had a promotion coming up and it was hers for the taking but it might mean moving to Baton Rouge. She avoided discussing Rainey or Creston. It was six o'clock and the oyster bar was starting to fill up with the early drinkers disguising themselves as diners but slow to order food.

"How about I get you a shrimp po'boy, dressed and fixed to go?" Big O asked. "You need to eat and get some rest. We can't do no more here."

"Yeah, guess I'm hungry after all. The sandwich would be great. And put a Dixie long neck in there for me.

Big O disappeared into the kitchen and came back out in five minutes with a small, brown paper bag, a long po'boy wrapped in white paper sticking half way out. He grabbed a Dixie from the cooler and told her to drink it for Rainey. Then O grabbed a Heineken, placed it into the bag and told her to drink this one for Creston. She took the bag and cradled it in arm, reached out and squeezed O's large hand, winked, and made her way out onto Iberville Street.

CHAPTER FOURTEEN

The search planes had been going out early each morning and returning for fuel before going right back out until after dark for several days. It was a typical search and rescue mission with the planes canvassing a grid defined by the U.S. Navy as their best guess as to where they thought the plane might have disappeared. Each day brought more frustration but no news of any survivors or plane wreckage. The navy had expended hours of manpower and tens of thousands of dollars amassing the forces to conduct the search. They halted rescue efforts after five days of searching and issued a report stating the plane and the occupants should be presumed lost at sea. The news might have been the final blow to some but not to Creston's parents, and certainly not to Rainey's and Creston's friends.

Captain Mike Striker had been in the U.S. Navy for thirty two years and in charge of rescue operations based out of Pearl Harbor for the last four. The operations should have been referred to as recovery rather than rescue, because the vast majority of the cases produced no survivors. When the navy found anyone after more than two or three days of searching it was usually a body and typically one badly decomposed. This would have hardened most men but Captain Striker had been hardened years ago from two tours of rescue operations in Vietnam. Even Hawaii had not softened him.

"Look, Senator…what'd you say your name is?"

"Senator Allain Comeaux from Louisiana."

"I don't give a rat's ass who it is or how much money they have. I followed the book, did the search in the proper procedure, then did it all some more. It didn't help when they weren't reported missing right away. We lost the first couple of days and they're the most important. We searched for five days, covered thousands of square miles, and found nothing. Not a trace, no signal from the ELT, nothing."

"What is the ELT?" asked Senator Comeaux.

"The emergency locator transmitter. It's standard on most small private planes."

"Well, Captain Striker, why can't you pick up the signal?"

"It doesn't operate off of satellites. It's a signal transmitted from the plane, and it's basically a line of sight signal. A plane or boat must be in the line of the signal to pick it up. Otherwise, no one receives it. If we get lucky, we get close enough and cross the signal. We haven't been lucky, and I'm not going to risk any more men or spend any more taxpayer money on a search that might last for months and months and still not produce a body, let alone a survivor. Please tell Mr. Labouef I'm sorry, but we have to stop the search. His son and the son's friend are casualties. There's nothing more we can do."

The senator had been ready for a big argument, but he heard the sincerity in Captain Striker's voice and he knew there was no argument to be made. He was the ranking member on the senate appropriations committee and Paris Labouef had been instrumental in his numerous re-elections. However, he had no choice but to call him and deliver the bad news. It was unlikely Paris Labouef would ever see his son again.

Paris Labouef hung up the phone and sat in silence. His son, his only child was missing and would probably never be seen or heard from again. His anger rose and he thought of his father. If Charles Labouef were alive today he would be cursing and wishing it had been Paris instead of Creston. Paris understood what people meant when they would say a parent should not outlive their child.

"Leslie, this is Paris Labouef. I've been in contact with Senator Comeaux and he advised me the U.S. Navy has abandoned the search for Creston and Rainey. They are presumed lost at sea."

The silence was expected but lasted longer than Paris Labouef was able to tolerate. His loss was greater than hers and he was sympathetic, but he was not used to pandering to someone.

"Leslie, did you hear me? They are presumed dead. We have to accept this and move on. Mrs. Labouef has taken this harder than you might imagine. She is resting with the help of sedatives."

"Mr. Labouef, I heard you. But I am not ready to, nor do I have to accept this. I have reason to believe Rainey is alive and is not alone. Don't ask me how because you wouldn't believe me anyway. But I'm not going to give up. If you're ready to start the legal proceedings on Creston's affairs, so be it. However, there is a minimum five year period before the bank or anyone else can do anything. He cannot be declared dead at this time and there is nothing I can do for you." Leslie responded with curtness and anger in her voice.

"You misjudge me Leslie. You have no idea what I'm feeling at this time, but let me be vulnerably candid with you. I love Creston as much as any father can love a son. But my love for him was more than a father-son relationship. Creston was the final link I had to my father. My father adored Creston and gave him all the attention and love he never had time to give me. Through Creston I was always able to feel connected to my father even though he's been dead for many years. So today I say goodbye to my son, but I must finally bury my father. Do you even begin to comprehend what I have admitted to you?"

"Mr. Labouef, I'm truly sorry for your loss, but I'm also sorry for my loss. Forgive me for being so straightforward, but maybe you should let your father go and start praying your son is found alive. I've not given up hope and I'll continue to pray and do anything I can think of to find Creston and Rainey."

Leslie sat at her desk staring out across St. Charles Avenue toward the Mississippi river. Her anger and disbelief were mixed with confusion following her conversation with Paris Labouef, and the confusion added to the anger. Grabbing her desk phone she dialed the Oyster House hoping it was not too early to reach Big O. She needed the comfort and encouragement of Big O especially when bearing bad news.

CHAPTER FIFTEEN

The tenth day was much like each day before except Rainey had adjusted to the island. He no longer awakened to the risen sun inundating his eyes the way his bedroom light had intruded upon him when his mother joyfully flipped the wall switch to wake him for school. Instead, the freshness of the new day roused his sense of smell, waking him before an edge of light crept above the horizon. He lay waiting while the sun appeared, tentatively, as if checking to make sure everything was in order before ascending to its rightful dominance in the sky.

Creston had no trouble sleeping through the sunrise. His health had improved and there were no signs of infection. The head wound was healing, but the bruises to his body were slow to dissipate. The dark, plum color of the bruises was gone, but traces of tan and yellow remained, the largest in his right hip area. Creston was almost recovered.

Creston stirred. He would soon awaken and Rainey would check the head wound and make sure he was comfortable. Each day Rainey told Creston how good he was looking, continuing to instill confidence in him. Creston had been fatalistic in the beginning, and Rainey believed healing was partly attitude. It was important Creston believe he was getting better.

The coffee had improved and by the tenth day Rainey had perfected the formula of water, coffee, boiling and steeping time. Or maybe he and Creston were becoming less particular. The honey buns were almost gone. The plane had been stocked with two boxes containing twenty four each. Rainey and Creston had eaten two apiece each morning. Rainey would place them on the make-shift grill while he boiled the coffee, warming them at the same time. The warm honey buns were a small treat at first, but by the tenth day every moment brought awareness and appreciation. Nothing was taken for granted, especially their dwindling supplies.

"There are a few things we should discuss, even if you've already figured out some on your own," Creston said soberly. "This is probably day ten, but we were so disoriented we might have missed a day. So unless a coconut falls on my head and kills me, I'm gonna make it. I owe you my life."

"I saved you so I could kill you later for getting me into this mess."

Creston adjusted himself, sitting up and leaning against the plane, the wing protecting him from the glare of the sun. "What have you salvaged from the cargo hold of the plane?"

Rainey glared at Creston, his brow furrowing upward and his lips pursing. His face turned red. He had seen the cargo door, mostly submerged in the sand, when he did the inspection of the plane. His intention had been to try to dig it out. The unsettling part was he had not thought about it one time since then.

Creston returned Rainey's stare and said, "You're shitting me, right? Don't tell me you forgot about the hold of the plane where we stowed the luggage. Plus the things I stowed before you showed up." Creston's tone angered Rainey.

"Yeah, there's gratitude for you. You're unbelievable." Rainey stood and looked at the plane. The hold contained supplies they were already in need of. The redness drained from his face. Maybe this was a better time to dig out the additional supplies than before, he thought.

Rainey looked at the left side of the fuselage while shaking his head. The cargo door was partially visible with most of it below the sand. Even with Creston's help it would be difficult and slow removing enough sand to uncover the door. He stared at the plane while mentally beating himself up. And then, he let it go. "Screw it!" he said. He turned toward Creston. "I'll fix breakfast, and then you can dig out the cargo door."

"This must be what it's like when you're married," Creston said.

The digging was not difficult. The coral sand was coarse and moved easily, even after years of almost daily rains. Rainey knew smaller grain sands had a much denser consistency and would have been more difficult to dig. The makeshift stove top had become a makeshift shovel. It was cumbersome to use but Rainey was soon excavating the sand like a drag line operator, digging and tossing it away from the cargo door. As he dug the hole a sense of accomplishment coupled with his determination. He was mentally removed from everything previously consuming him, and the first two hours went by as fast as watching a favorite movie. Rainey looked up from his task and scratched his head like a lost tourist. He had underestimated the size of the hole needed to expose the cargo door, and had failed to realize how much room would be necessary for the door to swing open. But he was making progress and it pleased him.

Creston was feeling well enough to be of help. As Rainey dug deeper it became increasingly more difficult to throw the sand far enough away from the plane and not have it fall back into the hole. Creston had taken an ice bucket from the plane and used it to scoop sand and toss it farther away. As he scooped he watched Rainey's laborious effort take its toll. The sand was becoming heavier, and Rainey's pace slowed.

The heat was draining and they were soon covered in sand and sweat. After two hours they were forced to take breaks in fifteen minute intervals. Six tiring hours after they started digging, the cargo door was clear and ready to be opened. Rainey's excitement waned and he looked around, one more step going nowhere he thought.

Rainey flipped the handle up, rotated it counter-clockwise and heard the latching mechanism release its grip on the metal fuselage. The door moved slightly and Rainey pulled it open, staring into the hold.

"What are you waiting for?" Creston bellowed.

Rainey shook his head and leaned into the opening. The compartment appeared smaller and more cramped than when he had viewed it from the tarmac. The sunlight invaded the space and Rainey could see the cargo netting had prevented displacement of the major items and they were all intact. A cardboard box approximately four feet long and close to the door caught Rainey's attention. He reached down and pulled the box from the cargo hold.

"Anything in here we might find helpful?" Rainey asked.

"Yeah, I think so. Those would be the fishing poles," Creston said ignoring Rainey's stare.

"Uh huh, so here I am in the middle of the ocean, on an island for TEN days, eating stale honey buns, canned soup, dry crackers and an occasional coconut, which by the way is DAMNED hard to open, and we have fishing poles, right?"

"Yep, that about sums it up," Creston replied. "And I'm not the one who forgot to open the cargo door for TEN days."

Rainey threw the box on the ground, brushed himself off and climbed out of the hole. He glanced in the direction of the sun and guessed there were at least four or five hours of daylight remaining. Grabbing a bottle of water, he turned and started toward the center of the island.

"Hey, you pissed off about something?" Creston said.

"No, I'm not pissed off. But I need a break, so I'm going for a walk. And I'm headed into the center of the island. I've been walking the beach and I need a change of scenery. Are you up to a stroll?"

"No, go ahead. I'll pull some of the other stuff from the hold. Maybe tomorrow," Creston said.

Nodding, Rainey turned and started walking. Creston watched him thinking maybe he should tell Rainey about the inflatable life raft also in the cargo hold. Or maybe it would be more fun to let him find it on his own.

CHAPTER SIXTEEN

The Times-Picayune newspaper had picked up the story on the missing home town aviators and had run several articles about the search efforts, as well as on Creston. There was almost no mention of Rainey. Leslie read each article several times; scouring them for details or new information she might have missed. Instead, she became increasingly upset with the inaccuracies they wove into their reporting. They pushed the limits of free speech with their creative license. The facts were dramatic enough and the paper's articles were laced with suggestions. The reader was left to question what they were doing, if theirs was a covert mission based on Creston's political connections, or even an illegal operation of some type centered around drugs, blood diamonds, or American currency. The article bothering her most was the one implying two single men from New Orleans were more than good friends. But it was all implied, nothing specific. She found herself throwing the newspaper down in disgust. She was helpless to do anything and this upset her the most.

Leslie's frustration increased daily. The newspaper had stopped covering the disappearance and the consensus was the missing travelers would never be found. Her parents had visited from Alabama, and though it helped to have them near for a few days, Leslie's feeling of helplessness returned as soon as they left.

Management at the bank had given her several days off, letting her come and go almost at will, and assigning work to others Leslie would normally be responsible for. But with all the understanding and help from her coworkers, she knew she needed positive direction and she also knew she would have to find it from within.

On the tenth day after their disappearance Leslie woke with a comfort she had not enjoyed in as many days. Her fear of the worst had overshadowed her true belief. Rainey and Creston were alive, this she was sure of. Calm settled over her like a warm fleece blanket and she was able to devise a plan of action long overdue.

Leslie walked into the bank and went straight to the office of the bank president. Jackson Aberdeen sat at his desk reading the morning paper while drinking coffee. He looked up as Leslie walked in.

"Jack, I need to discuss a few things with you."

"Sure Leslie, I have a few minutes before my first meeting."

"I have power of attorney with Creston's affairs. I intend to invoke this power immediately. Creston trusted me with this and I feel it's time for me to live up to his trust. I'm going to need your help."

"My first thought is it's a little early for this action. Do you believe Creston is dead? If so, there's no rush. Perhaps we should wait a while longer to see if…"

Creston is alive."

"And Rainey, too?" Jack said.

"Yes, and Rainey too, but this is about Creston."

"Ok, then let's hear what you have planned."

Leslie detailed her plan to appoint a small board to oversee all of Creston's affairs. The board would check all the companies involved in managing Creston's investments, properties, and private matters such as upkeep and maintenance of his residence and vehicles. Jackson Aberdeen agreed with everything, but questioned the last board appointee.

"Oscar Bourgeois, I don't think I've met him."

"I'm sure you have. Big O at The Oyster House, sound familiar?"

"The bartender Big O?"

"Yes, that Big O. Bartending and shucking oysters is what he does," Leslie said, "but it's not who he is."

"It's unorthodox but if you're sure then I'll support you completely."

"The board will meet randomly at my discretion to avoid predictability by anyone thinking this might be an opportunity to cash in at Creston's expense. It's strictly a precaution, but one I feel should be taken."

Leslie returned to her office and spent the rest of the morning catching up. She worked through lunch and readied herself for her next task. She picked up her purse, left her office and headed to the parking garage. Twenty minutes later she parked in front of Joan Dufrene's house.

Joan Winters Dufrene, born and reared in New Orleans, had been a big fan of Claude Raines and Mary Pickford, two movie stars she adored. She was proud of herself for ingeniously combining parts of both names and adorning her son, Rainsford Aloysius Dufrene, with a unique moniker. It reminded her often of, and was a tribute to, her favorite movie stars. Aloysius was simply a name she liked. St. Aloysius high school had been a prominent catholic school for boys in the neighborhood she had lived in at one time. The red brick structure with the white trim was long gone from New Orleans but it had still been there when Rainey was born and she had always liked the name.

She had married John Dufrene, Rainey's father. The surname dated back to France before Nova Scotia was established. Rainey's father was unsure from where his heritage stemmed other than France. It always sounded exciting and romantic to assume his people had come down from Nova Scotia as part of the Acadians migrating south, the Acadians who would eventually become the Cajuns of south Louisiana. But the truth was not easily determined and his people might as easily have landed in the new world directly from France fleeing the poverty and darkness of the pre-bourgeois uprising. John Dufrene died of cancer right after his fiftieth birthday.

Leslie had phoned Rainey's mother and told her of the lost plane. A faux pas and Leslie knew it as soon as Joan answered. She should have been more courageous and visited Joan at her home instead of calling by phone. Leslie believed Rainey's mother had resented Leslie leaving and causing her son such pain, and the truth, as Leslie believed, was Joan had never forgiven her. She hoped to rectify her mistake.

Leslie was uncomfortable as she rang the door bell. Joan opened the door and Leslie said, "I wouldn't blame you if you said no, but I'd like to come in, please."

"Of course you can come in," Joan said. She turned, walked to the sofa and sat.

"It was cowardly and insensitive of me to call you when I was told Rainey was missing. I should have come by to see you. But I was afraid you'd never want to see me again, and I wouldn't blame you."

Joan gently rocked back and forth on the sofa. "Certain things happen in life and we must let go of them or they will continue to do us harm. I was upset with how hurt and devastated Rainey was with losing you. But he told me it was as much his fault as yours, and as his mother I didn't want to believe him. We would sit and watch the old movies like we had years ago. He would point out examples in the movies of how things happen, how it is nobodies fault sometimes. But he never told me what happened, why you two didn't work out."

"Seldom is one person to blame in a break up," Leslie said. "And maybe he could have tried to stop it from happening, but I doubt it. Things were near perfect with me and Rainey for almost a year so when we got married it was great. And it stayed great...for a while. You saw us at our best, and it was all very real. But then I guess we became too used to each other. Rainey worked and I worked.

We were soon going different directions. We came to see you less and less. I got caught up in my career, spending more time at the bank, and not enough time working on my marriage. I thought Rainey was losing interest. Later he told me he was giving me space, thought he had been crowding me. So if he had any fault it was not keeping me close. But the worst part was I fell for an older man who worked at the bank and gave me too much attention. We saw each other every day. He was a prominent figure, and powerful. I thought we were a good fit even though he was much older than I. It was all about power and he used it to his advantage. I moved out. Rainey tried to stop me, but it was too late. I was way in over my head. Anyway, I think you can figure out the rest. And I'm sure Rainey told you all this."

Joan shifted in her seat and thought for a moment. "That's more than I realized. Rainey did not share any of this with me. He avoided discussing it except for what I told you earlier. I had trouble believing it was his fault, but I accepted it. He convinced me to forgive and forget. That's when I knew."

"Knew what?" Leslie said.

"He still loves you, and will all his life."

Tears ran down Leslie's face. She bowed her head and reached for a tissue from her purse. "I hope you're right."

"I haven't given up hope," Joan said, "but sometimes it's hard, especially when nothing has been found and they stopped searching."

"Don't quit believing, and don't stop praying."

"I think we need some coffee," Joan said. She rose and went into the kitchen.

They sat and drank coffee the rest of the afternoon. Tears flowed and the waste basket was full of tissues by the time Leslie said she must go.

"I have one more request," Leslie said. "I'd like to borrow your key to Rainey's apartment."

Joan tensed as she said, "I don't understand. Why would you want to see his apartment?"

"Mom," Leslie said, "I want to feel close to him again. I think going to his place might help."

"You haven't called me mom in a long time. I'll get the key."

Words spoken in anger can never be retracted, and some actions cannot be undone. Leslie was ashamed she had been so cowardly and insensitive to Joan and hoped she had repaired some of the hurt.

"Hang on to this," Joan said handing Leslie the key. "If I need it I'll call you."

Rainey had no housekeeper and it was evident to Leslie as soon as she let herself in. It looked the same as when she had visited him six months earlier. Men simply don't rearrange furniture or make changes, she thought. They are the epitome of creatures of habit content in their lot. She moved through his apartment with no real purpose, noticing magazines scattered on the coffee table, a pair of slippers on the floor by the couch, one upside down on top of the other, and a cup left on the dining room table with the residue of coffee starting to grow mold. She expected to see dishes in the kitchen sink and was surprised to find it empty. An empty wine bottle on the counter caught her eye and she picked it up, remembering her night with Rainey. It was the bottle they had shared and she wondered why he had not thrown it away. Leslie sniffed the bottle; it had been rinsed out and saved, not thrown away. She returned the bottle to the counter, moved back into the living room and then down the hall. Rainey's bedroom door was partly open. She stopped and flipped on the light. His closet door was closed but several pairs of slacks and a shirt had been left draped across his king size bed. Taking several hangers from the closet she returned the slacks and shirt to the closet and thought about their last night together in his apartment, the wine, the temptation, and the mutual succumbing. She sat on the edge of the bed and then lay across it, resting her head on his pillow. Rainey's scent was still present. She closed her eyes, inhaled deeply and prayed for his safety.

CHAPTER SEVENTEEN

Rainey had walked about five hundred yards into the center of the island when he stopped, drank from the water bottle and looked in all directions. The trees and foliage were thick but navigable. The simplicity of it all made him feel alive. Sweat ran from his forehead and he found himself admiring the lushness of the island. The frustration he had experienced earlier had waned, replaced by guilt for leaving Creston. As he turned to head back he noticed a tree to his right with large, green spheres hanging from it. They were about the same size as coconuts but with a berry-like skin. He looked around more closely and noticed several more trees with the strange, oversized berries. With a little luck they would prove edible, and with a little more luck they might even taste good. Curiosity pushed him to approach the tree and take one. As he pulled the fruit from the tree a chill ran down his spine. Rainey turned and hurled the fruit into the trees.

"KNOCK IT OFF!" he screamed. The sense of being watched like the first day on the beach returned. One moment he was like a warrior ready to battle, and the next moment he felt foolish. "Creston wouldn't understand," he said. "And neither do I." He grabbed another fruit and headed back to camp.

Rainey, holding the green fruit, watched Creston, on hands and knees backing out of the hold, resembling an over grown toddler. But Creston's movements were agile and sturdy, prompting encouragement. The healing process was well along and Creston had improved dramatically. Standing and holding a small duffle bag, he turned and noticed Rainey. He threw the duffle onto the sand. Rainey followed the flight of the duffle and watched it land near two suitcases and a large, yellow, vinyl and canvass bundle.

"Hey, I see you found a bread fruit," Creston said.

"Is that what this is?" Rainey asked. "What's bread fruit?"

"It's indigenous to the Pacific islands. And it's edible. But, I think you have to cook it first. It's supposed to have bread like taste and substance when cooked."

"So what do we do with it? How do we fix it?

"Hell, Rainey, I don't know. I guess we cut it open, clean out seeds or whatever and go from there."

Rainey glared at Creston, feeling edgy but thought better about responding. Both of them were wearing thin and remaining quiet might be the better part of valor. But it ate at him. He tossed the breadfruit on the ground near the fire pit and approached the pile of items from the cargo hold. Two suitcases, the box with fishing poles, his duffel bag, the large yellow bundle which was still a mystery, a case of Ramen Noodles of mixed flavors, and a plain, unmarked box about two feet square in size. He watched Creston back out of the cargo hold again, this time appearing empty handed.

"Maybe you better let me get the rest of the stuff out of there," Rainey said.

"Why, you think I can't handle it?"

"I don't know what you can or can't handle. But you're out of line with your attitude. What's eating at you?"

Creston climbed out of the hole and approached Rainey, stopping inches from him. Sweat covered his soiled shirt and beaded on his forehead, "This. All of this," he said loudly, throwing his arms up in the air, wincing with pain from the exaggerated motions. "The whole mess I've gotten us into. The minimal supplies we have, the limited water, no communication to the rest of the world." Creston stopped, resting with his hands on his knees. "The plane's a total loss. I'm beat up, you're beat up, and I don't have a clue as to what to do."

The two men glared at each other. Rainey nodded and then broke out in laughter.

"You think this is FUNNY!" Creston yelled. "Have you lost your mind?"

Rainey understood Creston's rage. His laughter subsided and he said, "You're about a week behind me. The difference is you were pretty much knocked out when this got the better of me. I ranted, I yelled, I stomped about the plane, and when I was finished nothing had changed," Rainey said. "We survived. We beat the devil, or father time, or however you want to look at it. That alone is reason to laugh, so get over it. Let's figure out what we can do about all this."

"All right, but think about this. We've been on this overgrown sandbar about ten days. And yeah, I'm much better, but what you see here is what we've got. Maybe we get found in two or three days, or twenty or thirty years, or never. Philosophize about *that*, why don't you."

"Like I said, you're a week behind me. We're stuck here and there's nothing we can do about what's happened. You know this. We'll make the most of what we have, and pray for the best." Rainey turned toward the pile of items from the hold. "What's the big yellow bundle over there by the luggage?"

Creston moved toward Rainey and put his arm around his shoulders. "Oh, well remember how I forgot to tell you about the fishing poles? I guess I forgot to tell you about the inflatable life raft, too."

"A life raft," Rainey said. "Shit, Creston, a life raft is important, don't you think? Anything else you forgot to tell me?"

"It's a life raft but it's not meant to sail across the seven seas. It's an eight foot, two man raft. One good wave in the open ocean and we'd be treading water until the sharks got us, or we gave in to exhaustion." Creston shook his head. "So no, there isn't anything else I forgot to tell you."

"Good," Rainey said. "Let's go over what we have and how to make the most of this."

The list of supplies and equipment was promising for the short term: two fishing poles, the life raft, suitcases and duffle bags with clothes and toiletries, a small tool box with pliers, screwdrivers, electrical tape, knife, tape measure, and ball-peen hammer, two more cases of water, three cases of soft drinks, more boxes of candy bars and chocolates, the case of Ramen noodles, and two cases of canned soup.

"All things considered, I'd say we're in pretty good shape," Creston said.

"All things considered, I'd rather be in New Orleans," Rainey said. "Let's move it into the plane.

"The rains come with such force the hole will fill back up with sand after one or two downpours. They remind me of the summer squalls blowing in from the gulf, like the May 3rd storm that flooded New Orleans years ago. A real mess and lots of water."

They gathered the items retrieved from the cargo hold and moved them into the plane, stacking them neatly toward the rear. Rainey closed the cargo hold door and turned the handle to seal it.

The day was almost gone. It had been much more productive than previous days, though the tasks had been simple. The sun was on the horizon and cast an elongated, fiery orange reflection across the lagoon, shimmering in the water like a thousand fireflies bunched together.

"Some of the prettiest sunsets I've ever seen," Creston said. "Better than the sun over Lake Ponchartrain, better even than Hawaii. I can't force myself to believe it all ends here. No matter how dire it gets, I can see us getting out of this."

Rainey watched the setting sun. "I never figured you for the eternal optimist. A realist maybe, so a little optimism is good. I need you to be encouraged. Maybe you can navigate us out of here."

"Let's start a fire, heat up the chicken soup, the Ramen noodles, and dine like kings. We've earned it. There are enough unbroken plates and bowls to make this gourmet dining. Damn I wish I had some wine. I guess the Jack Daniels and Sprite will have to do."

"What Jack Daniels?" Rainey asked. "I didn't see any whiskey in the plane. You have a sick sense of humor."

"I guarantee you there are two bottles of Jack safely stowed under the pilot seat, unbroken and safe." Creston rose. "Some things are sacred. I'll be right back."

The waves crashed in the distance, the sun had sizzled into the ocean, and a breeze caressed the island, gently massaging the trees. They dined and drank, then ate chocolate for dessert, and pushed their situation far from conscious thought, if but for the moment.

"You know what tomorrow is, don't you?" Rainey asked.

"Yeah, it's day eleven, so what?"

"True, it is day eleven, but it's also time to take out the stitches. I hope I have as much fun removing them as I did putting them in," Rainey said.

"You're demented," Creston said. "Sometimes I don't buy this good Catholic boy image you've portrayed so well. I think you must have a little sadistic side to you."

Rainey looked at Creston and nodded. It was a good evening, and for the moment their sense of humor had been found. They were enjoying their friendship, and not relying on it.

Morning winds, colder and more forceful than usual, swept across the island and both men shivered as they slept on blankets placed over the open ground. And as the blast of cool air traversed the island, heavy rain followed and poured down as they struggled to jump up and make for the open cabin door. Their bodies were well along in the healing process, but Creston still grimaced while awkwardly climbing into the plane. With Rainey in a hurry to get out of the almost violent rain he pushed Creston and they both fell onto the floor in a heap, cursing and struggling to sit up. The rains had occurred mostly in the afternoon so the morning storm caught them off guard. The downpour lasted about ten minutes, and as abruptly as it had started, it came to a stop.

The storm moved eastward, blocked the rising sun, and absorbed its flood of light. The inside of the plane was muggy and stale like an old deserted house. Rainey moved into the doorway and then jumped down. The sand was spongy from the downpour, but the rainwater had disappeared, absorbed deep into the island within a few minutes. He looked east at the fast moving storm clouds and watched the sun appear from behind them, casting light over the island that flickered through the trees. Creston had crawled to the door, maneuvered his legs out and sat, watching Rainey. With the exception of the early morning storm, day eleven brought nothing new.

Rainey looked back at Creston, shrugged his shoulders and said, "I guess we should have seen it coming one day. No harm done except the sand caved in a little by the cargo door. You ok?"

"Yeah, but wish I'd been prepared. I'd have grabbed some soap. How good would a shower feel?" Creston said. "I'm gonna help with breakfast. You've been doing all the food since we got here."

"I'm not keeping score, and what else was I going to do. You get the food and I'll make the coffee. I can start the fire even after the hard rain. We'll eat, and then I'll take care of the other matter I told you about."

Creston ran his fingers over the stitches. "You scare me sometimes."

Making coffee had become routine. The fire was blazing, water with coffee had been boiled, and the carafe of liquid steeped as Creston emerged from the plane with the usual honey buns.

"We're down to the last few honey buns. I don't have a clue on how to fix breadfruit but we better figure out how and gather some more."

"Yeah, and we better figure out how to catch and save some of this rain water, too. We're running low on bottles of water and we can't live on soft drinks. I can make something to catch rain water using the tool kit and parts from the plane," Rainey said.

"I've never thought of you as the mechanical type. I'm beginning to appreciate Swiss Family Robinson except this ain't no movie." Creston placed the honey buns on the panel over the fire.

"Let's eat and then get the stitches out. I think those swims in the lagoon's salty water must have done some good. It never looked infected, and the skin has grown together and closed the wound. How does it feel?"

"It doesn't. But I'm sure it will as soon as you pull the stitches out."

Rainey stood over Creston holding the tweezers and scissors. He took a deep breath and leaned forward. "Hold still, this might hurt a little." He considered his attack, wondering if he should start at the top of the cut or the bottom.

"What the hell are you looking at so hard? It's stitches. Cut the damn thread and pull them out." Creston looked for a snicker or grin from Rainey. "But go easy."

He looked closely, stopped, and turned toward the plane.

"NOW what?" Creston said.

"I need a bottle of water and a towel. The cut looks a little crusty where the stitches penetrate the skin. It might start bleeding a little when I cut and pull the stitches," he said.

Rainey poured water over the cut while holding the towel to absorb the excess. He dabbed at the wound with the wet towel to moisten it enough to allow the stitches to pull clean without bleeding, or worse, open the wound again.

"Don't move," he said, and leaned over Creston. With the scissors visibly shaking he snipped the first stitch at the bottom of the wound. Rainey cut all the stitches before removing them and a smile came to his face even though he tried to suppress it.

"WHAT? What are you grinning at?"

Rainey moved back one step and said, "I can't help it. All those stitches sticking out of your forehead, well, it looks like an upside down centipede."

"That's great. I need a doctor and I get a comedian. Use the tweezers and pull the damn things out."

Rainey gently, and with stern face, pulled each stitch from Creston's forehead, dabbing the wet towel on the wound after removing each one. Again he stepped back and looked intensely at his handy work. He crossed his arms over his chest, still holding the scissors and tweezers, tilted his head to the right, then back to the left, scrunched his mouth in a lopsided pucker and said nothing.

"Stop right there. You're not fooling me," Creston said. "No smart ass remarks, see. No scar face wisecracks, nothing, got it?"

Rainey remained stoic. "Truthfully, scar face would be an improvement."

"Man, it is HARD to get good help these days," Creston bellowed. He stood up and gently pressed the tip of his index finger up and down the freshly healed cut. "It doesn't feel half bad. Not the kind of souvenir I'd have chosen, but it'll have to do."

CHAPTER EIGHTEEN

Leslie sat in the conference room with the other members of the board. It was her intention to pay them a small stipend for their time but they had all refused. The reality was Creston made more in interest on his deposits in one day than all of them would have been paid combined.

Leslie explained the responsibilities of each board member and there was unanimous agreement to Leslie's plan. The meeting had lasted less than an hour. Big O lingered behind as the others left.

"What's on your mind, O?" Leslie asked.

"Rainey," Big O said. "I want to help. He ain't got nothin to do with this here, but I can't get him out my mind." Big O paused. "What's next for all of us?"

"Big O," Leslie said. "None of us is sure of what to do, but we all want to help. And we've all tried to do as much as we can. O, I'd like to see Momma Mary again. Maybe she might come up with something new or…"

"Leslie," Big O interrupted, "I told you before if Momma got some kind of feeling she'd have called me."

"But maybe she's waiting for us to visit her. It could be the push she needs to get a vision or new feeling. Let's go see her today at lunch. In fact, let's bring her lunch and eat over by the river, at the Moon Walk. So, what about it?"

"How I'm gonna tell you no, Leslie? Mama always liked her fried catfish po'boy, dressed. I'll get some for all of us from Maspero's and meet you at her stall. I'll call her and tell her we're comin."

"Excellent. I'll meet you there at noon. And I'll be hungry so don't forget my po'boy. I'll bring some drinks."

Big O moved toward the door as Leslie put the conference room in order. She was feeling remarkably better and was pleased to be moving forward. Leslie was looking forward to lunch but she had much work to do until then. The bank had been tolerant of her lack of focus but it was time to pick up the pace. It was time to give her mind a rest from Rainey and Creston.

Leslie spent the morning reviewing the commercial loan applications stacked on her desk. The minor loan requests had been handled by Lynnette Small but the larger ones required Leslie's scrutiny. She was meticulous in her review process and had learned to spot the potential high risk loans. Leslie was so engrossed in catching up her neglected work the phone on her desk startled her when it rang. She knew she was late as soon as she heard Big O's voice. She relaxed when O told her he and Mama Mary would wait for her at the Moon Walk instead of Mama's stall. But he also reminded her the catfish po'boys would get cold.

Leslie caught a taxi and in less than ten minutes was getting out on Decatur Street across from Jackson Square. The ten dollars for the four dollar ride provided too big a tip, but she was in a hurry and didn't wait for change.

The street alongside the building where Jax Beer was once brewed rises with a modest incline and crests at the top of a levee that for years has protected the French Quarter from the Mississippi river during the flood season. Two sets of railroad tracks run atop the levee and intersect the street where it flattens out across the barrier. Reaching the top of the twenty foot rise, Leslie made her way across the tracks, sure to stay in the painted pedestrian crossing, and looked down upon the Moon Walk promenade.

Big O and Mama Mary were seated on a bench, talking, and occasionally looking out over the water at the busy river traffic. Tug boats pushed barges, the Algiers ferry shuttled cars and pedestrians across the river to the foot of Canal Street, large cargo vessels were tied up to the docks on both sides of the river. It was an almost typical late October day, sunny and clear with the temperature in the low seventies, unusually low humidity and mild wind. An unusual phenomenon created a greenish blue Mississippi River instead of the usual muddy brown.

The river was similar in color to the coastal waters of the gulf. The water level of the Mississippi river can drop so low the Gulf of Mexico will move upriver as far as New Orleans and sometimes even farther. The salt water intrusion causes air whiffing off the river to smell of ocean and can be reminiscent of a day at the beach. In years past there had been reports of sharks sighted in the river, and of fisherman catching red fish and speckled trout in lieu of the usual fresh water river cats. This was an exceptional day.

Leslie approached and said, "O, I'm sorry but I forgot the drinks. I was late and left in a hurry."

"I thought you might forget. You been way too busy and occupied, so I put some drinks in with the sandwiches. Come sit with us and eat." Big O handed Leslie one of the catfish po'boys.

Leslie reached for the sandwich. "Mama, how have you been?" Leslie said. "It's only been about a week since I met you and yet, it seems so long ago."

"Baby, I been real good. My life is the way it's supposed to be. I wish I had some good news to tell you two, but there's nothing new. It's the same as last time. I guess maybe the good news is nothing has changed. I still feel Rainey is alive and doing ok. And, I'm pretty sure Creston is ok too, but I don't get nothin on him, not yet anyway." Mama Mary looked out at the river and said, "I'm sorry you're disappointed."

"You've been a God send, please don't feel bad or worry about anything else. You've given me peace when I couldn't find it. I believe if you say they're alive then it's true. I wish we knew where they were and how long it'll be until we see them again, but believing they're alive is good enough." Leslie stared at Mama Mary, who was lost in thought.

Mama Mary turned from watching the river and looked at Leslie. "It won't be too long child, before they get back. I don't know yet how long but maybe less than a year."

Big O stopped short of taking his first bite of sandwich, holding it inches from his mouth. "Mama, you shore? We can't be making no mistakes. Not about this. We got to know for shore…"

Mama Mary tilted her head and raised her eyebrows. "Oscar, I don't come with no guarantee, remember?"

Big O was blushing with embarrassment, and was thankful his dark skin did not give him away. He knew better than to question her or put pressure on her about anything she said. Sometimes, it didn't happen the way she said or thought it would. But most of the time she was right.

"Never mind, forget I said anything, Mama."

She reached over and patted his knee. "You betta eat your sandwich."

They sat on the bench and ate. The French bread was crisp and had been toasted so the outer skin was flakey. Small bits of the crust would flake off with each bite and float to the ground, resembling pieces of paper riding on the wind. The local pigeons gathered excitedly around the bench, bravely inching closer and closer to the fragments of bread, skittish but determined. The bravest of the flock scurried under the bench from behind, grabbed a speck of bread and retreated to safety. The others soon followed and virtually picked the area clean of the crumbs.

After they finished their sandwiches they stood, brushed off crumbs from their laps, and shook the sandwich paper, making sure the remaining bits of bread fell to the ground for the pigeons. They deposited the trash in the wrought-iron enclosed receptacle and walked along the river. Talk flowed easily and natural, much like the river, and they discussed random topics, but did not discuss Rainey and Creston. If Mama Mary was correct, there was nothing they could do but wait. Lack of patience was their most formidable challenge, but one they would have to overcome despite their frustration with the lack of progress.

It was a long walk back to the bank but Leslie enjoyed it immensely. She had new hope. Mama Mary's prediction of Rainey and Creston possibly returning in less than a year was encouraging. Half way back to the bank, amid a sea of unknown faces, the idea

Mama Mary might be wrong clouded over her and erased her exhilaration. She stopped for a moment on St. Charles Avenue, resting against a building. Her attitude had changed and she resented the change as much as she resented the loss of Rainey. A paper cup lying on the sidewalk flew off her foot as she kicked it. With her head thrown back she tramped un-lady like down the avenue to the bank building.

CHAPTER NINETEEN

"What's on your mind? You look like you're thinking too much and way too hard," Creston said.

"It's day twelve and we haven't seen anything. I've scanned the sky looking for a sign of a plane but nothing, and no ships far off in the distance with smoke stacks billowing into the air, nothing."

"We're not going to see anything."

"Why not?" Rainey asked.

"Because," Creston said. "We must be too far from the shipping lanes and commercial flight patterns. They don't set sail or take off and then figure out which way they're going. If we were close we'd have seen a jet, maybe a ship. The search planes stopped looking days ago."

"So nobody's coming," Rainey said.

"Unless somebody in a sailboat happens to go cruising by, randomly sailing around the world, but I wouldn't count on it."

Rainey stood, turned and walked a few paces toward the lagoon. He turned back toward Creston and yelled, "HEY, guess what I'm doing. I'm looking for the sailboat." Looking back over the lagoon he whispered, "But it ain't coming." Rainey paced back and forth a couple of times and then walked back.

"Screw it, getting rescued probably isn't what it's cracked up to be. I've walked around the perimeter of the island a couple of times and nothing changes. All I've seen is the reef, waves crashing, the lagoon, trees and sand, lots of sand. And all I've gotten from the walks is exercise. I'm going into the middle of the island and see if I can find some more breadfruit or something, anything. Maybe I'll find some pineapples," Rainey said. "No telling what's out there."

"More likely a bunch of trees and bushes, but no pineapples, city boy."

"From a distance some of the bushes sort of look like pineapple plants. And since when did you become Mr. Green Jeans? You're more city than me," Rainey said.

"Maybe so, but I *learned* a few things along the way."

"Yeah, well did you learn how to kiss my ass while you were at it?"

"Spoken like a true southern gentleman."

"I can always tell when you're feeling better," Rainey said. "The brain stops working and the insults start." Rainey went about picking up and storing the provisions safely in the plane to protect them from the almost daily rains.

"Look, before you take off, don't you think we should try to figure out what we can do about our water supply? We're running low and the two cases from the cargo hold will be gone in a few more days. We can't stand out in the rain like a bunch of long neck geese trying to capture water forever. What about when the rains don't come for days at a time? We need a reserve of water."

"I already figured it out. Come on, I'll show you. I don't think this will take too long." Rainey headed toward the plane. "And even if it does take a while, time is one thing we have plenty of."

Rainey retrieved the small tool box from the plane and placed it on the sand by the fire pit. Taking a screwdriver from the tool box he returned to the plane. It took him almost twenty minutes but when he emerged he carried a piece of sheet metal taken from one of the seat-backs similar to the one they used as a cook top. Creston watched as Rainey headed toward the lagoon, carrying the panel. He rinsed the panel in the lagoon, turned and placed it flat on the sand close to the water's edge. Back and forth he worked the panel over the sand and in less than ten minutes he stopped, held it up and nodded with approval. He walked back and sat on the ground next to the tool box. Creston never took his eyes off Rainey. Inside the tool box, Rainey found the ball peen hammer. Methodically,

Rainey hammered at the panel, turning it in a circle making sure he never hit the same place twice. The panel proved more rigid and stubborn than Rainey had expected. Harder and harder he delivered blows with the hammer, and soon the panel bent inward and took shape. For more than thirty minutes Rainey labored, but when finished the sheet metal seat-back resembled the better part of a large oblong serving dish with hammer marks completely covering the interior surface.

"That's it? A big bowl?" Creston asked.

"Well, not just a big bowl. I'm going to use a Phillips head screwdriver and punch a small hole right in the center of the panel and use a screw from the plane to make a plug. We can place it on the wing, prop it up with some tree limbs, and when it rains the water will collect in the bowl. After it's full we remove the plug and drain the water into the empty bottles. So while I go out on safari you can make another one."

"I have to say, I'm impressed. You and I know each other better than we know anyone else. And yet, I'm seeing a side of you I've never seen."

"I did what I had to do," Rainey said. "No big deal."

"No, it's more than a big deal. When I was leaning against the tree, the day you found me, I could have given up then and waited to die. But not you, if you have one breath left you'll fight for one more. I've learned you're a survivor. And I like it."

"Thanks," Rainey said.

Creston removed another seat-back panel, looking forward to his task. The need to be productive was strong and his competitive nature had him convinced his rain bowl would be better than Rainey's. As the panel took shape, he did not see Rainey set off.

After walking out about a hundred yards, Rainey stopped and looked back at the camp site. Creston was working diligently on the panel. His mind raced through the events of the last twelve days and a reality was gnawing at him. The harsh reality of possibly being lost forever was swallowing him as he stood motionless. He was stuck, his eyes lost focus and his mind escaped to New Orleans. A falling coconut, dislodged by a strong gust of wind, hit the ground and disturbed his moment of self pity.

Rainey turned, unsure of what he might encounter. The breadfruit was less exciting to eat than it had been to find. Creston had cleaned it and roasted it on their improvised grill. It was bland but edible.

Strong winds gusted, belying the calm, cloudless sky and shook the trees. Rainey moved farther into the center of the island. The breeze coming off the ocean was swirling and cooled him. He stopped, closed his eyes and the wind on his face brought him back to the shotgun house on Banks street in New Orleans. It was his early years, before air conditioning, and he was standing in front of the large window fan turning at full speed throwing warm outside air on his face. The image brought a determination to his psyche and he was grateful.

The plane and campsite was a mile behind him and the trees were denser. The lack of insects was surprising. There had been no mosquitoes or gnats attacking him and he remembered how bothersome they were in Louisiana. Another good sign was the absence of snakes, but he was still careful as he placed his feet when close to fallen tree limbs, bushes and trees. The thickness of the trees and flora had increased and moving forward was turning into a formidable task. It was as he had anticipated. His first trip around the island had brought him to a spot where gazing through the trees to the other side of the island was impossible. Up close the density was even greater.

Rainey stopped and concentrated on the various trees. There was an abundance of coconut trees, each with clusters of six or eight coconuts. He counted ten breadfruit trees at least thirty to forty feet tall and all with ovoid shaped fruit hanging. If the trees are this thick throughout the island, there must be hundreds of them he thought. "At least we won't starve anytime soon," he said.

He moved forward between two palm trees less than two feet apart causing him to turn at an angle to squeeze through. Stopping as he placed his left foot, he peered straight ahead at more trees and thick flora. What's the use he thought, why move on?

Rainey retreated by moving his right foot far enough behind to balance himself and twisted his body back through the palm trees. He lifted his firmly planted left foot. The ground was covered with grass, fallen leaves, limbs, and countless vines growing from tree to tree. His right foot snagged in the thick ground cover, making it impossible to reposition as he tried to move backward. The tangled footing, coupled with his body's momentum, precipitated his fall and Rainey found himself face down, mouth crusted with sand, and a pain emanating from his right shoulder, having slammed against a palm tree as he fell. Propping himself up, he spit out the small amount of sand and wiped his mouth with his right hand.

"Jesus, Rainey," he said in frustration. "How stupid are you going to stay for the rest of your..."

He froze. Ten feet away, his eyes locked on what he was sure was a bare, human foot protruding from a cluster of trees. His heart ached with an adrenaline rush, sweat beaded on his forehead and he gasped. Not releasing his stare from the foot, he managed to rise and regain his footing. He tried to calm himself. "Holy shit," he muttered. It was a real human foot, he was sure, even though it had not moved. Confused, as if lost on a strange highway and not knowing which way to go, he did nothing.

The foot pulled back and disappeared behind the tree and he yelled out, "Wait!"

Rainey bounded after it brushing against trees then stopping, his right hand on the trunk of the palm tree where the foot had been. He hesitated, his head was pounding and his breath caught in his throat. Expecting to see nothing Rainey leaned to his left and peered around the tree. Two brilliant blues eyes less than six inches from his own looked back at him. The shock of seeing the piercing blues eyes sent him jumping back. He again found himself on the ground after bouncing off another tree, this time on his back, and looking up.

A woman stared down at Rainey. "Oh my God," he said.

Rainey sat up making no quick movements, and not averting his eyes. His heart was pounding and his chest tightened as he finished rising. He stood three feet from her and his stare traveled from her blue eyes downward, taking in her form. Stringy, dirty blond and auburn hair hung to her waist, partly concealing her naked breasts. A stained and tattered white sarong barely covered her hips. She wore nothing else and made no attempt to cover herself.

Rainey shook his head, blinked and exhaled. The fear waned as he stared at her, and she at him. "Rainey," he said tapping his closed fist several times against his chest.

She stared back at him for a long moment then shifted her eyes away and looked skyward with a puzzled expression.

"Are you kidding me?" he said in a low voice. "No, Rainey is my name." He waited but she had no response. "What…is your… name? Do you speak English?"

Her expression remained blank as she stared at him.

Rainey extended his hand but she did not move. He pulled his hand back and wiped it on his shirt as if dirt was the reason she had not taken it. She looked at him but there was emptiness to her stare. Rainey studied her more completely. Her skin was dark from the sun and there were small creases in the corners of her eyes. She had a long neck and a firm jaw. The stringy hair had not been brushed in years. Her hands were rough, weathered, but strong, almost masculine except for long slender fingers. The nails were short, rough, and not manicured in a long time, if ever.

Rainey took a step to the right, and she turned her head following his movement, her bare feet remaining firmly planted. He studied her flat abdomen and found himself admiring her physique. Very bohemian he thought, but then realized he might be the odd one here. The blank stare did not change and her face stayed emotionless. Rainey figured her to be at least five foot eight or ten inches, tall for a woman, definitely Anglo-Saxon, and somewhere between forty and fifty years old.

"So where do we go from here?" he said. "Who are you, and where do you come from?" Each question went unanswered and she gave no indication she understood him.

Rainey turned away from her and stepped in the direction of the campsite. Perhaps he and Creston could figure this out together he thought. Maybe she holds the key to where they are. A tingling of fear gripped him and the chill returned, running down his spine. Were there others? Was he being watched? Fear gripped him as he considered each question.

"How long have you been here?" he said as he turned back toward her.

She was gone. But how did she disappear so quickly? It was early afternoon. The sun's rays of light cast shadows through the trees and they moved eerily as the wind rustled the limbs and palm fronds. Rainey perspired even more, despite standing almost motionless. Turning a complete circle he scanned the area. Nothing appeared out of sorts. Anger replaced his fear and he admitted she was imagined, his desperation, but not real.

The walk back to the plane was a blur. Rainey struggled to erase the trick his mind had played on him. Was this the beginning of going crazy? Would his mind continue to fool him? He wanted to believe the encounter had happened, but she had not spoken nor accepted his hand. It makes sense, he thought. You can't shake hands with a figment of your imagination. The mind gives and the mind takes away, he thought so yes, his mind would continue to fool him and he was scared.

Creston was relaxing under the wing of the plane, out of the sun and looking almost like he was on vacation. His newly formed bowl for collecting water was on the ground next to him and he made no movement as Rainey approached. He looked up and said nothing, but watched as Rainey stopped, stared at the ground for a minute, then lifted his head and looked around, not cognizant Creston was within ten feet of where he stood. He plopped down on the bare sand without acknowledging Creston or saying anything.

"Well, it's not as if I'm expecting a big hug and a kiss, but maybe a ...Rainey, you ok? You look sick."

A long moment passed. "I'm ok," Rainey said. "But I think the island is getting to me. Or maybe it's being stuck here like this. I can't put my finger on it, but I've had about enough of this crap."

Creston rose, brushing off sand with both hands. Rainey was visibly different and obviously bothered. Being sensitive was not typical of Creston. He contemplated his choice of words longer than normal. Rainey rolled his eyes up, as if looking over reading glasses. He did not move, waiting for Creston to speak.

"I don't think it's the island that's getting to you. It's everything we've been through, being stuck here and not having a solution to our situation. And you've had to take care of me and all of this without any help. But we're both better, and on the right track. We can figure this all out." Creston had not convinced Rainey or himself.

Rainey rose and took several steps toward the interior of the island, stared into the trees, and then turned back toward Creston.

"I don't feel like being positive or bullshitting either one of us. The island's not fine, and I'm not fine with the island. I didn't want to say anything because I don't want you thinking I'm crazy or losing it, but something happened out there." The two friends stared at each other. Rainey drooped his head until his chin rested on his chest. He then lifted his head while raising both arms out to his sides, and with palms up he shrugged his shoulders as if he had no idea what was going on, or even what he was talking about.

"I don't think you're crazy or losing it. When you start planting sticks in the sand and watering and singing to them, then I might think you're crazy." Creston's humor did not faze Rainey.

"Ok, then let's try this on for size." Rainey told Creston everything, the abundance of coconuts and breadfruits, having to squeeze through the trees, falling, seeing the foot, scrambling toward it and coming face to face with a tall blonde lady. He explained every detail, turning away for a moment and her quick disappearance. Rainey stopped and cleared his throat. "A figment of my imagination. Crazy, right?"

"Go on, I'm listening," Creston said.

"Go on?" Rainey said. "There isn't any more. It's my mind playing tricks on me." Creston was staring toward the center of the island. "Hey, are you listening to me? Did you hear what I said? I said I'm...."

"Maybe you're not as crazy as you think," Creston said.

Rainey turned and his jaw dropped. The figment of his imagination had appeared from behind a palm tree no more than a hundred feet away. His mouth hung open and anger washed over him as he remembered how he had doubted what had happened. She walked toward them and carried a small bunch of bananas. Neither moved nor spoke as they watched her approach. Rainey's gaping mouth closed as the anger left him.

"You were saying?" Creston asked without turning toward Rainey.

"I doubted my sanity, thought I was seeing things. I didn't think she was real."

"She's real," Creston said. "We've been here almost two weeks. Where the hell was she hiding?"

She stopped and held out the bananas as an offering. Creston took them, broke one off, peeled it and ate it in three bites. In the open light of the day, and away from the shadows of the trees, Rainey was able to get a much better look at her. The emptiness of her expression was still prevalent. Fear, or at least apprehension, would be understandable, but there was nothing.

"My name is Creston, and his name is Rainey," Creston said softly. She stared at him, watching his mouth move. "This is our plane. We crashed here, and now we can't leave." Creston looked at Rainey and then back at her.

"Play...ane?" She moved to the tip of the damaged wing, placed a hand on it, and turned. "Plane?"

Creston took a step toward her but Rainey grabbed his arm, stopping him. He stepped back.

"What...is... your name?" Rainey said.

Her expression changed slightly, as if remembering and then said, "Amy?"

"Your name is Amy?" Rainey asked.

Rainey and Creston looked at each other. "Amy, are there others here with you?" Rainey asked. "Are you alone? How long have you been here on this island?"

"Slow down," Creston whispered.

She looked at Rainey, as if considering the questions. But no answers came. She looked at Creston.

Rainey moved toward their fire pit and sat. "Amy, come, sit with us." Creston followed and sat next to Rainey. She hesitated, then walked to them and squatted down on her haunches, as a young toddler would, the back of her thighs resting against her calves. Her long hair fell between her legs but was not enough to cover her exposed pubic area no longer concealed by the sarong. Amy's lack of inhibition did little to relax them. They squirmed, trying to avoid looking directly at her. Not looking was like trying to not breathe. She gently rocked back and forth. Rainey raised his head to avoid looking in her direction and then moved toward her, sitting to her right.

Creston cleared his throat and looked at Rainey. "I'll get some water." He got up and moved toward the plane, taking the bananas.

Rainey resisted the temptation to get up and follow Creston, afraid she would take off again if he left, and he had too many questions. He again took note of Amy. Her long hair was scraggly at best. The hair on her legs was light blond, long, thick, and not shaved in a long time, maybe never. The same was true for the hair under her arms. She was not beautiful but her features were pleasant. Rainey thought she might be modestly attractive if she had the advantages most women applied. There was nothing sexual about her presence and she was not the stereotypical image of a woman on a deserted island. He looked up and she was staring at him, her face expressionless, her demeanor unchanged. Rainey squirmed, uncomfortable and embarrassed for so blatantly scrutinizing her.

Creston returned with three bottles of water, handed one to Rainey, one to Amy, and then sat next to her. She looked at the bottle, clearly unsure of what to do. They watched her turn the bottle upside down, then right side up, shake it slightly and look at Creston. He took the bottle from her, twisted the top off and handed it back. He removed the cap of his bottle, placed the opening to his lips and turned it up. The water flowed into his mouth while his eyes remained fixed on Amy. She brought the bottle to her mouth but turned it up before placing it against her lips. Water spilled out and ran down her chin. She held the bottle in front of her, looked at it and again tilted it up to drink but this time without spilling any of the water.

Rainey shook his head several times, got up and motioned for Creston to follow him. He stopped several feet away from Amy. "She couldn't open the bottle. Can this be real or do you think maybe she's playing with us, pulling our leg?"

"It's real. Look at her. We've been here at least ten days and there was no sign of her or anyone else. She's been watching us, deciding if she should come out of hiding. But, where the hell was she hiding? Why didn't you see something when you went around the island? Three times you went out and came back with nothing. And yet, she's been here the entire time.

"Twelve."

"Twelve?" Creston asked.

"Twelve days. I'm sure we've been here twelve days, not ten."

"Fine, twelve days. It doesn't really matter, does it?"

"Every day matters to me," Rainey said.

Creston nodded. "Anyway, I think she's been here a long time. And I think she's alone."

They turned their heads toward her and realized she had been watching them. They had spoken softly and she had not heard anything. It was apparent from her lack of expression she thought nothing of their whispering. Amy stood up and handed Creston the empty water bottle. She turned her head in the direction of the sun as if acknowledging it and walked away, back toward the trees.

"Amy?" Rainey called.

She stopped, turned and pointed toward the center of the island, turned back and walked away. Rainey and Creston watched her, staring hard but did not try to stop her.

"Maybe she'll come back tomorrow, and if not I guess we can go looking for her," Creston said as he watched her.

"This is a strange feeling," Rainey said. "First I think she's there, then I think she isn't there, and then she shows up here. Now she's gone again. I feel like I'm in suspended animation."

"Would you relax and get a grip on yourself?" Creston said. "Yeah it's weird, but somehow we'll get to the bottom of this. I'd like to know where she's going, where she stays at night. It's kind of creepy to think she's been watching us all this time, like we were being spied on, eyes following us and every move we make."

"I think she's alone and was scared. Can you imagine what she must have thought when she heard the plane crash? I'm surprised she came out of hiding this soon."

"Her expression never changed," Creston said. "No smile, no excitement, nothing. Deadpan and emotionless."

"She doesn't know how to interact. And it also makes me wonder if she'll show up tomorrow."

"Then we'll go looking for her," Creston said. He looked toward the sun. "We've got a couple of hours of daylight left so let's see if we can rig up those fishing poles. I'm getting damned tired of soup. Not to mention we both look like we've lost about ten pounds. Besides, I think better when I'm moving around."

Rainey and Creston spoke little of the day's events as they assembled the fishing poles, reorganized the supplies, and straightened around the plane. Countless thoughts swirled inside Rainey's head as he stayed busy. But all he got was more questions and no answers.

The sun setting over the Pacific started the evening ritual for Rainey and Creston. They prepared for sleep and then stood by the tail of the plane looking out over the lagoon as the western sky changed from blue to orange. Darkness from the east traversed the sky, pushing the orange glow above the horizon into the ocean while the heat of the day was swept away by the cooler evening winds. The night sky came alive with a million stars, all reflected in the lagoon which magnified the vastness of it all.

CHAPTER TWENTY

Morning of the thirteenth day was cloudy with stormy weather looming in the distance and approaching at a fast pace. Several times before, similar looking storms had raced across the island, drenched everything and then moved on across the Pacific Ocean. This time they had the bowls to catch rain water and the storm was eagerly anticipated. Creston took both bowls, set them on the wing of the plane and propped them up with several large palm fronds. He and Rainey moved inside the plane to wait out the storm. The rain poured down hard enough to puddle on the coarse sand before being absorbed into it.

"I've been working on figuring out, as closely as possible, where we are. There's a book on celestial navigation in the cabinet next to the bulkhead. I never paid much attention to it before. All the planes have navigation computers and radar so it wasn't important. But when I started feeling better I got it out and read most of it. There are charts in the plane so with a little luck I believe we should be able to come pretty close to where we are. By *shooting the stars,* as they say, or whatever it takes. I'm not real sure how, but I'll figure it out."

Rainey nodded. "I'm sure you will. I didn't have any idea where to start but it's been on my mind." He looked out the door. The rain was heavy and the winds were strong. "I don't think this will last long."

In twenty minutes the worst of the storm had passed. They stood by the wing looking at the water bowls, each of which was almost full and held what they guessed to be about three gallons of water. Rainey scooped out a handful of water and tasted it.

"It tastes a little salty. We need to keep these inside the plane and covered up. The sea air must be depositing salt inside the bowls. But at least they work and we can collect water." Rainey picked up his bowl and without looking at Creston threw the contents of the bowl directly onto him. "You need a bath anyway." Rainey turned his back to Creston fully expecting what was to come next and Creston did not disappoint him. The water was cool, refreshing as it splashed over him. He walked in the direction of the rising sun, vigorously shaking his head. Beads of water flew from his hair in all directions.

Rainey started his morning routine of fixing coffee. Creston, in his improved physical state, started scrounging up their breakfast, which this morning included bananas, courtesy of Amy.

"We're running out of honey buns," Creston said. "But we've got the grilled breadfruit. Not as tasty but it's sustenance, and healthier."

They were quietly reflective as they ate. Rainey broke the silence. "Care to make a guess as to who she is and where she came from?"

"A guess is all it would be," Creston said. "But a couple of things come to mind."

"You're way ahead of me then because I have nothing, not even a guess. So, what are you thinking?" Rainey asked.

"One possibility is she fell overboard from a ship, or sailboat, and maybe drifted in the ocean and eventually waded ashore here on the island. A little farfetched perhaps, but I guess possible. Or maybe a sailboat got lost at sea or dismasted and drifted until it crashed against the reef. She and whoever else might have been with her walked across the reef at low tide and settled here."

"I agree with the farfetched part." Rainey said. "It's hard to imagine how she's managed to survive, unless she wasn't alone. Look how hard it's been on us, and we have food, water, resources. What else?"

"Europeans have had a small presence in the Pacific for decades. Amy looks like she could be from Europe, maybe Germany. Her physical features are definitely not of an islander from this area.

It's possible she has German parents. Parents who maybe were abandoned here or maybe went missing on purpose. It could be they wanted away from the German regime."

"Sounds like a bit of a stretch. After all, she does speak English."

"She doesn't speak it well," Creston said. "It was pretty basic to say the least. I'm not sure English is her first language because she struggled with most of it. And I'm not sure how much of what we said was understood."

"True, so are those your theories? Nothing else you can think of?" Rainey asked.

"There is one more thought," Creston said. "Maybe a stork got lost and left her here by mistake."

"Try to be serious."

"Well feel free to come up with your own idea!" Creston said.

"Damn, you're a little touchy, don't you think?"

"It's frustrating, ok? Look, I'm open to suggestions."

Creston studied the book on celestial navigation while Rainey busied himself stowing their provisions. He picked up one of the fishing poles contemplating the idea of venturing to the lagoon to test his luck at catching a fish. Rainey turned to head toward the lagoon. Amy was standing by the wing of the plane holding what looked to be a large mango. She wore the same soiled sarong.

Amy took a bite of the mango, wiped a runnel of juice from the corner of her mouth and then offered the mango to Rainey. She dragged her hand across her sarong and wiped it clean.

Rainey looked at Creston, shrugged, and accepted the mango. He took a large bite and the juice ran down his chin the way a large overripe peach explodes with juice when bitten. Creston took the mango when offered and bit the fruit, nodding with approval at the sweet taste. He passed it back to Amy and they shared the mango until only the large pit remained.

The awkwardness of the previous day was still present. Rainey and Creston knew they had to move carefully and not pressure Amy, but they also burned with questions. Creston motioned Amy to the fire pit, offering her his hand after wiping them on his pants. She ignored the offer of his hand, but not rudely. They sat on the sand but this time Amy sat Indian style, the sarong falling between her thighs and covering her. Creston picked up his coffee mug, grateful the temptation to stare was gone. He offered it to Amy and she leaned forward, sniffed the strong aroma and backed off.

"I don't think she's ready for coffee," Rainey said as he took a big sip. "Amy, will you take us to where you went yesterday when you left?"

Amy stood and started walking away. She looked back and motioned for them to follow her.

"She sure isn't a woman of many words," Creston said.

"I think she understands us more than we first thought. Maybe she hasn't had anyone to speak with and maybe she's out of practice. I'd guess she hasn't spoken in the last few years, or even longer." Rainey stopped. "Hey, you think this is smart, both of us going with her?"

"Are you kidding? What do you think is out there? A trap? Look, we were easy pickings the first few days. There's no one else. So get up and let's go."

Rainey shook his head, feeling foolish for being intimidated. They followed Amy into the center of the island. When they reached the area where the trees and foliage became much denser Rainey recognized the spot where he first saw her. He and Creston were covered with sweat, breathing hard, and laboring to keep up with Amy as she moved to the right, following the thick tree line. Without any warning, Amy turned to the left and disappeared behind several palm trees. Creston followed her and Rainey right behind him. A small path two feet wide and almost eight feet long appeared between the trees. At the end of the path Amy turned and again disappeared. Creston and Rainey followed the maze until they emerged into a large clearing. They stopped, mouths agape, and gazed upon a parcel of the island obviously cleared by men. The surrounding perimeter had been intentionally left dense and hard to penetrate.

"How many times did you pass by this area?" Creston asked.

"Half a dozen at least, and I never had a clue this was here. You can't see it from the beach. I don't think it's meant to be seen."

"Then why the hell is it here? What's the point, I mean why clear this area and leave it surrounded by trees?" Creston said.

The cleared area was rectangular in shape, approximately half the size of a football field. They moved about twenty feet from the edge of the clearing into the open area and stopped.

Eight banana trees, planted in a zigzag pattern of two rows, were confusing to Rainey. Why not plant them in a straight row he wondered. Beyond the banana trees and toward the far end of the hidden area were more trees which had also been planted. He was sure several were mango trees. Their hanging fruit looked like the one Amy had brought with her. Several breadfruit trees and lemon trees were also scattered about. Rainey thought it all looked out of place.

Creston's hand grabbed Rainey's shoulder and turned him. Creston was pointing at a raised area. Most of the ground was flat but one section, rectangular in shape, had a rise of about three feet. All four sides sloped from the level top to the ground. It was blanketed with sparse grass, leaves and vines, the same ground coverage as the surrounding area. From a distance and with a quick glance it would be almost impossible to detect the rise.

Rainey approached the protruding mound and estimated the area to be about sixty feet long and thirty feet wide. He looked back at Creston and shrugged, but Creston was looking up, scanning the tree tops. Rainey did likewise.

"What am I missing because all I see is trees?" Rainey said.

"This might change my theories completely. Or, it maybe substantiate at least one of them," Creston said. He moved several steps closer to the trees and looked straight up.

CHAPTER TWENTY ONE

The emotional roller coaster was taking its toll on Leslie. Each day became more difficult and her resolve was draining like air escaping from a worn tire. Her zeal had prompted her to take charge of Creston's affairs and be Rainey's representative, but it was abandoning her. Still, the commitment was made and there was no backing out.

Leslie sat at her desk and stared through the glass separating her office from the open cubicles where the majority of the junior bank executives toiled away, looking like a silent movie until someone would open her door and she would hear the controlled chaos. She thought it was almost comical until she remembered her early days in the *pit*. A single tear emerged from her eye, ran down her cheek, and fell onto her desk blotter. Closing her eyes, she took a deep breath, rose from her desk and headed to the ladies room to touch up her make up when the phone rang. She gazed at the phone like it was some kind of demon, and considered not answering it.

"Hello, this is Leslie Duf....Leslie Fremin."

"Leslie, this is Joan," Rainey's mother said.

Leslie winced, angst rising and feeling regret for using her maiden name.

"Hi mom. Are you ok?"

"Yes, but I'm concerned about you. I'm downstairs at the food court. I was hoping you would meet me and have some coffee."

"I would love to. I'll be right down." She read 10:37 on the digital desk clock.

The food court was mostly empty and the vendors busied themselves getting ready for the lunch crowd. Rainey's mother sat at a small table with two cups of coffee. Leslie leaned down and kissed Joan on the cheek before sitting.

"Is café au lait alright with you?" Joan asked.

"It's perfect. I never drank café au lait before moving to New Orleans. Now it's my favorite. Mom, this is a pleasant surprise, especially today. But is there some reason you are here?"

"I have some business to take care of downtown. Nothing important and I could handle it by mail, but coming downtown as a young girl was always a big treat to me. It's a nice reminder of way back when, even though so much has changed," Joan said as she opened her purse.

"I understand." Leslie watched as Rainey's mother pulled out a postcard and handed it to her.

"I got this in the mail the day after Rainey…and Creston were declared officially missing."

Leslie looked at the postcard of Pearl Harbor. She turned it over and read the message to his mother, and stared at it. She took a deep breath and fought back the tears. Joan watched her through misty eyes.

"I knew you would want to see the card. And I knew Rainey would want you to read it." She took a sip of her coffee.

"I'm not so sure he would have wanted me to see it. I didn't tell you earlier, but he stood me up the day he and Creston left. I asked him to meet me at Hillary's in the Quarter because I had a few things to tell him. I waited, but he didn't show up. I suppose I can't blame him." Leslie thought for a moment. "Rainey never said anything about an Uncle Larry. I didn't know you had a brother."

"He was killed in the attack on Pearl Harbor. He went down with the Arizona. I was young and it was a great loss. But I accepted it a long time ago."

"And now you think you've lost Rainey," Leslie said. This time the tears came for both ladies. They smiled at each other through their blurry eyes. "I don't believe we have lost him," Leslie said. "He will return. I am certain of it."

"Faith is wonderful medicine. You can't buy it or sell it, and yet it works miracles." Joan picked up a paper napkin from the table and dabbed at her eyes. "I want to believe you might be right."

They finished their coffees while discussing Rainey's imminent return. Twice Leslie picked up her empty cup to take a sip, not wanting anything to change, afraid doubt and confusion were waiting at her desk.

Joan rose first. "I'm going to the St. Louis Cathedral to pray for the return of Rainey and Creston."

Leslie stood and they embraced each other as a mother and daughter should hug and held it longer than usual. Leslie was calm and secure for the moment, thankful for Joan's kindness, understanding, and forgiveness.

Joan took the escalator down to the first floor while Leslie walked to the elevators. The dark wood paneling and inadequate lighting of the cab was uncomfortable. She pushed the button for her floor, and as the doors closed the automated voice spoke "going up" in the robotic monotone sound she had come to ignore.

Leslie stood next to her desk and wondered if faith was self perpetuating. Would it keep her steady and moving forward, or would it desert her in the hectic daily pace and cause her to lapse into moments of doubt. Was doubt an element of faith, or the absence of faith, or simply confusion? She shook her head for thinking too much. A pink message note had been placed on her desk blotter. She picked it up and read Paris Labouef had called. She collapsed into her chair, dropping her arms over the side of the armrests. They dangled aimlessly and the nuisance of worry entered into her mind.

The phone number Paris had left was local and not surprising. Leslie had expected his return to New Orleans as soon as Creston and Rainey had been reported missing. Gathering her thoughts, she returned his call.

"I fear I was unkind and selfish when we last spoke," Paris said.

"I think it's understandable given the circumstances."

"I expect more of myself, regardless of the circumstances. I am sorry and sincerely appreciate all you've done. I admire your loyalty and persistence."

Taken aback Leslie said, "Thank you. I can't imagine not doing all possible until they are found and return."

"Optimism, a wonderful trait I need more of."

"Faith," Leslie said, "I prefer faith."

"Creston's mother and I will be in New Orleans for a while. Please, if there is anything I can do, let me know. You have done an excellent job of taking care of everything. I don't want to interfere, I want you to continue. But I feel like a spectator when I want desperately to be involved."

"Then be involved in getting ready for his return. It will help all of us."

"How did Rainsford let you get away?" Paris said. There was silence for a moment. "I'm sorry. I should not have said anything."

"No, it's all right. It made me think for a minute. I seldom heard him called Rainsford. But to your question, he did not let me get away, I ran away, unfortunately. I hope to change this when he returns."

"Faith, I believe you said. Good advice, and you should follow your own," Paris said and hung up.

Leslie sat at her desk, bewildered and almost in shock. Paris had been understanding and almost gentle. Perhaps, she thought, he found in her what he lacked in himself. The tension drained from her neck and she blushed as the image of her last night with Rainey flashed before her. The digital desk clock read 12:43. She admitted to herself she had wasted the morning on anything but bank business. She would work through her lunch and on into the evening until she was caught up. Then, on her way home she would pick up a bottle of red wine, stop by Rainey's apartment and drink a glass or two while planning for his return. But an element of doubt invaded her. She shook off the brief moment of doubt and thought, no way will he get off so easy.

CHAPTER TWENTY TWO

Rainey glanced up into the trees and asked, "What are you looking at?"

"Look closely. I'm pretty sure there's no Spanish moss in the Pacific Islands. So, what's the fine stringy stuff way up there at the top of the trees?"

"No idea," Rainey said looking around. "Where the hell did Amy go?"

"She disappears more than Houdini."

The sun was straight up and the cooler morning air had burned off. The noon air trapped amid the trees was hot, heavy with humidity and created sauna like conditions. Creston walked toward the edge of the clearing while watching the tops of the trees. Rainey followed but was looking around for Amy. Creston stopped and Rainey bumped into him.

"What the hell has you so distracted?" Creston asked.

"I'm not sure. I can't get a grip on all of this. We're going deeper into our situation instead of away from it."

"Nothing changes our situation so get your *head* out of your ass and start paying attention. Maybe together we can figure this all out."

Rainey was angered by Creston's comment and it took all his fortitude to keep from mouthing off. Creston knew he had crossed the line and stared at the ground.

"Forget it," Rainey said. "But, you aren't perfect either,"

"Far from it." Creston turned his gaze back to the top of the trees. "Look, up there," he said, pointing.

Rainey missed it with his first glance and looked back at Creston. "Look, right there," Creston said again. Rainey looked up again. The group of palm trees was at least thirty feet high. A large, undistinguishable mass obscured in the shadowy underside of the palm fronds was easily missed at first glance. It was dark in color, but had random contrasting hues which caused it to blend into the trees. Rainey and Creston moved closer, approaching more with curiosity than caution.

Rainey looked up again. A large cylindrical object was wedged between the two trees and a large, iron band helped keep it secure in place. A small pipe connected to the bottom of the cylinder had been attached to the tree on their left and extended downward. The pipe stopped about five feet above the ground.

"I've sold enough stainless steel pipe to the oil fields to recognize it when I see it," Rainey said. "And this piece here, connected to the bottom of the pipe is a manual valve. This lever opens and closes it." Rainey took a closer look. "It's one inch pipe, but the wall thickness is heavier than what I'm used to seeing. It's pitted and discolored from the salt air but, it's high quality steel. I'm guessing the cylinder up there is a water tank, placed there to collect rain and made from the same stainless steel as this pipe."

"How the hell did it get up there? It must weigh a ton, especially when it's full of water. How does it stay up there?"

"More questions and still no answers," Rainey said. "This whole thing gets more confusing by the minute."

Standing shoulder to shoulder they stared at the cylinder in the trees. Neither heard Amy approach from behind. Creston turned around to find himself mere inches from her.

"Damn, Amy, at least make some noise when you come sneaking up on us."

Amy did not react to Creston's outburst. She moved between them toward the pipe, bent slightly and leaned forward, put her face under the pipe and turned the lever. Clear water poured forth and drenched her face. She opened her mouth and drank, like a child will drink from a garden hose after dousing his head with cool water in the heat of summer. She turned the valve off, threw her head back and beads of water flew from her face sparkling like crystals as the sunlight refracted through the drops. Amy wiped the excess water from her face with her hand and then dried it on her sarong.

Creston moved to the pipe, bent down and opened the valve.

"Hey!" Rainey shouted. "I wouldn't drink the water!" Amy jumped at his booming voice. "It might be safe for her because she's been drinking it for a long time, but it might make you sick, or worse.

Creston heeded the warning for a few seconds but then took a small sip. "Guess we'll find out soon enough," he said as he closed the valve. "Rainey, the ever conservative and protective one."

"You didn't complain when I was watching over you and trying to save your life. Maybe *she* can take care of you when you get sick this time." Rainey turned toward her and asked, "Amy, where did you go?" Her face was somber and she looked confused. "A few minutes ago, you were gone. Where were you?"

He stared for a moment and then turned back to Creston, shrugging his shoulders and shaking his head.

Creston moved closer to Amy. Her ease at disappearing made him uncomfortable. He lowered his head like a young boy will do when searching for an answer to a teacher's question. After a moment he spoke.

"Here's my theory on all this. I already told you the Germans had a real presence in the Pacific long before World War II. And the Germans were excellent at making tools and surgical instruments from stainless steel. The water tank and pipe are stainless steel. Amy looks more German Caucasian than anything else. I think she's German descent. If there were others then they either died here, or maybe she was abandoned."

"I guess it makes as much sense as anything else," Rainey said. "But, you're talking, what, sixty years ago, or more. Amy can't be that old. And, I haven't seen anything resembling a grave. If they abandoned her, why? And how long ago? How long has she been alone?"

"No answers, not even a clue."

"So what does all this mean to us?"

"At this point, not a damn thing," Creston said. "But, she has fruit bearing trees and a fresh water supply which is how she survives. As much as it rains here, and as big as the tank is, I imagine she's never had a water shortage." Creston looked at Amy. "Some diet, huh. Water and fruit day after day, but she doesn't know anything else."

Amy watched as they spoke, expressionless, as if their words meant nothing to her. She glanced at each of them and started walking away. Her movements were dispassionate, perpetuating the mystery.

"Damn, there she goes again," Creston said.

"I don't think she does it on purpose. She does what she does and gives it no thought," Rainey said. "She's a creature of habit and we mean nothing to her, and why I think she's been here a long time."

"Maybe you're right. But it still doesn't answer any questions, does it?"

Rainey shrugged, his eyes focused on Amy. "No, but she could be the key to the answers even if she doesn't understand us."

Amy had reached the far end of the rectangular mound, turned back toward Rainey and Creston, tentatively raised her arm and motioned for them to come to her, as they had motioned to her at the plane. She was less than fifty feet away and waited.

"Hell, maybe we're getting somewhere." Creston grabbed Rainey's arm above the elbow and moved toward Amy.

Rainey followed, pulling his arm from Creston's grasp. They were ten feet from her when she stooped down and gently moved an obscure cover. Without looking at them and with an easy and deft movement she dropped down into an opening and disappeared.

They bounded to the narrow opening and looked down at where Amy had vanished. Rainey's heart pounded as be kneeled down and bent forward, leaning into the opening. Creston grabbed him by the back of his shirt and pulled.

"What are you doing? We don't know what's down there," Creston said. "Look, she's been almost like a zombie at times. This is a little too spooky."

Rainey stopped. "Are you kidding me? What happened to 'nobody being here', 'easy pickings the first few days' and 'if they wanted us they'd have done something then'?" he said.

Creston released Rainey's shirt. He sat in a squat position, leaned toward the opening and his eyes adjusted to the darkness. Amy sat cross legged on the ground waiting for them to join her.

"What the hell," Creston said. He sat on the ground, draped his legs into the opening and slid inside.

Rainey followed and found himself in a crouch position. The darkness enveloped him, and he imagined himself a spelunker in a new cave. His eyes struggled to adjust but soon shadowed images appeared. He looked toward Amy sitting on the floor and moved toward her, hitting his head on the ceiling which was six to eight inches shorter than his six foot height. He crouched back down, resting on his haunches and duck walked toward Amy as his eyes adjusted to the dim light. The ground was cool and damp, comfortable compared to outside, but musky with an odor born from age.

"What is this place?" Rainey asked.

Rainey relaxed and took a sitting position in the corner near the entrance and close to Amy. The floor was hard and smooth, of compacted coral sand from years of Amy walking on it. The room was consistent with the shape of the outside mound, but smaller, maybe 20 feet wide and fifty feet long. Three columns spaced equally down the center of the room supported a ceiling of galvanized, corrugated tin. Rainey realized the mound outside was the tin ceiling covered with a thick layer of sand. He counted eight openings in the ceiling located around the perimeter of the room. The openings were square and Rainey estimated them to be about twelve inches by twelve inches. There were three openings on each long side and one each on the ends. Thin rays of splintered light entered the room through the openings and did not totally illuminate the space.

Creston rose, still bent over enough to avoid hitting his head on the low ceiling, and moved along the wall to his left taking stock of the room. Rainey moved in the opposite direction but with the same intent. Amy remained sitting, watching them move around the room, and swayed ever so slightly back and forth.

The underground space was almost empty, devoid of but a few furnishings, and was odd, even creepy to Rainey. In a far corner he came upon two metal bed frames completely rusted and old. They were single beds, basic, each end the same as the other, and thus no head or foot discernable. They had been pushed together and the remains of what appeared to be mattresses lay upon the frames. Each had an old and tattered blanket neatly folded and placed at the end of the bed. Rainey, his lower back cramping from bending over, tried to straighten up and hit his head on the metal ceiling. Rubbing his head he heard Creston's muffled chuckle. He moved back into a slightly bent position, resembling an old man out for a Sunday stroll. To his right in the opposing corner was a single bed frame, identical to those he stood beside. He looked at the two beds, then at the single bed in the opposite corner. His mind raced as he looked at Amy, sure of the answer before asking the question.

"Whose beds are these, who sleeps here?" Rainey said.

Creston watched Amy. Neither he nor Rainey moved as they waited for an answer.

"Mommy and daddy dead," Amy said. She spoke child like but sans emotion.

Rainey's heart pained with her words. The juvenile use of "mommy and daddy" jolted him. The misfortune of Amy's existence washed over him.

"Amy, how long ago did your mom and dad die?" Creston said.

She sat, gently swaying, no answer forthcoming. Her stare returned to the floor.

"Let's take it easy on her," Rainey said. "Jesus, I'm beginning to think she's been alone a long time. The way she said mommy and daddy, her lack of emotion and her limited speech is telling." Rainey dropped to a knee and breathed deeply. Creston sat Indian style next to the bed in the opposite corner. The coolness of the floor permeated his pants. Rainey wiped his brow and tried to imagine how Amy survived and what she had lived through. The thought of the loneliness and boredom over years unending crushed him. Bolts of light shining on the floor caught his focus and calmed him.

"Look over there," Creston said pointing at two cabinets against the wall closest to Amy.

The cabinets were five feet tall, four feet wide, and almost touched the ceiling. They were divided in the middle, the bottom half metal with three drawers, and the top half also metal, but with two glass front doors. Rainey sidled to the cabinets. The light from the openings was projected away from the cabinets and Rainey had difficulty seeing through the glass.

"This is it?" he said. "Two cabinets and a couple of beds in this big space? Why dig out a hole this big, build the walls, put up support beams, cover it with a corrugated tin roof and then disguise it with ground cover, all for a couple of beds and cabinets? This makes no sense."

Creston shrugged and shook his head. "She gets more and more mysterious. I feel like I'm going backwards. When she said 'mommy and daddy dead,' well it tells me they were here, and the beds probably confirm this. So, any suggestions?"

"No, but the answers, or at least some of the answers, are here. We have to find them. How long ago would the Germans have been in this part of the Pacific?"

"What are you thinking?"

"Let's assume she's fifty, which I think is close. This suggests she was born about nineteen forty five or so. The Germans weren't here in 1945. More likely it was someone else, maybe from the Netherlands. The Dutch were sailors. They settled in the Caribbean and I guess they could have come here."

"So instead of narrowing things down you add more possibilities. Yeah, I guess it might have been the Dutch, or some other Anglo-Saxon type. But I'm sticking with the Germans, maybe a lone couple escaping Europe. It makes the most sense to me," Creston said.

Rainey turned toward the cabinets and moved closer, looking through the glass doors. Several mangos and breadfruit were stored on the shelves but nothing else. At least this makes sense, he thought.

The top drawer of the cabinet to his right screeched as he pulled it open. A piece of cloth, old, stained and frayed, similar to the sarong Amy wore, was folded and lay on the bottom of the drawer. Amy watched as Rainey opened the second and third drawer, each as noisy as the first. He stopped for a moment.

"I feel a little guilty, like I'm peeping at someone through a cracked door."

"I think this is different," Creston said. "And it's pretty obvious she's not bothered by it."

"You're right, this is different.

In the darkness the top drawer of the cabinet on his left appeared empty and he almost missed it when a slight reflection of light caught his eye as he was closing the drawer. Pulling it open again, he placed his hand into the drawer and felt a smooth finish, unlike the bottom of the other drawers. Rainey ran his hand across the bottom of the drawer, feeling for the edge of the thin, vinyl-like material. He removed it, turned toward the closest opening in the ceiling and held it up to the dim light filtering past the vines and ground cover over the openings. Creston moved to Rainey's side and looked at the X-ray film.

The outline of a chest, complete with ribcage, sternum and vertebrae was evident in the picture. Two small, darker objects, foreign to the body, appeared suspended in the chest cavity and close to where Rainey assumed the heart would be. They meant nothing to him. As he held the film higher, vying for better light and a clearer view he noticed the print at the bottom.

"The markings aren't German or Dutch," Rainey said. He held the film for Creston to see. "They're Japanese."

"This complicates things even more. How does Amy fit into this with the Japanese? We keep adding pieces to the puzzle but can't make any of them fit," Creston said.

"I need to get out of here," Rainey said. He put the X-ray film back in the drawer and moved to the opening. Placing his foot into a small cavity in the wall, he lifted himself out of the underground room. Creston followed, but Amy remained sitting and watched as they left.

A slight breeze swirled, refreshing and cool on Rainey's face. He had become unaware of how still it had been below. Creston breathed deeply of the fresh breeze and wiped his hands on his pants.

"Let's go back to the plane and give this some thought. I'm hungry and I think better when I've eaten," Rainey said.

"What about Amy? Are we gonna leave her here?"

"In case you hadn't noticed, she comes and goes when she wants. She'll either show up at the plane or she won't."

"You're right, but since we've found her I feel like we're supposed to take care of her," Creston said.

"You're being very chivalrous, but I'm not sure who's taking care of who."

"Whom, who's taking care of whom," Creston said.

"I thought you minored in history, not being a smart ass."

Backtracking through the small maze they soon emerged from the trees close to the lagoon. The water was calm and still, glass like, and a whisper of a mid-day breeze, too gentle to disturb the trees, swirled around them. They turned away from the lagoon and headed back toward the plane. All was quiet as they approached, but they walked around looking for signs of disturbance.

"It's the three of us. There is no one else. But there were others, there were *definitely* others," Creston said.

"Ok, so tell me what you think about the X-ray film and the Japanese markings?"

Creston ignored Rainey's question, deep in thought. His theories were falling apart and even more so because of the X-ray film with the Japanese markings. Inside he was grasping at straws but not gathering enough to make sense of what they had found.

"You're thinking a little too hard there, aren't you?" Rainey said.

"The X-ray film is confusing me. The Japanese fought most of World War II in the Pacific. They were all over. But there isn't anything here other than the film, and Amy has no oriental features at all. Those beds and cabinet could be from anywhere. If the Japanese were here why isn't there more equipment or signs of them, more oriental objects to indicate they were here?"

"Let's give it a rest and clear our minds," Rainey said. "Nothing's going to change in the next ten minutes, or the next ten hours. Besides, you look like hell. I've seen more energy in a rock."

Creston checked the location of the sun and guessed it to be two or three o'clock. "I'm tired but I can't take a nap. Grab us a couple of waters and let's sit in the shade and go over what we've discovered so far."

In the shadow of the plane's wing they sat and discussed the events of the last two days. Creston was more frustrated than Rainey. He was used to figuring things out but this was not going well.

"You still think she's about fifty years old?" Creston said.

"Well, she's been exposed to the weather for years, and her skin has lines of age so it's hard to tell. Tropic sun can make you look older than you are. So, yeah, my guess is she's in her late forties give or take, say, five years or so. One thing bothers me. When we asked her about the two beds pushed together she responded by saying 'mommy and daddy dead'. That's what a little kid or maybe a young girl might say, but certainly not a mature, older woman. In one sense she's as old as you and me, and in another she's almost like a child."

"It's as if she grew older but never matured," Creston said. "Hard to fathom, I mean, can you imagine if she's been here for twenty or thirty years by herself."

"No, I can't imagine. What makes you think she's been alone that long?"

"There's almost nothing here. The water tank, the beds, and the cabinets are all old and rusted. There's not a sign of any modern equipment. Nothing."

"So I guess we wait and we watch," Rainey said. "Nothing else we can do. But I'm afraid we might not find many pieces to put together. This whole situation bothers the hell out of me. We're not any better off than her. In fact, we're worse off. She expects nothing other than what she has. You and I have much greater expectations. If there are answers out there we need to find them, and soon."

Rainey shrugged and reclined where he sat. Creston leaned back and soon they dozed off.

After two weeks the pattern was set and unchanging, as strict as life itself. Night time was total darkness with the exception of distant stars illuminating nothing but their imagination. The moon had been waning when they crashed and the night's darkness had been ominous at times, waiting on the new waxing moon. Rainey and Creston had stopped taking naps. The sun set, the island was in darkness, and they slept.

Rainey woke first. Looking around, and gauging from the position of the sun he had slept about two hours. The nap would definitely interrupt his sleep pattern and he would be sitting up after sunset, not tired enough to fall asleep. But he was too hungry and thirsty to be aggravated about it. He looked at Creston, reached with his foot and nudged him awake. Rainey sat upright and his thoughts focused on the events of the last two days

Creston interrupted Rainey's thoughts. "Since when do we skip lunch and take naps?"

"It was too much and wore us out mentally. At least if the clouds stay away it'll be a great night to watch the skies." Rainey rose and started moving toward the plane. "I'll look inside and see what we have left in the soup category. What are you in the mood for?"

"Anything you pick will be fine, but I was dreaming about some oysters with Big O, and a cold beer. What about you?"

Rainey said nothing but a slight grin appeared on his face as he thought of Big O, New Orleans, then for some reason, Leslie, and the grin disappeared. What the hell, and why her he asked himself, but he knew. The loneliness and desperate situation revealed to him what he missed and needed most. He pushed it out of his mind and excused it as weakness. He picked up two cans of soup and read the label. Creole chicken gumbo from a can would be a sore disappointment. He stood in the doorway and again thought of Big O and wondered what he was doing.

CHAPTER TWENTY THREE

Big O was behind the oyster bar readying for the evening rush. In the next hour the crowd of diners would fill up the restaurant and form a line down Iberville Street. October brought the biggest conventions and the most tourists. Conventioneers, men and women alike, were eager to leave their normal lives at home. New Orleans, a city with an excess of food, drink, passion and mystery, would lull one's inhibitions as easily as a baby sleeps. Most of them did not miss an opportunity or forego the opulence.

A presence at the bar caused Big O to look up. Paris Labouef reached across the stainless steel counter and offered his hand. They had met years ago on a rare occasion when Paris and Creston had dinner together. Big O had been uneasy then and it was obvious he was uncomfortable now, but he took the offered hand and shook it firmly.

"Mr. Paris, what brings you in here?"

"Hello, O. It's been a long time. How have you been?"

"I been fine, sir. It has been a long time. How you doing?"

"You ask a tough question. Usually I'm good, but these days it's harder to get a grip on things." Paris paused. "A man makes mistakes in his life. If he's lucky he gets the opportunity to rectify them, but more often than he would like to admit, he must live with the consequences of his decisions."

Big O nodded but said nothing. Paris Labouef was in a situation no one but he understood. He wore his self pity on his sleeve and exposed a vulnerability seldom seen on men of his wealth and stature. Big O witnessed a man desperate and in pain.

"You gonna find this hard to believe, Mr. Paris, but I'm convinced they're alive. I believe it sure as I'm standing here in front of you." O reached down and picked up a tray of half a dozen raw oysters on the half shell. He placed them on the bar in front of Paris and said, "Here, these are on me."

Paris looked at the oysters for a few seconds and then laughed. "It's funny. I was born and reared in Louisiana, lived here most of my life, but I never acquired a taste for oysters. Makes me feel almost unpatriotic at times, but I don't eat them."

Big O stared at Paris as if he had heard blasphemy and then laughed. The humor turned awkward as both men looked at each other in silence. O took the tray of oysters from the bar and placed them on the drain board of the stainless steel sink.

"Can I get ya somethin else, Mr. Paris?" Big O asked.

"Yes, yes you can. I'll have a Heineken. Creston's beer of choice, isn't it?"

"Well, it was at one time but him and Rainey mostly drank Dixie beer. It goes way back to when they first met. Kind of a tradition."

"OK then, give me a Dixie. May I buy you one, Big O?" Paris asked.

"I don't drink when I'm working, but, I'd like to drink a beer with you." Big O took the towel from his waist, wiped his hands and placed it over the long neck faucet.

"Johnny Tap, bring us two Dixies," Big O called out as he sat next to Paris.

"What makes you so sure they're alive? There's been no sighting of plane wreckage, and in fact, the navy called off the search. I wish I shared your enthusiasm but it's hard for me to be optimistic."

Big O thought for a moment, took a long drink of his beer, and questioned how much he should tell Paris. "Some things aren't known, but ya feel em. If a man is honest with hisself and learns to trust his feelings, he usually makes better decisions. Don't get hisself in as much trouble. I learned this a long time ago, but I had the help of a special lady. My life been better ever since."

"I think you're a wise man, O. I feel it too, but I didn't know what to do. Thanks for setting me straight." Paris raised his beer bottle and offered it to O in a toast. Their bottles clinked and they each took a big drink of beer. For an hour they nursed the one beer and talked, but not about Creston and Rainey.

The nights had become peaceful and comforting, not foreboding as Rainey had perceived them the first few days. He and Creston reclined and admired the vastness of the open sky filled with stars brighter than either had ever seen. In less than ten minutes the first shooting star, a burning light streaked across the sky pulling a long sparkling tail through God's heaven and was gone in two seconds. Neither said anything for a while. Rainey spoke first.

"Eight shooting stars in less than thirty minutes. I don't think I've seen eight in my life. I read somewhere there are thousands of shooting stars every night. Most you can't see because they're too far off or there's too much ambient light. "

"I've seen a few while flying at night but nothing like this. It makes me wonder what else I've missed," Creston said.

"Look, right there. It's the brightest star yet." Rainey watched the star race through the darkness toward the lost horizon, and disappear in the night.

"Sitting here, it's easy to understand why you wanted to fly around the world," Rainey said. "I think I owe you an apology. Truthfully, and I hate to admit this, I thought it was mostly a rich boy thing, something to do when money was no object."

"Since we're being truthful, I'll admit it was a whim, and mostly a rich American showing off, being different. I had other motives, but they came later. Such as the soft drinks and candy for the kids we'd meet in the third world countries. Pretty shallow when I think about it. I'm not showing off too much right now."

"I think you've beaten yourself up enough for one night. Save the self flagellation for when we get the hell off this island," Rainey said.

The shooting stars reigned in the tropical sky. Rainey quit counting and watched as they danced in the night. A crescent moon crept above the tree line and a new, diffuse luster glimmered across their campsite. Rainey was aware his senses were much more acute. He anticipated the wind before it rustled the palm fronds. The different scents of the island, such as the sea air, the reef at low tide, vegetation, and even an occasional dead fish on the beach, were easily discernible. His sense of taste, even with the limited offerings of food and drink, had developed keenness and sharpness he was unaccustomed to. Every sound penetrated his awareness. He listened to the island and ocean and heard more completely. And this night his sleep was deep, peaceful, and he drifted with the stars.

The morning sun surprised Rainey awake. For the past week he had awoken before the sun crested the horizon, but this day found him sleeping later because he had taken a nap. Rainey watched Creston, deciding to wake him or let him sleep. Creston turned, opened his eyes and then shut them tight to block out the sun. He turned back and squinted from the brightness.

"Great, you let me oversleep. We're gonna be late for work."

"You're sense of humor is lost on me. I wish we had work to go to," Rainey said shifting to look at Creston.

"Well, we do have work to do. After we eat breakfast and drink some coffee I say we head back to Amy's underground and see what we can find. Yesterday was too much to process. Today we can do some digging around. Speaking of digging, if there were others, where do you suppose they're buried?"

"Buried? I don't care where they're buried. What the hell would make you think of dead bodies?" Rainey said.

"Death is a part of life. Maybe some of the answers are buried with them. I'm not saying we exhume the bodies but I am suggesting there's more to this than Amy's telling us, more than she realizes." Creston shrugged. "Lighten up pal. We can't change the past, but maybe we can learn from it."

"What we need to learn is how to get off this island. It doesn't matter what we find or don't find if we're stuck here forever. And all your money and your ego won't change anything."

"It's funny how things change. My money and ego never bothered you before. The point you're missing is maybe the information she holds inside is the key to our getting off the island," Creston argued.

"Well, it hasn't helped her," Rainey said. "I'll start the fire and fix the coffee. Slice us some breadfruit and throw it on the grill."

They had agreed to ration the coffee to one cup a day for each of them, hoping to stretch the remainder for at least several more months. The morning coffee had become a much anticipated start to the day; much like an evening martini is anticipated after work. Conversely, the breadfruit was as uneventful as plain bread is to a prisoner. They ate and drank in silence. Cleaning up after breakfast could be done in ten minutes but they took twenty and still had time to kill before heading back to the compound.

The walk to Amy's was so deliberate and with such purpose they failed to notice her as they moved along the beach and approached the entrance to the maze. They stopped in front of the opening, gathering their thoughts. Rainey considered what they might expect to accomplish.

Amy stepped closer behind them and said, "Amy here."

"DAMN!" Rainey bellowed as he turned. "Amy!" he shouted as he looked her in the eyes. "Don't sneak up on us like that. Do you hear me?"

Creston took a step back and stared in disbelief. He had never seen Rainey display such an outburst of temper. "What's *wrong* with you?" he said. "We're both wearing a little thin, but even so, you were way out of line."

Rainey bit his lower lip, ashamed of his reaction toward Amy. She looked at the ground and did not look up as Rainey approached her. He wrapped his arms around her and pulled her closer to him, nestling her head against his shoulder. She remained stoic, did not pull back, but did not return the hug.

"Jesus Christ," Rainey said in frustration.

Amy lifted her head and a quizzical expression appeared, as if she might have recognized the name. Rainey blushed again as the blasphemous retort consumed him with guilt, making him feel like an altar boy in need of confession.

He released her from his grasp and turned back toward Creston. "You're right," Rainey said. "I have been wearing thin. But it stops right here." They moved through the maze and into the clearing.

CHAPTER TWENTY FOUR

Rainey stood in front of the entrance, compelled to enter, but the underground was mostly empty and devoid of any clues of how Amy came to be on the island, or what island they were on. Rainey grabbed the cover to the opening and pushed it to the side and turned, looking for Creston and Amy.

"What the hell are you doing?" Rainey shouted. Creston was half way up a palm tree and struggling. "Have you lost your mind? I already patched you up once. I don't want to have to fix you again. You're not strong enough yet to be climbing a tree."

Creston had stopped his laborious climb. It was obvious he had tired and would never make it the rest of the way up. He was breathing hard and resting, his legs wrapped around the skinny palm tree and locked together.

Amy had watched Creston attempt to climb the palm tree. She approached a similar tree to the right of the one Creston was hugging. It was curved more and bending away from her, unlike the straighter, more vertical tree Creston had chosen. Placing her right foot at a forty five degree angle against the tree trunk she leaned forward and grabbed the tree with both hands. Rainey watched as Amy placed her left foot on the tree, opposed and slightly above her right foot, and started up the tree, her arms remaining extended and her hands working one over the other, pulling herself up as her busy feet walked the trunk. She reached the canopy and grabbed a coconut, plucked the fruit and dropped it to the ground. Creston relaxed his grip and inched his way down the tree where Amy waited, offering him the coconut.

Creston took the coconut from Amy and said, "Thanks, but I was trying to reach moss hanging at the top of the tree. Amy, can you reach it and bring it back to me?"

Amy did not answer but turned and approached the tree Creston was pointing to, grasped the trunk, placed her feet as before and climbed. The more vertical trunk did little to slow her ascent. In less than a minute she had reached out, grabbed a large handful of the hanging moss and maneuvered her way back down. She handed the tangled moss to Creston. It was coarse and brittle, falling apart as Amy handed it to him. He studied the moss, rubbing it between his fingers, causing it to fall apart even more. Rainey watched, a puzzled look on his face. Amy stood quiet.

"It's not moss. In fact, it's not a plant at all. It's man made." Creston looked at Rainey.

"Man made?" Rainey said. "What is it, and what's it doing up there?"

"Maybe it's left over from the Germans or Dutch." Creston tossed the tangled mass to the side. It hit the ground, fell apart, and a small puff of dust rose less than six inches above the ground. He watched Amy walk away. "I'm not sure she holds any answers for us."

"Maybe, but I'm not ready to let go of this."

Amy wandered around the compound, bending over to pull an undesirable plant or sapling from the ground. The area was like a parade ground, clean of random growth, and it was obvious as to why.

The sun was almost straight up and the heat inside the clearing intensified. Rainey and Creston had acclimated to the island and no longer dwelled on the hot, still air. Rainey moved back toward the opening to the underground, hesitated and looked at Creston.

"I need another look down there," Rainey said and dropped into the darkness.

The noonday sun splayed minimal light through the opening and into the space but it was enough to aid Rainey. His eyes adjusted. He knelt on one knee and scanned the interior again. The cool dampness provided a short respite from the above ground heat. Creston descended and interrupted him.

"Rainey, we've been over this place already. There's nothing here."

"You said you didn't want to let it go so let's dig a little deeper." Rainey stopped and watched Amy descend through the opening, stealth and catlike. "This is scary. I'm starting to sense her, like I knew she was about to enter. I'll go this way along the wall, you go that way. Pay attention."

"I'll pay attention, but let's not spend too much time down here. I'm tired of it already." Creston shook his head. "And I have no idea of what we're looking for, anyway."

Rainey took a deep breath. The air was not as stale, or maybe he was adjusting to it. Futility crept over him and he questioned the point of this task. Even with more light he strained his eyes to see, as if in a sleazy bar on Iberville Street. He shook his head and followed the wall closely, missing the first set of small circular imprints on the floor less than two inches from the wall. Kneeling down he placed his index finger in a circle and traced the imprint several times. Nothing clicked until he looked at the bed against the opposite wall. The legs of the bed were made of round tubular steel. Rainey stayed close to the ground and moved along the walls, finding many more imprints indicating there had been other beds, or Amy had moved her bed many times. The first thought made much more sense. Why would she keep moving the bed?

"It pains me greatly to suggest you might have been right about coming back down here, but come look at this." Creston was crouched by the two beds pushed together.

Rainey rose to a semi-crouch position and moved to the beds. Creston had moved the top blanket off to the side and though it was dark Rainey could see what looked to be a book lying on the second blanket.

"I wasn't paying much attention," Creston confessed. "I was watching you do whatever it was you were doing, and my hand brushed across the blankets as I walked by. I felt a slight bulge. I stopped and flipped the blanket over and found this book. But it looks more like a journal than a book.

Rainey looked at Amy and without picking up the book asked, "Amy, what is this book?"

"Mommy's book," Amy said.

Rainey gently picked up the book. It was long and narrow with hard covers, resembling an accountant's journal. In the darkness of the underground it appeared to be dark gray with a cloth-like texture, a half inch thick, and maybe a hundred pages.

"The journal's in fairly good shape. It must have been wrapped in those blankets for a long time," Rainey said. "Let's get out of here and find out what's in it."

Rainey passed Amy moving toward the exit. She reached out at the book but Rainey did not notice her outstretched hand. Creston took Amy's extended hand, helped her up, and together they exited the underground.

Rainey sat with his back resting against a sturdy palm tree, the large fronds at the top stretching out like giant fans protecting him from the sun. He held the book in his lap, unopened, waiting while Creston and Amy approached. Rainey looked at Amy and thought he detected a slight hint of anxiety, the first sign of emotion since he had run into her hiding behind the trees. Creston held her hand as they sat down and watched Rainey carefully open the front cover. The binding was stiff and crackled with a noise like stepping on a sun dried leaf. The book had not been opened in years. The first page was blank, yellowed with age, but still firm even though the edges were thin and worn. The blankets had provided protection from the air and preserved the book. It was in remarkable shape, if, as he also assumed, it was at least as old as Amy, and probably older.

Rainey turned to the second page, careful with the aged journal, focused on the hand written script and silently read.

1943
They tell me it is 1943. I don't know if this is correct. I gave up counting full moons long ago but I know there had been at least forty when frustration got the better of me. Captain Matsunaga

finally answered my request and gave me this journal. He tells me the great war wages and Japan will be victorious in defeating America. I have no idea what he is talking about. If it is 1943 then we have been here six years.

"Hey!" Creston's outburst startled Rainey. "Would you care to share what has you so captivated? I don't want to sit here and watch you."

"God, you're a piece of work. Have a little respect. It's a journal with hand written entries. I got caught up in it, ok?"

"Ok, but read out loud."

"Guess what. It's not German or Dutch, it's written in English."

Creston's grin disappeared and his face turned as solemn as a priest's in the confessional. He looked at Amy who sat quietly. If she's not German, or Dutch, and certainly not Japanese, then what he wondered?

Rainey reread the first passage aloud and continued.

"It is hard for me to imagine America at war with Japan. Captain Matsunaga told us quite a long time ago Japan and America are at war. At first I did not believe him but the wounded Japanese soldiers have been coming for a while. Also, he continues to assure me Pearl Harbor was destroyed, the American navy was crippled and soon Japan will rule the Pacific and then the world. This is too hard for me to comprehend. If this is true then this journal is futile as no one will ever read it. However, I write and hope by chance, should we never leave this place, this writing will find itself into the hands of someone who will care to know the truth.
Amelia Earhart

Creston bolted upright, his mouth agape. He looked at Amy and then back at Rainey. "Holy crap! I can't believe…this must be some kind of joke. This can NOT be real. "

"I…I'm not sure. It reads sincere and matter of fact. Besides, why would someone go to the trouble of making this up, especially way out here with no real hope of anyone ever finding it? And we know about the war and Pearl Harbor and how it turns out. It's as if the writer doesn't know what happens, at least at this point in the journal." Rainey stopped. "Amy said it was mommy's book which means Amelia Earhart is Amy's mommy, I mean mother."

Amy moved toward Rainey. Reaching out she took the journal, closed it, stood up and clutched the book to her breast. Rainey did not resist her. Expressions of confusion turned to looks of understanding as Amy walked away. They said nothing until Amy disappeared into the underground.

"I'm open to suggestions," Creston said.

"Yeah, well I don't have any except this isn't the time to push it. We'll get another chance to read the journal. Whatever we do, we have to go slow, if nothing else but out of respect for Amy." Rainey stopped and looked toward the underground. "Hopefully, there are answers in the journal and we'll find out what happened here."

"Well, I'm not a patient man especially when I want something. And, I want to find out what's in the journal."

"This isn't about you," Rainey shot back. "You got us here but so far you haven't done much to get us off this island."

"Right, I got us here, but I'm also the guy who woke up in time to wrestle the plane to a reasonable crash landing and saved our lives. So drop it before you *piss* me off."

"For the record, I saved *your* life." Rainey regretted his words as soon as he spoke.

Amy approached them, listening to the argument. They looked at her, embarrassed for the tiff but it was lost on Amy. She held out her hand to Creston. He hesitated but then took her hand. She clasped it in hers, caressing his fingers as if familiarizing herself with every detail. The innocence of it humbled him.

Rainey, as he had in years past, came to Creston's rescue. "Amy, come back to the plane with us. We have some fishing poles and we might be able to catch a fish and cook it for dinner."

"Fish?" Amy said. "Amy has fish."

Amy turned and walked away, stopped by a palm tree and picked up a long stick with a distinct point. With her back to Rainey and Creston she vanished between the trees in the direction of the ocean.

"Let's go. I want to see what she's up to." He took off at a quick pace leaving Creston behind.

"Slow down, you dick. I'm not a hundred percent yet."

Rainey ignored Creston as he followed Amy. They struggled through the thick trees and stood on the soft sand less than ten yards from the reef. It was low tide and much of the coral reef was exposed. Amy stood at the water's edge, pulled her sarong off and dropped it on the ground.

"Nice butt," Creston said.

"Right now you'd think Lizzie, the three hundred pound stripper on Bourbon Street has a nice butt."

"Lizzie, how do you know about Lizzie? A good catholic boy like you."

Rainey ignored Creston and watched Amy. Carefully, but with confidence, she walked the reef, stopped as if looking for the perfect spot, and then moved on.

"Tidal pools," Creston said. "When the ocean recedes at low tide it leaves pools of water in the deep holes of the reef. Sometimes fish get caught in the holes and have to wait for the tide to come back in and the water to rise before they can swim out. I think she's looking for fish in the tidal pools." Creston watched Rainey's dumbfounded expression. "Maybe you should read more," he said.

"Maybe you should …" Rainey stopped. "Maybe I should."

Amy had reached a spot about twenty yards from shore. She raised the stick in the air and thrust it into a tidal pool without releasing it. Using both hands she lifted the stick. A large reddish fish, wriggling to get free, was impaled on her spear. Turning from the pool she placed the tip of the spear on the reef and using her right foot, slid the fish down the spear. She held it in place as she pulled the spear free. Still pinning the fish, she turned toward the tidal pool and again jabbed the spear into the water. She pulled the spear from the water with another fish cleanly impaled like the first one. Without hesitation she moved her right foot, and simultaneously as one motion, she re-impaled the first fish. She maneuvered her way back across the treacherously slippery reef with the spear resting on her right shoulder.

"Imagine," Creston remarked.

"Yes, pretty amazing when you think about it," Rainey added.

"Exactly. She's a natural brunette."

"You're going to hell; you do realize this, don't you?"

"Not a chance. God loves a smart ass. Why else would he make so many of us."

Amy stopped before them, the spear still resting on her right shoulder. Rainey relieved Amy of the spear and fish, placed them on his shoulder and headed back to the compound. They entered the clearing and Rainey kneeled down, picked up Amy's sarong and handed it to her without looking. Amy tied a simple left over right half knot and cinched it tight while they walked. She gave no thought to her nudity and a succinct awareness settled over Rainey. He envied her freedom and lack of inhibition, a trait he knew he did not possess. Amy walked to the water tank, opened the valve and drank freely of the water gushing forth. Creston did likewise when Amy finished but Rainey still refused to take of the water from the tank. He turned and headed toward the exit, the fish and spear still on his shoulder.

Their walk back to the plane was interrupted by a ten minute downpour. They were soon drenched as if they had walked under a waterfall. Rainey dropped the spear on the ground and he and Creston stretched out their arms letting the rain wash over them until they were completely soaked. Rainey shook his head wildly while Creston used his hands to squeegee the excess water from his hair. Amy did nothing but stand and watch. They were mostly dry by the time they reached the plane.

Creston had gone into the plane and returned with a knife from the galley and saw Amy had taken the fish, still impaled on the spear, to the lagoon's edge. He watched as she removed the fish from the spear, picked one up and placed the point of the spear into the anus and then ran the spear completely through the fish and out the underside of the lower jaw. With a forceful pull she disemboweled the fish and dumped the innards into the lagoon. Bending down she rinsed the fish and threw it onto the sand, then repeated the process with the other fish and carried them back to the plane, handing the larger fish to Creston. With the smaller fish in her left hand she plunged two fingers into the fleshy part of the red snapper and dug out a strip of flesh. Creston's eyes opened wide, caught off guard by how fast she ripped the meat from the fish and placed it into her mouth. She watched with an expression indicating to Creston she expected him to indulge in the delicacy she had presented.

"Wait, wait a minute," Creston said. "Rainey, you better hurry up with the fire while we still have some fish to cook."

CHAPTER TWENTY FIVE

Leslie was sorely disappointed after the second board meeting. None of the members questioned anything or had offered any suggestions to help, even after all she had done. Big O had been far too complacent. She was irritated, upset and confused. Self pity was driving her like a runaway locomotive and she had no control over her emotions. Four weeks had passed since Rainey and Creston were reported missing, and Leslie was finding it more and more difficult to be optimistic. She slammed her open palm on the table and rose from her chair. Leaving the papers, coffee cups, and water pitcher on the table she forcefully pushed the conference room door open wide and marched down the hall to the elevators.

"I figured you'd be coming out soon," Big O said as Leslie exited the building. "I'm worried about you. You're wound a little too tight."

The November afternoon air was cool on her face but intensified her ire instead of calming her. Leslie looked at O, the background noise of the city was fading, and her head buzzed with confusion. She stepped toward Big O and collapsed against him.

"Stress, most likely, and her blood sugar's a little low, probably not eating right. We see it from time to time with the big executive types."

Leslie heard the paramedic talking as she came to with the help of the ammonia capsule. She turned her head toward the voice and a paramedic was on one knee, stethoscope hanging from her neck, explaining the situation to Big O and several people from the bank.

"Well, hello dawlin, feelin betta?" she asked.

Leslie recognized the strong ninth ward accent, one unique and different from the uptown people, different from the Cajun and bayou people. The exception to the uniqueness was a slight similarity to a Brooklyn, New York accent, the inflection and dropping of the letter R in some words. She had come to love the culture of the old New Orleans people, how they talked, how they lived life, and the fun they had at a moments notice.

"Yes, I am feeling better, thank you. I...I don't know what happened."

"It's simple. The body has a way of takin care of itself. You overload enough and it shuts down like a car out a gas. Not sure what's got you so worked up, but you need to chill out, honey."

Leslie thought for a moment and said, "My ex-husband is missing. I guess that and my job got the better of me."

"Hell, is that all, I wish my ex was missing. I'd *pay* for him to go missin," she said. "But he was pretty good in the sack."

Leslie laughed at the brashness of the paramedic. She made note that her name tag had Natalie etched into it. The dizziness left her as she sat on a chair from one of the shops in the lobby of the Place St. Charles building. The ambulance was parked, it's flashing lights calling attention to their presence like neon in Las Vegas. She stood up, inhaled deeply and looked at Big O.

"I've been told if you breathe through your nose the oxygen gets to your brain quicker. I think it works," Leslie said.

"Whateva gets you through the night, sweetie, works for me." Natalie placed her stethoscope in her bag, closed it and stood up. "I don't think you need to go to the hospital but we'll take you if you want."

"No, I'll be fine. Thank you very much."

"Would you like me to call you later? Just to see how you're doin, it's part of the job. No extra charge."

"No, I'll be fine." Leslie waited a moment, then said, "Say, listen, if you're not doing anything later, Big O here, he'll be shuckin at the restaurant, and I'm buyin if you want some oysters."

"Yeah, well tell ya what. I can eat a mess of ershters, especially if someone else is buyin so I'll be there at six. Be a good chance to check up on ya so don't stand me up you two."

Leslie hugged Big O and hustled over to the elevator bank. She had much to do and recovered well enough to work before meeting Big O and Natalie.

"Where ya at?" The greeting, unique to New Orleans traveled across the restaurant as Natalie made a loud entrance. The restaurant was busy and no one bothered looking up from their meals. Leslie was sitting on a stool and Big O was behind the bar.

"Ain't nowhere, baby," O yelled back. He wore a smile as bright as the flashing Dixie Beer sign in the window.

Natalie perched her pleasantly large backside on the bar stool next to Leslie and ordered a Dixie Beer. O picked out a bottle from deep inside the cooler where the coldest beers resided and placed the dripping bottle in front of her.

"Here's to ya," she said as she lifted the bottle to Leslie and then Big O. And…don't forget them pearl huggers."

Big O shucked a dozen of the biggest and juiciest oysters, placed them on a tray and slid it in front of Natalie and Leslie. A smaller tray with horseradish, ketchup, lemon, hot sauce, two small forks and paper cups for mixing the cocktail sauce was placed next to the oysters. Natalie went to work, first scooping the spicy, and sinus clearing horseradish into a paper cup. Taking a lemon slice between her thumb and two fingers, she squeezed it onto the horseradish, poured a small offering of the ketchup, shook out three drops of hot sauce over the lemon, and stirred it all together. She dipped a cracker into the sauce and silently proclaimed it near perfect with a nod of her head.

"How bout a little more horseradish?"

Big O looked up from the oysters. "What'd you say?" he asked.

"Horseradish, I need a little more horseradish," Natalie said. "What, you rationing it or somethin?"

"No, you just caught me off guard. Comin at ya."

"Tell me bout this missin ex-husband of yours," she said.

"The short version is he and his friend took off from the lakefront airport, made it to Hawaii, spent the night and took off again. Then they disappeared. Neither of them nor the plane has been found. It's been almost a month. What bothers me is they were too well prepared. I can't help thinking maybe someone had a hand in making this happen."

"Say, I read about them guys. One of em's filthy rich. Is he your ex?"

"No, my ex is the other one."

"Damn, ain't it always the way? C'est la vie, as we say. Maybe would have been a huge inheritance, dawlin."

"I don't care about the money. I want my ex, his name is Rainey, to be all right. The other man is Creston and I want him to be safe and return as well."

"Right, and I'm Mother Goose. Who you kiddin? I know what you want. We ladies is all the same."

A commotion arose from a table several feet behind Leslie and Natalie. A large man had stood up grabbing his throat, choking. Natalie turned and moved behind the man in distress. Wrapping her arms around his oversized girth she constricted hard in a Heimlich maneuver. Again she squeezed with no result. Once more she squeezed as hard as she was able. The big man coughed, and wheezed lowly, sounding like a balloon as the final hiss of air escaped through the stretched neck. A large oyster followed the last wheeze of air and the man caught it between his teeth. Half of the oyster was hanging from of his mouth and the big guy sucked it back in swallowing it whole.

"Slow down and take a breath next time. There's plenty for everyone." She slapped him across his buttocks and walked back to the bar. "All in a day's work. Where were we? Oh yeah, the ex. What happened between you and him?"

"You don't mince words, do you?"

"Look honey, we're friends for life. I know a keeper when I see one. Well, except for husbands. But I know who'll be a good friend and you is one."

Leslie thought for a moment and said, "It's an old story. I put too much time into work, building my career, trying to advance and prove myself. Rainey gave me plenty of room which I justified as neglect. Then I fell for an older man. He was smart and forceful. By the time I finally figured out I was another notch in his belt, Rainey and I had separated. The divorce came soon after. The older man moved away after telling me it wouldn't work between us. And I was left here. I don't expect to get back with Rainey, but I need him to be ok." Leslie cleared her throat and looked at the clock.

"That's it, nothing else since the divorce?" Natalie said.

"We've remained friends and even…yeah, nothing else."

"Boy, are you a bad liar. So how does the other guy figure in all this?"

"He's a whole story and we don't have time. How about we give it a rest? I can't believe I'm telling you all this," Leslie said. "Tell us a little about yourself? I get the feeling you've had an interesting life."

"Ah, not much to tell, I grew up in the lower ninth ward, other side of the industrial canal. Me and my family survived Hurricane Betsy in '65. I graduated high school from Nicholls on St. Claude Ave. It's still there but the name has changed. Went to Southeastern in Hammond, thought I wanted to be a nurse, but I knew pretty early I needed to be on the move, working outside with people. So after graduation I decided to be an EMT. Oh yeah, been married twice, and divorced three times.

"Interesting trick, divorced more times than you've been married." Leslie glanced at Big O then back at Natalie.

"The third divorce was from the idea of getting married again. I divorced myself from ALL men. Well, from marryin em anyway." She grinned and took another big drink from her beer. "I love being in love. But you might have noticed, I'm a little overbearing. Most men can't handle it. I guess I wear em out."

Leslie and Big O took turns telling stories and filling Natalie in on Rainey and Creston. Three hours, several more beers, and another dozen oysters disappeared faster than any of them wanted.

Natalie looked at the clock above the bar, slid from her stool, both feet slapping the tiled floor simultaneously and said, "I got the early shift in the morning so I need to go. Thanks for a good time. You two are all right. Here, take my card, give me a call some time." Natalie handed Leslie and then Big O a card with the name of the ambulance service boldly printed across the top with her name underneath. "You know, if you think about it."

"I'm here most nights shucking," Big O said. "Drop by anytime you feel like it. And when Rainey and Creston get back we'd like you to meet them, right, Leslie?"

"Right," Leslie said. "The story isn't over, not yet by a long shot."

"My, you're optimistic, but I like it. Y'all take care and have a good night. And you," she said, pointing at Leslie, "get some rest and let the trivial stuff go." She waved as she walked out onto Iberville Street.

Leslie finished her beer chatting with Big O as he shucked oysters almost non stop. Johnny Tap hustled the trays of raw oysters to the waiters and waitresses with a smile and an occasional three step tap dance and a twirl. The clock on the wall behind O showed almost ten and she pondered where the evening had gone. And then wondered where the last month had gone. The restaurant was still packed, bustling like Grand Central Station at rush hour when she said good night and walked out into the night air. She inhaled deeply through her nose and felt the oxygen rush to her brain, giving her a mild natural high. It made her feel like a young school girl.

She walked into the parking garage next to the restaurant, paid and waited as the attendant stepped on the man lift to the upper floor to retrieve her car. The squealing tires caused her to clench her jaw, but she said nothing as the attendant held the car door open for her.

It was late and the start of a physical and emotional crash was coming on. This night would bring contented sleep like a cat on an old lady's lap. In the morning she would call Joan and Paris. She had nothing new to report but hopefully her positive attitude would encourage them.

CHAPTER TWENTY SIX

"Amy, please give me the book," Rainey said, reaching toward her.

"NO!" she yelled. "Mommy's book."

Rainey looked at Creston. "Whoa, that's the most emotion we've seen from her. She thinks I'm taking it away from her." Rainey looked back at Amy. "I want to read it then I'll give it back to you. I don't want to keep it."

She clutched the book tighter to her chest, shaking her head, hair flying wildly. Creston started moving toward her.

"Wait, give her some room. Let's not push it too fast. She doesn't understand."

"Okay, but how do we find out what's in the journal?" Creston said.

"Amy," Rainey said softly, "can you read to us from the book?"

She rocked back and forth, looking from Rainey to Creston. They took a step back. Amy opened the book to the middle, ran her hand over the page and then looked back at Rainey. A tear ran down her cheek.

Creston said in a low voice, "I think I liked it better when she showed no emotion."

Rainey moved to Amy, closed the journal and pushed it against her chest. "It's ok. Maybe we'll read it later." He turned toward Creston and said, "Let's go back to the plane. This has got me feeling pretty shitty."

"We haven't seen Amy in a couple of days," Creston said placing his coffee cup on the sand. "Do you think she is still upset about the book?"

"I don't think so. We didn't push the issue or threaten her. She got over it soon after we left."

"So why hasn't she shown up?"

Rainey stood up, crossed his arms across his chest and looked out at the lagoon. "The Indians called it moon time," Rainey said.

"Moon time? What the hell is moon time?"

"Her monthly cycle," Rainey said. "Her period? In some tribes the squaws weren't allowed into the lodge when they were on their moon time. I guess maybe it's a natural understanding in women. I think she went off, well stayed in her underground, until it's over. And, if she is as old as I think the periods are shorter in time than when she was young. Maybe explains her display of emotions. I should have figured it out right then."

"How the hell do you know all this?" Creston asked.

"I was married remember? And you're not the only one who reads," Rainey said.

"Moon time, huh? I've got a moon for ya."

"I think I liked it better when...never mind," Rainey said. "Come on, I've got to move around and be active to stay sane."

They busied themselves during the day doing aimless work, moving things around then moving them back like a housewife rearranging furniture all day before putting it back in its original place. They had collected water in their hand made bowls and refilled plastic bottles almost daily. They were no longer in danger of running out of water and they had become more liberal in using it to clean, bathe and drink. Fishing with poles was seldom necessary as Amy had provided fish on an almost daily basis. But the poles had come in handy during her absences. Rainey managed to catch a couple of small sea bass while fishing the reef during high tide. They had both lost weight, stopped shaving, gotten tanned, scruffy and castaway looking. Their injuries had healed and they were feeling more fit than they had in years.

Neither had spoken anymore about getting off the island, but both thought about it constantly. Rainey had decided if death was inevitable then he would rather die at sea trying to survive than end up like Amy, years on the island with monotony dire enough to challenge a cloistered nun. He had decided to discuss it with Creston, later, after they had eaten.

Amy walked back into their camp, her sarong clean and an unusual freshness about her face. She carried the journal in her arms, pressed to her breast.

"Read," she said handing the journal to Rainey. "I like ...you read."

Rainey flushed with excitement as he took the journal noting Amy's English was getting better. Emotion coursed through him as he slid his hand over the cover, brushing off fine particles of sand, and then opening it to the first entry he had read. He stared at the script feeling as though he were treading on hallowed ground or invading someone's privacy. He turned the page and read.

First, let me explain I'm sure we have been here for about six years. I was able to get this journal from Captain Matsunaga by asking no, begging, please let me write my story. I believe he thinks it doesn't matter. I pray he is wrong.

I don't know what happened but we were terribly off course after traveling more than eighteen hundred miles. The radio had quit working properly and we could not make contact with anyone. We tried many times to make contact with Howland Island. Eventually running out of fuel we ditched at sea. I maneuvered the plane into a reasonably good landing on water. The small inflatable raft probably saved our lives. I don't know how but in a short amount of time we were picked up by a Japanese patrol boat launched from a large naval vessel. At first I was relieved thinking we would soon be headed back to America. Captain Matsunaga informed us he was on maneuvers and he would not jeopardize his mission. He avoided answering me when I requested he try to contact an American vessel. We were confined to quarters, given daily rations of a clear broth with a bowl of rice, and visited by various Japanese officers, most of whom did not speak English and showed little respect to me.

I'm not sure but I believe it was on the second or third day we were delivered to this island. The large ship was able to navigate into a channel almost all the way up to the island.

Rainey stopped for a moment and recalled the large open channel through the reef he had encountered on his first trip around the island. It made sense a large military ship would be able to approach the island through this opening. Rainey read aloud.

We were escorted onto the island by a group of Japanese sailors, each armed, and delivered to the open area near the center of the island. Part of the area had been excavated and then covered with a ceiling. This was to be their hidden underground hospital. The rest of the open area surrounding the hospital had been created by the clearing of trees and large netting had been placed over the area, stretched from one side to the other and supported by the various trees around the perimeter. Fred later told me it was

Rainey stopped abruptly and went into deep thought. Creston had been staring at the coral sand, lost in the reading but looked up when Rainey paused.

"What is it? Why'd you stop?" Creston asked.

"Fred would be Fred Noonan. He was her navigator. I had forgotten about him. It's who she's referring to when she says "we". It's her and Fred."

"Ok, but why'd you stop?"

"It made me remember something my mother told me when I was a boy. Most people think of Fred Noonan as Amelia Earhart's navigator, but before he got into aviation he was a seaman. He started as a mate and worked his way up to a responsible position on ships. He got married in Jackson and moved to New Orleans with his new bride to work out of the port. And my mother, as a young girl, lived next door to him. I had forgotten all about it. She told me the story many times when I was young. I guess it was her fifteen minutes of fame so to speak."

"You never told me the story of Fred Noonan," Creston said. "Where do you think Amy fits into all of this?"

"I'm not sure," Rainey said, "but if what Amy said about this being mommy's book is correct then she must be Amelia Earhart's daughter." He nodded, deep in thought for a moment before resuming.

Fred later told me the netting was camouflage material used to hide the area from planes. From the sky they would not be able to see the open area and from the higher altitude it would look like a mass of trees. We were left here on the island with minimal provisions. They returned after what must have been months, bringing with them hospital beds and equipment. This happened several times over a period of what I guessed to be several years. At the time we were both confused as to the purpose of building a secret underground hospital. We later learned of the war and realized the purpose of the hospital and why we had been detained.

One evening Captain Matsunaga told me he had been educated at a small university in California but he refused to tell me which one. I am not sure why but I am sure he is a very calculating man and not one to take chances. He is tolerable and polite but unbending in his mission.

My training as a nurse is probably the reason we are still alive. I spend my time taking care of wounded Japanese sailors and on occasion a soldier. They are brought here and put into the hospital where the doctors try to save them and put them back into the war. As a woman I am given little respect. Fred is assumed to be in charge and most orders are directed at him. He is a good man and does as much as possible to protect me. Most of the wounded do not survive and are taken back onto the ship to be buried at sea. As of this writing Captain Matsunaga has told us the war has lasted over two years but Japan will soon be victorious. I can not imagine this to be true but if it is then I do not know what will happen to us.

Rainey read as Creston and Amy sat in silence. Many of the entries were somewhat repetitive, describing daily routines, but Rainey spoke each word. He read for over an hour before pausing to look up. He watched Amy unable to determine if she was happy with the reading, or sad.

"I think I've read enough," Rainey said. "Besides, I need a break. Amy, thank you for sharing the journal. It has been helpful."

"We would like to read more later if it is ok with you," Creston said.

She nodded. "Amy read…too."

She leaned toward Rainey and took the journal into her hands. Standing with it cradled in her arms, she turned and started back to her compound.

Rainey stopped Creston before he stood and objected to Amy leaving. Creston nodded in agreement.

"Rather ironic isn't it?" Rainey said. "Maybe the biggest mystery of the century and we hold the answer to what happened, and no one to tell. How cruel is this?"

"Maybe not so cruel when you think about it."

"What do you mean?" Rainey asked.

"Some things are better left alone. Can you imagine the uproar if the rest of the world found out about this. It would go on for years. Maybe it's best to let it die here. The world has mostly accepted the fact Amelia Earhart is gone and the truth might never be known. There's still a few out there who think they'll find her remains, solve the mystery. Why spoil it for them? Maybe solving the mystery would be the cruel part."

"Sounds almost logical," Rainey said.

"Amelia Earhart never made it to Howland Island and was lost at sea. And then, like magic, the Japanese pick her up in the middle of a vast ocean. What are the odds, and don't tell me coincidence. I'm not a big believer in coincidence. The whole world knew about her attempt to circle the globe. I think the Japanese were tracking her. She disappears and they pick her up within a few hours. Not a coincidence, they knew about her all along. Think about it. The Japanese are getting ready for war, building up their forces or positions in the Pacific. There's no way they want her stumbling across their fleet or maybe making a forced landing on one of their bases. I think they knew and weren't taking any chances. If her plane went down they didn't want any sighting or evidence. Maybe it's a long shot, but I don't think so."

"I think you're right. It makes sense. So they bring her and Fred to this island, finish building the hospital and then put them to work. She and Fred work day in and day out tending to the wounded and getting the dead ready for burial. And this goes on for years, or at least until the war ends. The ship and Captain Matsunaga came back from time to time bringing more wounded. Most probably didn't survive."

"Man, I can't imagine how they survived for so long," Creston said. "The war ended in 1945, so then what? They were left here? Too hard to believe, but I don't see any other possibility."

"There's more and we can read it tomorrow. Amy wants us to read it," Rainey said.

"Let's get some rest tonight. The sun is sinking fast. I think I can hear the hiss as it hits the water."

Rainey shook his head and said, "Why me?"

CHAPTER TWENTY SEVEN

Rainey and Creston entered the compound. Amy was sitting, her back against the palm tree where Rainey had read the first entry in the journal. The journal rested in her lap. Rainey was beginning to piece things together. Years of solitude had numbed her from any expectations. He knew she would have sat on the sand with her back against the tree for hours. And had he and Creston not come she would have eventually gotten up, returned to the underground, replaced the journal and done nothing. Understanding how she had endured for years was unfathomable to him.

Rainey sat next to her, his back against the palm tree. He adjusted his sitting position, purposely leaning in toward Amy until their shoulders touched. She did not move away but sat quiet and still. Rainey reached for the journal. Emptiness consumed him but then he understood. Even though the journal was important it had caused Amy to become secondary, and Rainey was ashamed by his thoughts and actions. She was constantly in the back of his mind, but the journal consumed his first thoughts.

Before opening the journal and reading he contemplated his situation. Luck, fate, destiny, or whatever one might want to call it, he believed he was here for a reason. Amy was not a coincidence, happenstance, or simply a fluke. And with this his priorities changed. Rainey opened the journal.

I believe Captain Matsunaga's ship must be some type of hospital ship. The doctor only stays on the island with us if he is tending to the severely wounded. As soon as they are well enough the ship returns and he leaves. Sometimes the wounded survived and other times they did not. The hospital has been empty for some time now. Two soldiers survived and left with Captain Matsunaga months ago. The others did not survive but they left also, for burial at sea. Fred and I have been alone and we have taken excellent care of each other. We survive on fresh fish, coconuts and other fruits from the trees planted years ago by the Japanese.

Captain Matsunaga returned but he brought no wounded to tend to. It is late in the year 1945. He has informed me the great war is over and Japan has surrendered to the United States of America. Fred and I could hardly contain our joy when told of this great news. But our joy was quickly replaced with confusion and disappointment. Captain Matsunaga has told us since the war is over and Japan has lost he must return home. We would not be going with him he said. It was then I realized what he meant. He would be going home but not to Japan. Everything from the hospital has been loaded onto the ship except a few beds and a cabinet I pleaded with him to leave with us. His shame is evident and I know he will take his ship back to sea and it, along with all his men, will die a noble death.

The morning was somber and yet, there appeared to be contentment in the eyes of Captain Matsunaga. He refused to answer when I asked him what would become of me and Fred. I believe he would have done something if he could but his mission was not complete and we would not be allowed to interfere. He was a proud man, loyal to his emperor but his fate was unavoidable. Fred and I watched as his ship sailed, knowing it was a ghost ship on the water headed to its grave. I wonder if we will ever be found.

Rainey took a deep breath as he thought of what had happened. They had been abandoned, left to survive or die, and it bothered him this many years later. Creston was deep in thought. Amy sat quiet, waiting for Rainey to read more.

The next page was uneventful but the journal offered a decided turn as he read.

I have lost track of time and I don't care. It must be five or six years since we were abandoned here, left to die. I am guessing I must be approaching fifty years of age. Fred and I have become as man and wife and even though I never looked at him in that way he has been a good husband. We both are healthy and fit although my body is changing somewhat. We eat fish daily and they are easy to catch in the reef pools at low tide. At first we fell many times, slipping on the wet coral but not anymore. We walk together around the island and sometimes swim in the lagoon. We have two knives and a hammer left by the Japanese. Not much but enough to open coconuts and clean the fish.

It is years later since my last entry. I am filled with joy and fear at the same time. I believe I am pregnant which, under different circumstances, should be cause for celebration. But I fear I am too old. I have heard of "change of life babies" and I believe this is the case with me. I worry if Fred and I can deliver a baby and save it.

Again Rainey stopped reading. He turned toward Amy and a chill swept over him. It was as if he were reading from Amy's life.

My best guess is it would be 1950 or 1951 but I am truly not sure. This means we have been here for fourteen years or so. It is hard to imagine this could happen to us. I will do better with keeping track of time after the baby is born. I don't know why but I feel hugely confident Fred and I will have this baby and it will survive. If it is a boy I will name him Fred junior but if it is a girl I think I shall name her Amy.

My belly is very large, much larger than I would ever have imagined. I am at least eight months pregnant and I feel the baby move most of the day. I think the baby is ready to come into this world. Fred stays busy making sure I am comfortable, bringing me food and water and anything I want. Although, there is not much at our disposal. He has moved the beds together, separated them and then moved them together again. There is little to do and far too much time to do it all. Most days I take a walk to the beach, resting along the way, and then return. I spend time sitting under my favorite palm tree right outside the hospital, which is not a hospital anymore but our home. The curve of the tree fits my back nicely and gives me good support. It affords me shade and protects me from the sun.

Again Rainey stopped. He looked at Amy and noticed how the tree they were leaning against curved much like a large easy chair, fitting her back and supporting her. What are the chances this is the tree Amelia made reference to. But looking around, he realized almost all of the palm trees were similar. Creston was staring at him.

"Did we miss something?" Creston asked.

"No, you didn't miss anything. I was lost for a moment, overwhelmed with the whole idea of what has happened here. Let's face it, if someone was to tell us this story we'd laugh them back into sobriety. But here we are in the middle of it."

"And we'll make the most of it. Somehow, one way or another, we'll survive this." Creston looked at Amy. "Keep reading."

The contractions have started and this will probably be the last entry for a while. The pain is intensifying as the contractions get closer together. I pray everything will be all right. I am proud of Fred. He has proven strong and confident. This comforts me greatly.

Amy is a week old today, whatever day this is, and she is strong and alert. She suckles constantly but I think it is more she is learning to nurse. I'm not sure she is getting as much milk as she needs. Perhaps I am a worrisome mother. This is new to Fred and me even though I had training as a nurse. It is certainly different when it is your own child.

Rainey learned of Amy's early months and then years. But the journal entries were becoming shorter and more to the point. It was obvious they were spread out over time more than the previous entries. Rainey surmised a young toddler had her too busy and tired to write many entries. She was resting when she wasn't chasing after Amy.

Amy is ten years old. She seems tall for her age. I wish I could bake a cake for her or have a party for her, but I now know that will never happen. I am tired and feel worn and old most of the time. Amy keeps me and Fred going but we have been here to the point of insanity. And yet, I look at Amy and get new energy, but it is short lived. I feel guilt but worse is I have abandoned hope. It has been so many years, at least twenty five I think, to the point giving up is the appropriate result of all this. Perhaps tomorrow, or the next day, or the day after, I might feel better again.

"Stop," Creston said. "I think Amy's getting upset. And it's depressing the hell out of me."

"Amy," Rainey said, "are you all right? Should I stop reading?"

"No..." she said. "It is ok to read."

Rainey hurt for Amy and tried to conceive of her pain and loss. And then a thought occurred to him.

"Amy, can you read?" he asked.

"Amy...Amy once read. But, no more."

Rainey looked at Creston with empathy for Amy but did not speak. Creston nodded with understanding. Rainey cleared his throat.

It is cruel in so many ways. I have lashed out in anger at my God almost daily. What else will he do to us? And now, my last pencil is almost too short to write with but I have more life to live and write about. How shall I do this?

Amy is almost at puberty. Soon she will be a woman but there is nothing for her here and no hopes of ever leaving this island. Why did no one find us?

Fred and I have taught Amy all we can. She learned her alphabet by writing her letters with a stick in the sand. I use this journal to teach her to read. She is a lovely girl who could have done so much in another place.

I am tired and have no energy anymore. Fred has died. I don't know why but I think he grew too tired and gave up. And I don't blame him. We wrapped him in a blanket, dragged him to the channel the ship used and at low tide floated his body as far out as possible while walking along the reef. It was a fitting burial. Fred was a ships officer at one time and we have returned him to the sea. Amy is confused and I hurt for her as much as I hurt for myself.

Amy and I have celebrated her fourteenth birthday even though I have no idea when her birthday is. But it doesn't matter. It is close enough to her birthday and is all I care about. I believe it must be about 1965 or so. This means I am fast approaching seventy years of age. My time is short. I can feel it in my bones and in my soul. I have made peace with God and I know he has heard me. Only He can save Amy when I am gone and I pray each day He will be kind.

It must have been several years since my last entry in this journal. I will write no more after this. I have told Amy it is my time to join her father and this upset her greatly. My entire body aches and it has taken hours to write this entry. I must pass and I cry for Amy as any mother would cry for her daughter. Another day or perhaps another week at the most, but no more. She will take me to sea as we took Fred. I do not want my body on the island for her to mourn over. I know this is right. I pray she will be saved. I have done my best.

Amelia Earhart

Rainey cleared his throat, his eyes watering as he looked at Creston. Misty eyes stared back at him. This was the first time he had ever seen Creston this emotional. He nodded in understanding and wiped his own eyes dry. Rainey closed the journal and placed it on Amy's lap, holding it firm against her thighs with his hand, his fingers stretched out like a starfish. He was slow to remove his hand, feeling a connection.

"Why us?" Rainey said.

"Well, as a great philosopher once declared, Why not?"

Rainey was confused. One side of him wanted to return to the plane and sort things out, but the other side did not want to leave Amy. If the journal was anywhere close to correct, and if Amelia had passed in 1965 or even as late as 1970, Amy had been alone for twenty five or thirty years. It tore at his emotions to think of the loneliness of Amy's last twenty five years. He sat and watched her stare off into the trees.

"Stay here," Creston said. "I'm going to the plane. Give me an hour or so and then head back. Bring Amy if she'll come." Creston got up from the sand, his eyes narrowed and his jaw set firm. "I've got something I need to take a look at. We're not gonna be here for the rest of our lives, I promise you."

"Okay, I'll stay with Amy and head back later."

Creston walked toward the trees and disappeared into the maze. Rainey sat, watching Amy with his peripheral vision, while he searched for the right words. It was easy to understand why she was silent, and why she had no need to speak. After almost thirty years, Rainey was surprised she spoke at all.

"Amy, I know about your mother, who she was and where she came from. Now I know what happened to her, and your father, too. My mother knew your father many years ago." Rainey was not sure his words made sense. "Amy, do you know what a promise is?" he asked.

Amy looked at Rainey. "Mommy promised... never leave."

The blood drained from Rainey's face. He had made Amy a promise to take care of her and get her off the island. But with her words he realized how insignificant his promise would be.

Creston moved with a new energy. Rainey smiled watching Creston move back and forth, hurriedly, as if late for an appointment. The sun was two hours above the horizon, bouncing reflected light off the smooth surface of the lagoon. A predictable early evening breeze was wafting across the campsite but was not enough to cool the air. Creston concentrated on his mission. Rainey wondered what had Creston so busy and driven.

The campsite was neat and orderly. Most of the supplies had been removed from the plane and organized. Rainey walked along the line of supplies as if on a military inspection and made mental notes of the limited goods. He turned toward Creston.

"I take it you have a plan," he said. "Care to share it with me?"

"Sure, I plan to be home for Thanksgiving…this year!"

"Ok, let's see, Amy has been here for almost fifty years but you think you'll be home in two weeks or so. Interesting plan."

"Ah, ye of little faith. I'm surprised at you. Especially you. Ya gotta have faith my friend," Creston said.

"Well, let's see what we have," Rainey said. "Oh, that's right. We have NOTHING! Hell, we don't even know where we are. We have no idea…

"Hold it right there, pal. YOU don't know where we are, but I have a pretty good idea as to our location." Creston scratched his head. "Give or take five hundred miles or so."

"FIVE HUNDRED?" Rainey laughed. "It might as well be five thousand miles. What were you thinking of doing? Putting on some floaties and drifting around out there?'

"Cynicism is a little ugly coming from you," Creston said.

Creston's words stung and Rainey looked inward for what was bothering him. "I guess it's the fact of how long Amy has been here since her parents died. I was foolish enough to make myself a promise to get her off the island. Walking back here I had to admit how stupid it was. I was beating myself up a little."

"Hey, I'll be happy to beat you up if it'll make you feel better," Creston said.

"A true friend." Rainey relaxed and said, "So what's your plan?"

"Ok, try to follow me and keep up. I've studied the book on celestial navigation, and even though we don't have a sextant or other instruments, I think I have a pretty good idea of where we are. Like I said, give or take five hundred miles, which is not as insurmountable as you might think. We had maps and charts on the plane and I feel pretty confident in my findings. We've been on the island for about a month. I figure it's early November, maybe the second week. So, with a little luck we can make Thanksgiving."

"What the hell do you mean, make Thanksgiving? Rainey said.

"Calm down and let me finish. This might sound a little crazy, but I think we can build a wood frame around the inflatable life raft, add some floatation using the seat cushions from the plane and secure it all with some of the wiring from the plane. I can store some water and food by tying it down with more of the wiring. Then I'll launch in the channel the Japanese ship used to access the island. At low tide there is no surf line at the reef opening to worry about. With a little *more* luck I can…"

"Wait a minute. It was *we,* and all of a sudden it's *I,* as in just you?" Rainey said. "You think you're sailing off and leaving me here, alone?"

"You won't be alone. You have Amy to look out for."

"Amy doesn't need looking after. Besides, we stand a better chance of surviving if we stay together. So, add me to your plan, no argument. Got it?" There was no compromise in Rainey's voice.

Creston cupped his chin in his hand, partially covering his mouth. He starred at the ground. Dropping his hand to his side he looked back at Rainey, nodding.

"I suppose it's foolish to try to rationalize my position with you. But I was thinking should I not make it out there, I didn't want you with me. Enough of this, WE have other things to discuss. We'll need twice as much water and food so the frame will have to be a little bigger than I planned. We have plenty of fallen trees and branches to work with. We'll start in the morning. I figure we can do this in about three days or so. Creston put his hand on Rainey's shoulder. "Hey, we can do this. And, we can make it."

"What about Amy?" Rainey said.

CHAPTER TWENTY EIGHT

It was late afternoon and quiet inside the restaurant. Big O had done all his prep work and was ready for the tourist crowd. Johnny Tap swayed to music no one else could hear. Big O let his mind wander, his right foot propped up on the stainless steel sink. He didn't notice as she walked in and approached his bar.

"Oscar, you thinking awful hard," Mama Mary said.

"Mama, what you doin here? You never come here no more. If you wanted some oysters I'd a brought em to ya. All ya had to do was call me."

"I didn't come here for no oysters. I needed a change of scenery."

"Mama, I know you better than that." Big O placed his foot on the floor and leaned into the bar. "What's botherin you?"

"Oscar, sometimes I get worked up and fool myself. I think of things that never happen. I learned not to take any of them too serious. Besides, I've been wrong plenty a times. I don't tell no one bout all the times I'm off. Sometimes I think maybe I have too good of a imagination and it fools me. So, I didn't think nothin of it at first. I figured it was maybe my mind going crazy."

"This ain't makin no sense to me Mama. Didn't think nothin about what?" Big O said interrupting her.

"Your two friends. I been thinkin of them more than usual. I seen them here and there was some big celebration. First, I figured it was because you and your friend wants them to come home and it was a nice thought. But it got real clear and I couldn't ignore it no more. It come to me a couple of times. But I told you already,

198

maybe I'm right, maybe not. I don't want you tellin no one about this. Not yet. But I feel pretty strong about it. Even more so cause I'm here talkin to you." Mama Mary turned, looking around the restaurant. "Kinda quiet in here for a change," she said.

O stood tall and said, "I sure hope you're right Mama. What should I do?"

"All you can do is pray. Them boys ain't safe yet."

"Let me get you some oysters and a cold drink. Stay here with me a little longer." Big O moved to the cooler, put his hand into the icy water and grabbed a root beer.

Leslie was having trouble sleeping at night. Thanksgiving was less than two weeks away and her intuition, aided by Mama Mary and hope, had convinced her Rainey and Creston would return soon. Faith and believing were necessary, but at some point a sign or any positive indication became essential to keep the faith fueled and the hope alive. But occasionally a lapse of faith occurred, especially when she was alone. She asked herself if her doubt clouded reality until she was left confused and embarrassed. And, sometimes at night she would lie awake trying to believe. The sleep came, but never soon enough, and never lasted long enough.

In the distance, as if from another world, came a faint ringing. Leslie opened her eyes as her phone stopped ringing and the answer machine picked up the call. She placed her head under her pillow and pulled it tight around her ears. Whoever it was and whatever they had to say would wait. She held no hope it was good news, and bad news was as welcome as the next hurricane.

The voice stopped and Leslie removed the pillow. Rising from the bed she made her way into her bathroom, stopped in front of the mirror and waited for the pitiful reflection to smile at her. Not today she thought, and turned around to start the shower. Leslie stood motionless for several minutes, her mind empty. The trance released her and she slipped her nightgown from her shoulders, letting it fall to the tile floor on top of water dripping from the shower curtain she had failed to place inside the tub.

Leslie fixed the shower curtain, entered the tub, and tilted her head back as the pulsating water hit her. The force of the center jet vibrated against her chest like a soothing massage, relaxed her, and she squatted into a sitting position with her legs crossed. The porcelain enamel of the tub was cool to her buttocks and startled her. She reclined, her back supported by the rear of the tub, and stretched out her legs. The swirling steam was cloud-like and comforted her. Rising to a standing position she waved her arm upward and scattered the clouds. She finished showering, stepped from the tub and looked into the mirror which had completely fogged over. Perhaps my problem, she thought, is I'm not seeing things clearly.

Before leaving her apartment she pushed the play button on the answering machine. She hit delete before the recorded advertisement finished. "At least it isn't bad news," she said.

CHAPTER TWENTY NINE

"What do you miss the most?"

Rainey gave the question some thought for a moment while staring out at the lagoon. "It varies with the time of day, but I think what I miss most is the comfort, the comfort of being home, knowing what to expect most of the time. I mean, I miss the things you'd expect, like the food, friends, even work, but comfort is the main thing for me. What about you?"

"Well, I guess I miss my boat."

Rainey nodded. "Yeah, a boat would be helpful."

"This is why we're building a raft."

Rainey and Creston had scavenged the island, gathering enough tree limbs and fallen palm trees to attempt constructing a frame large enough, and sturdy enough to float out to the open ocean. The gathering of the smaller limbs was tedious, requiring scrutiny of the limbs, making sure they were large enough and not dry rotted. Most of the tree limbs were two or three inches in diameter and easy to drag to the inlet on the reef side of the island. The palm trees, being large and heavy, were a different matter. Rainey and Creston, working together, lifted the palm tree trunks to their shoulders and carried them one at a time to the inlet. It proved more laborious than expected. The soft sand swallowed their feet under the added weight of the palm tree, causing them to stumble several times. The trees and underbrush were thick and challenging, continually slowing them down. But mostly the task tested their patience and resolve. They repeatedly gasped air then exhaled loudly, as much from frustration as effort. Cursing and sweating while bumping into trees and working against each other, they persevered. After resting several times they had eventually managed to drop the first tree onto the sand and return to find a companion palm tree. It took all of the first day to gather the four palm trees needed for the frame. Creston had decided against stripping the plane of electrical wiring to lash the raft together after a suggestion from Rainey. Removing the leather covers and cutting them into one inch wide strips made more sense to Rainey than trying to dismantle the plane to harvest wiring. Creston had complemented Rainey for his suggestion while inwardly kicking himself for not thinking of it first.

They had agreed the sides of the raft would be approximately fifteen feet long and the front and back ten to twelve feet across. They had no basis for the size other than a guess as to what might be right. The shorter palms were placed across the ends of the longer palms and tied together with two strips of leather at each intersection. The first attempt did not prove satisfactory to either of them. They pulled the leather straps as tight as possible but the joints were not firm enough, much like two pipes bolted together wobble and are less secure when the nut is not tight enough. Rainey struggled to untie the leather straps while Creston returned to the plane for the hammer and largest screwdriver.

Creston chiseled a six inch wide notch about twelve inches from the end of a longer palm. He labored for almost an hour and was able to notch two ends. Rainey took over for the next two, sweating as he worked, his arms weary from the unfamiliar hammering motion, but accomplishing his task in about the same amount of time as Creston. They took turns notching the palms until all were finished and the logs intersected more securely. Again Rainey and Creston tied the leather strips around the palms and secured them together, this time confident the logs would remain in place.

Their next step was to place four limbs across what they decided was the front of the frame and four across the back. The smaller limbs proved easier to secure to the larger palms and did not require notching to hold firm. The sides had ten limbs each crossed on top of the front and back limbs. All were strapped together with shorter pieces of leather. After all the limbs were tied in place an opening in the center of the raft remained. It was large enough to accommodate the small inflatable raft.

There was less than two hours until darkness shrouded the island. The building of the raft had been encouraging, but as they stood looking at the vast ocean stretched out beyond the reef, the size of the raft caused them to question their decision of setting to sea. With a tilt of his head Rainey indicated they should return to the plane. They walked back, not speaking, each deep in thought about what was left to do and what might be ahead of them.

Amy had been sitting patiently waiting for Rainey and Creston to return. Two large fish, grayish brown in color, large mouthed with oversized, fleshy lips had been placed on the sand close to her feet. Creston plopped down next to Amy. His head fell back and his eyes closed. Rainey took three refilled bottles of water from the plane, grabbed a large knife and returned to where Amy and Creston sat. Too exhausted to do anything more, Rainey lifted the larger fish by placing two fingers into the gills, sliced it open, filleted a strip of flesh and handed it to Amy. He did the same to the other side of the fish and handed the filet to Creston. Without saying anything Rainey raised the fish to his mouth and nibbled at the remaining raw flesh. They consumed the second fish and sat in a silence familiar to Amy, a silence she had known for over thirty years.

CHAPTER THIRTY

Floatation cushions had been strapped to the underside of the smaller limbs to give the raft as much buoyancy as possible. Two eight foot long limbs had been formed into a V and strapped to the left side of the raft near the center of the opening for the inflatable raft. Two additional eight foot limbs were similarly secured to the right side. Rainey had taken their largest blanket and tied it to the V limbs. When raised they would provide shade from the intense sun, but were easily folded down. Cargo netting from the hold of the plane was used to tie up their supplies of water bottles and food. The raft was completed. Rainey and Creston had checked the straps, and then checked them again. All was secure and tight and they were calmed by their accomplishment. They had thought of and considered every detail except how heavy the raft had become as a single unit, and how difficult it would be to move it the twenty feet to the inlet. Rainey checked all the ties one more time.

"I'm impressed," Rainey said. "I never figured you for one to improvise and construct something."

"You forget my grandfather made the family fortune by improvising, making things happen even when everyone else said they couldn't be done. He spoiled me but at the same time he taught me much that I've been able to use. I don't know how many stories he told me about the oil companies needing something done and when all the others gave up somehow he almost always managed. He mellowed in his old age, had more patience with me than he'd had with my father. Later, I could tell it in my grandfather's eyes, the regret for missing the time he should have spent with my father. That's why my dad and I have been so close. He didn't want to make the mistakes his dad made." Creston looked down for a moment. Looking back up he said, "And none of this has anything to do with the raft."

"Well I'm glad you learned from him. I don't think I would have figured this out on my own. I'm surprised you didn't share some helpful suggestions before."

"You had it all under control and figured out on your own by the time I was well enough to help. I think you'd survive being lost in the wilderness with nothing but a Swiss Army knife," Creston said.

"Let's get this raft into the water."

Rainey lifted and pulled while Creston lifted and pushed, moving the raft less than two feet at a time, but it was progress. They were cautious and slow as they moved the raft, studying it for faults. They knew the ocean was powerful and would prove ruthless.

An hour after they had started moving the raft they were able to float it in the cove described in the journal as the unloading area for the Japanese war ship. The raft would sit on the water for two days, secured by a long rope tied to the nearest palm tree, being watched and checked for signs of weaknesses. The final touch before loading the minimal supplies would be to place the inflatable raft into the center opening and secure it to the frame.

"Amy has been scarce," Creston said as they worked around the plane, searching for anything they could take with them.

"I think she's scared. She's been watching us build the raft at the inlet, the same place she took her parents to sea after they died. She doesn't understand what we're doing."

"We'd tell her if she'd show up. But she still won't understand," Creston said.

"Amy isn't stupid. She's uneducated and hasn't seen much, but she watches us and learns from what we do. It bothers me to think we have to leave her here."

"I'm fairly certain about where we are. With a little luck, no, with a lot of luck and good weather we might be out there for less than a week. In a month we'll be back here to get her. Can you imagine how the world will take to her, considering who her mom was, and all she's been through? What do you know about Amelia Earhart?" Creston asked.

"Not much, probably as much as the next guy."

"She's a legend in aviation circles, at least with the old flyers. But it's all the same rhetoric. Everyone knows she took off trying to be the first woman to circle the globe in a plane. She got lost and was never found. But there's more to the story. Her life was complicated but she was strong willed, forceful and determined. She almost made it but she became a bigger celebrity because of her disappearance. More so than if she had succeeded."

"I don't think we can…"

"Can't do what?" Creston interrupted. "You're not saying we shouldn't come back for Amy are you?"

"No, I'm not saying we don't come back. What I *am* saying is the world would tear her apart. We can't dump her in the real world. She wouldn't survive. They'll examine her, poke her all over, hook her up to machines, take constant readings of her temperature, pulse, blood pressure, and anything else they can think to do. They'll ask her a thousand questions about her mother and father she can't possibly answer. They'll try to compare her to Amelia, try to make some big dramatic story about destiny, fate, whatever. They won't give a shit about her. She'll be a big experiment. And when they put her in the psyche ward of Charity Hospital they'll abandon her. We can't let that happen."

"You're kidding me, right? You can't be serious. The story of the century and you want to suppress it, make like it doesn't exist, like it's a foolish dream you can't explain to someone. What the hell are you thinking?"

"I'm thinking about Amy."

Creston thought for a moment. "I hate it when you're right. But worse, I should have figured this out before you."

"Why? You saying you're smarter than me?"

"No, I'm not saying I'm smarter." Creston hesitated. "My mother made sure I went to several therapists when I was growing up. Seeing a therapist was a status symbol, or so my mother thought. They weren't too bad, and a couple were even fun to talk with at times. But you're right, it won't be about Amy. So I guess this changes things. Do we still come back for her or keep this to ourselves?"

"I say we come back, but it's up to you since I don't know where we are or how we would get back."

Rainey and Creston finished gathering all the supplies for the raft. Anxiety gripped Rainey as he examined and reexamined all they had gathered for the trip. He worried the supplies were not enough to last a week but it was all they could take. They had been on the island for over a month and there had not been one sighting of a plane or ship so they had no choice. In two days, at low tide, they would cast off and pray for a miracle.

The morning sun of the next day woke Rainey from a sound sleep. Constructing the raft had pushed him to the point of exhaustion and he did not wake before the rising sun as he had become accustomed. Their frugalness with the coffee afforded them more than enough for the next two days. Rainey got up and went about making the coffee, waking Creston.

Rainey and Creston stood on the beach at the inlet, watching the raft gently bob up and down with the subtle movement of the calm afternoon water. The raft was holding strong, ready for the supplies to be loaded and secured to the decking. Rainey ran his hand through his long, scraggly hair, covered his mouth, and thought for a moment before speaking.

"We forgot a critical part."

"What are you talking about? What'd we forget?" asked Creston.

"We have no way to steer or maneuver the raft. We need a rudder or a tiller like on a sailboat. The inflatable raft has a small paddle but it won't be good for anything other than trying to swat away an overly zealous shark or two, and not much good for that. Without a tiller we drift, and what's to stop us from drifting onto another island?"

"Why didn't you think of this earlier?" Creston said. "We can't afford any more delays."

Rainey ignored Creston's frustration. "We better get busy," Rainey said. "One way or another we still sail tomorrow."

Rainey headed toward the thick of the trees where they had found numerous fallen branches. Stopping abruptly, almost causing Creston to bump into him, Rainey turned around.

"There's no sense in both of us looking for one tree limb. Go back to the plane and find something to use as the rudder, maybe another metal seat-back and bring it here with more of the leather straps. We don't have much time. We've made the commitment and I'm ready."

Three hours later Rainey and Creston had fashioned a tiller and rudder from two tree limbs and a piece of flooring from the cargo hold. Using the pointed Phillips screwdriver and hammer, Creston had made a square pattern of four holes in one corner of the rudder and then a similar pattern of holes near the trailing edge. The leather strips were laced through the holes and around both limbs, firmly securing the metal. Two longer strips of leather were made into small loops large enough for the tiller limbs to slide through. The loops were secured around the rear log and should one become loose the second would hopefully remain tied. A twelve inch limb was also tied perpendicular between the tiller limbs to prevent it from slipping through the loops.

"Low tide should be about mid-morning. We'll be able to walk along the side of the inlet and pull the raft to the edge of the reef and launch from there. Using the tiller in a back and forth pattern we should be able to put to sea and not be pushed back to the island," Creston said.

"You sound pretty sure of this. We're going to need luck, some good weather, and God smiling on us, but we can make it."

"Let's find Amy and spend the evening with her. We'll have time in the morning to load the raft and still make low tide," Creston said. He moved in the direction of the compound with purpose in his walk.

Amy was moving lithely, almost poetically, as she tended to her compound, picking at weed-like foliage. She stopped when she noticed Rainey and Creston. As if they weren't there she turned back to her task at hand. They looked at each other and Rainey shrugged his shoulders. Creston nodded and his eyes followed Amy's movements.

"She can tell we're leaving," Rainey said. "Her attitude is as if we were never here. I'd guess a sort of self preservation. She's going back to her life of the last thirty plus years alone. She might be the only person I've ever known who has no concept of reality, or at least no concept of our reality. Maybe we shouldn't come back."

"It's too late. We have a plan and I say we stick to it."

"Do we have a plan?" Rainey asked. "What's our plan? To come flying back here and rescue her, to take her away from all this and bring her back to *our* civilization."

"Damn Rainey, what's gotten into you? We've already discussed this. So yes, we have a plan. But it's not complete. We have more to work out but not here. When we get back to New Orleans we'll work out the rest of the details, including how we can convince Amy to leave with us, which, by the way, won't be easy."

Rainey was second guessing their decision to leave, but knew if they stayed he would be second guessing that decision as well. The odds of their survival were against them, and he knew it.

"You're thinking too much, as usual," Creston said.

"Maybe so, but let me ask you something. Have you ever faced death? I mean not just thought about it but stared it in the face?"

Creston looked around the compound deep in thought and then said, "When you found me after the plane crash, when I was leaning against the palm tree, I thought I was already dead. Not then, but in a matter of time I knew I would take my last breath and it would be over. I assumed you were dead, because of me. I had contributed to your death, and it made me give up. But as usual, you show up and try to make it all right, like nothing bad is going to happen. I couldn't even die in peace. You drag me back to the plane and patch me up. So yeah, I guess I've faced death. I can tell you I'm not ready to face it again. We'll figure out what to do about Amy after we get home." Creston watched Amy for a minute. "I don't think she's in a big hurry."

Creston's explanation and confidence was partially reassuring. Fear is a good thing, Rainey thought. It would keep them from making fatal mistakes. Rainey looked at Amy and then motioned for Creston to follow him back to the plane.

Rainey's internal clock was back on schedule and woke him before sunrise. He sat up and watched the eastern sky start the change from a deep black into a calming orange pushed by a hint of blue creeping in from a later time of day in a different time zone, a different world miles away. There were no clouds and Rainey watched as the stars disappeared, almost row by row. There was time for a final cup of island coffee so he rose to start their journey. The aroma of the coffee coupled with the increasing brightness of the morning woke Creston. He moved toward Rainey and helped himself to the coffee.

The typical morning breeze was absent and the air was still. Rainey's senses, while on the island, had become more acute. Waves breaking over the reef, a hundred yards from where he sat, thundered, and yet at home he had been oblivious to a running faucet a few feet away. Some favorite aromas such as coffee brewing at Café du Monde, the chili from the Lucky Dog vendor selling hot dogs on Canal Street, or the heavy grease from fried shrimp and oysters in the French Quarter were hard to miss because he would seek them out. But he often was unaware of the heady aroma of magnolias in the air, or the night blooming jasmine growing on a fence he walked by on his way home. He attributed this new sensitive awareness to the absence of daily distractions, a slower pace and because he had come to appreciate the purity of his setting. Even though the air was still and the sky cloudless, Rainey knew when a morning shower was an hour away.

"Rain's coming," Rainey said as he and Creston stood and studied the horizon while drinking their coffee.

"Yep, but it'll pass before we lose the tide."

"Are you scared?" Rainey asked.

"Sure I'm a little scared. But I'm more scared of staying, dying here years from now, never being found."

"We'll be a speck on the ocean, almost like a grain of sand on the beach."

"We found a needle in the haystack," Creston said. "I'm ready to take the chance."

"We'll make it. Somehow, someway, we'll make it."

It took several trips before they had water, coconuts less the outer husk, mangos and lemons, a few cans of soup, and candy loaded onto the raft. Creston had inflated the two man raft and secured it into the center opening. The small raft also came with a kit containing a whistle, mirror, and a flare gun. Rainey studied the raft almost as one might admire a new car, thinking it looked smaller floating in the water than it did on the beach. The quick drop in air temperature caused him to look up. The anticipated rain came and the intense storm showered down on them fiercely. Rainey tilted his head back and stretched his arms out to his side, and remained still for several minutes, enjoying the last shower he would take for a while. Twenty minutes after the rain started it came to an abrupt end as the large gray cloud, resembling a huge dirigible, lumbered across the sky and headed out to sea, moving in a southern direction. They checked all the straps. Rainey pulled hard on all the joints. Each held firm and remained tight and secure. Creston walked across the raft, testing the limbs, shifting his weight from side to side. The raft dipped, listing slightly but not sinking. He nodded while stepping off the raft. Rainey and Creston returned to the plane for a final inspection of all they were leaving.

"Nothing's been missed. All the supplies and gear are stowed in the plane."

"I'll feel better when the site is in order," Rainey said. "Especially since we'll be coming back."

"I thought you were procrastinating for some reason."

"I didn't want it to look like an abandoned post, like someone left in a hurry. It's secure, and I'm ready."

Creston looked at Rainey and held up the last piece of equipment they would take. "The compass Big O gave me," he said. "Maybe the most crucial piece of equipment we have. Plus, I wouldn't leave it behind anyway."

Rainey stared at the ground thinking of Big O, New Orleans, Leslie, and his mother. He was far away in a second. Creston slapped him on the shoulder and his mind cleared. As Rainey looked up Amy was approaching. They watched her, neither of them moving.

"You…go?" Amy asked.

"Creston and I must leave," Rainey said. Amy turned to walk off.

"Wait!" Creston yelled. "Amy, stop and wait a minute."

Amy stopped but did not turn around. Rainey approached and put his hand on her shoulder, gently, like approaching a stranger for directions or to ask for help. Her tenseness emanated into him, but he did not remove his hand.

"Amy," he said, "I don't expect you to understand what's going on. And, I don't expect you to believe in miracles. But I do, I believe in miracles. I believe in God and I believe it's a miracle from God Creston and I are here. We survived and found you so the miracle won't end, not here. Creston and I will make it home. And after we do, we'll come back for you." Rainey thought for a moment. "I promise, we *will* come back."

Creston watched Amy. From her expression it was obvious she did not comprehend what Rainey had said. Rainey stepped closer to Amy, wrapped his arms around her and pulled her into him. She stood with her arms stiff at her sides. Tentatively, and with an awkward movement, Amy placed her arms around Rainey's waist.

"Hey, this is real cute but we have a mission, and it's time to get started," Creston said. Rainey released Amy and moved closer to Creston. "The tide's falling and we have to make it out of the inlet before it starts rising again. If not, we'll lose a day. We'd never be able to fight the incoming tide and get past the surge at the opening of the reef."

A warm, silky breeze rustled through the trees and the time to leave had come. Rainey labored to breathe, his heart raced, and fear of the unknown gripped him. His confidence of a few minutes ago had deserted him and he was filled with doubt.

"Rainey, you don't look good," Creston said. "Don't go south on me, pal. Almost since the day I met you I've relied on you to keep me down to earth, grounded as they say. The first night we met, and the big fight in the Quarter, you kept it together." Creston placed his hand on Rainey's shoulder. "We can do this."

Rainey squared his shoulders and straightened his back. "You're full of shit, but it's working." Amy had moved away, headed back to her compound. "Amy, take care of all of this until we get back." He looked at Creston and motioned toward the reef. "Let's go. It's not gonna get any better than right now."

Low tide exposed the reef for several hours each day. The slippery, algae covered, grey-green surface made walking difficult. Each step was calculated, either stepping around a tidal pool or over the many holes scattered throughout the reef. Several times Rainey and Creston lost their footing and slipped as they pulled the raft through the water of the inlet. It took an hour to cover the two hundred yards from the beach to the edge of the ocean.

The two friends stood less than ten feet from where the outside edge of the reef plunged hundreds of feet to the ocean floor. Rainey looked back toward the beach, knowing he would not see Amy. Turning, he inhaled deeply, and then entered the water of the inlet. The rear of the raft was the easiest spot to climb on board. He hoisted himself up and sat on the larger palm log. The raft dipped lower into the water than he had anticipated and for a moment he was thrown off balance. He steadied himself as the raft leveled and then inched his way forward. The inflatable raft was a two man version but it looked too small for both of them over an extended period of time. Rainey dropped into the center raft, grabbed the tiller and motioned for Creston to board. Creston pulled the raft tight to the reef, took two steps across the smaller branches and plopped down. Rainey felt the craft rise several inches and move forward into open water as he maneuvered the tiller back and forth.

CHAPTER THIRTY ONE

Amy walked among the remains of Rainey's and Creston's time on the island. Her feet tread softly, gently slicing through the sand where they had sat, ate, talked, and slept. She looked at everything, touching certain objects as if making sure they were real, and not understanding much of anything since the day Rainey had stumbled upon her. Two other people had been in her life and were gone. She no longer understood all she remembered. Her solitary confinement on the island had been like living in a well, unable to emerge until Rainey and Creston arrived. With their departure, she was plunged back into her well of solitude.

Amy turned away from the camp, took several steps toward her compound, and then stopped. In her mind's eye everything behind was gone, the plane, the fire pit, refuse, all of it and she was again alone.

The rising tide first brought small waves lapping over the reef. They would increase and intensify until high tide culminated, again covered the reef and larger waves pounded repeatedly until the tide started to fall. Amy watched the inlet Rainey and Creston had sailed from for several hours. When the tide had risen completely she walked to the other side of the island, blocking out all that had happened. The lagoon was calm and she was again in her own world, as she had been for years and years.

Two days and two nights at sea, and they had seen nothing. The weather had cooperated, almost to a fault. The massive Pacific Ocean had been calm, feeling more like a small lake than an endless sea, and their movement was practically undetectable. Rainey thought of the doldrums sailors wrote about. The calm with nonexistent winds had stranded many sailors before them. The ocean's vastness consumed them like they were in a giant plastic bubble. Neither he nor Creston mentioned it, but both knew they would not survive many days like this.

It was impossible to calculate how far they had traveled in the two days. The island had disappeared from view several hours after launching. Rainey worked the tiller back and forth more out of boredom than necessity. Late in the evening of day two the raft entered an ocean current and it moved them, albeit slow and almost undetectable, in a northeast direction. Creston would check his compass to a point of annoyance, each time repeating their direction and stating they were on course. Several times a day they would change positions and Creston would man the tiller. Rainey would check the compass and shake his head, having no idea if they were sailing toward being rescued or farther into the emptiness.

During the hottest part of the day they lifted the V shaped limbs into an upright position raising the blanket to provide cover from the burning sun. The limbs were secured with long strips of leather to the front and back at a forty five degree angle, giving resistance each way, holding them in place. They had eaten little and drank sparingly as well. Conserving their supplies was paramount, and the first two days had proven this. Rainey had taken a positive attitude onto the raft as they launched, but the endless drifting had erased his hope. Rainey feared they might be adrift for weeks, adrift beyond survival.

"We had no choice. We had to do this," Creston said as he looked toward the setting sun. The orange sky was clear and stretched beyond the horizon.

"Yes, I know."

"Well you haven't said anything all day, and you look like you're feeling sorry for yourself. If we had stayed on the island we'd be standing on the beach convincing ourselves to try. So, here we are."

A sense of dismay had settled upon Rainey like a heavy fog. What was the point in discussing it? He turned toward Creston and noticed the grim look. In a moment, his shame replaced his lack of courage.

"Jesus, Rainey you look worse than a moment ago," Creston said.

Rainey looked out to sea, thought for a moment and then smiled. "Two days out here and I've been so consumed with myself I've even forgotten to pray, to ask for help."

"Well, get busy pal. God helps those who help themselves, right?" Creston chided Rainey, his grin almost appearing.

"Of course, if God is ready for us then there's nothing we can do. You're aware of this, aren't you?" Rainey said.

"NOT the encouragement I was looking for."

Rainey turned his head toward the horizon where the sun was fast disappearing. Tonight would be a good night despite the cramped conditions. The sky was filled with stars, crowding the heavens, almost appearing in layer upon layer, with the occasional renegade shooting star breaking free to race across the sky. He inhaled deeply, held his breath, his lungs pressing against his ribs, and the feeling of life flooding his senses.

"A storm is coming. Probably hit us before morning."

"The smell is in the air," Creston responded.

The first wave broke over the raft, drenching Rainey and Creston like they had passed under a waterfall. They awoke, trying to sit up as their legs tangled and they fell to the side, pushing their arms through the small limbs on the side of the raft. The second wave crashed over them and filled the inflatable raft with water before they had time to right themselves. Rainey grabbed the tiller and started moving it back and forth, at first much too hard causing the limb to bend and almost break. Sitting in water to his waist he backed off the tiller and held it firmly in place. His face dripped with the salty residue of the waves, and as soon as he wiped it from his face, another wave drenched them. The raft strained under the movement of the ocean and Rainey prayed the leather straps would hold. The sky was dark as a canvas of storm clouds obscured the moon and stars. Rainey and Creston could not see the next wave about to pour over them. Cold rain pelted them and they shivered until a wave of warmer ocean water washed over them.

Rainey managed to maneuver the raft perpendicular to the waves, and as he held firm to the tiller the raft surged forward with each swell of ocean. Creston sat upright, watching Rainey as they rode each new wave. The sun was rising and hints of light filtered through the dark clouds disrupting the veil of darkness. Creston watched the ocean rising behind them and Rainey panicked when Creston's eyes flashed wide open. Before he was able to turn around a ten foot wall of water tumbled over them, pushed the raft below the surface and submerged them. Rainey swallowed a mouthful of sea water while flailing his arms trying to rise out of the sea. He coughed and choked, ingesting more water while the ocean refused to release them. The salt water burned his eyes but he kept them open, watching Creston. Rainey reached out and grabbed Creston's leg as the wave pushed Creston out of the smaller raft. With the top of his head exposed and his eyes barely even with the water his chest ached from lack of air. The tiller was wedged in Rainey's armpit, pressed against his side and he gripped it tightly. It was less than a minute before the raft rose and they emerged enough to breathe.

"Enough!" Creston yelled. "Give us a break."

Rainey took a deep breath, coughed, and said, "You ok?"

"I lost my grip on the small limb when the last wave hit. I panicked, thought I was going overboard."

"It was close," Rainey said.

Ten minutes later the rain stopped, the wind calmed down to a gentle but consistent breeze, and the ominous clouds had moved away, clearing the sky for the morning sun. A new, stronger current had caught the raft and was pushing it forward. Creston checked his compass and told Rainey to adjust the tiller to the right, steering the raft in a more northerly direction. The storm had pushed them almost due east and though they had no idea what lay due east,

Creston was committed to a northeast route. If correct this would at least bring them closer to the shipping lanes than an easterly course would.

Creston stretched out across the left side of the raft and checked all the leather strapping. Several had been stretched into a loose knot but none had broken or come untied. As Rainey manned the tiller Creston inspected the cargo netting. Some of the water bottles were lodged in the openings of the cargo net, but secure. He worked on the loose straps, untying them and then re-securing them, sat up in the inflatable raft and watched Rainey handle the tiller.

"Ease off the prayers," he said. "We got a little too much help with the storm."

"Don't let your humor be blasphemous," Rainey said. He leaned his head back, closed his eyes, and the warmth of the sun bathed him in comfort. With his head still drooped back, he opened his eyes, stared and then tried to focus. After a few seconds he recognized two contrails, miles overhead, and moving southwest.

"Headed to Australia I'd bet."

Creston looked up at the contrails. "Like the dying nomad said upon seeing the oasis, that might be the most beautiful thing I've ever seen."

Rainey laughed. "Dying nomad is the best you can come up with?" They watched the contrails disappear, but it did not dampen their spirits.

The rest of the third day was calm as the ocean current pushed the raft at a constant pace of at least five or six knots. A slight wake trailed from the raft, and their spirits were lifted.

Rainey believed luck was a relative thing and most of the time one had to make one's own. But on occasion, and without explanation, an exceptionally good day occurred. Things fall into place and unexpected positive risings occur such as a forgotten twenty dollar bill in a pocket, or a line at the bank with no waiting, a friend buying a beer, or a beautiful lady smiling for no reason. Day three was such a day.

A flying fish left the water, sailed over the bow of the raft and startled Rainey. Creston was sleeping and looked like an old man partaking of an afternoon nap. Another flying fish landed on the deck next to the inflatable raft and flopped several times before flipping itself back into the water. He sat up and scanned the ocean in the direction of the flying fish. In a minute another fish left the water and was sailing straight at him like an errant and wild pitch. Rainey defensively swatted at the fish and knocked it from the air into the inflatable raft. His mouth agape, he looked at the fish but did not know what his next move should be.

"Creston, wake up and give me a hand," Rainey yelled as he tried to watch the fish in the raft and look for another rising from the water.

Creston stirred and jumped as the fish flapped against his leg. "What the hell is it and where did it come from?" Before Rainey answered another fish was flying over the bow of the raft and disappeared into the ocean. Creston was fully awake, squirming and twisting in the confines of the inflatable raft, grabbing at the fish.

Rainey watched for more fish and yelled, "Quit playing around and grab the damn fish."

"This one's not going anywhere," Creston said. He gripped the fish, reached into the tool bag and brought out a knife. Another fish landed on the deck of the raft next to Creston and he stabbed the fish with the knife before it slipped through the limbs and back into the ocean. "And neither is this one," he said. Creston glanced at Rainey and said, "The proverbial better to be lucky than good, don't you think?"

Rainey shook his head and laughed. "Hey, you have the knife, clean the fish." He bowed his head and gave thanks.

"Maybe the worst tasting raw fish I've ever eaten," Rainey said. He was grateful for the fish but not sated of his hunger.

"I might have to agree with you. But I think it's time to try a little trolling."

"What are you talking about?" Rainey asked.

"Ok, we take the remains of the flying fish, the head and body, tie it to a piece of the fishing line I brought and trail it from the front of the raft. I'm sure a fish will come looking for the source of the scent. And with a little luck it won't be a shark but maybe a bigger, more edible fish."

"But how do we catch the fish? You didn't bring a hook."

"Yeah, pretty stupid, wasn't it?" Creston said. "As I hold onto the line and trail the fish in the water, you try to grab the tail of the new fish when it comes up for a closer look. You should be able to push your hand through the deck of the raft and maybe grab it before it gets away."

"Sure, because I have nothing better to do, otherwise I'd tell you what a lame idea this is." Rainey, impressed with Creston's initiative, refused to acknowledge this.

Several hours passed and they had not seen one fish approach the raft and the flying fish had long ago disappeared. Creston pulled in the fishing line and examined the bait. There was nothing left but the head and vertebrae. The bits of flesh left on the skeleton had washed away rendering the fish less a morsel for unsuspecting predators than when they first dropped it into the water.

"Let's drop the blanket," Rainey said. "It'll be dark in several hours. We can try again later. This isn't the first time I went fishing and came away with nothing to show for it."

Creston untied the V limbs and placed them toward the back of the raft. Rainey was right, there had been many fruitless fishing trips but this was different. Maybe they should have used one of the flying fish whole as bait he thought. They shared a coconut and piece of fruit. Each drank a bottle of water. Darkness fell across the ocean and they lay in the raft, marveling once again at the starry night.

A light rain fell but did not produce the violent seas they had experienced the night before. Rainey woke and straightened his back from the slumped over position his body had settled into as he slept. He let his head fall back exposing his face to the rain and rinsed the salty sea away. The rain was teasingly sweet in contrast to the sea water, the taste intoxicating, refreshing, and pure. Creston had awoken as well, and using his hands vigorously scrubbed his face in the falling rain. For twenty minutes they rubbed, rinsed, drank, and rinsed again until the rain had stopped. Their long, unkempt hair was matted to their scalps. Their untrimmed beards, after more than a month of growth, were scraggly and clumped from the excess water. Sunrise was several hours away. They settled back and dozed until the morning sun woke them.

Creston lifted the carcass of the flying fish, laughed at the unappetizing condition but threw the fish over the front of the raft and held onto the fishing line. Rainey, a look of doubt about him, said nothing.

Creston sat up and pointed, "Dorado!" he yelled.

Rainey turned toward the back of the raft and watched as a small Dorado swam toward the trailing bait. The fish was mere inches from the surface as it closed in on the bait. Rainey sat still, made no sudden movement, and watched as the flat, bull nose head of the fish came closer, its phosphorescent blue, green, yellow, and silver body gliding through the water like a perfect aquatic specimen. Rainey placed his hand into the water, careful not to startle the fish as it came along side the inflatable raft. With a quick sure movement he grabbed the tail of the fish, yanked it from the water, and placed it in the raft, refusing to let go. The two foot long fish thrashed and flopped, desperate to return to the water but Rainey would not relinquish his grip on their next meal.

"I don't think anyone would believe us if we told them we caught a fish with our bare hands," Rainey said.

"Let's see, we survived a plane crash, managed to stay alive on the island for over a month, discovered Amelia Earhart's fate, found her daughter, set to sea in a home made raft which is nothing close to seaworthy, and you think they won't believe we caught a fish, right?

"Look, have I told you lately... give me the damn knife, or would you like to take a bite as is?"

Rainey used the knife to slice open the Dorado. He held the fish over the side and disemboweled it easily with his fingers. The knife was dull but he managed to fillet a large slab of flesh from one side of the Dorado, handed it to Creston and then filleted the other side for himself.

"I would never have thought raw fish would be so sweet and moist," Rainey said. "The next challenge is to catch another fish, and hopefully one as tasty as the Dorado."

"This is turning out better than I expected. We have fresh fish to eat and a strong current pushing us along."

"I wonder how far we've traveled. Sometimes it's like we're barely moving. But we're making a small wake so I'm sure we are."

"Stay positive and keep praying," Creston said. "We could get spotted and picked up at any time."

Two more days passed and they drifted. Rainey manned the tiller but with far less enthusiasm and energy. Creston said little and had checked their bearing with the compass one time then ignored it. They remained on their northerly course, adrift and fearful they were moving farther away from being rescued.

By the sixth day they were hungry, thirsty, and weak. There had been no rain for two days and their water was gone. Their luck with catching fish had abandoned them and Rainey cursed the cruelness of the first catch. It had been too easy and it spawned anticipation that another catch would be forthcoming. They managed to lift the V limbs into place, secured them with the straps and settled in the shade of the blanket before slipping into unconsciousness.

CHAPTER THIRTY TWO

A sport-fishing cabin-cruiser pulled alongside the raft. It was early morning and there was no wind. The ocean was calm, slick like glass for miles. The deck hand from the boat knelt down on the transom of the vessel and stared under the blanket canopy trying to determine if the two people were alive.

"Captain, I can't tell if they still breathin or not," he yelled while keeping his eyes on Rainey and Creston. "But they ain't moving. I'm gonna need some help if we want to get them on board."

The captain yelled down from the flying bridge to the two men who had chartered the boat for an afternoon of deep sea fishing, "Gentlemen, the fishing for today is over. Throw Kimmy a line and tie the raft to the transom until we get those two on board. Kimmy, climb out on the raft and do your best to get those men closer to the boat. Mr. Green, Mr. Winslow, get down on the transom and help get them on board."

Kimmy, the first mate, managed to maneuver himself across the deck of the raft and lift Rainey up from the slumped over position. A gasp escaped Rainey as he fell back. Kimmy jumped, startled at the sudden noise, and then looked closely at Rainey. He watched for a few seconds and then Rainey labored for air. Before Kimmy turned around to check, Creston moaned and his body tilted to the side.

"Captain, they's both alive!" Kimmy yelled. "You two, help me here."

Rainey was first to be pulled on board. The two fishermen struggled with his limp body while Kimmy crept carefully back across the raft for Creston as the captain kept the boat steady from the flying bridge. With Kimmy's help Mr. Green and Mr. Winslow had an easier time bringing Creston on board and settling him on the cabin berth next to Rainey.

"Cut the raft away," the captain yelled to Kimmy. "It's twenty miles back to port and we can't get slowed down hauling it behind us."

The thirty six foot sport fishing vessel ran full throttle back to port, the twin diesel engines roaring, vibrating the boat and pushing its limits. The captain had radioed the harbor officer, requested an ambulance and gave an estimated time of arrival at the dock of forty to forty five minutes. Kimmy and the two fishermen tended to Rainey and Creston, wiping their faces and gently pressing the cool, wet towels to the swollen and sunburned lips. Drops of water ran down their cheeks, but a few drops at a time would caress the swollen tongue of each man, resulting in an unconscious attempt at suckling, much like a new puppy, eyes not yet open.

An ambulance waited at the dock, the two attendants searching the lagoon for a sign of the fishing boat. Less than forty minutes after radioing the harbor master the captain sped through the pass cut out of the reef and entered the lagoon running at twenty knots, much faster than the accepted speed for the calm, interior waters. A hard turn to starboard without cutting back on the throttle caused the sport fishing boat to kick up a large rooster tail before returning to plane and heading toward the dock. It was a half mile to the ell shaped pier. The captain raced past the end of the dock, cut back on the throttle to idle speed and turned the boat in a one eighty maneuver, positioning the boat less than ten feet from the side of the pier where the ambulance waited.

Large tire bumpers lined the edge of the pier at the water line and provided a cushion as the captain came in too fast and too hard. The momentum carried the boat into the tires before the captain reversed thrust and eased up to dock as he normally would. Kimmy jumped onto the pier holding a line and tied the boat firm to a bollard. The captain gripped the rails of the stairway, threw his feet out and slid down from the bridge without touching a single step.

Before Green and Winslow had time to lift Rainey or Creston from their berths the emergency medical technicians placed two stretchers on deck and were headed into the cabin. It took mere minutes to secure Rainey and Creston to the stretchers, lift them to the dock and then into the ambulance. Neither man had regained consciousness.

Rainey woke first, his eyelids fluttering enough before opening to perceive a hazy, dim light overhead. His head ached even as he lay still, and his arms were heavy and useless. He rolled his head to the right, his eyes following an intravenous tube running from his arm upward to a bag containing a clear liquid hanging from a stand next to the bed. The room had come into focus and Rainey knew he was in a hospital. He turned to his left. Creston lay still in another bed, apparently asleep.

In a gravely voice Rainey said, "Don't you die on me you son of a bitch. I'm not through with you yet." He stared at Creston, hoping for a sign of life.

"Shut up! I have a headache." Creston did not move.

Rainey turned and stared at the ceiling. "Where the hell are we?" he asked

"Perhaps I can help."

Rainey rolled his head on his pillow. A boyish looking man was standing in the doorway. He had tousled blonde hair but was neatly shaven, deeply tanned, and wore baggy, white surfer shorts, a lime green T shirt and black flip-flop sandals. He came into the room and stopped between the two beds.

"And you are...?" Rainey asked.

"Oh, right...I usually wear the doctor's coat but today is Sunday and there's not much happening on the island today so I didn't expect much activity. You guys are a real diversion from the usual Sunday here on the island. You came in about eleven this morning. I got the message on my pager while I was at mass. It said the captain's gig was bringing in two men found floating on a homemade raft in the ocean. You two caused a huge stir…" He looked at Creston. "Around here we don't get tourists or visitors… I must say, that's an interesting scar you have on your face. Sort of homemade looking, crude stitches to say the least."

Creston gave Rainey a sideways glance. Rainey refused to acknowledge him.

"Anyway, oh yeah, Father gave me a quizzical look when I got up to leave before communion. I assumed you guys were alive so I got here as quick as I could. The ambulance showed up about twenty minutes after me. Considering your ordeal, you two looked pretty good. Not nearly as bad as Wesley when Miracle Max had to bring him back to life. You know, *The Princess Bride*, anyway, you're a little dehydrated and weak but nothing too …"

"AND, you are…" Rainey repeated.

"Sorry, I can talk a little too much sometime, unusual for a doctor, or so I'm told. Dr. Neil Banyan, like the tree but purely a coincidence because I'm from California and not Hawaii. I'm the emergency room physician. Well, pretty much you name it and I'm responsible. Emergency room, deliver babies, patch up kids, even counsel some of the adults but honestly, most of them are older than me. I've been here almost a year and don't plan on leaving…"

"Doc, give it a rest. Where are we?" Rainey said. The constant talking came at his sensitive head like machine gun bursts.

"Look, you two need some rest and I'm talking too much."

A nurse came in, clearing her throat. Dr. Banyan stopped talking. She was tall, slightly plump in the bottom but not unattractively so, freckled, with dirty blond hair, also dark tanned, wearing a lab coat over blue Bermuda shorts and a flower print blouse. "Zip it for a few minutes or these guys are gonna want to get back on the raft. I'm Sue, your nurse."

"Ok," Creston said, "let me ask you. Where are we?"

Sue looked at Dr. Banyan, then turned back to Creston and said, "Kwajalein, the Marshall Islands. You're in the middle of the Pacific Ocean. This is the island hospital, small but all the latest equipment, the best the government can buy, so to speak. Who are you two?"

"Rainey, I mean Rainsford Dufrene, and he's Creston Labouef. What is Kwajalein?"

"We can explain later. You're probably not a history buff as most people aren't and don't..."

"World War Two, the Japanese held the island. It took us three days to get it away from them." Creston spoke softly. "It became a trust territory for the U.S. We took it from the natives, that is, I guess we didn't give it back, and turned it into a base of operations. The U.S. has had it ever since. They were doing some top secret stuff with ICBMs back in the 60s I think."

"Not bad," Sue said. "Still run by the military but lots of private contractor defense stuff going on but it ..."

"Hey," Dr. Banyan blurted. "I remember. We got word about you guys weeks ago. You two disappeared but nobody knew where. You were flying around the world but never made it across the Pacific. All the islands and bases were alerted but none of us gave you guys much hope. Even the navy gave up. They sent out search planes but they didn't have any idea as to where to look. This is incredible. Honestly, I never gave it another thought. You know how many people go missing every year, even though some of them do so by choice. Now, here you guys are and...."

"Neil, shut up for a minute," Sue said. "Is he right? Are you the guys he's talking about?"

"Yeah," Rainey said, "Look, we're both hungry and thirsty, and for some reason I need to use the bathroom."

Dr. Banyan nodded. "It's because of the IVs. We pumped lots of fluid into you guys. You were pretty out of it, plus you'd become dehydrated."

"Doc, go order them some food, and make sure it's light and cool. I'll help him into the bathroom." Sue looked at Rainey. "Don't get any ideas, I'm not gonna hold it for you."

Rainey blushed as she unhooked the IV bag, held it up high and helped him from the bed. Creston groaned as his head pounded.

CHAPTER THIRTY THREE

Leslie collapsed onto her sofa. She clutched the receiver to her chest, tears rolled down her cheeks, and she lost her breath, unable to speak. Paris Labouef waited patiently for Leslie to regain her composure.

"Leslie, are you there?" He waited for a moment, "Leslie?"

"Yes, yes, I'm here. Sorry, I…I wanted this phone call for so long but maybe I had given up any real hope and you call and I…I'm at a loss for what to say."

"Don't say anything, but please listen for a minute. I've already called Rainey's mother. And of course Creston's mother has been told, but no one else. I spoke with Creston late last night. He and Rainey are doing well considering what they've been through. Creston is going to call you in a few minutes. He wants to talk…"

"Where are they?" she blurted.

"Kwajalein, an island in the middle of the Pacific Ocean. They have been there for two days. There's a six hour time difference plus one day. So it's tomorrow over there. It's Wednesday, November 29th here but Thursday, November 30th where they are. It doesn't matter. What's important is he specifically asked you not tell anyone. He'll call soon. I have some arrangements to handle for their return. I'm sure he'll explain everything when he calls." Paris hung up without saying goodbye.

Ten minutes passed while Leslie chewed on her lower lip trying to think of what she would say when Creston called. The phone rang and her heart raced as she tried to catch her breath.

"Creston, is it you? Please tell me it is…"

"No, sorry, it's Rainey."

As hard as her heart pounded seconds before, it seemed to stop and her voice was lost. She blushed with heat as she stood up from the couch and stared into the receiver.

"You son of a bitch, you stood me up."

Rainey handed the phone to Creston. "Here, it's for you."

"Hi, Leslie." Creston listened to Leslie's sobbing.

Paris assumed the task of making arrangements for the return of Creston and Rainey. Normally, travel was worked out by Paris's assistant. He never meddled with the menial chore of making travel plans. But he would not ask anyone for help, feeling joy and purpose as he checked the list of things to do, excited for their return.

Creston's request was simple, but there were complications. Both men had left their wallets and passports in the plane. They had no identification and no money or credit cards. Paris made a phone call to his local state senator to whom he had made generous campaign contributions. He requested duplicate driver's licenses be made for Creston and Rainey and he needed them right away. The senator assured him the duplicates would be delivered to his home by currier from Baton Rouge before noon the next day. Paris enjoyed wielding his power, and like the old days, some things in Louisiana were still done with a phone call and a promise. U.S. Senator Allain Comeaux was his next call. A military attaché would meet the arriving plane from Kwajalein at the Honolulu airport and escort Creston and Rainey through the airport and deliver them to the Hyatt hotel. Because Kwajalein was a U.S. trust territory there would be no need for passports or customs clearance. It was going as well as Paris had expected it would.

CHAPTER THIRTY FOUR

Under different circumstances Rainey and Creston would have checked into the bachelor officer's quarters and spent the two days on the island waiting for the next flight to Hawaii. But Dr. Banyan wanted to keep a close eye on them. Their second day in the hospital showed remarkable recovery. Both men were rested, alert, and anxious to get up and move around, maybe see the island. Dr. Banyan provided them with surgical scrubs, hospital slippers, and walked them over to the small Base Exchange store. It took them less than twenty minutes to twice scrounge through the complete offering of men's clothing. Reluctantly, they both picked out a flowery Hawaiian shirt, pair of shorts, underwear and flip-flop sandals. The walk back to the hospital took less than ten minutes and neither man was satisfied with the minimal excursion.

"Doc, there must be something else we can do, right?" Creston said. "The island is small but maybe we could get a tour."

"Look, you wanted to keep it quiet, remember, and I'm trying to honor your request. And you do understand the military and island police are fully aware about this, don't you? People don't come and go on this island. However, the officer's club has a table for you tonight and some of the island big wigs including the army captain in charge would like you to join them for dinner. I took the liberty of telling them you were both well enough to attend and you'd be there. My advice is grin and bear it, go with the flow, so to speak. I'll tag along and try to bail you guys out if the questioning gets too intense. But as you've seen, the island is small and we don't get much excitement around here, so you two are in for a grilling. At least the food is good and there'll be plenty of drinks. And I strongly suggest you limit it to one and certainly no more than two beers, max. Your systems are still off and I don't want any problems with you before you catch your plane tomorrow."

"Do you ever say anything in two words or less?" Rainey asked.

"Nope." Dr. Banyan smiled and turned toward the door.

"Hey, what time is dinner?"

Dr. Banyan held up his right index finger and his left hand with all fingers extended indicating six o'clock, and said nothing as he left the room.

Lilly answered her page, identified herself and then listened as Paris Labouef explained who he was and why he was calling. Lilly told Paris she remembered Rainey and Creston and would be happy to accommodate the request. Two adjoining suites would be prepared for their arrival, with fully stocked bars, fruit baskets, robes, slippers and essential toiletries to make them comfortable. A chauffeured limousine would be at their disposal should they require one. Ten thousand dollars would be wired to the hotel in Creston's name to cover expenses. Lilly was to expect an overnight package and to hold it for Creston and Rainey. Lastly, Paris insisted all of this be kept quiet. Lilly promised the utmost discretion which pleased Paris.

The Boeing 737 arrived from Kwajalein at Honolulu International airport on December 1st, the day before it took off. The passengers disembarked while Rainey and Creston waited in the back row, the last to leave the plane. Clean shaven and hair freshly cut, courtesy of the barber on Kwajalein, they looked like mainland tourists dressed in Bermuda shorts, flowered Hawaiian shirts and flip-flop sandals. As they exited the Jet way two naval officers waited. Creston sensed they were the welcoming party.

"Captain Mike Striker, navy search and rescue from Pearl Harbor. It's good to meet you. This is Lieutenant Burns, media liaison to the local government. We have a car waiting downstairs to take you to the Hyatt hotel."

"Creston Labouef and this is Rainey Dufrene. Thanks for meeting us, but who asked you to meet us and...why?"

"Well," Captain Striker said, "your senator called our senator, asked for a favor and the navy wound up obliging. Normally I wouldn't be here, but the search and rescue mission I commanded looking for you two didn't pan out. So, I wanted to see you guys for myself. You're the exception. Most are never found."

"I imagine my dad is responsible for this," Creston said.

"There's an official car out front, courtesy of the U.S. Navy. We were asked to bring you to the Hyatt Hotel on Waikiki Beach." Lieutenant Burns led them through the concourse and out the doors to the waiting vehicle.

Rainey and Creston stood in the lobby of the Hyatt. They had come through Hawaii on October 11, left the next day, and now it was December 1st, a month and a half later. But in that short period they had experienced a life time. They crossed the lobby and approached the front desk.

"I don't suppose you being here is a coincidence," Creston said.

"I've been expecting you," Lilly said. She looked at Rainey, "My, you two are quite the adventurers aren't you?" She turned to Creston. "Mr. Labouef called and made arrangements for both of you. He also told me a small portion of the story, but not much. I'd love to hear about it. There was nothing on the news and nothing in the papers. Why do you suppose it's so hush, hush?"

"We're private citizens, and all of this is a private matter. It's very simple. And Mr. Labouef wants it quiet."

"You," she said, as she pointed at Rainey, "Call your mother, and call Leslie." Lilly slid a piece of paper across the counter with his mother's home phone number as well as Leslie's. Rainey stared at the paper before putting it in his shirt pocket.

"Two adjoining suites are ready for you. Your father insisted on the arrangements. Also, there's ten thousand dollars on deposit with the hotel for your incidentals. A limo will take you shopping for new clothes whenever you're ready. And this packet came for you this morning. I was instructed to hold it for you." Lilly handed Creston the large envelope.

Creston opened the envelope and emptied the contents on the counter. A duplicate driver's license for him and one for Rainey spilled out. Two United Airlines ticket holders came to rest on the counter as well. Creston picked up the folded piece of paper addressed to him and read it silently.

"Rainey, let's go up to the rooms." He turned to Lilly and said, "Have the limo out front for us in twenty minutes. Tell the driver we want to go to a local men's clothier. We'll need about a thousand dollars from the hotel safe. Put it in an envelope and wait for us here." He headed toward the elevators.

"He gets like this sometimes. Used to getting his way and can be a little forceful about it." Rainey looked at Lilly. "I'm sure it's what attracted you to him."

"Grown men can be such boys. I was attracted to you. I simply found him intriguing and interesting," Lilly said.

"Why didn't you tell me before? I could have died out there and never have known. You crushed me, had me thinking it was Creston you were interested in.

"Come back and see me if it doesn't work out with you and Leslie."

"Leslie and I are divorced. I want to make it work, but I'm not sure she's up to giving it another try."

Lilly nodded, "It's true what they say. The good ones are either married or gay. And you're still married, at least in your heart, which is what truly matters."

Rainey spoke to his mother for ten minutes with most of the time spent asking her not to cry. He hung up after promising to see her as soon as they landed in New Orleans, knowing she would be waiting at the airport. He stared at the phone and five minutes dragged on before he mustered the courage to dial. Leslie answered on the first ring, her voice tinged with anxiety.

"I'm sorry about the way I jumped on you but I was upset and I've been so worried about you and Creston. You have no idea what I've been through."

"Leslie, you have no idea what I've been through." Leslie's silence prompted him to continue. "But I don't want to get into it. There will be time to discuss it when we get back to New Orleans. Creston and I are going out to buy some clothes. We have a flight to San Diego in the morning, then a private jet to New Orleans. I think we'll be back late tomorrow night."

Leslie waited and then said, "Anything else you want to say?"

"Hey, did you call Big O and tell him about us?"

"NO! I did not call O. I was told not to say anything to anyone. And I try to do what you want."

"Come on Leslie, O would want to be one of the first to know. Call him right now and tell him. I can't believe you didn't tell him."

"Hey! Are your fingers broke? Why didn't you call him?"

"That's more like it," Rainey said. "Now, please call Big O. Tell him we should be home tomorrow night, barring another plane crash."

"I suppose you think you're being funny. Well, you're not, and I don't appreciate your humor. I'll call O, and I'll see you tomorrow night, even if you didn't ask me to meet you at the airport." Leslie slammed the phone down.

"Ouch," Rainey said and hung up. On the table by the window was the fruit basket elegantly displayed. Looking at it Rainey appreciated the painter's quest to capture it on canvas. He took a red delicious apple, turned toward the large picture window, looked out over Waikiki Beach and watched the waves breaking far offshore. The sweet juice of the apple exploded into his mouth with the first bite and the crunching of the fruit echoed in his ears.

CHAPTER THIRTY FIVE

Big O was talking to tourists in the habit of eating much earlier than people in New Orleans. It was six o'clock but the Oyster House was filling up with early diners. The street lights were coming on and dusk was settling over the French Quarter. Johnny Tap was anxious to get O's attention.

"Big O, telephone. I think it's important. Miss Leslie wants to talk wit you."

"Leslie?"

"Big O, I'm sorry I didn't call sooner, but I was told not to say anything. O, Rainey and Creston are in Hawaii. They should be home tomorrow night." Leslie waited for a response. In her mind's eye she saw his big grin and knew the diners had to wonder what was going on. "O, are you ok? I'm sorry I didn't call as soon as I knew. I found out yesterday and I was too crazy with relief and wonder. I think maybe I was preparing myself to give up on their coming back. I didn't want to give up, but then I reached a point at which I couldn't help thinking about it. Then the phone call came and I went into a spin. I'm sorry I didn't call you right away."

Big O stood for a moment, turned around and leaned back against the wall, looking up as he spoke to Leslie over the noise of the restaurant. "It's okay Leslie. It don't matter cause I knew they were okay. This is good, real good."

"They want to keep this quiet and don't want it spread around."

"Leslie, I don't have nobody to tell cept one person. And, she ain't gonna say nothing. But I have to tell her. Mama Mary would

235

never forgive me if I didn't call and tell her. It was her kept me going most of the time. Call me tomorrow when you know more."

Big O hung up and dialed Mama Mary's number. The phone rang several times before she picked up.

"Mama, it's O. Do I need to tell you or do you already know?"

"Oscar, I'm not a mind reader. Now tell me why you called."

"It's my friends, Rainey and Creston; they should be home tomorrow night. It's hard to believe after all this time but they coming home. Leslie called and told me a few minutes ago. I thought you'd want to know. You was right when you said they was still alive."

"Well, I think there's more to this story, O. Don't know what, but I guess we'll see what we see. You take care and let me know when they get home."

Big O hung up, puzzled by Mama Mary's lack of excitement, and wondered if she knew more than she could share with him. He shook it off and returned to his work with thoughts of his friends soon sitting at his oyster bar.

The 747 took off on time and climbed to cruising altitude for the flight to San Diego. Rainey settled into his first class seat, sipping on a glass of fresh pineapple juice the flight attendant had served prior to take off. He wondered why he didn't feel anxious about the return, why he was so content. Maybe it's the calm before the storm he thought, or maybe it would hit him right before landing in New Orleans. For the moment he was grateful pondering his confusion.

Breakfast was served and even though they had eaten at the Hyatt before leaving for the airport they accepted the food and ate again as if they had been gone ten years instead of a month and a half. The attendant offered them more food but this time they declined. Four days earlier they had been adrift at sea, unconscious and close to death. Dr. Banyan had marveled at their quick recovery but warned them about overdoing anything or exerting themselves too much at least for the next month or so. He had told them it would take several weeks for them to fully recover.

The plane would land in about five hours and less than an hour after landing they would be airborne again headed for New Orleans.

Creston pushed on Rainey and woke him up from a deep sleep. "We land in about thirty or forty minutes. You were out like a newborn taking a nap. I've been flirting with the flight attendant but she's married and not interested. Can you believe it? Not interested in me?"

"Yeah, I can. Let me out. I have to use the head. Never thought I'd be excited to see a real toilet."

The jumbo jet landed at Lindbergh Field. Creston remained in the plush seat, reclined and stared at the ceiling. Rainey watched his friend and refused to rush. They sat and listened to the passengers grab their carry on belongings, jostle for position like school children, and wait impatiently for the door of the large jet to open, and release them back into the tension of the real world. The plane emptied while Rainey and Creston remained seated.

"You two plan on returning to Hawaii?" the flight attendant asked. "It's a turnaround. The plane's headed back to Honolulu but with a new crew after a four hour layover." She handed each of them the small grip they had brought on board. "You two travel light."

"Not yet," Creston said, "but I'm starting to."

They exited the plane and followed the jet way to the lobby. They were again connected to the mainland, but both possessed a feeling of being worlds away.

The waiting area at the arriving gate was empty of passengers. A lone man stood twenty feet from the door of the jet way holding a small white placard with *C. Labouef* handwritten across it. He wore black slacks and a white shirt with gold striped epaulets atop the shoulders. Aviator sunglasses hung from the pocket.

"I'm Creston," he said extending his hand to the pilot. "And this is Rainey."

"Call me Rob," he said as he shook hands with Creston and then Rainey. "I'm your pilot. We can take the stairs down to ground level. I've got a cart we can drive over to the plane. Are you ready?"

It was three o'clock and the air was cool even though the sky was clear and the afternoon sun burned high overhead. Rainey closed his eyes and inhaled deeply. The wind blowing in from the ocean invaded his sense of smell with the familiar aroma of the sea and he hoped he would never become as desensitized as he had been.

Rainey and Creston looked at each other, hesitating at the entrance to the plane. Each knew what the other was thinking. The last month and a half rushed at them as they looked at the private charter jet and contemplated whether they should get on board. Rainey shrugged his shoulders thinking what are the odds of another crash? He moved in front of Creston and climbed the three steps into the cabin and Creston followed. The co-pilot, busy with pre-flight check out, turned back toward his passengers and waved without saying anything.

"Joey's our co-pilot and getting us ready for takeoff. Sometimes I think he's a better pilot than me, but then I come to my senses and realize how foolish I'm being." Rob's humor was lost on Joey but Creston appreciated the sparring and knew it was a regular routine with the two pilots.

"All set...captain," Joey said. "You are the captain, remember, even though I do all the work."

"It's good to be the captain," Rob responded. "Let's get moving. I'm sure you two are more than ready to get home. Strap in gentlemen and let's get this bird off the ground."

Takeoff was smooth. They climbed to thirty nine thousand feet and leveled off. The cabin was quiet except for the constant drone of the engines. The flight would arrive about nine o'clock, depending on the jet stream. Rob stepped into the cabin and offered Creston a turn at the pilot's seat but he declined, explaining his last flight had not ended well.

"Yeah, so I understand. But what happened out there?" Rob asked.

Creston thought about the question, recalling the time right before the crash. "I'm not real sure. Rainey started feeling tired and went to lie down. I was having trouble staying awake, got sleepy, like we weren't getting any oxygen. Next thing I know I'm fighting to right the plane and keep it from plunging into the sea. Somehow

I managed and we hit the water hard, sliding over the beach and into the trees."

Rainey listened and watched the pilot. The expression on Rob's face made Rainey think he knew more than he was sharing with Creston.

"You might want to check with head of maintenance at Total Aviation, where you kept your jet." Creston lifted his hands, palms up, unclear what Rob was referring to. "Total Aviation had a mechanic working for them who got fired and then arrested. He was tampering with some of the private jets, causing the systems to malfunction then making himself look good by finding the problem and fixing it. But, he went too far. One of the jets crashed at the airport on take off. No one was killed but there were injuries. It was traced back to his maintenance records. One of the NTSB guys started digging and several other reported close calls pointed at the same guy.

"The alarm didn't go off when we had low oxygen, and the masks didn't deploy," Rainey said. "Maybe this guy disabled the alarms and sabotaged the oxygen supply."

"Yeah, maybe so," Creston said. "We're solving all kinds of mysteries, aren't we?"

Rob nodded, stood up and turned back toward the cockpit where Joey had kept things under control.

Flying east accelerated the coming of night about the cabin. The rest of the flight was quiet. Rainey and Creston woke when they heard Rob yell they would be landing in twenty minutes.

They taxied to a hanger with the help of a lone, ground crewman directing the jet as it got closer. Before the door was opened a white limousine pulled up alongside of the jet. The driver got out and waited by the passenger door for Rainey and Creston. Inside the limo Paris Labouef sat impatiently. Mrs. Labouef sat demurely, belying her anxiousness to see her son.

"Uh, oh," Creston said as he moved in front of Rainey and started down the three small steps. "I should have been expecting this."

They stepped into a cool, light breeze blowing in from across Lake Ponchartrain. The orange-hued, high pressure sodium lights on the exterior of the hanger and other lights scattered around the fence line glowed, casting an upward haze, obscuring the stars and reminding them they were home. It was nine-thirty and Creston anticipated a long drawn out reunion, listening to his mother softly weep tears of joy while holding a lace embroidered handkerchief, and his father asking endless questions with unspoken but obvious castigation.

"There's no way we're going to get out of this," Creston said over his shoulder.

The driver held the door open. Creston stepped out of the way allowing Rainey to approach the open door first. "Coward," Rainey said as he stepped past Creston and got into the limousine.

Creston had seated himself across from his mother and father. Rainey's mother sat to Paris's right while Kimberly, Creston's mother, sat to his left. Rainey moved to the center of the seat and held out his hand to his mother, motioning for her to change seats and sit next to him. She leaned into Rainey as she settled next to him.

"Mom, we can't talk to each other if you don't stop crying," Rainey said.

"I've cried so much the last month I told myself no more crying. Then you get in and it starts all over." Joan wiped her tears.

"I'm sorry for what I put you through. I knew you were taking it hard. It was hard on me too, not being able to contact you, to tell you I was okay."

"Okay? You were not okay, alone in the middle of the ocean is not okay."

"Give your mother a kiss and a hug," Paris said. Creston leaned toward his mother.

"My God, Creston. What happened to your face? I've never seen such a hideous scar," Kimberly said.

"I cut my head in the crash. Rainey sewed me up." Creston sat back down.

"Well, this will never do. We'll get it fixed right away. I have the perfect plastic surgeon. He does excellent face work."

Creston leaned toward his mother, kissed her on the cheek and said, "I like it the way it is. No surgeon, no fixing anything." He then grasped his father's hand, leaned into him and put his left arm around Paris's shoulders. "Thanks for all you've done. Rainey and I have a pretty good idea what happened and why. I'll explain it later."

Rainey said nothing more but grasped his mother's hand and quietly thanked God for this moment.

"I'm sorry I worried you both so much. There were many times I didn't think we would be back here. I can't find the right words to say. Rainey and I…"

Paris had held up his hand, interrupting him. "Stop, we can discuss this further and in depth tomorrow. We all realize you and Rainey can't wait to inhale the aroma of the French Quarter. It was the trade off I made with your friends and why Leslie isn't here, although she objected the most. We wanted this first moment alone with you two, and they all wanted to come out here and greet you. I didn't want a big scene out here. It would have taken you and Rainey from us. They're waiting for you at the restaurant. The limo will drop you off, take us and Joan to our homes, and come back for you. But don't stay out too late. We have much to discuss tomorrow. Breakfast at our house, nine o'clock, and the limo will call for both of you. Rainey, your mother insists on coming early to help out and we can't convince her to relax and let us handle this." Paris looked at both men. "I must say, except for the scar you two look remarkably fit, especially considering your ordeal."

The limousine took Downman Road from the lakefront airport, merged onto the interstate and pulled up in front of the restaurant at ten-o-five. The French Quarter was as crowded as on a Mardi Gras weekend. Rainey and Creston stood outside the limo and marveled at how nothing had changed. A familiar odor of spilled beer mixed with stale gutter water wafted up, grabbed their sense of smell and Rainey nodded with remembrance of many years past. The crowd noise intensified, musicians performed on the corner at Bourbon Street, and Charley, the same legless man in a wheelchair, sat across the street with the same tin can he had held out to tourists and locals for years.

"Who said you can never go home again?" Creston asked.

"The Moody Blues," Rainey answered, "but, I don't think this is what they meant."

From behind them came a familiar loud voice. "Hey, would you two get in here!"

"Big O," Rainey whispered without turning around.

Creston placed his right arm around Rainey's shoulders and together they turned toward the open door and Big O.

CHAPTER THIRTY SIX

Saturday night in the quarter and even at ten o'clock the restaurant was packed. There were people at every table and half a dozen waiting outside, lined up along the wall in the direction of Bourbon Street. No one bothered to look up or pay any attention to Rainey and Creston as they entered. Big O stretched out his massive arms and drew both men into him by their necks. Big O released them, turned away and moved toward the oyster bar, his eyes watering.

"What we went through on the island will never leave us," Rainey said. "It'll always be tucked away in the back of our minds. But this, this had escaped me. Over twenty years you and I have been coming here and it was never a conscious thought like it should have been."

"The possibility of death will make you think of inconsequential things differently, the day to day things at the core of our being. I learned this on the island when I was leaning against the tree before you found me, when I thought it was over."

"I'm looking forward to life's challenges, but I hope the island doesn't get in the way, make me too cautious, afraid to take on a challenge."

"You're careful, but you'll answer the bell," Creston said. "Come on, let's get this party started."

"Hey you two," Big O yelled. O was pointing toward the rear of the main dining area where Leslie stood in the opening of the hall leading to the back tables. Rainey moved toward Leslie with Creston close behind him.

"Hello Leslie," Rainey said.

Leslie blocked the entrance to the hall. She threw her arms around Rainey's neck. He stood rigid, not sure how to proceed while Creston squeezed by Leslie, smacking Rainey on the butt as he went. He turned toward Leslie and delivered an equally hard smack with his hand to her backside, turned and walked straight into Natalie.

"Hey, partner, you're getting a little too familiar there aren't you?"

Creston stepped back. "And you might be…?" Creston asked.

"No might about it. I'm Natalie, and this lady is my friend." She relaxed her hard stare. "I'm kidding with ya, although you coulda been some drunk tourist lookin to cop a free feel. The quarter is full of em tonight. You must be Rainey or Creston, which is it?"

"Natalie, he's Creston. This is Rainey," Leslie said still holding onto him. "Guys, this is Natalie. I met her a couple of weeks ago, but it's like we've known each other for years. She grows on you… almost instantly."

"Yeah? Well you better lighten up your grip honey, I think he's starting to turn blue around the edges there. I might have to give him some CPR. But then, a little mouth to mouth might not be so bad." She turned toward the back room. "Come on, Cress, buy me a beer…my goodness, some scar you have there, and it looks kinda new." Grabbing Creston's hand she led him to the table in the back where they had impatiently waited since nine o'clock.

Creston looked over his shoulder at Leslie. She had released Rainey and was motioning for him to lead the way. Creston shook his head as he was led down the hall. He had lost control and it was a new experience for him.

The back room was as noisy and crowded as the front dining room. The waitresses hustled bringing food and drink to all the tables, clearing dishes to make room for more food and pitchers of beer, yelling at the busboys as well as rowdy patrons, and taking money and making change. And it was all a blur to Rainey.

"So, who's gonna go first?" Big O asked.

Creston stood and said, "Look, you all know the story. We crashed, built a raft, got rescued, and here we are. I don't think Rainey and I have any energy to go into the details, not tonight."

"We'll tell you the whole story," Rainey said. "But tonight we want to celebrate. Have a few beers, eat some New Orleans food, and be with the best friends we could have."

"Right, but we have to take it easy on the celebrating. Dr. Banyan, the one who got us back on track and checked us out, told us to take it easy, especially in New Orleans. He spent a couple of college breaks here," Creston said.

"I concur with the doc," Natalie said. "But the rest of us, we can make up for what you're missin."

Leslie looked at Creston. "You're right, we can wait on the details, but tell us one thing, how did the crash occur? It's so hard to believe you crashed. You, of all people, mister check and double check. I don't see it."

"Okay, fair enough," Creston said. "As it turns out, my jet was tampered with and intentionally made to have a malfunction. But the mechanic went a bit too far. So it wasn't totally pilot error. But I have to file a report with the feds. They're investigating several incidents including another crash."

"You're right, we don't have to go into this tonight," Big O said. "But I got to tell ya both, I was real bothered when y'all was reported missin. I'd stand behind the bar up front and get lost in my mind, not knowin if y'all was comin back. So I'm drinkin a beer to you guys tonight. I'm glad you're home." Big O lifted his glass and then drank half of it. "One more thing, I got someone I want you both to meet, not tonight, but soon."

"I agree with O. Let's drink and celebrate," Leslie said. "But don't go running off anytime soon."

Leslie, Big O, Creston, Natalie, and Rainey talked until midnight. Rainey and Creston heeded Dr. Banyan's advice, and took it easy on the oysters and beer, but with much difficulty. Both men were feeling almost claustrophobic.

"I need some fresh air," Rainey whispered to Leslie. He got up from the table and headed toward the front of the restaurant and then out the door onto Iberville street. The cool night air washed across his face and revived him. He placed his palm against a cast iron street-lamp post and steadied himself, took a deep breath and then moved across the street. He leaned against the building with his back hard to the brick wall. Bourbon Street was crowded with people in perpetual motion. Leslie was standing outside the door of the restaurant watching him with a worried look.

"What are you doing?" she yelled. "Why'd you leave the table?"

Rainey walked back across the street to Leslie. "I'm taking my life back," he said.

"What the hell do you mean? Rainey, you're driving me crazy."

Rainey leaned into Leslie and hugged her tighter than he had in years. "It means I want to be in control of my life again. Since the plane crash everything I've done has been a reaction. Survival instinct, trying to stay alive, getting by, so I want to do something positive, unprovoked." He leaned into Leslie and kissed her tenderly. "Something like that."

"Not the hottest kiss you've given me but it's a nice start."

"I need to take it slow. And I couldn't do anything in there with the others."

"Come on, they're waiting. But I expect another kiss, and soon."

The welcome home party lasted an hour longer than planned. At one o'clock the two guests of honor climbed into the limousine and fell into the plush seats as their heads spun from jet lag and the night's excitement. Leslie stood outside the open door of the limo waiting for Rainey to ask her to get in.

"Get in here," Natalie yelled. "You could freeze to death before these two speak up."

"I need to know you two get home safely," Leslie said. "I'll feel better when you're both tucked away, safe in your own beds."

Rainey let his head drop back against the plush leather seat. Dizziness engulfed him and in a second he was back on the beach of the island and disoriented. He righted himself, and the feeling disappeared.

The limousine pulled through the gate and stopped in front of Creston's townhouse condominium. Natalie got out and waited for Creston. He looked at Leslie.

"Natalie's an EMT and I thought it would be a good idea if she sat up with you tonight while you slept. You've been through so much and I'm worried abut you. It's your first night back. Precaution, nothing more." Creston glared at her, speechless and less than pleased.

Rainey smiled and said, "Hurry up and get out, your babysitter's waiting."

"Yeah, and if you don't change your attitude I'd say babysitter is about right," Natalie added.

"Go on, get out of here," Rainey said. "We have an early morning."

"Yeah, well looks like somebody else has a baby sitter, too," Creston said.

Rainey slouched down into the seat. Leslie's eyes burned into him like a branding iron. With his heart pounding, he was oblivious to the slam of the door and the acceleration of the limousine as it pulled away from the curb and made its way back onto the street.

Inside his apartment Rainey relaxed with a comfort borne of familiarity.

"You're about as subtle as a five alarm fire on Saturday night," Leslie said. "I don't think you could be more distant."

"Sorry," Rainey said. He walked toward his bedroom, hesitated as he looked at the wine bottle still on the counter in the kitchen, and then entered his room.

Rainey stripped off his clothes except the silk boxer shorts Creston had insisted they buy at the clothier in Honolulu. He grabbed the comforter and top sheet, threw them back and sat on the edge of his bed and stared at the open bedroom door.

"Sorry, is all you have to say?" Leslie asked.

"There's plenty I could say, and most of it would be wrong. Would you like me to say thanks, again?"

"No, you told me thanks, thanks for everything, as I recall. How considerate of you."

"Sometimes saying nothing is best," he said. "I'm dealing with things more complicated than you might understand. The island was small but it had become my entire world. I had accepted I might never be back. There were times I had given up and it left me empty. This is almost surreal. It'll pass, but like I told you earlier, I have to take it slow."

"This is funny. I wasn't offering anything and yet I feel like I'm being rejected."

"Rejected, I don't remember you being rejected the last time you were here."

"True but afterwards you made me feel like it was a mistake," Leslie said. "I didn't say anything about last time but..." Leslie stopped. "Never mind, it doesn't matter. I think you're right, let's get some sleep. I'll be on the couch if you need anything."

Rainey watched Leslie move from the doorway. The lights went out and he was lost in the darkness. His mind called out to Leslie but his voice was silent. "I miss the stars," he said softly.

The phone rang at eight o'clock. Rainey heard Leslie answer. His eyes opened and he stared at the ceiling.

Leslie appeared in the doorway. "It's time to get up," she said. "The limo will be here soon to take you to breakfast at the Labouefs house. I'm leaving." Leslie turned, stopped, turned back toward Rainey and said, "You talk in your sleep. Or rather, you mumble. I tried not to listen but you were loud.'

"What did I say?"

"You kept saying 'I'll be back' and then 'aim here' but more as a question. At first I thought you were saying Amy because aim here made no sense, especially since you're not a hunter. It was so mumbled I couldn't be sure what you were saying."

Rainey did not respond for fear of saying the wrong thing. He shook his head, but then thought of showering in his own bath and it comforted him for the moment.

"One more thing, you're welcome." Leslie turned and left the apartment.

The image in the full length closet mirror was laughable. The weight he had shed on the island showed in his clothes. The pants and shirt hung on his body. His stomach had gotten flat, his legs muscular from daily walks on the loose sand, and his butt was smaller and tighter. He imagined his clothes as a badge of honor for surviving the ordeal he and Creston had been through. And then his thoughts turned to Amy. He and Creston had made a vow to not mention her to anyone until they had a plan. Standing in front of the mirror he had an urgency to formulate a plan and start working it, but not without Creston.

The limousine was waiting when he walked out of his apartment into the cool morning, the sun shining brightly, the sky clear as new ice. The driver opened the door for Rainey and he entered. He took the seat across from Creston. The smell of new leather was strong and Rainey inhaled deeply.

"How was it last night?"

"I slept well," Rainey said. "Better than I expected. What about you?"

"Yeah, pretty good but not until I got Florence Nightingale to shut up and stop taking care of me," Creston said. "But she meant well. Told me Leslie and our parents were worried about us on our first night home and wanted us looked after. I'm not sure what the hell she meant."

"Leslie slept on the sofa. I didn't move until the phone rang this morning. She was upset when she left."

"Is Leslie what's bothering you?" Creston asked.

Rainey thought for a moment and then said, "Amy is what's bothering me. I think about her all the time and I worry about her and what might happen."

"You don't have to try and save the world," Creston said. "But it is one of your better traits. Amy can do fine without us for a while."

"Maybe she got upset with us leaving. But what's bothering me is I made a promise I can't keep without your help, and I'm not sure it's fair to ask you to go back."

"WE… got it, WE made a promise. You don't have to ask me anything. We're going back. I don't know how or when, but we're going. For once in my life I'm not sure where to start." Creston looked at the driver, hoping he had not heard their discussion.

Rainey clenched his jaw, nodded and said, "Like Scarecrow told Dorothy, I've always found it best to start at the beginning."

"You and your old movies."

The limousine pulled into a large driveway on St. Charles Ave. in the uptown garden district and stopped in front of a wrought-iron gate bordered by two large brick pilasters. An eight foot high, solid brick fence stretched out from each pilaster and encircled the property, obscuring the grounds and most of the lower level of the main house from the view of tourists walking along the avenue admiring the garden district homes. The driver entered a code on the push button pad and the gate rolled to the right, granting them access to the large Labouef mansion.

Rainey had been to the Labouef mansion many times for various events, including Thanksgiving, and once for an elaborate Christmas party Creston had hosted. He had always admired the house. The mansion dated back to 1878 and had been completely renovated twice, the last time by Mr. Labouef twenty years ago. A deep veranda fronted the house with large white columns supporting the second floor balcony. From the balcony the viewer was afforded a panorama of St. Charles Ave., the electric street cars, and the stately oak trees, most of which were well over one hundred years old. The mansion floors were solid wood finished with a clear acrylic compound and polished to a mirror-like sheen. The ceilings were fourteen feet high and one would feel small upon entering the rooms. Windows were strategically placed in opposing positions to allow for cross ventilation which was necessary in the days before air conditioning. The mansion was more than enough house for ten people, and yet it fit the Labouefs like a glove.

Breakfast was served in the solarium where Rainey's mother waited with the Labouefs. Eight places had been set for five people. Paris Labouef sat at the head of the table, Mrs. Labouef sat to his right and Rainey's mother next to her. Sunlight splashed through the solarium and bathed the room, not unlike an early morning on the island, Rainey thought. A large bowl of fresh fruit consisting of seedless watermelon chunks, strawberries, diced cantaloupe, sliced kiwi, and green grapes was the centerpiece on the large rectangular table. Ham, slices of bacon, and sausage patties covered a silver platter glistening in their own grease as the sunlight played across the table. Large biscuits, mounded on an identical silver platter, had been placed on the opposite side of the bowl of fruit beside a plate of Creole cream cheese. Coffee and orange juice had been poured and steam swirled upward from the coffee cups. Creston sat to his father's left, across from his mother, and Rainey sat next to Creston.

"What, no honey buns?" Rainey said.

"I suppose you think you're funny," Creston said.

"See, your problem is you have no sense of humor. No sense, and no humor."

Paris Labouef interrupted the repartee. "I am truly amazed at the ability of you two to revert back to your adolescence without so much as a thought or moment's hesitation. But then, maybe I shouldn't be surprised. Creston has more money than he will ever need. And Rainey couldn't care less about money, admittedly a trait I admire but can't grasp." Paris waited but only for a moment. "No reply? Good. Your mothers and I would like to hear your story, what happened and how you survived. And, how you managed to make it to a safe island."

The story flowed, but then would abruptly slow like a quiet creek. Rainey and Creston played off each other, each crediting the other with their survival, and neither placing blame. Paris, Kimberly, and Joan listened, concentrating on every word. There was little expression as they sat quietly until Rainey explained how he found Creston, and fearing he might die, dragged him to the plane, made him comfortable, and stitched his forehead. Kimberly looked at Creston and a tear rolled down her face as she was back in the reality of how close she came to losing her son. They refrained from interrupting but occasionally a clarification was needed as they would hurry in telling their story, omitting details understood by them, but lost on their audience.

After an hour Creston said, "And, here we are."

"Fascinating," said Paris. "Can I presume such carefree adventures are over for you two?" He watched their blank stares. "Yes... I didn't think so. However, since I have done as you requested and kept all of this quiet and out of the papers I am due some consideration. I don't care that you are both in your forties and grown men... the grown men part being questionable at times. I simply don't want you running off on these adventures anymore. Use a damn travel agent, for God's sake. I'd like to live a few more years and you two came close to putting us in our graves. Do you both understand?"

Rainey and Creston stared back at Paris Labouef then glanced over at their mothers. The silence was as uncomfortable as sitting in a confessional, searching for the words to say to the priest to make the list of sins less unappeasable.

"I see," Paris said. "Mary, would you come in here, please?"

Rainey and Creston looked at each other and then turned toward the sound of footsteps, a loud clicking noise made with the heels of a woman's shoes against the hardwood floor. Mama Mary entered the room and stopped next to Paris. Rainey watched her and was hit by the emanation of her understanding. Mama Mary smiled at Rainey as if she had known him for years. She glanced at the others and the tension in the room evaporated as soon as she spoke.

"So you two was the missing boys caused so much grief to all these people. I was sittin in the other room there and heard the whole story, and a wonderful story it was, too."

Rainey and Creston rose from their chairs. Mama Mary looked at Creston briefly but then locked on Rainey's face and delved deep into his eyes. She said nothing for several seconds, then smiled again as she confirmed her earlier intuition.

Creston stood, his mouth hanging open, then said, "What is this about, and who is this lady?"

"My name is Mary but some people call me Mama Mary. Like your friend Big O, he calls me Mama Mary. I ain't nobody, just an old lady been livin here in New Orleans all her life."

"Well, she left out one important detail," Paris said. "Some people believe Mary has a gift of seeing things, things other people don't see. Big O called on her when you two went missing."

Creston looked at his father and said, "Are you kidding? She's a fortune teller? I can't believe…

Rainey grabbed Creston's forearm and squeezed hard enough to leave impressions in his arm.

"HEY! Damn, that hurts," Creston yelped.

"It don't bother me none. Lots of people have the same reaction." Mary paused and then added in a stern, maternal voice, "But, I ain't no fortune teller." She turned toward Paris Labouef. "I don't think you got nothing to worry about with these two. I don't see nothing bad." She looked at Rainey again, then back at Paris and said, "I got to get to my shop in the French Market Mr. Paris so I'd like the ride we talked about."

"I'll have the driver bring you," Paris said.

"You're petty quick," Rainey asked. "Nothing else?"

"Honey, you been watching too much psychic TV. It's either there or it ain't." Mary shifted her shoulders back and said, "It was shore nice to meet you two. Leslie is a fine lady and did her best to take care of y'all while you was gone." She directed her next comment to Rainey. "Stop by my shop in the French Market and see me, soon."

Her words fell gently on Rainey like a warm mist. His eyes had locked with Mary's and he understood she knew.

"Boys, it's Sunday and the Saints are playing New England today. I'd like you to stay and watch the game with us," Paris said. "Your mothers deserve your time and presence today." Paris was used to making his point.

Rainey nodded as he thought about the Saints. He had always been a fan but not once while on the island had he thought about the Saints. With time he knew he would realize other things the island had temporarily robbed him of. The Saints won and life was a little more normal.

CHAPTER THIRTY SEVEN

Rainey picked up his phone and put it down several times before dialing Leslie's number. His stomach churned as each ring echoed through his head. On the seventh ring he was about to hang up when he heard the click of her phone as she picked up.

"Hello," she said after a moment, her voice emotionless.

Rainey hesitated, his confidence abandoning him, disappointment gripping his throat. "I didn't think you were home. I was about to hang up."

"Yeah, well I didn't think it was you and wasn't going to answer. But you're home, and I need to stop running my life around you."

"And Creston."

"What?" she asked.

"You were running your life around Creston, too," he responded.

"Damn you Rainey, this isn't about him. But I at least got paid to take care of most of his affairs." Leslie flushed with anger. "Look, your car is in your parking lot and the keys are in the kitchen drawer where you always kept them. It's Sunday evening and I'm not doing anything tonight. Drive over here and we can continue this conversation. Or not, it's up to you."

"I think I still have time to make the evening Mass at St. Louis Cathedral. Meet me there and we can continue this banter after Mass. I'd offer to buy you dinner but I don't have any cash on me, have no idea how much is in my account, and all my credit cards and stuff were left on the island."

"Well if your ego hadn't been so damned big, and if you'd have continued to bank with me then I'd have taken care of you too, and you'd know how much money is in your account." She waited, but all she heard was Rainey breathing into the phone. "I'll buy if you'll still have dinner with me," she said.

"I'll park at the Moon Walk. If I don't see you in the Cathedral then I'll figure you changed your mind."

"God, you're pissing me off," she said. Her irritation caused words to flow which otherwise would have remained unsaid.

Rainey heard the frustration in her words. He perceived a change in Leslie and he liked it. She was stronger than he remembered and he related this to himself. He was stronger, but also more aware of his vulnerability. Life was not guaranteed, and he had come to accept this. And listening to Leslie he reveled in it. He hung up without saying goodbye.

Jackson Square was usually quiet on a Sunday evening and this Sunday was typical. Many of the artists, tarot card readers, and street performers had gone for the day. The evening air was cool but the humidity was high and Rainey took comfort knowing he was home. He entered Jackson Square through the large gates on Decatur Street and crossed through the historic site toward the Cathedral. In the center of the square he stopped and looked up at the large bronze statue of Andrew Jackson, heroically seated atop a horse rearing up on two back legs. Jackson's right hand held his military head dress as if welcoming visitors while at the same time standing guard over the city. And he had stood guard, vigilant for more than a hundred years. Rainey inhaled deeply, the air rushing into his lungs. Many times, like this day, he had walked through the square, nodded to Old Hickory, and wound up in front of the cathedral. He pulled open the large wooden door and entered in time for the evening mass.

Rainey knelt in the aisle, genuflecting toward the Crucifix behind the altar, made the sign of the cross before rising and taking a seat in the last pew. He was alone. Most of the locals, tourists, and regular parishioners were seated toward the front of the Cathedral, closer to where the elderly priest would serve the mass and deliver his homily.

He sat quietly and remembered being ushered in by the nuns, and then being watched over by them. The front of the church, he thought, they always marched us to the front. It was an old habit he did not feel guilty about breaking. He enjoyed the different perspective and appreciated the Cathedral as never before. The ceiling, with its intricate hand painted murals and phrases in Latin towered over head. Light from the large chandeliers caused it to practically vibrate with life. There was no choir for the evening Mass and the two lofts were empty. Every whisper, cough and shuffle of feet echoed through the large Cathedral. Rainey remembered being a young boy, holding his father's hand, knowing no harm would come to him. The Mass was over in forty five minutes but Rainey lingered. He was the last to leave. As he stood and exited the pew he noticed Leslie in the far corner. He approached her and held out his hand.

"Tujague's, I'd like to eat at Tujague's tonight."

"So what do you want me to say? What do you want to hear?" Leslie said. She placed her fork in her plate. "Sometimes you can be so damn difficult. You sit there picking at the food, eating slower than I've ever seen and not saying anything. If I had ordered for you then you'd have said nothing at all."

"Maybe I simply want to enjoy the meal and…"

"And what?" she shot back at him.

"And maybe nothing. Being alive, and getting another chance…"

"Another chance," Leslie said interrupting him. "Interesting choice of words. Let's see, what *does* one have to do to get another chance?"

"Maybe one simply has to take a chance and not wait for it. I did and here I am, alive to tell about it."

Leslie looked down and realized the waiter had removed the dish of half eaten food and replaced it with a bowl of warm bread pudding covered in hot rum sauce. She picked up the dessert spoon, dipped it into the mushy, sweet treat and savored the first bite.

"I don't know you anymore, not like I thought I did. And I'm not going to make you promises I can't keep."

Her words jolted him as if someone had carelessly barged into his chair. Thoughts of Amy swarmed his consciousness and his stare became distant.

"What is it?" she asked.

"Nothing," he said. "I remembered...had a flashback, it's nothing." He straightened up in the chair. "I don't want any promises. A day at a time is all, a day at a time and see what happens."

"Rainey, there is something else I need to tell you."

"And I have things I need to tell you. But I'm asking you, not here, whatever it is. I'm still processing as much as I can, but it's difficult. Even though I was gone less than two months, it can feel like a lifetime." His eyes again lost their focus.

Leslie lifted her head, watching him drift in and out, wondering where he was or worse, where he wanted to be. "Where the hell do you keep going?"

"Please, pay the bill and let's leave. I'm tired and I'd like to get some sleep. Tomorrow is Monday and I think I still have a job. I plan to go into work and see if I can pick things up where I left off."

"I took a cab so I need you to bring me home. You can drop me off."

The ride to Leslie's house took fifteen minutes, most of it in silence. Rainey drove as if he were a chauffeur instead of an ex-husband. Leslie's smile concealed her anger, and the more she silently chastised herself for trying too hard the angrier she became. Rainey turned off St. Charles Avenue and drove toward the river, stopping in front of Leslie's uptown duplex.

"Don't bother walking me to the door. I can manage. It certainly isn't any colder outside than it is in here." Leslie opened the car door and slid her legs out, placing her feet on the curb without waiting for a response.

"There are things you don't understand and I'm not ready to explain," Rainey said loudly.

"Then there's no reason to explain to you the things *you* don't understand. But at least I was willing to try."

Rainey drove off toward Tchoupitoulas Street. He turned left and headed back into the Quarter with no purpose other than to drive and take in his city. Two hours later he pulled into the parking lot of his apartment.

CHAPTER THIRTY EIGHT

"So, what you're telling me is, I don't have a job anymore." Rainey sat across from his boss and watched him squirm in his chair.

"Look Rainey, you've been gone for two months and the truth is everybody gave up on you after a couple of weeks. We all thought you had died. Nobody expected you to return. Hey, I feel terrible about this and maybe there's something I can do or work out. But not today."

Abraham Capdeville sat restless in his chair as he spoke and Rainey refused to make it easy on him. Mr. Capdeville had been a good boss but his lack of compassion had kept him at a distance from most of the salesmen and Rainey was no exception.

"I hired a young guy to take your place three weeks ago. I can't cut him. It wouldn't look right."

"And not having a job for me after the ordeal I've been through does look right?" Rainey tried to contain himself but he was not successful.

"Let's be honest with each other," Rainey started. "You hired a new, young guy at a much smaller, fixed salary and gave him all my accounts. Accounts already generating high profit sales for the company, and when you switch him to commission it'll be at a reduced percentage. He'll never know the difference and the company will increase its profit margin." Rainey managed a Cheshire cat-like smile. "So, *Abe*, what about it?"

"Yeah, maybe you're right but I can't create another job or find some imaginary place for you. Private companies aren't like the government. The government gets bigger and bigger. People are added all the time but we can't work so carefree. We have to justify and account for all expenses to the last penny. I'd love to have you back, but I'm not sure when I can make it happen."

Rainey stood up. "Mr. Capdeville, no hard feelings, ok? Who knows what the future holds. I've got other business to take care of. By the way, I'm sure I have some money coming to me from my accounts before you wrote me off. Have accounting figure out how much and mail it to me, but don't take too long. I'd like it this week."

Rainey offered his hand to Abraham Capdeville. They shook and Rainey made his way out of the office leaving the tension behind. What's next he thought? He stopped at the receptionist's desk and used her phone to call Creston. They agreed to meet for lunch but Rainey made it clear Creston had to buy, especially with his new circumstances.

The weeks since their return were a blur. Creston had resumed managing his fortune and soon it was as if he had never been gone. But Rainey had become distant, and spent much of his days in his apartment. He contacted Leslie and his mother assuring them he was doing well and twice agreed to a quick visit. Big O had called and asked him to come to the restaurant. Rainey went one time, didn't eat, had one beer and left.

The Times-Picayune had kept the story of their return to a minimum, no doubt at the request of Paris Labouef. He had accompanied his request with a considerably generous donation to the paper's annual Christmas fund, and threatened a law suite based on the less than honest articles published about Rainey and Creston.

Club Louisiane occupied the top floor of a five story building on Canal Street. The private club dated back before the civil war. There existed minimal records and the earliest were from 1882. There were references to some events prior to 1850 but no one was able to determine when the club was founded.

Through the years the members enjoyed their secrecy until one member, ashamed of the club's unwritten policy of racism, anti-Semitism, and quiet contributions to corrupt government officials, leaked it all to the newspaper.

Creston had convinced his father to join him in resigning from the club a year before the paper ran the expose of Club Louisiane. The club was shamed into disbanding and not one member came forward to protest the allegations brought forth, or defend the club. The long term lease of the fifth floor was transferred to a holding company located in the Cayman Islands and Club Louisiane became a banquet hall, rentable to anyone for any social event. The first function was a dance for a prominent black Mardi Gras carnival group. Creston attended as the guest of Oscar Bourgeois.

Creston had arranged to rent Club Louisiane for an early Christmas Eve dinner party. The guest list was small but included all the people involved in his and Rainey's support while they were missing. There were also a few family members and friends and the list totaled twenty people.

The invitation was simple and direct. Reception from six to six thirty and dinner would start promptly at six forty five. The dinner would be over by eight o'clock so all attending would be able to return home to their families for Christmas Eve celebration. The menu was light fare by New Orleans standards. Oyster artichoke soup followed by sautéed speckled trout with lump crab in a cream sauce ladled over the fish. There was no dessert since most people would be attending parties later with an abundance of food.

Rainey was the last to arrive. Everyone else was seated at a large table in the center of the main ballroom. He took the last seat between Leslie and his mother, turned and kissed his mother on her cheek and smiled as he looked into her eyes. Leslie said nothing and did not move as he glanced in her direction. He patted her thigh and returned his hand to the table. Creston stood at the head of the table as the soup was being served, picked up his glass of wine and cleared his throat.

"Thank you all for coming to this little celebration. I'm sure Rainey shares my sentiment when I say he and I thought of you all often. Our desire to return and see you contributed greatly to our survival, so if not for you we might not have made it back." Creston held his glass high and toasted his guests. "Rainey, would you like to say a few words?" he asked.

"You pretty much covered it, but yes, thank you all very much." Rainey neither stood nor raised his glass.

"Please enjoy the dinner," Creston said, and then sat without looking at Rainey.

The wine poured freely, the food was served and they all shared stories of the past year, and most had nothing to do with Rainey or Creston. The table was cleared of the elegant china and more wine was poured. Creston again stood, and the chatter ceased.

"I thought you might like to say a few more words, maybe share your feelings a little," Creston said as he looked at Rainey. "I'm sure our guests would like to hear from you."

"Merry Christmas and thanks again," Rainey said.

"Isn't there anything else you'd like to say?" Creston said.

"What would you like me to say?" Rainey asked.

"Maybe how much you appreciate our guests, or maybe how you feel. This is about them, you know."

"About them?" Rainey asked. "Come on, let's face it. This is not about them or even me. This is about Creston Labouef. It is always about Creston Labouef, isn't it?" Rainey was standing. Leslie grabbed his arm.

"I think you're out of line, old friend. Perhaps it would be better if you sat down." Creston tried to smile at his parents and guests. "Yes, we have heard enough. I guess you were cooped up in your apartment a little too long."

"Maybe I was cooped up on the island with you a little too long."

Rainey stared straight ahead, his hands trembled. "I've had enough. Sorry to dampen the spirit here, but I'm leaving." Rainey stood and threw his napkin on the table.

"Yes, perhaps it's best if you left," Creston said. Rainey was out the large double doors of the massive room and did not hear Creston continue. "Don't think badly of Rainey. This is not like him. He had it much harder than I while on the island. I think it might be depression or stress or whatever. I'm sure he'll be fine."

The phone was ringing as Rainey walked into his apartment. He stared at it, the ringing stopped and he walked toward his bedroom. The phone started ringing again. He picked it up without saying anything.

"What the hell is wrong with you?" Leslie barked. "You were rude and inconsiderate and should be ashamed. I don't care what you went through, there's no excuse."

"Well I'm not sure what is wrong with me, but if you'd like to get together tomorrow we can discuss it."

"I can't get together tomorrow," Leslie said. "I'm leaving for Alabama in a few minutes. I packed my car before going to the dinner. I need some time with my family and to get...clear my mind."

"Of course," Rainey said. "Tell them all I said hello. They do remember me don't they?"

"Yes, they remember you. I remember you, but I don't think I know who you are anymore. But what makes it worse is, I don't think you know who you are."

Leslie's words stung. "Or maybe," Rainey said, "I know exactly who I am and I've decided to start acting like it." His voice became slightly softer. "Be careful driving over there. And come back safe."

"Thanks," Leslie said. "I have to be at work the day after New Year's. Maybe we can continue this conversation then."

"I'm going to spend Christmas day with my mother and then I might take off for a couple of weeks, maybe head over to Florida." Leslie had no response. "I'll call you when I get back," he said.

"Is this any way to spend Christmas day? Fighting with your best friend, and especially after all you two went through," Joan said. "I love you and I'm proud of you, but I don't understand what's going on, and you don't want to talk about it."

Rainey smiled at his mother and shrugged. He moved closer, hugged her and kissed her on the cheek.

"I was looking forward to a day alone with you like old times, when we sat and watched those black and white movies you were always so crazy about. I know we can find one on cable today, maybe White Christmas with Bing Crosby," Rainey said taking a step back.

"Does a mother ever get to quit worrying about her children?" Joan turned and walked toward the kitchen to check on her Christmas dinner.

Joan had cooked a simple dinner of baked ham, sweet potato casserole, green beans and bread. They shared a bottle of wine as they ate. Rainey was more relaxed and Joan welcomed this. She had long ago released Rainey from her motherly grip. He had done well, made many good decisions, and she was pleased and proud of him. She had confidence in him and knew whatever was going on in his life she would one day understand. But, she wondered what had happened on the island and why he was different, why he was so distant one day and then the next day act as if nothing had ever happened. She rose and smiled at him as she picked up their plates.

"Much better," she said.

"What's better?"

"The little grin you had, and the distant look in your eyes. Wherever you were, it pleased you," Joan said.

Rainey's face flushed. Thoughts of Amy and the island were ever present and he would drift away as he had while his mother watched.

"Rainey, you can never fool a mother's love. One day I expect to hear what has happened, one day when you are ready."

Rainey looked at his mother, then turned his gaze to his wine glass and lifted it to his mouth. The smooth, red liquid was sweet and he thought for a moment of telling his mother about Amy, the island, the promise he had made, and of his vast confusion at times. He swallowed the wine and decided today was not the day.

"I love you, mom," he said without looking at her. "It's a Wonderful Life with James Stewart is on and I'd like to watch it with you."

"I'll get the coffee and pecan pie. And yes, I'd like to watch it again." She gazed at Rainey. "With you."

A warm feeling came over Rainey as he sank into the sofa, realizing how he had missed these special times with his mother. He knew they would sit and talk for a long time, and he anticipated this as if he were a young boy again.

The movie was over, the pie eaten, and the coffee drunk. Rainey picked up the remote and turned off the TV. Joan gave him a curious look but said nothing. He replaced the remote on the coffee table and sat back.

"I think I need to take a couple of weeks off and get out of New Orleans." He waited, anticipating she would chastise him for his selfishness. She looked at him and said nothing.

"I have a friend who owns a condo at Buttonwood Bay on Key Largo. I thought I might head down there and stay a couple of weeks or so. I don't have a job, and it would be good to get away and do some thinking, try to sort things out."

"You're a grown man, and you can do what you want. You don't need my approval, but I don't have to like it either. I just got you back and you want to go off again," she said. "And what about Leslie? Rainey, she still loves you and the whole time you and Creston were gone she lived in fear she had lost you again."

"Mom, I've been back almost a month and things still feel out of sorts, like a part of my life is missing. Leslie is one of the things I need to sort out and think about. I still love her. I never stopped loving her, but it doesn't mean trying again is the right thing to do. I want to try with all I have in me. I thought about her constantly while on the island. Before leaving on the trip I used to think there would always be time and I'd be able to try again when I was ready. The time on the island changed my thinking. I need a couple of weeks is all. Like I said, I have a few things to sort out. I need you to understand and not be upset with me. I'll be back…"

"This is a fine Christmas present you give me," Joan said. Her lower lip quivered.

"I almost forgot, I have a present for you," Rainey said. He rose from the sofa, walked across the room and picked up a bag he had placed on the floor. He handed it to her and said, "Merry Christmas."

Joan reached into the bag and pulled out a ball-like object hand painted a lustrous light blue. It was approximately four inches in diameter, slightly misshaped, and had a rough texture even though there had been an attempt to sand-paper it smooth. The object was hollow with no way to open it. She rotated it in her hand and stopped when she came to an inscription written by Rainey. Not wanting to get up and hunt for her glasses she held it out at arm's length and read:

1995-Somewhere in the Pacific-
Miles from you but never far away-
Love, Rainey."

Joan wiped a small tear from her cheek. Leaning toward Rainey she hugged him tightly for a long moment.

"Go do whatever it is you have to do, but please stay in touch. The two months without you and not hearing from you took years off my life, and I don't have too many left."

"You have plenty of years left, and I'm going to be around to share them with you. But yes, I have some things to work out. I'm leaving in a few days but I'll be back soon, a couple of weeks at the most, I think." Rainey watched his mother for a sign of acceptance or understanding.

"I hope so," she said. "Let's watch another movie before you go."
"Yes, I'd like that."

At midnight Rainey hugged his mother at the door and left. Joan watched him go, crossed herself and said a prayer asking for understanding and his quick return.

CHAPTER THIRTY NINE

Rainey was packed the day after New Years. He checked his bag, and then looked around his apartment one more time for anything he might have missed, picked up his phone and dialed Leslie's home phone to leave a message, sure she would be at the bank.

"Hello," she said. Rainey heard a soft tremor in her voice.

Rainey froze. She said hello again and Rainey cleared his throat.

"Hi…I was calling to leave you a message. I thought you'd be at work. Are you sick?"

"No," she said, and cleared her throat. "I'm not sick. I took a few extra days off. How was your Christmas and New Year's?"

"They were good I…I spent Christmas with my mom and New Year's day I spent here at the apartment and watched bowl games. Stayed in and did nothing."

"Good for you," Leslie said. "What message were you going to leave me?"

"I'm headed over to Florida, like I said before. But also, I'll be gone a couple of weeks figuring some things out and doing some thinking. And, I wanted to apologize for the way I've acted toward you. I've not been as good to you in my return as you were to me in my absence."

"Wow," she said. "Did you come up with that all by yourself?"

Rainey clenched his teeth together then continued. "I guess I deserve this and why I wanted to leave you a message. You have the right to be upset with me. Anyway, I'll be back in a couple of weeks.

Hopefully we can pick back up with this conversation. I think I can clear some things up."

"I've got a few things to clear up too, so I hope you do come back."

"What are you doing today?" he asked.

"I'm having lunch with Natalie. She had a great time with Creston on Christmas Eve after you stomped out like a spoiled child. Nothing intimate or racy, but fun. It was depressing, to tell you the truth.

"I want to counsel her a little and keep her from getting attached," Leslie said. "You and I both know how Creston is, or at least how he was. I'm not sure either one of you is the same, which is all the more reason for me to talk some sense into her."

"Creston will come around, so don't go trying to fix something when it might not be broken. In the meantime, take care of yourself and don't do anything foolish…at least not until I come back."

Leslie hung up, looked at the receiver. "You are a big ass… but I love you."

Rainey grabbed his bag and walked out of his apartment locking the door behind him. He drove to the airport, parked in the long term lot across Airline Highway, and caught the shuttle bus to the outside ticket counter.

CHAPTER FORTY

The baggage carousel started turning and Rainey was surprised to see his bag was the second one to come out of the hole in the wall. He picked up his bag from the carousel, looked around to get his bearings and headed toward the door with the sign marked ground transportation. A voice called out behind him.

"Hey, Rainsford, you're late."

"Turning, Rainey said, "Yeah, and you'll never change."

Rainey grasped Creston's hand in his and placed his arm around the shoulders and gave him a hug.

"You have any problems?" Creston asked.

"No, but the flight from San Diego was fogged in and we were two hours late taking off. What about you?"

"I had a little trouble picking up the jet in Los Angeles. The company I leased it from got a little nervous when they realized I was flying solo to Hawaii. I think they might have suspected I was smuggling drugs. They held me up a while. I figured they were worried about getting their plane back. I had to get a letter of credit. Do you know how hard it is to get something done between Christmas and New Years?" Creston said. "Especially without Leslie's help. Guess I've been a little spoiled."

"Maybe *a lot* spoiled," Rainey said. "Thank God it never went to your head."

"The old Rainey returns, I see. Not like the dumb ass at the dinner party."

"The ruse was your idea. I hated acting so rude and insensitive. But I'm sure nobody thinks we're together so I guess it worked."

"The people who matter will know the truth soon enough. Anyway, I got the letter of credit authorizing certified funds in case I don't return the plane. I should have remembered this, but years ago before I bought the first jet the guys at the airport always set this up, and it was never a problem. Anyway, I told them thirty days on the letter then they could cash it in so let's not blow this." Creston smiled, "I think I shocked them a little."

"So where do we go from here?"

"I've got a car outside. There's a quiet resort on the north shore where I've been staying since I got here last week. We'll spend the night there and leave early in the morning. The jet's at the private airport I flew into instead of Hilo."

It was late afternoon and the sky was a rich azure blue not unlike the sky Rainey had marveled at on the island. He stopped at the curb and waited before entering the crosswalk. The enormity of the last few months pressed down on him, intensified by the task of finding Amy. Rainey shook his head and caught up with Creston.

He followed Creston into the parking lot expecting a Mercedes or Jaguar rental car. When Creston stopped at a pink, open air jeep with a white and pink striped canvas canopy Rainey hesitated before stopping. No way, he thought. Creston was standing at the rear of the jeep, grasping the roll bar, his left foot resting on the bumper.

"You can't be serious," Rainey said.

"It's all they had left. I forgot to reserve a car. Usually my assistant takes care of these things but I handled it all myself." Creston avoided Rainey's blank stare. "It's only until tomorrow. I've been driving this thing *all* week waiting on your happy ass to get here."

Rainey walked toward the jeep. The long flight was wearing on him and his bag felt heavier in his hand than when he grabbed it off the carousel. "The reporter in New Orleans would have a field day with this," he said as he threw his bag in the rear of the jeep and walked around to the passenger side. Bowing his head he grasped the handle on the windshield frame, placed his foot on the running board, and pulled himself into the jeep. He fastened the seatbelt thinking this should be an interesting ride.

Creston maneuvered the jeep onto the highway and headed west. The open jeep was noisy and the wind whipped around them. The striped canopy flapped like sheets left on a clothes line during a summer squall. Several times Rainey tried to ask a question or make a point but knew it was futile and decided to enjoy the drive. Mountainous, volcanic outcroppings, pinnacles covered with deep, green foliage separated by deep valleys to their right contrasted with the flat Pacific to the left, and both were as beautiful as anything Rainey had ever seen. He relaxed and thought of Amy. There was an hour of daylight left when Creston turned into the driveway of the north shore resort, a magnificent version of a modern Hawaiian village. He drove to a bungalow and parked.

Rainey climbed out of the jeep, bent and touched his toes, then stood erect, his arms stretched out straight above his head. Creston grabbed Rainey's bag and headed into the bungalow.

"This will do," Rainey said as he looked around the spacious room. The lava stone fire place looked out of place and he wondered how cold it gets in Hawaii.

"The restaurant is walking distance, takes about five minutes," Creston said. "It's nice and the food's excellent. It's located on the highest elevation of the property and was built on ten foot pilings as well. There's a great view of the ocean, inspiring in fact. Each night as I ate and looked out I thought of Amy and..." He looked at Rainey, who was scouting the bungalow. "No sense in getting too comfortable, we leave early in the morning. Put your bag in your room and let's walk to the restaurant for dinner."

Creston and Rainey sat at a table located next to a glass wall which offered a view of the deep blue, nearly black Pacific stretching for hundreds of miles. The sun would set in thirty minutes and the view would turn to infinity of darkness.

They both ordered the grilled mahi-mahi served over oriental rice with a pineapple mango salsa piled on top and shared a bottle of wine. They talked for two hours about what each had accomplished.

"Have you heard from Leslie?" Rainey said as they walked back to the bungalow. "I got some grief from her and my mother about throwing a fit and storming out of your Christmas dinner, about acting like a child."

"My parents thought I was a little cold when I told them to let you go and not worry about it. They told me I needed to have more compassion and understanding. Blamed your behavior on stress and losing your job. They think I'm in California on business and shopping for a new plane."

"Mom and Leslie think I was headed to Florida for a couple of weeks, maybe spend some time in Key Largo. I'm sure it worked. They don't think we're together."

"I haven't heard from Leslie because I told her I'd contact her if I needed anything. I didn't want her asking any questions."

Rainey was tired from the long plane rides. They agreed to get some sleep and continue fine tuning their plan on the flight to Guam.

CHAPTER FORTY ONE

New Orleans was suffering the effects of unusually cold, January weather. People returning from lunch scurried like ants as they fought the bone chilling gusts of wind accelerating through the wind tunnels formed by the downtown high rise buildings. Men held their coats closed tight against their chests, and those with a hat were forced to hold it or risk losing it in the winds. The ladies gathered a handful of skirt or dress and held it as close to the knee as possible, and still an occasional gust ripped through the air and lifted a dress above a lady's waist.

Leslie was seated at her desk, looking out the window and watching the activity on the street below. She smiled in sympathy for the poor souls fighting the elements. The chaos was so comic she shook her head, grateful to be inside. She and Rainey had not patched things up and were not moving forward together. Hopefully he would be back in a couple of weeks. She would make the clean break then and move on with her life. In the meanwhile she would start the wheels in motion for a transfer to a branch of the bank in Alabama. She loved living in New Orleans and maybe one day would return, but it was time for a change. In spite of the cold Leslie needed to visit Mama Mary. She was desperate for some guidance and matronly advice from a woman she trusted as much as her own mother.

Walking in the cold and windy weather was out of the question. Leslie called a cab and waited in the lobby, entertained by the patrons and employees dashing inside, often colliding with each other. The cab pulled up in front of the bank and Leslie ran outside, partly because of the cold, but also to make sure no one tried to jump in the cab ahead of her. She did not hold her dress and coat. A strong gust of wind caught her dress and raised it above her waist. Embarrassed, she spun around trying to catch her dress, laughing at herself as she realized she had become one of the actors in the play she had watched from upstairs.

The cab was warm and the drone of the tires on the road was calming. In ten minutes Leslie was on North Peters Street close to Mama Mary's shop. She hesitated, handed the driver his fare and then asked him to come back for her in twenty minutes. The gusting winds had ceased but the outside air was still cold. Leslie entered Mama Mary's stall and scanned the colorful displays of clothing and hand carved African art.

"Hey, honey, what you lookin for so hard?" a sales attendant asked.

"My name is Leslie, and I was looking for Mama Mary. We're friends and I wanted to talk with her about a few things."

"She's not here today. In fact, she been gone for a few days and I don't suppose I'll see her anytime soon. Hell, I wouldn't be here today cept these crazy tourists think this is a nice spring day compared to where they live up north." She noticed the confused look on Leslie's face. "You ok honey?"

"Yes, I'm fine, but disappointed. I thought Mama Mary was always here and I didn't think she'd take a vacation this time of year."

"Oh no, it ain't no vacation. I don't know what, but she's off somewhere helping out those two white boys that was lost."

"What?" Leslie shot back. "What two white boys?"

"Calm down honey, before you get yourself all upset. She's comin back. Said it may be a few weeks, maybe a month. She left me the store with instructions on how to take care of things. I already know how, but I let her tell me anyways. I been with her for a few years. If it weren't for me she'd have a tough time."

"What two white boys came to see her?" Leslie asked, sure of the answer.

"Them white boys what got lost in their fancy plane one of em was flyin. She introduced em to me but I ain't real good with names. Guess I'm gettin a little old."

"When did they come to see Mama?"

"It was about four days before Christmas the first time when they came together. They each came back separate the next day or so but yeah, they came in here and was all laughing and having a good time with Mama. I couldn't hear what it was they was sayin, but they all had a good laugh. Then it got kinda serious for a little bit. Mama put her hands on the one boy and I knew then somethin was up. She hugged him and said not to worry. They left outta here and a little later she told me she might have to be gone some. I told her don't make no never mind to me cause I'd handle it. She came back the day after Christmas, helped me get things in order and said she'd be seein me later. No problem I told her and that was that."

"You're sure, aren't you? I mean, you are sure it was the two boys, I mean men who had been lost after the plane crash"

"Honey, I already *toll* you it was them. I'm as sure as I'm sure you standin here." She waited and when Leslie did not respond she asked, "Girl, you sure you ok? Can I get you somethin to drink or maybe a chair to sit in?"

Leslie smiled. "No, I don't need anything. You've been a big help. Maybe even bigger than Mama would have been." She gave her a hug and kiss on the cheek. As she left she said, "I don't know what those two are up to, but I'm going to find out."

"Yeah, I bet you will. Good luck honey. Come back and see me when you figure it out."

The cab was waiting and the ride back to the bank was too short for Leslie to process all she was thinking. "Those two," she said. "I should have known."

CHAPTER FORTY TWO

The take off was not typical Creston, but more reserved and near perfect none the less. As they leveled off Rainey looked out across the clear sky and the dark blue ocean below. Night was in front of them and he was unable to determine where the sky and ocean came together. The low morning sun cast a faint orange hue behind as they flew west into darkness.

"If you did your homework you know it's about 3900 nautical miles to Guam. It'll take us about eight hours or so, maybe a little more depending on the head winds. This is a long range jet similar to the one *we* left on the island."

"Let's not start even if you are joking," Rainey said. "Guam's much farther from the search area we outlined than some other islands we could land on."

"It is but like I told you, Guam is a U.S. territory and we can fly in and out without passports. All we need is U.S. identification. Some of the other island territories are restricted, like Kwajalein. We can't even land there without special permission and even then we can't leave the plane. Guam is much larger than most of the islands so we'll be less conspicuous. We're a couple of tourists on a fishing trip."

"We covered it," Rainey said. "But we're going farther west simply to work our way back east looking for the island. And the farther west we go, the longer this takes. I've been over the charts too many times to count and I can tell you there are thousands of square miles of empty ocean down there, and hundreds of tiny dots they call islands. I hate to think so, but this might be totally futile."

"Ye of little faith. I don't need you getting negative on me."

"Quit with the guilt trip. And especially quit with the biblical references before this plane crashes like the last one."

"Sometimes you have a demented sense of humor," Creston said.

Creston had engaged the auto pilot and they flew for several hours but he refused to get up and stretch his legs or ask Rainey to take a turn watching the controls. He was harboring his failure on their trip around the world, and it was hard for him to relax. Rainey busied himself checking the charts he had worked on for two weeks in his apartment. He had plotted a grid onto the charts over the search area Creston had suggested. Rainey rolled up the charts and stowed them behind the co-pilot seat.

"Are you going to sit there the whole time until you pee on yourself? It's a long flight and we're only half way," Rainey said.

"I'm starting to get a little nervous about all this. I was fine but we're getting closer to Guam and I guess it's settling in on me. I keep checking and rechecking."

"There's nothing wrong with this plane. Your plane was sabotaged. The mechanic was fired, arrested, and confessed. His days in the airplane mechanic business are over."

"All right, I do have to pee, so sit here and pay attention. Don't touch anything, but keep an eye on it. I'll be right back."

Creston released his harness and made his way to the back of the plane. Rainey was slumped over in his seat, loud snoring emanating from his mouth when he returned.

"Don't be a smart ass. I suppose you're trying to make me feel better," Creston said and strapped himself back into the pilot's seat.

"No, but it made me feel better."

Creston shook his head. "You're a piece of work," he said. "But I do feel better. Make yourself useful. There are sandwiches in the refrigerator and coffee in the thermos. Fetch it for me Luke."

The sandwiches were filling. They shared a cup of coffee and Rainey thought of the many times he had made their morning coffee on the island, and the trouble he had gone through to get it as close to right as possible without a coffee pot. Creston nodded as if he understood what Rainey was thinking.

They were an hour from Guam when Creston started his check list for landing. Satisfied all was in order he turned toward Rainey. "Let's go over this one more time. After we land we go inside and produce our identification. We're on vacation, just a couple of guys looking to do some fly fishing in some remote lagoons in the islands. If they want to search the plane, no problem. There's nothing on board we have to worry about, at least not yet."

"We spend the night in the hotel and in the morning we catch a ride over to Apra Harbor and make arrangements to pick up the sea plane. No problem, right?"

"Right," Creston said. "No problem, but we'll have to convince them we're going to fly fish off a big seaplane. A challenge, but we've had bigger ones."

"Much bigger so we can pull this off."

The landing was smooth and Rainey sat at ease. Creston taxied to the designated area and shut down all systems. He released his harness, made his way through the cabin, opened the door and stepped onto the tarmac with Rainey right behind him.

"So you guys are taking a seaplane out of Apra to do some fly fishing in some remote islands?" A large man in uniform, with a holstered pistol, questioned them as they checked in at the flight office. "I'm Captain Powell, head of airport security. I don't think I've heard of anyone doing this before. We get lots of divers, fishermen using big game boats with outriggers, but fly fishing off a seaplane?" His eyebrows scrunched, his lips pursed. He smiled. "Nope, don't think I have. You boys might start a trend here. Everybody is always looking for a new way to do things. Where's your gear?"

"It's in the jet. I've arranged for a truck to meet us here, load it up and bring it over to the harbor where the seaplane's waiting. I've got fly rods, tackle, all the usual stuff. I even have a large, insulated anvil case full of food and drinks, water, and uh, maybe a beer or two. And in case I catch a trophy fish I'll be able to bring it back in the case. You never know, we might hook into a large sailfish or Wahoo. Got a guy back in Hawaii who will mount it."

"Good luck on your trip. How long you boys gonna be?"

"We've scheduled a week but it depends. If we get lucky we'll cut it short but, if we *really* like it, hell, we might even go a couple extra days."

"The truck's outside to pick you up. You need any help with your stuff?"

Rainey spoke up. "Nah, we got it. It's not much but thanks for the offer. Come on, let's load up." Rainey knew Powell's eyes were watching him as they left and he hoped they were safe.

Rainey and Creston loaded all their gear into the truck with the help of the driver. Creston waited for Powell's men to finish their inspection and then got back into the jet, taxied it to the holding area as instructed by security and powered down the engines. It would be tied down and secured until they were ready to return to Hawaii. The jet alone was costing him what the average person would earn in two years, extravagant even for Creston, but it did not faze him.

The driver took them to Apra Harbor and straight to the office which Creston had made arrangements with for the seaplane. The driver told them they would find Hannibal inside.

"Who's Hannibal?" Rainey asked.

"Hannibal is the owner of the seaplane and runs this flight line. He's the guy I made all the arrangements with."

A large Grumman HU-16 Albatross was parked within twenty feet of the office close to a concrete ramp with a slope to the water. The plane looked ready to go. Creston went inside to finish the paper work while Rainey talked with the driver. After ten minutes Creston emerged from the office with a large and commanding person in tow.

"Step back out of the way guys. The owner here insists I get checked out on the Albatross before he hands it over. I tried to tell him I cut my aviator teeth in one of these on Lake Ponchartrain but he insists."

Rainey walked up to Creston and slapped him on the back, trying to exude a sense of confidence. Whispering he said, "I hope you know what you're doing." He turned and walked back toward the office.

"I can take off and land on water all day," Creston said. He spoke loud enough for all of them to hear. "In fact, landing on water is one of my favorite parts of flying. There's nothing like it." He climbed into the seaplane and took the pilot seat.

Creston did a complete preflight routine, started the engines and was about to yell at Rainey to remove the tire chocks when Hannibal told him he had seen enough, convinced Creston knew what he was doing.

"I'd like you to top this bird off with fuel and make sure we have maximum capacity. We'll do an overnighter out there if we find a promising lagoon. If we don't then we'll be back, refuel, and take off again."

The gear was taken from the truck and loaded into the cabin of the seaplane. The anvil case was the last piece placed on board. It was strapped in place and all was in order. In the morning they would be taking off to find Amy. They contained their excitement in front of Hannibal but they were anxious to get started. There was no margin for error and Creston did not consider the possibility of mistakes.

They walked to the truck. Creston stopped, turned and walked back to Hannibal. "Can you get someone to fill up the big case with ice first thing in the morning? Leave the drinks in it but take the boxes of food out. I'd like the case full of ice. In case we get lucky and catch a big one, and if it takes us a day or so to get back the ice will keep the trophy from spoiling. We're taking off at seven sharp."

"I'll have it all ready," Hannibal said. "You two gonna have a good time. Wish I was going with ya."

They spent the evening in their hotel room going over charts and determining, based on their best guess, where they should start looking. They agreed on the route for the first attempt. Later, Rainey lay in bed and thought of Amy and questioned if they were doing the right thing, disrupting her almost perfect world, bringing her into theirs. He had trouble sleeping as he wrestled with the different possibilities.

CHAPTER FORTY THREE

Rainey and Creston had arrived at the harbor, anxious to take off. The sun was barely over the horizon, the sky bright orange and pulsing with the new day. The salt air invaded their noses. The breeze was heavy with humidity and reminded Rainey of the island. He inhaled deeply and an image of Amy rushed at him.

The seaplane was in position and two men, obviously native to the island, were loading the last of the ice into the case. Creston scanned the harbor and then looked toward the sky. Conditions were perfect. Scattered clouds floated lazily across the sky and the surface wind was almost non-existent. The water of the harbor was like glass. The takeoff would be smooth.

"You boys sure are in a hurry to get going," Hannibal said as he walked up behind Rainey and Creston.

"We've come a long way for this little adventure so maybe we are in a hurry. I assume you have everything ready for us," Creston said.

"Well, there is one last thing before you go. I'd like a contact name and phone number back in the states. It's a standard precaution in case we don't hear from you guys for a couple of weeks."

A chill went through Rainey as he thought of someone again calling his mother and Leslie, telling them the plane was missing. His chest tightened and the image caused him ire. He turned toward Hannibal.

"We'll leave the names and numbers," Rainey said. "But under no circumstances can you contact anyone for at least two weeks. If we come back in two days, the clock starts all over. Are we clear on this?"

"Not a problem, so relax. You guys will be back bragging about the great time you had and all the islands you discovered. There are still some small islands out there no one's ever stepped on. Hard to believe, but it's true. The thing is no one knows which islands are virgin and which ones aren't. Guess it doesn't matter, does it?"

"It doesn't matter to us," Creston said as he and Rainey walked toward the seaplane.

The sun was not high enough in the sky to have warmed the inside of the seaplane and the temperature in the cockpit was comfortable. Creston strapped in, and after making sure Rainey had done so as well he repeated the preflight routine he had gone through for Hannibal. The twin prop engines roared to life, and after warming up Creston taxied the big plane down the ramp and into the harbor. He maneuvered the Albatross into position and readied her for take off. The tower granted clearance, and Creston revved the engines. Rainey's heart pounded and he gripped the armrests as the plane fought the pull of the water and then lifted off, trailing a rain-like mist. His grip eased and he exhaled, unaware he had been holding his breath. Creston shook his head, laughing at Rainey.

Talking through the headset Creston said, "Relax, partner and enjoy the ride. Was it smooth or what? The draw back is these beauties aren't fast. The cruising speed on this jewel is about 130 knots. It takes eight to ten hours to cover a little over a thousand miles but it's worth it."

"It was smooth, unbelievable in fact. Shouldn't you be paying attention and not laughing at me?"

"Yeah, but sometimes laughing at you is so damned easy. Break out the main chart and let's check our headings."

Rainey released the seat belt and took the head set off. It was then he realized how noisy the plane was. It would be almost impossible to talk normally and be heard. He maneuvered his way out of the seat and stood in the cabin behind the cockpit. He took notice of the interior. The cabin was comfortable but not outfitted like the private jets he had flown in with Creston. The interior was battleship-gray with four sets of back to back seats covered in a heavy orange canvas, two sets on each side. The area aft of the seats was for storage. The gear Rainey and Creston brought had been neatly stacked on the starboard side while the anvil case was snug up against the port side, secured with tie-downs looped through the cargo clips on the wall of the cabin. Rainey took the main chart from his bag and returned to the co-pilot seat, fastened the seat belt and put the head set back on.

"I see they didn't spend a lot of money fixing this bird up," Rainey said.

"Hey, she's been refitted and upgraded. The avionics are the latest available, engines were rebuilt, new gas tanks, the fuselage was sealed and reinforced, and it has longer range than the standard model. This plane can travel three thousand miles, which is about five hundred more than typical." He looked at Rainey. "You didn't think I'd go off without checking this bird out first did you?"

"No, but I also didn't realize how much had to be verified."

"These are great old planes. The navy and coast guard used them for search and rescue for years. There aren't too many of them left in service. Another reason we had to go to Guam. The best plane available was this one. Hannibal did a great job fixing her up." Creston got quiet then said, "Rainey, there's no margin for error, but we can pull this off. Nothing else matters."

Rainey placed the chart across the co-pilot controls "Let's start right here," he said putting his finger inside a grid he had drawn on the chart. "Change the headings to this grid."

Creston leveled off at twelve thousand feet, checked the markings on the chart, and adjusted his headings. "What makes you so sure about this grid instead of the other hundred or so we mapped out?"

Rainey did not respond. He removed his head set, and remembered back to the week before Christmas.

Mama Mary was quietly working about her store, fixing the modest displays and arranging the latest African clothing she had received. Rainey was quiet and watched her work.

"Rainey, what you doin here?" She glanced down at the rolled up paper in his hand.

"Mama, I need a little help."

The understanding smile she had shared with him at Paris Labouef's house returned. She took Rainey by the arm and led him to a small room with enough space for a two foot diameter table and two chairs.

"Sit there honey and tell me what's on your mind."

"It's kind of funny. I have this feeling you already know and it makes me feel like I'm walking on eggshells. There were a few things Creston and I didn't tell you when we were here yesterday. I know what Creston said about needing help and you were willing to help, so maybe we figured you knew."

"Look Rainey, I never pretend to be what I'm not."

"Mama, Creston and I left something on the island. We want to go back and get it but we're not sure where the island is. We have a good idea, but it's a huge ocean and it could take weeks or months to find it. We might not ever find it but we have to try." He searched her face for some expression to ease his anxiety.

She reached over, took his hand and placed it on the table with hers resting on top. "I knew you was bothered by something when I met you, but I first thought it was Leslie, thought maybe she was your problem. But the image wasn't her. I wasn't sure what it was, but because I'm getting old I don't dwell on things too much. But I can't ignore them when they are there. Tell me what you want me to do?"

Rainey placed the chart on the small table and rolled it open. She looked at the map, at the red lines, the red squares he had drawn as a grid, and studied it before looking back at Rainey.

"The point where all the lines begin is where we have to fly from when we start our search," Rainey said. The boxes are fifty miles square. We studied this over and over, and based on where we were found, we narrowed it down to this search area. It's about six hundred miles by six hundred miles. It would take a long time if we had to cover it all. We're using a seaplane because they can land on water. There's no other way."

Mama Mary balled her right hand into a fist and extended her index finger. Still holding his hand, looking Rainey in the eye, she moved her right hand in a circular pattern over the grid. She didn't blink or take her eyes off of his. Her hand stopped and her finger rested in a box with no islands.

"I'd start right here if it was me."

Rainey took a red marker from his pocket and traced over the box, making the outline darker and more distinct than the others. "Thank you, thank you," he said trying to contain his excitement. He placed the marker back in his pocket and rolled up the chart and sat for a moment. Mama broke the silence.

"I hope you find her."

"You amaze me," Rainey said as he shook his head. "How do you do it?"

"What's wrong with you?" she said. "I told you before, I don't do nothing." She thought for a moment, "But I do see you're a good man Rainey, and so is Creston.

"He came back to see me yesterday after you two left, but I suppose he told you already," she said.

"Yes, but he didn't tell me why. And I was afraid to talk to him about this."

"Well, he knows more than you think. He told me to keep it quiet he was here. But he also said you might be comin to see me. How you suppose he knew?"

"He's a pretty smart guy. Guess I underestimate him sometimes, but you'd think I would have learned. I don't suppose you can tell me why he came to see you?"

"Maybe you should ask him."

He stood up and hugged her tightly. Her energy surged through him and he kissed her on the cheek before turning to walk away.

"You need to ask him, ya hear me?"

"Hey, where are you?" Creston yelled.

Rainey placed his head set on and said, "I'm right here. But I was thinking of a few things. Are we on the heading for the area I pointed out?"

"Yes, we're on the right heading, but tell me why this spot."

"Maybe we should trade stories." Rainey shifted in his seat to get comfortable and speak directly at Creston, even though he still had to use the head set. "I'll go first. I got this spot from Mama Mary. I went to see her the week before Christmas, the day after we paid her a visit. We talked for a while and then she pointed to this spot on the chart. Even if she's way off it's as good a place to start as any. Except I'd feel better if the chart at least indicated some islands were there." He paused. "So, what's your story?"

Creston cleared his throat, checked the heading of the seaplane. "Ok, but understand I wanted to surprise you, give you a charge or a thrill, especially after all we've been through and what you did for me. You saved my life and I haven't forgotten."

"Please," Rainey interrupted, "We're not keeping score so let it go."

"Maybe so," Creston said. "Anyway, let me finish.

"I leased a private island in the Bahamas. I went through a broker in Miami. I didn't tell Leslie about this, like I never told her I have a lot of money in one of her bank's big rivals. She'd be more than pissed if she found out. I couldn't involve her with the lease of the island because I used the other bank."

"What the hell does this have to do..." Rainey stopped as it hit him. "Are you kidding me?"

"I asked Mama Mary to house sit for me. I told her you and I had some unfinished business and it was more important. I hired her to take care of the house, but the real reason is I think she's the perfect person to help Amy once we find her and bring her back with us."

Rainey nodded. "I wish I had thought of it. But how would I have hired her?"

"The good thing is I can hire her. She's already on the island. I talked Big O into escorting her down to the island; make sure it was safe, and no problems. I chartered a private jet at the lakefront airport to fly them to Freeport. I told Big O to protect her like she was his mother, which was pretty stupid on my part, since she saved his life when he was young. I feel sorry for anybody who gives Mama a hard time if O's around. Anyway, I gave O a list of food and supplies to pick up in Freeport. Then he was to go back to the airport where he and Mama Mary would take a small seaplane to the island. O was supposed to stay with her a couple of days, make sure everything checked out and was safe, then if he was ok with it he'd call the seaplane captain to come back and pick him up. He was back in New Orleans so I'm sure it's all good. All I told him was I had business to take care of in California, which was not a lie, but not the whole truth. Mama's down there taking it easy. The house has electricity, but also has a backup generator. It comes with a pool, air conditioning, satellite television, phone and a twenty-one foot boat with twin outboard Yamaha 225 motors."

Rainey shook his head. "I can't imagine how much this is costing, and yet you act like it's another day at the office."

"It is not about the money. It's not about you, or me, or anything else. It's about keeping our promise and finding Amy. As far as how much this whole excursion is costing, including the island lease, it's all relative. I make more in interest on money sitting in the banks in one year than all of this is costing." Creston stopped, then said, "Plus, when you consider the two months you and I were stranded and I didn't spend a penny, I might even be ahead of the game."

"Right, I got a king size picture of that," Rainey said. "I'm hungry. You ready to eat?"

"Food's in the back, unless those guys loading the gear left it off by mistake, or on purpose."

Rainey again made his way to the back of the cabin, found a box with store-bought turkey sandwiches, grabbed two bottles of water and returned to the cockpit. They ate and Rainey thought of the times on the island they had eaten meager provisions, rationing their food, making it last longer. He took a bite of the sandwich and realized he had already settled into a comfort zone devoid of island memories.

They maintained the same heading for several hours more. The sky in the distance was turning black and Creston knew they were headed toward a thunderstorm. He checked their location and decided to stay on course for a while longer. It was possible the storm would break up or be less intense than it appeared. But there was also a chance the storm would intensify. Rainey looked at Creston and cleared his throat.

"Relax, I see the storm," Creston said. "It looks big, maybe two hundred miles across, but it's hard to tell from this far away."

"Well, as big as it looks I say we need a new plan," Rainey shot back.

"I told you to relax. Guess I thought we might get lucky and miss any bad weather. I have a back up plan."

"We got rained on almost every day we were on the island, and sometimes it was severe. We should have figured this would happen." Rainey stared straight ahead. "Speak up and make it quick. I'm not feeling good about this."

"I told you this plane's not fast, so it makes no sense to try to outrun the storm. And flying around it would take us outside our search grid. Not to mention it would compromise our fuel and put us short."

"So far, I'm not liking this back up plan. Please don't tell me our next move is to fly into the teeth of it. I don't care how strong this plane is built."

"This is a good plane and built strong. You forget she's a *sea*plane."

Rainey gritted his teeth. "I guess you mean to put her down on the water and wait out the storm."

"I told you to relax. We're already into the search area, so we land on the water and hopefully in a lagoon on the leeward side of an island. But first we have to find one, and from this altitude I don't see anything but blue water. We're going to drop down to a thousand feet and then head north parallel to the storm. We'll land when we find a promising lagoon."

This was Creston's element. Rainey unhooked his seat belt and moved to the cabin to get the other charts, returning with the larger scale map depicting the islands more clearly than the first one. He opened the chart and double checked his finding before looking up.

"I think we need to fly south instead of north. According to this enlarged area on the chart we have a better chance of making it to a group of islands quicker if we head south."

Creston said, "You might make a good navigator after all."

Creston turned the seaplane to make the hundred and eighty degree change in direction and head south. He leveled off at a thousand feet and flew for almost an hour before the deep blue sea turned turquoise; a sure indication the water was becoming shallower. Rainey pointed off the port side at a lone island about a half mile long, covered in coconut palms with a sandy beach on the opposite side of the approaching storm. Creston nodded.

"First we have to do a slow fly by and make sure there are no large coral heads close to the water's surface. We hit one of those and the plane will flip and we'd be back where we were a couple of months ago."

Creston slowed the plane, dropped down to fifty feet above the surface and scanned the shallow water for the best approach. He made two passes and then decided. He circled back around and lined up his approach.

"This is it, the smoothest landing you'll ever make. It's like landing on an endless silk pillow."

The seaplane gradually descended. Rainey's vantage point from the co-pilot seat had great visibility of the oncoming island but not so of the water underneath the plane. The island was getting closer and closer and he spoke up, "shouldn't we be in the water soon, real soon?" he asked.

Creston reached for the throttle and cut back on the engines. "We've been in the water for thirty seconds," he said.

The aircraft came off plane and settled in the water, drifting toward the beach. Creston remained ready, prepared to use the engines to keep the Albatross on course. He revved both engines giving the plane a needed push to reach the beach. Rainey reached up and cut the engines as Creston had shown him during the preflight routine.

"Good job, but we're not finished yet," Creston said. "Hannibal showed me where he stows two Danforth anchors. We have to attach the ropes to the fuselage and then make sure the anchors have a secure grip, especially with the storm and wind approaching.

With the anchors set, Rainey and Creston stood on the beach and looked in the direction of the storm. "Be here in less than thirty minutes," Rainey said. Creston nodded agreement and they returned to the plane to wait for the storm to pass.

Heavy raindrops pelted the plane, making the windshield look as if they were going through a carwash. "It's not as bad down here as it looked flying around up there," Rainey said. "Guess we could have made it through the weather without landing. Much ado about nothing I guess."

"Shakespeare," Creston responded.

"What?"

"Much ado about nothing, Shakespeare wrote the play," Creston explained.

"All this time I figured you for a Puck."

"Puck?" Creston said.

"A Midsummer Night's Dream, more Shakespeare.

"I know," Creston said. "I didn't think you knew."

"Maybe some of you rubbed off on me through the years but doesn't show."

The storm lasted almost three hours. The sky cleared and Rainey checked his watch. There were two hours of daylight remaining. He slid the side window open and the scent of ocean air entered the cockpit. Creston did likewise and a cool cross breeze filtered through the plane. Indolence befell both men and each longed for an island nap.

"Almost like a déjà vu kind of thing," Creston said.

"It's more like an epiphany," Rainey said. "The whole time we were stranded we had a dire need to get off the island because it was on the island's terms, not ours. We thought we weren't in control. But we were in control which is why we survived. Sitting here, I see the beauty of it all, the epiphany is the beauty in the hopeless situation we found ourselves in. I see things differently at this moment."

"I envy how you see things," Creston said. "But we have work to do. I'd planned on flying about a thousand miles, scout the grid for another seven hundred miles or so and then return to Guam if we didn't find the island. That way we'd have a three or four hundred mile cushion on fuel. The storm threw us a little bit of a curve, but no real damage done. We have a couple hours of light left so let's get out of here and head back to our original destination. I think we'll cruise lower this time, maybe a thousand feet or so. We'll need to find another island like this one to spend the night. We can't chance landing at night so let's get going. Oh, and by the way, you're gonna get a little wet."

"Let me guess, I get the anchors, push the plane back and then wade through the water and hop back on."

"Yep, and try not to get too much water in the plane when you hop back in," Creston said. "Don't say it, whatever it is you're thinking." He looked forward. "Get the anchors."

They flew for two hours, crisscrossing the grid Mama Mary had selected. It was getting close to dark and Creston decided to put down on a small island with an inviting beach. Another pillow-soft landing, setting of the anchors, and they were put in for the night. They decided to sleep on the plane and not bother with setting up camp on the beach. The windows in the cabin were operable and Rainey opened them on both sides. Even though it was warm, the ocean breeze softly billowing through the cabin was cool, short of air conditioning, but comfortable. The seats in the cabin folded open and resembled a cot, making for a bed, but not as plush as those on the jet.

By sunrise they were awake and had busied themselves fixing breakfast. There was coffee in a thermos, still warm enough to satisfy but not as hot as Rainey's island coffee. They ate while watching the sun rise like a beacon and remembered where they had been.

After breakfast they were eager to start. Rainey jumped from the plane, released the anchors, and stowed them away. He pushed the plane into position while Creston waited for him to jump on board before starting the engines. The seaplane vibrated as Creston pushed the throttles and soon they were airborne.

"We have enough fuel to search one more grid box, but no more. If we don't find anything then we have to return to Guam and refuel. We'll spend the night and start over again in the morning."

They eliminated another box of the grid with no sign of anything even closely resembling the island where they had crashed. Rainey used binoculars as Creston stayed focused on flying the seaplane. It had taken over two hours of back and forth flying to cover the grid. Creston checked the fuel and made the decision to head back to Guam.

The flight back was quiet with frustration. They had covered two boxes of the grid, but most discouraging was they had covered the area Mama Mary had chosen and found nothing. An hour out of Guam Creston used the radio and called Hannibal.

"We're about an hour out. We'll be refueling, spending the night and taking off in the morning."

"Yeah, well, uh bring her in and let's see what we can work out," Hannibal said.

Creston was unsteadied by the tone in Hannibal's voice. Rainey, listening to the conversation, covered his mouth piece and yelled, "What do you suppose is up with him?"

Creston strained to hear Rainey. "I'm not sure but something's not right." He uncovered his mike and said, "Right, clear the ramp and I'll bring her in."

Rainey enjoyed the water landings but the plane was slow. He had become spoiled with the speed of the private jets and was having a hard time adjusting to the leisurely pace of the Albatross. Creston steered through the harbor and taxied onto the ramp. Two police jeeps and four large and heavily armed policemen waited to greet them.

"Holy shit," Creston said.

"What the hell is this about?"

"No idea. You were listening same as me so shake it off and stay calm."

"Right, why don't you tell me to stop my heart from beating," Rainey said. "That would be easier."

Creston parked the plane and powered down the engines, did a post-flight check of all systems before he and Rainey disembarked. Hannibal was waiting as they approached his office.

"Hello boys, it's good to see you back. It seems we have a little problem."

Rainey stood with his mouth open, his face flushed as Hannibal explained.

Creston stammered, collected himself and said, "What do you mean the credit card has been denied and the previous charges rescinded? That's impossible. Rainey, tell them this never happens. NEVER! There's a big mistake and I didn't make it." Creston rambled on but Hannibal and the police were not budging.

"This is more than a couple of hundred dollars we're talking about," Hannibal said. "This is thousands of dollars in fuel, plane rental, and insurance. What are we going to do about this?"

"It's too late to call back home and get this glitch corrected, so how about this. Rainey and I will go to the hotel, have dinner, get a good night sleep and be back here first thing in the morning. I'll call back home from your office and fix this. Then, with the Albatross refueled, we'll take off and get back to our fly fishing."

The expressions on the faces of the police officers were unchanging and it was obvious they were anxious for Hannibal to say the word and they would take Rainey and Creston to jail. Creston, usually calm, was moving, shifting his weight from side to side, worse than a woman in a long restroom line. He was fearful of what might come next.

"Ok, but only because your jet is locked down and you can't take off. Get some food, get some rest, but be back here at seven sharp. If this isn't fixed, your next stop will be jail," Hannibal said.

CHAPTER FORTY FOUR

Creston was moving fast to fix the problem. He and Rainey were standing in front of Hannibal's office before seven o'clock. The same four policemen were waiting but Creston was not deterred.

"Good morning! I see you guys get up early. Well you're going to see you wasted your time." Creston stepped inside and Rainey followed. "Give me the phone and we'll fix this thing," he said.

Hannibal handed Creston his desk phone. "Make it collect. The charges are on you," Hannibal said.

"Calm down a little," Rainey whispered. "Once you fix this we're gonna need Hannibal on our side."

Creston nodded and waited for the operator to place the call.

"CRESTON!" Leslie exclaimed. "I'm soooo glad you called. How's California? Look, I'm sorry to have to tell you this but your credit card must have been stolen. I was checking the account and came across exorbitant charges made on the island of Guam. I knew the charges were drastically wrong so I called the company and had the card suspended until we could get to the bottom of this."

"Leslie," he said.

"Creston, how did you let this happen? It must have been stolen."

"LESLIE," he yelled. "It was not stolen. I have it with me right now."

"What?" she feigned. "I don't understand. You must not have heard me. The charges were made on GUAM, not California. Normally I would call Rainey and try to find out what was amiss, but he's in Florida for God only knows what so I didn't even bother trying to reach him."

"Ok, Leslie, I get it. I suppose you think you're being cute."

Leslie dropped the act. "What are you doing in Guam? And don't lie to me. I know Rainey is with you, isn't he? God, you two drive me crazy. What are you up to?"

"Yes, Rainey is with me, but I can't go into it today, or tomorrow, or the next day. We'll explain it all later, but I need you to fix the credit card and fast before these guys throw us in jail."

"Give me twenty minutes and then call back. It's later here, so I can make a phone call and take care of this. But when you get back I want a full explanation. Not because I work for you, but because I'm your friend and I deserve better."

"You call me back in twenty minutes, or sooner," Creston said. He looked at Hannibal. "You got any coffee?"

In twenty minutes Leslie called. The credit card issue was resolved and all the charges had been reinstated. Creston handed the phone to Hannibal. "Mr. Hannibal, is it?" Leslie said. "Please take care of those two. Help them and give them whatever they need. I don't know what they're up to but I promise you they're both good men."

"Yes, I understand," Hannibal said.

"One more thing," Leslie added. "I've seen Creston tip someone a month's salary because he liked them." She hung up.

Laughing, Hannibal dismissed the police, assuring them all was under control.

"What's so funny?" Rainey asked.

"You two must have pissed off somebody pretty bad. You were so close to jail the humor in this situation was long gone. It's funny now though. Take the plane, enjoy your trip, and me, I'm gonna enjoy your money."

"We need more ice," Creston said.

They were approaching the grid after flying for eight hours but this time they were following Rainey's gut instinct, compelled to search an area several boxes north of the one Mama Mary had chosen.

"This is a little spooky," Creston said. "You superseding Mama Mary in the psychic department."

"I'm not superseding her, and she isn't psychic. This is a feeling I have so I want to check it out. If we miss then we'll move on to another area."

Creston brought the Albatross down to five hundred feet maneuvering the plane in a typical reconnaissance pattern. An hour passed with Rainey using the binoculars to scan the ocean. There was nothing more than a few coral outcroppings, too small to be islands.

"Over there," Rainey said holding the glasses to his eyes and pointing in the distance. "A larger island's out there. I want to take a closer look."

"You're the navigator."

The hair on the back of Rainey's neck stood up as they approached the larger island. They circled it once, recognized the wreckage of Creston's jet and then sat, speechless. Creston recovered, checked his coordinates, and scribbled them on the chart while Rainey stared at the island.

"Snap out of it Rainey. This is what we came for. If we had gone south we might never have found it. Let's make another circle of the island while I reduce altitude. Take a look at the clearing and tell me if you see anything. I'll come back around and land on the lagoon close to the wreckage. Keep your fingers crossed."

"Suppose there's been an accident or she doesn't want to go with us."

"She's survived almost fifty years, I'm sure she's fine. Let's put this bird on the water and worry about one thing at a time."

Rainey leaned tight against the side glass while looking down on the island. They passed over the clearing and Rainey strained to get a good look, but the plane was still flying too fast and all he managed was a glimpse. Creston took the Albatross out over the lagoon away from the island. Making a large turn to port he changed his direction and was headed straight to the beach, the same beach he had crashed on.

Rainey watched Creston manage the approach with the care and precision of a surgeon. The seaplane descended, cleared the outer edge of the reef and settled into the water on a perfect line to the beach. Rainey was up and out of his seat as soon as the belly of the seaplane nudged the beach leaving Creston to kill the engines and shut down all the systems. The anchors were set before Creston jumped from the cabin door into the shallow water and waded onto the familiar beach.

Rainey stood rigid, hands on his hips, staring into the dense foliage.

"Rainey, relax and take it easy. I'm as anxious as you. Let's take a look at the jet and camp site."

Rainey nodded. They moved with caution as if walking into a dark alley. Nothing had been disturbed and all was as they had left it. Rainey broke the tension.

"What the hell were we expecting? Two months we were here and there was never so much as a single plane in the sky, and we walk up like we're invading a secret ritual."

"I was following your lead, walking up like we we're gonna get shot."

"Fresh footprints, she's been here since we left," Rainey said, pointing to the ground. "I was afraid she would block us out of her memory as if we were never here, but she's been back and recently."

"What makes you so sure?"

"As much as it rained while we were here, the footprints would be washed out almost daily. So, the good news is she's still here."

"Where the hell was she going to go?" Creston said.

"I didn't say anything earlier but I was afraid she would take a walk on the reef at high tide."

Creston realized the seriousness of Rainey's concern. "I don't think so," he said. "I'm more concerned she blocked us out of her memory right after we left."

"Maybe at first, but she's been back. We've got a couple of hours of daylight left. Let's find her."

"All of a sudden I'm nervous," Creston said.

Rainey started walking along the lagoon side of the island in the direction of the compound. The twenty minute walk was tiring and he perspired heavily. "Damn, we were home for a month and already we're getting soft," he said.

Rainey found the entrance and zigzagged through the palm trees. Creston was close behind him, breathing heavily as they entered Amy's compound. Rainey looked around and his throat tightened. Amy was nowhere to be seen. They walked to the entrance of the underground Japanese hospital and called out her name, knelt down at the entrance and called her name again. There was no response. Rainey dropped into the opening, landed in a crouching position, and knew instantly she was not there.

Creston helped Rainey out of the underground. Rainey paced back and forth for a few minutes, stopped, and then took off running.

"She's back at the plane," he yelled running toward the way out. "She's waiting at the plane for us," he yelled again, even though Creston was right behind him.

They ran back covering the distance in less than twenty minutes. Out of breath, gasping and wheezing, Rainey stopped short of their old campsite. Creston almost ran into Rainey and cursed under his breath. Bent over, both hands resting on his knees, Rainey caught his breath.

"You sure she's here?" Creston asked, kneeling, bent forward and his hands pushing into the sand.

Rainey took a deep breath and stood. "She's here. Come on, get up."

"I'm getting too old for this," Creston complained. "And I thought we got in shape."

They entered their campsite and stopped when they reached the left wing of the jet. Rainey called out Amy's name, his eyes moving from side to side, waiting, and sure she was close. Amy stepped from behind the rear of the plane and moved into view. She was the same; long stringy hair, dirty sarong, glassy eyed stare, and beautiful to Rainey.

"We promised we'd be back," Rainey said as he took her hands into his.

"Amy here," she said.

Rainey led Amy to the fire pit and sat on the sand, encouraging her to sit with him. Creston sat next to Amy, at a loss for words.

"Amy, we have a lot to talk about and it might be hard for you to understand," Rainey said. "Creston and I came back because we promised we would. But we don't want to stay." Rainey hoped Amy understood. "We want you to go with us."

"Amy with you," she said.

"Yes, Amy is with us, but we want to go, to fly in the plane," he said pointing toward the sky. "We want you to go in the plane with us."

Amy had no reaction and Rainey realized this would be even more difficult than he thought. Using his index finger he drew a big circle in the sand, placed a small line on the left side of the circle and then drew a large rectangle on the right side.

"Amy lives here," Rainey said pointing at the small line. "Rainey and Creston live here." He placed his finger in the rectangle. "All this is ocean for miles and miles." He watched but her expression didn't change.

"Let's stop for tonight," Creston interrupted. "She needs time and we need to go slow. We can eat and take it easy. We'll stay here an extra day if necessary but maybe she'll be better in the morning." Creston stood up and moved toward the seaplane. "I'll get some food and drinks. Wait here with her."

Creston returned and placed the food on the wing of the jet, went back to the seaplane and returned with an overnight suitcase.

"What are you doing?" Rainey asked.

"I got a few things from the plane I packed in case… no, hoping she'd be willing to come back with us."

"No kidding," Rainey said. "What's in the bag?"

"I have some panties, a couple of bras, two dresses, sandals, a toothbrush, lady stuff." He turned his back to Amy.

"Panties and bras? Are you kidding? She's never worn a bra in her life. It would be a stretch getting the dress on her, and the shoes are real iffy. How do you propose we talk her into getting into the panties and bra?"

"Yeah, well, I'm counting on you," Creston stammered.

"Me! Why me?"

"Because you were married, and I figured you know about these things. You must have helped Leslie at times, or at least watched her."

"That doesn't make me an expert on these things any more than you. And as many women as you've known, I'm sure you helped more than one of them get dressed."

"Maybe, but those situations were usually sexual. This is not. You told me more than once, after being married for a while you became one with Leslie. You knew what she needed, how to help her, when to be there for her, and when to leave her alone. I'm sure you helped her get dressed many times. And you enjoyed it, and it wasn't about sex."

"Right, and look what it got me," Rainey said.

"Damn it Rainey, stop feeling sorry for yourself. It got you a second chance. Can't you see? Wise up before you blow it. Leslie won't be there forever."

Rainey looked at the ground. Creston's words stung with truth. He glanced at Amy. "Where'd you get all these things anyway, and how'd you know to pick out the right stuff?"

"I had a little help." Creston waited then said, "Natalie helped me."

"You told Natalie about this?"

"No, you big dumb ass. Jesus, Rainey, give me some credit."

"I told Natalie they were for a lady who runs an orphanage in Mexico, and I was sending them to her. I said it was a friend's friend kind of thing. I described the size by pointing out women I thought were similar in size to how I remembered Amy. It wasn't hard…"

"Wait a minute. Why Natalie? You hardly know her."

"We sort of hit it off the first night back after the restaurant. She helped me get settled at my place, and then we sat up and talked for a couple of hours. She checked on me while I slept. But nothing else. We sort of hung out a few times over the holiday before I left for California."

Rainey said nothing, staring at Creston.

"Look, this whole experience has taught me a few things," Creston said. "I look at life differently. I'm not going to be a seventy year old man with money and loneliness all I have to live with." He looked up, distracted by two seagulls flying by. "Natalie is strong, independent, and confident. It made me think."

"Do you have anything else for Amy?" Rainey said. "I didn't bring her anything."

"You didn't need to. The basics are covered. We'll go over the rest in the morning. It'll be dark soon and we need to get some sleep. If the weather cooperates we're taking off early, and there are some things we have to do first."

The sun would set in an hour. They had finished eating and Amy stayed with them, not like before when she would spontaneously get up and walk off. As night settled on the island Rainey reclined and listened to the waves break over the reef and thought of Leslie.

CHAPTER FORTY FIVE

Rainey was restless through the night, dozing off several times, and each time waking with a start. At first he thought it was the excitement of taking Amy back home, but realized he was afraid he would wake up and she'd be gone. After they had come so far he worried Amy would refuse to leave, worried she would panic during the flight, and worried they were not doing the right thing for the right reason. He propped himself up on one elbow, looking at Amy and Creston. The challenge of convincing Amy to leave bothered him. Creston sleeps so peacefully, he thought. A gentle wind drifted across the island. The stars were magnificent, brilliant against the jet black sky. Reposing he silently spoke to God, and was comforted with the warmth of His answer. With a few hours left before sunrise, he drifted off to sleep.

Rainey woke to the sound of Creston rhythmically snoring. Amy was sitting up, her legs bent, knees pulled tightly against her chest with her arms wrapped around them, and her hands clasped together. His eyes dropped and then he averted them. We need the panties he thought.

Rainey nudged Creston with his foot until he woke and grumbled incoherently. Creston pushed himself up and stumbled as his feet settled into the sand. Stretching his arms out over his head, he let out a low moan. "Let's get started."

"I'll make coffee," Rainey said. One last time he thought, build a fire, heat the water, and brew island coffee. The making of coffee had been symbolic of their will to survive.

"I think that's a great idea," Creston said. "But can we skip the raw fish for breakfast?"

"Yeah, I think so," Rainey replied. "I've had enough raw fish to last a while." But he was grateful to have had the raw fish, and for the memory.

He poured the coffee and they drank, shaking his head with the strong taste. Not as smooth as he remembered, but neither had been their time on the island.

Creston disappeared into the wreckage of his plane while Rainey sat and attempted to explain to Amy why they had returned, how she had helped to save their lives, all she had done for them, and how they wanted to help her. Amy did not respond and looked away from him most of the time as he spoke. As he tried to reorganize his thoughts and words he heard Creston stumble out of the jet and curse as he almost fell. Creston approached carrying two bags and a briefcase.

"What's all that?" he asked.

"Stuff. We all have stuff and I needed to get some of mine to take back with me."

Rainey thought about the things he had also not been able to take on the raft. "What's so important?"

"A couple of books, a few clothes. It's bad enough I have to leave the jet, but I don't have to leave everything."

Rainey looked at the briefcase.

Creston shook his head. "This is nothing much," he said. "Ten K, cash."

"Ten thousand dollars, in cash?" Rainey said. "A little excessive don't you think?"

"*I'm* excessive," Creston said placing the briefcase on the sand. "We were flying around the world, and let me tell you, there are lots of unfriendly people in this world. Truthfully, I wasn't sure ten K was enough. I brought it as extra insurance because you never know what might happen. I'm sure as hell not going to leave it here."

The banter had Amy's attention. He smiled hoping to reassure her nothing was wrong. Creston watched Amy, and then also smiled.

"Here we are two grinning idiots and one dumbfounded, innocent lady."

"Well, at least one idiot," Rainey said.

"I think we're trying too hard," Creston said. "We spent more than a month with her and yet we tiptoe around like she's going to break. Let's cut to the chase and see what happens. Besides, I have an idea."

"Your ideas make me nervous," Rainey said. "Look, take it easy. Amy's tough but we can't predict what she might do."

"The sure bet is to leave her here. Otherwise, we have to take a chance." Creston turned and said, "Amy, come with me in the plane. Let me show you what your mother loved so much." Creston took Amy's hand and helped her up.

Rainey stood in water up to his knees and helped Amy into the Albatross. Creston took her hand, helped her into the co-pilot's seat and fastened the seatbelt. Creston returned to secure the door. "Go to the inlet, I'll land there."

In a few minutes the engines roared to life and Rainey released the anchor chains, pushed the seaplane out from the beach and gave the thumbs up to Creston. He watched the plane lift from the lagoon and start to bank left. It was almost as exhilarating watching them take off as when he sat next to Creston.

Ten minutes after take off Rainey was kneeling on the narrow beach at the inlet, gasping for breath. The drone of the engines approached and he scanned the sky. Beyond the reef line the Albatross was descending as Creston lined up for a landing.

The seaplane slid into the water and coasted toward the beach as Creston used the engines to maintain a straight line and avoid drifting into the reef on either side. The Albatross nudged the beach and Creston indicated Rainey should set the anchors. Rainey searched for a way to tell him the anchors and anchor chains were on the beach at the lagoon. The engines feathered to a stop and Creston opened the side window.

"Well, what happened was," Rainey stopped. "What happened was I was in a hurry to get here and forgot to put the anchors back on board."

"Another person at a time like this would use the opportunity to make a derogatory comment, demean someone, but I'm not going to. You're my friend, hell you saved my life right here so I'm not going to say anything." Rainey fumed as Creston gloated. "There's a heavy rope in the front compartment of the nose. Take it out, tie it to a palm tree and secure the damn plane," Creston said.

Rainey reached for Amy's hand and pulled, helping her jump from the plane's pontoon to the beach, narrowly missing the steep drop-off. Creston stood near the open door, judging the distance to the narrow beach.

"I forgot about the drop-off being so close to the shore," Creston said. He held out his hand and jumped as Rainey released the rope and let the plane drift away from the beach. Creston missed the beach by a foot and plunged into the deep water.

"Guess I let go too soon."

Rainey extended his hand to Creston and helped him out of the water. "That was damn funny," he said. "I thought sure it would make her laugh. Guess I'll have to try something else."

"I wish she would have laughed. Then it *might* have been worth it. Don't think this makes us even, not by a long shot."

"You'll dry off and it'll be like nothing happened," Rainey said.

Amy walked to Creston, took off her sarong and dried his face, then tied it back on. She stepped back several feet and squatted, looking toward the plane. "Is compassion a natural instinct?" Rainey asked.

"It must be. Amy's pure and innocent. She's had no outside influence. Her life has been simple and matter of fact. Probably why she didn't laugh when I went into the water. She accepts everything at face value and doesn't question anything." Creston looked at Amy. "I hope we are doing the right thing."

"How we do it is the issue. We're doing the right thing, but we have to protect her. She's not ready for the real world."

"Then let's get busy."

"Why do you want to be here instead of the lagoon?" Rainey asked.

"I'm hoping leaving from here will be positive for Amy, not like the times she floated her parents out of here after they died," Creston said. "It's a gamble but maybe this will be a good memory when we take off."

"Big gamble," Rainey said.

"Plus we need some fish to bring back with us. Hopefully some large fish we can catch or get from the tidal pools. But if not I still have a plan."

"What the hell are you talking about? I thought the fly fishing was a story for Hannibal, to throw him off."

"It was, but we need a diversion. We can't show up without any fish. And we certainly can't show up with Amy. It *was* just you and me. Do you think we can land; march Amy off the plane and onto the jet like nothing is amiss? Remember, Guam is a U.S. trust territory. It's similar to a state with all the same laws."

"What about Amy? What did she say about the flight?"

"She didn't say anything, like she almost never says anything. But I found out what they mean when they say *eyes as big as saucers*."

"So what's next?" Rainey asked.

"We need to spend the rest of the day here and get anything onto the plane we want to take. It'll be too late to leave by the time we finish loading. I don't want to land in Guam after dark. Hopefully, we convince Amy she's going with us. She doesn't have anything to bring except her journal. We'll take off in the morning and make Guam before night."

"Landing after dark might work to our advantage."

"The best place to hide is in plain site. People ignore the obvious. After dark would bring more scrutiny and I don't want those policemen snooping around. It's going to be hard enough getting past Hannibal."

"One more thing," Rainey said. "I want to walk the island and take pictures before closing this chapter of our lives."

CHAPTER FORTY SIX

Rainey and Creston were ready by the time the sun crested the horizon. They had packed the day before, the anchors had been retrieved, and they had agreed to forgo the coffee. Six large fish from the tidal pools were iced in the anvil case. Rainey paced the beach while Amy squatted, watching them, and Creston checked the plane.

"You checked the plane yesterday. Nothing has changed. Can we get going?" Rainey said.

"I'm as anxious as you but I don't take chances." Creston finished the inspection and nodded. "Let's turn her around and point her toward the ocean."

The nose of the plane pointed toward the open water and away from the island. They pulled it back until the pontoons settled on the edge of the beach and the tail of the plane hung over the sand. Amy had agreed to leave with them but they were unsure she understood. Rainey wondered if maybe she thought she was going for another ride around the island. He hoped it was human instinct to be with other humans regardless of how long someone had been secluded.

Creston started the engines and checked the gauges, then checked them again and signaled for Rainey to jump on. He locked the door and the plane moved toward the open ocean. Low tide and a calm day made the ocean as smooth as the inlet. Creston throttled up the engines and the Albatross cleared the edge of the reef and started a slow climb out over the Pacific. Soon the island was no more than a speck, undetectable from a normal cruising altitude.

Amy sat in the co-pilot seat while Rainey had strapped into the jump seat directly behind Creston. This is too easy, Rainey thought trying to relax. They had ten hours before landing in Guam and much to do before they were home free.

Several hours into the flight Rainey noticed Amy was restless and fidgeting. He unfastened his seatbelt and moved between the pilot and co-pilot seats and got down on one knee. Amy looked out the window, but at twelve thousand feet Rainey knew there was nothing to see. Then it hit him. Reaching in with his left hand he unfastened the seatbelt, gently took her hand and encouraged her to get up and follow him. He heard Creston mumble, "This ought to be good."

The head was small but adequate. The one thing missing, Rainey thought, was instructions for the woman who had never used a commode. Amy was uninhibited and had no reservations at all about squatting in the sand and urinating. Rainey envied her unabashed straightforwardness, but he would have had better success trying to explain quantum physics. As Rainey tried to muster the courage to demonstrate by sitting on the commode, Amy was squirming and looking at the floor.

"Here, right here." Taking her by the waist, he turned her around, pushed her into the head and as gently as possible forced her to sit on the metal toilet. "It's ok. This is the same as on the island when you squat down and…and…" his hands waving in circles, "do what you always do. It's ok…" And then he heard the sound of her bladder emptying into the stainless steel bowl.

Rainey let out a large sigh of relief and stepped aside as Amy got up and walked back to the cockpit. Too many unforeseen challenges, he thought as he strapped back in.

They snacked on sandwiches, fruit, and cheese, but Amy was slow to eat. All but the fruit was new to her. She nibbled at the sandwich, not sure what to make of it even though Rainey demonstrated. The bottled water was cold, having been covered with ice in the anvil case and Amy jumped as the near freezing water touched her lips.

Hours later Creston said, "It's time to get your nerves in check, get rid of any negative thoughts and remember what we went over."

Creston radioed the island and was told the weather was clear and a slight head wind out of the north would facilitate their landing. Amy had not donned the head set and looked curiously at Creston as he talked into the air.

"It's got to be the way we rehearsed it," Creston said looking back and yelling loudly. Rainey did thumbs up and rose from his seat, stowed the food, secured the case, and checked the cabin. Guam appeared in the distance. Rainey again did the thumbs up and Creston began the descent for landing.

The Albatross floated into the water and slowed gradually. Amy sat transfixed, her eyes wide and her mouth agape at the size of Guam, all the buildings, vehicles, and people as the seaplane approached the ramp. Amy exuded a sense of panic, wringing her hands together and breathing in shallow gulps of air. Rainey took her hand, unclasped the harness and hustled her to the rear of the plane.

Creston opened the door and stepped down onto the ground.

"Hello boys," Hannibal shouted, as if the engines were still running. "I must admit I'm glad to see you guys. I wasn't too sure with all the commotion we had here last time you guys might not be too happy with me."

"Hey, a little misunderstanding is all. We don't have a problem except Rainey and I have to head back to the states. I got a call on this new satellite phone I brought with us. There's a small crisis back home with one of my companies. The union is trying to strike and I've got to get back home and negotiate a new contract and fast. Is the jet all gassed up and ready to go? We want to leave early in the morning, about five or so, right before sunup. I want to be in the air when the sun breaks the horizon."

"Yep, she's all ready. I had her fueled and moved over here the first day you two left on your fishing trip." Rainey was standing in the doorway as if waiting for assistance. Hannibal waved. "I'm sorry to hear you have to cut the trip short," he said. "I don't guess you got much fishing in this time."

"Oh no, we did pretty good," Creston said. "There was one island out there, about eight hundred miles or so from here, had a perfect crescent shaped inlet with a white sandy beach. Not a trace anyone had ever been there before, and lots of fish. We would have stayed out a few more days if it wasn't for the crisis back home." He pointed toward the side of the office. "Mind if we use one of those carts over there? I need some help getting my case into the jet. It's too heavy for me and Rainey to carry."

"Sure, "Hannibal said. "Mind if I take a look at your catch?"

"Sure but help me unload it onto the cart first."

Creston grabbed the handle on the end of the case and with Hannibal's assistance, pulled it from the plane while Rainey held the rear handle and pushed the case to the edge of the door. He jumped down, grabbed the handle and helped place the case onto the cart.

"Easy, *easy*," Rainey said.

"Okay, but it's just some dead fish," Hannibal said.

Creston unsnapped the latches and lifted the top of the anvil case. There was nothing visible except the shadowy outline of what appeared to be a large fish under the ice. Creston reached into the ice at the end of the case and pulled up a large sea bass. It weighed almost ten pounds.

Hannibal grinned with approval at the beauty of the fish Creston held high in his hand, his arm outstretched. "What else you boys got in your case?" he asked.

Creston motioned for Hannibal to come closer. He moved the ice in the center of the case to expose the bright colors of a bull dolphin. "Almost six feet long and barely fits in the case. I'm dropping it off in Hawaii to have it mounted and then shipped home to New Orleans. I need to keep it on ice so I hope you don't mind if I don't take it out. Not to mention the damn thing is heavy and slippery," Creston said.

"Nice catch. Send me a picture when you get it mounted."

"Here, take this home, maybe the little lady will cook it up for you nice and proper," Creston said as he handed the sea bass to Hannibal and closed the lid on the case.

"I'm the little lady, and the old man, and everything else at my house," Hannibal said and broke into a raucous laugh.

Creston forced a laugh and motioned for Rainey to move the cart to the jet. Again with the help of Hannibal, they lifted the case into the jet and pushed it toward the rear of the plane. Rainey secured the case while Creston returned to the Albatross to retrieve the rest of their gear. Twenty minutes later they had loaded the jet, thanked Hannibal for his help, and told him they were off to the hotel for a meal, shower, and some sleep.

Rainey and Creston watched the sun set from the lobby of the hotel. An hour later, having borrowed a van from the hotel, they returned to the airport and parked along side the jet. Creston unlocked the door and stood watch as Rainey entered the plane, a small bag in his hand. He looked around but there was no one moving about or vehicles approaching. He leaned into the plane and motioned to Rainey, indicating all was quiet and clear. Rainey had convinced Amy to slip the dress over her head and nodded with approval as it fell around her, stopping several inches below her knees. She pulled the dress up and held it out in front of her, then let it drop again, not understanding the necessity of the garment. The flip-flop sandals were uncomfortable and Amy tried twice to step out of them, but each time Rainey insisted she leave them on. There was not enough time to convince her bra and panties were necessary, so Rainey did not remove them from the bag. Back at the hotel, and after a shower, he would try to explain the bra and panties, but he was less than optimistic about success.

Rainey led her from the darkness inside the jet to the door. Creston helped her down and into the van. After they drove off and were out of site, Hannibal stepped from the cover of his building and walked to his jeep he had parked out of site. He maneuvered onto the road, not following them but determined to find out who the third person was.

The hotel lobby was small and they ushered Amy to the stairs and up to the second floor. All was deserted except for the front desk clerk whose head was buried in a magazine. The trio went unnoticed.

"You get her showered, wash her hair and whatever else you think needs doing while I go back downstairs and get us some food. I'm starving and I know Amy must be hungry. There's a small restaurant and maybe they can cook up something to go."

"Why do I have to do the babysitting? I'm sure you…"

"Like I told you before, you know about these things with women." Creston was out the door leaving Rainey with Amy.

Rainey turned to Amy. The sandals had been kicked off and the dress was heaped in a pile on top of them. She stood before him with nothing on but her sarong. Shaking his head he mumbled "this will never work," and went into the bathroom to turn on the shower.

Creston returned with three bacon, lettuce, and tomato sandwiches, Hawaiian kettle potato chips, and two apples. Rainey was dressed in fresh clothes and Amy sat on the floor stroking her hair as it fell across her breasts and down her back. Curiously, the sarong was gone and she sat wearing a pair of panties. He looked at Rainey. "This looks almost hopeful. How did it go?"

"I tried to explain the shower to her but it wasn't working. She stared at the water but wouldn't get into the stall, so I got in, and after a minute or two coaxed her to get in with me."

"You took a shower with her! You can't be serious," Creston said. "You showered together."

"I couldn't get her to step into the shower. She's never experienced hot water before. I turned it on, and when she placed her hand in to feel the water she jerked it back so fast she hit herself in the face. And it wasn't even hot. I kept trying to convince her, but she shook her head. I stripped down to my boxer shorts and stepped into the tub. After a minute or two she took my hand and got in."

"What happened next?"

"Nothing happened. I used the little bottle of hotel shampoo and lathered my hair, and then I lathered her hair. I think she likes the smell of the shampoo, she almost smiled. It took two times lathering her hair to wash it all. She has lots of hair. Next, I got the washcloth, soaped it up and started washing my body with it."

"Stop right there. Please tell me you didn't wash her. Please tell me."

"Well, at first I sort of had to get her started by washing her back, but then I placed the wash cloth in her hand and she figured out the rest. She almost tasted the soap but I was quick enough to stop her and tell her yuck."

"Yuck? You told her Yuck?" Creston laughed and Amy starred at him.

"Yuck," Amy said. "Soap yuck."

Rainey realized Amy was dealing with too much and decided to slow things down. "Let's eat and get some sleep," he said. They finished the sandwiches and Rainey turned off the lights, plunging the room into darkness.

At four in the morning, two hours before sunrise, Rainey awoke in the twin bed. Amy's bed was empty. She lay curled in a fetal position asleep on the floor.

Rainey threw a pillow at the couch where Creston slept, his snoring at a modest and tolerable level. Creston sprang up, cursing at Rainey. Turning toward Amy, intending to wake her, he was surprised to see she was sitting up looking at him.

"We don't have much time," Rainey said. "It's a long way home so let's get going."

"Amy goes home?" she said.

"Amy, we have a new home for you. We want to take you to the new home."

With her head down she rose from the floor and moved in the darkness toward the bathroom. Rainey turned on the lamp by the bed and watched Amy move amidst the clutter.

"You'd think there would be at least one suite in this place," Creston said.

"Yeah, that's what we needed, to draw more attention to ourselves. Did you order the food for the flight back to Hawaii?"

"Yes, it's supposed to be ready at five and at the front desk for us. We can pick it up, check out and take the van to the airport. The manager said they'd send someone to pick up the van later." Creston looked around the room. "What's next?"

"You don't want to know." Rainey picked up the bag and headed to the bathroom.

Creston busied himself packing while waiting for Rainey and Amy to emerge from the bathroom. At ten minutes to five Rainey came out with Amy behind him. Her hair had been brushed and flowed to the small of her back. She wore the dress Rainey had given her, had the flip-flop sandals on and, Creston noticed, her breasts were firm and pointed.

"You should open a beauty parlor. She looks great. We might pull this off if we make it to Hawaii."

"First we have to get her on the plane and take off before this place wakes up. Then we'll worry about Hawaii, which is a serious concern I have."

It was five fifteen and still dark when they pulled the van up alongside the jet. Creston scanned the premises, determined no one was near and got out. He moved around to the passenger side and opened the middle door. Rainey had already gotten out and was unlatching the door of the plane. He lifted the door and a beam of light blinded him for the moment.

"Good morning, *boys*. I thought I'd wait inside the plane. I didn't want to miss you two." The large voice of Hannibal stunned them.

Rainey, his vision slow to adjust to the darkness after being hit by the bright light, turned toward the voice of Hannibal and demanded, "What is this about, and why are you on our plane?"

"Rainey, take it easy," Creston said.

"I've been here for thirty years renting and chartering planes, setting up guides for fishing trips, scuba diving, and pretty much anything else someone wants to do. I've about seen it all. And some of those things I don't like. I've seen guys from Asia come in here and fly out to certain islands and make a deal for some of the young girls. They promise the natives they're gonna take care of the girls, get them educated, provide a better life. They give them a couple of hundred dollars U.S. money and the natives think they're rich. Then they smuggle them young girls out of here and into a sex trade business over in the orient. Ten, twelve years old some of them."

Rainey and Creston said nothing as Hannibal told his story.

"I had a daughter once, but she ran off. It wasn't such a good life for her here. First her mom left us, and I didn't do so good with my daughter. She left me a note one day saying she had a ride to the states. But I don't think so. I think she got hooked up with someone and they lied to her like these guys I told you about. I've never seen or heard from her since. It's been almost twenty years. I might have grandkids." Even in the darkness Hannibal's face showed the pain of lost years.

"Hannibal, this is different. What gave it away there was someone with us," Rainey asked.

"The story about the crisis back home didn't wash with me. And when you got back you showed me the one fish and the so called bull dolphin. I've seen more dolphins than anybody and yours didn't look like the ones from around here. I figured you brought it with you. The colors were close but not the same. Where did you get the fish?"

"Salt Water Jack's down in the Florida keys. It's a fishing and outfitting store for tourists. They have lots of different pillows made to look like fish. They have marlin, dolphins, sharks, barracuda and the like. It's a pillow but it looks like a real dolphin from a distance. Hard to tell it's fake," Creston explained.

"A pillow?" Hannibal thought about what Creston had said. "You guys keep coming up with firsts for me. You boys was in too big a hurry to get the case into the plane. You were pretty smooth, but not convincing enough, especially since I have a suspicious nature to begin with." Hannibal held his arm out and pointed toward Amy. "She was in the bottom of the case wasn't she? That's why you wanted to get it into the plane and why you," he said pointing at Rainey, "jumped up in there so quickly. I wasn't sure but I smelled some bad fish you might say, so I watched you boys real close. You came back after dark. I was parked over by the office where you couldn't see me, but I saw the whole thing, including you help this lady out of the plane and into the van. One thing's for certain. If you're smuggling women, you two are amateurs."

"We're not smuggling women," Rainey said. Then he realized in fact they were trying to smuggle Amy back into the states. "Well, not the way you think."

"You better talk fast, because Captain Powell will be coming around here in about twenty minutes. He likes to make early rounds at the airport before he heads off to breakfast."

Rainey told the entire story. He told of the plane trip around the world, the stop in Hawaii and Pearl Harbor, the crash, finding Amy on the island, the raft, getting rescued and returning to New Orleans. But he did not tell Hannibal who Amy's parents were. Hannibal listened and never took his eyes off Rainey's.

"We think she's been on the island her entire life, almost fifty years and the last thirty alone. We want to take her back and give her all the things she's never had. But it has to stay a secret. The doctors and shrinks would ruin her. We think she'd end up in an asylum, and there'd be nothing we could do about it."

"You boys are telling the truth, aren't you?"

"Hannibal, we don't have much time. We need to get out of here," Creston said.

"Sometimes, when I have some extra money and I'm not too busy, I fly out to the islands and bring food and things to the natives. I can usually talk one of the navy fly boys into piloting the plane with me. So maybe I understand what you're doing and why you're doing it." Hannibal stopped for a moment staring at the ground. "I'm gonna be mighty disappointed in you boys if you're bullshitting me. Ok, let's get you loaded up and get her on the plane before anyone else shows up."

Creston started the engines and returned to the open door to secure it. Hannibal was starting to shut the door when Creston handed him his briefcase. "Don't open this until we're gone. Put it to good use." He secured the door, hurried back to the pilot's seat, and after fastening his harness taxied into position. Captain Powell's police jeep pulled into the area as the jet raced down the runway.

CHAPTER FORTY SEVEN

Amy paced the cabin as Rainey and Creston concentrated on the approach into Hawaii. Being out of her element was taking a toll on her. She rubbed her hands along her hair, clasped them together, released them, looked out the window, sat down, got up, and paced again. Rainey unfastened his harness and moved to the center of the cabin to calm her. Amy was confused and nervous to a point of panting. She had removed the dress as well as the bra and panties and replaced them with her stained sarong. She sat on the floor of the cabin and rocked back and forth.

Rainey had no training in how to deal with a person, let alone a woman, who was bewildered and panicking. His recourse was to rely on his faith and God's guidance. He sat down cross legged on the floor in front of her.

"Creston and I will take care of you," he said. "There is nothing to fear." He took her hands. "All we want is to take care of you. Look at me and please tell me you understand, tell me you trust me and know what I'm saying."

"Amy miss home," she said as she looked around the plane.

"Soon we'll be back on another island, but one much bigger than home. We'll go to another hotel like the one with the hot water shower…"

Amy perked up. "We shower again?" The panic was gone from her middle-aged face.

Rainey nodded. "Yes, we can shower again."

Amy's innocence was contagious. He held her hands for thirty minutes until Creston called from the cockpit and said Hawaii was less than twenty minutes away.

Still holding her hands Rainey said, "It is time to land again, like we did before. You need to sit in the chair and I'll help you fasten the seatbelt.

Amy looked at Rainey and her calm surprised him. She got up, removed the sarong and dropped it. Amy then picked up the panties and donned them again, pulling them up as Rainey had taught her in the hotel room. The bra was more of a challenge and after several minutes he took the clasps in his hands and fastened them. Amy slipped the dress over her head letting it fall into place. Rainey stepped back and admired her, feeling a breakthrough had been made. She settled into the overstuffed cabin chair, holding her sandals, and waited for Rainey to fasten the seatbelt.

Rainey secured the belt, and on impulse leaned forward and kissed her on the cheek. Amy stared straight ahead and did not react to the kiss.

Creston taxied to the terminal at the private airport from which they had departed for Guam. He shut down the engines and all systems, unfastened his harness, grabbed his flight bag and rushed into the cabin.

"One more thing before we get off the plane," he said as Rainey followed him. "Hold this bag open for a minute." He removed a Polaroid camera and said, "Amy, be still for a few seconds and try to smile."

Creston crouched down to eye level with Amy and took her picture. The flash splashed a bright light in her face causing her to jump and grip the arm rests of her seat. She glanced at Rainey obviously frightened. He took her hand and smiled. "It's ok," he said. "The light can't hurt you." He turned to Creston. "Give us a warning next time. I got her calmed down and the flash scared the hell out of her."

"Sorry, but I'm trying to hurry. Hold the camera and hand me the bag," Creston said.

The picture developed as Creston waved it in the air, trying to hasten the drying process. He used scissors and neatly trimmed the photograph of Amy into a one inch square. Rainey watched Creston pull an official looking passport and a small container of glue from the bag.

"What the hell is that and where'd you get it?" Rainey asked.

"This, my friend, is a great fake passport. And in a minute Amy will become Jean Smith from Florida."

"Jean Smith? Who the hell is Jean Smith?"

"Hopefully, she is one of at least several thousand in the United States," Creston replied.

"This is a major felony, do you hear me, a major felony. Have you lost your mind? And, where the hell did you get a fake passport?" Rainey said.

"A major felony? We have committed several major felonies. It's a little late to start worrying. Besides, it's only a problem if we get caught, so relax before we get off the plane or you'll give it all away. You heard Hannibal; we look like a couple of amateurs, so let's tighten up."

Rainey stewed for several seconds, irked because Creston was right, and because he should have already had his act together. "You didn't answer my question. Where did you get the passport?"

"Better. I like it when you get stoic and determined. It saved my life."

"Quit stalling and tell me where the passport came from."

"Big O is well connected but he keeps it quiet. If you ask the right questions you'd be surprised what you can learn."

"Big O! You got Big O involved in this? I can't believe you used him to break the law. Have you no conscience?"

"Jesus, Rainey, would you shut up? You're getting Amy upset. And I didn't use Big O. He gave me a name and I did the rest. He didn't ask any questions, and I didn't volunteer any information. See, I didn't tell you about this because I was afraid of how you'd react. Your conscience would eat at you and might compromise your judgment. Hurry up and let's get the hell off the plane before someone gets suspicious."

Creston opened the door as the ground attendant knocked on the fuselage.

Security at the small airport was lax, and in fact, closer to non-existent. The security personnel talked to each other more than scrutinizing the bags and people from the private jet. The attendant gave a cursory look at the passport of Jean Smith from Florida and did not look at Amy as he handed it back to her. He managed to mutter a most insincere "have a nice day" and returned to his conversation with his coworker.

They had cleared security and there was nothing to hide from. They were safe at least until they got to California, and with a little more luck, there as well. Creston made arrangements to have the plane serviced, refueled, and ready for an eight o'clock morning departure.

They entered the open air lobby of the private resort after a short taxi ride to the hotel. Amy walked between Rainey and Creston, stumbling as she looked up at the high ceiling, her eyes darting back and forth, trying hard to absorb it all. Rainey couldn't stop the anxiety building in her, the quick breathing, and her fast head turns. She moved toward him until she was practically stepping on his feet, her hands clasped at her chest as if she were praying or making a wish. He placed his arm around her shoulders to comfort her, knowing they needed to get to the room before she fainted or collapsed.

The suite was luxurious and Amy stood in awe more so than in the lobby. There were two bedrooms, one with twin queen beds and the other with a large king-size four-poster bed. A mosquito net canopy hung over the king bed and fluttered with the wind blowing in from the ocean. There were two bathrooms and the master bath was almost as big as the room they had shared on Guam.

"Amy, you can sleep in the room with the big bed," Rainey said.

Amy entered the large bathroom, looked at the shower stall next to the Jacuzzi tub and turned toward Rainey. "We shower?" she said.

"Excellent idea!" Creston proclaimed.

"No, it's Creston's turn," Rainey said. "Amy, you can show Creston how to shower."

Her expression did not change but there was sincerity in her eyes as she held out her hand to Creston.

"A word of advice," Rainey said. "Enjoy the innocence." He stopped in the doorway of the smaller bedroom. "This might be the purest experience you'll ever have. I'll be in the other bath getting ready for supper. Let's eat in the restaurant overlooking the Pacific." This should be interesting Rainey thought, Amy's first restaurant experience. He moved toward the second bath. So far they had been successful, even if most of it was dumb luck.

Rainey stripped down to his boxer shorts and fell across the queen sized bed closest to the large sliding glass doors which opened onto the Lanai. He heard the shower running and the temptation was too great to resist. He forced himself up from the comfortable bed and walked back toward the master bath and stood in the doorway. Creston was standing in the shower wearing jockey underwear, his arms at his sides. Amy had lathered his hair with shampoo and was working the lather into a heaping snow white skull cap. She had the look of a child with a new toy. Creston held up his hand as Rainey approached, gesturing him to stop. Rainey suppressed a laugh and went back to shower.

"I'm not sure the same dress is appropriate for dinner tonight. And the flip-flops are pushing it a bit too much," Rainey said. "The last thing we want is bring attention to ourselves."

"The resort has a ladies apparel store. I can give it a try, or we can take her down there and let the sales lady help. But there might be too many questions and we don't have enough answers to avoid suspicion."

"Ok, then you go to the dress shop and find more appropriate clothing that won't draw too much attention to us. Hopefully Amy will wear it."

Amy came out of the bedroom wearing the new one piece dress, a floral print on yellow with an open back. The bodice was supportive and the dress did not require wearing a brassiere, a feature Creston knew Rainey would appreciate. The shoes were open-toe flats with white mesh that would mold around the foot. Her long hair had been brushed and her suntanned complexion contrasted dramatically with the brightness of the dress and shining hair. She looked at least ten years younger than her age.

Rainey had requested a table in the farthest corner, forgoing the view of the Pacific. Showing Amy how to use a knife, fork and spoon would take several tries and risk drawing too much attention.

"Let's order the mahi again. Rice pilaf and bread should be enough," Rainey said. "And water to drink; her system isn't ready for wine or soft drinks. We can start slow and see what she can handle."

The waiter and two assistants, each carrying a plate, positioned themselves and on the waiter's nod, placed the food on the table precisely at the same time. "The chef prepares a wonderful presentation. Enjoy."

Creston placed his fork on the table. "Is anyone looking?" Creston asked.

"How would I know? You can see I have my back to the dining room. I'm trying to conceal her as much as possible. Try to show her again."

"I've shown her twice already. She's holding the fork like she wants to stab something. Thank God it's not a steak. I'm afraid to give her the knife."

"We should have ordered room service," Rainey said. "Give her the spoon, hold her hand and shovel the rice into her mouth. Maybe she'll get it this time."

The waiter approached, looked at Amy and asked, "Was the silverware dirty?"

"Our friend's not from around here," Creston said. "She prefers her fingers."

"May I suggest the crème brulee with fresh raspberries for dessert?" the waiter said. "I can bring another spoon."

"Amy likes fish," she said placing a piece into her mouth as the waiter walked away.

The servers brought the crème brulee and placed in on the table as they had the dinner plates. The waiter glazed the dessert with a torch, ladled the raspberries on top and placed a spoon by Amy.

Creston placed a spoonful of the dessert into Amy's mouth. Her expression was like a toddler's with his first birthday cake. Her eyes widened and she held the bite of dessert in her mouth, not swallowing.

"I think she likes the dessert," Rainey said.

"Amy, swallow and I'll give you another bite."

Amy swallowed, took the spoon from Creston and fed herself another bite, again savoring it for several seconds.

"The right motivation is what she needed," Rainey said.

Creston doted on Amy, wiping her hands with the napkin, dabbing at her mouth, and making sure she was comfortable. Rainey discovered a side of Creston he had never seen before and knew Creston would take care of Amy forever. They were best friends, but you never know everything about someone, no matter how long you know them. Or, he thought, even if you're married to them. Maybe you're not supposed to.

CHAPTER FORTY EIGHT

Miles above the Pacific, halfway between Hawaii and California, Creston turned on the auto pilot and they cruised smoothly, as if suspended like a toy plane on a string. With three hours left before landing in California, Rainey unfastened his harness and walked back to where Amy sat staring out the window. Rainey had strapped her into one of the single seats for takeoff but she had moved to the sofa during the flight. He sat next to her. We are almost home, he thought.

Flying into a small airport with private flight line service affords benefits owners of private planes understand and appreciate. Rainey had made many trips with Creston, although none as far as the trip to Guam and back. He, too, had become accustomed to the ease of flying into the airport, taxiing to the hanger and stepping out almost directly into a waiting vehicle. There were never any lines, security check points, or baggage checks. And because the trips were legitimate and on the up and up, there was never reason to be nervous. Rainey's stomach churned as he sat next to Amy and wondered if his guilty conscience would give him away. He released Amy's hand and walked back to the cockpit and strapped himself in.

"I never worried about it before," Rainey said. "The landing, or taking off, the coming and going, or anything. But now I'm concerned about everything."

"Guilt is a powerful enemy," Creston said. "It's usually best if you can avoid it."

"Good advice, but let's see what we have here. A bogus passport, so I'm sure it's good for at least one felony conviction. And then we have bringing someone into the country illegally, so another felony conviction waiting to happen. Then we take her back out of the country which is the Mann act, or whatever you call it. We're up to at least three felonies each and we haven't even landed yet. So, what were you saying about guilt?"

"The Mann Act?" Creston said. "It might be breaking some law, but it's definitely not the Mann Act. That has more to do with white slavery and bringing women across state lines for immoral purposes." Creston stopped as he remembered what Hannibal had told them about the native island girls who were enticed into leaving for a better life but wind up in a sex trade business somewhere. He was sickened to his core men could be so vile. Rainey sat quietly and appeared as deep in thought as Creston.

"You're right, screw the guilt. Laws are meant to be broken, right?" Rainey said.

"No, but it happens."

A winter storm churned off the coast of southern California and Creston had been instructed by the tower at John Wayne Airport to change his course and altitude to fly higher and around the densest concentration of weather. Rainey had moved to the cabin to make sure Amy was seated properly with the seat belt attached. He sat next to her and talked as the plane bumped and drifted through the rough weather. Rainey held her hand, continuing to talk, until Creston had artfully landed the private jet and taxied to the hanger.

"This might be a slight problem," Creston said pointing out the window. "U.S. Customs is here."

"What do you think this is about? What are we going to do?"

"First," Creston answered, "we calm down. There isn't anything we can do but think fast. I'm sure they're going to want to come aboard and search the plane. Keep your fingers crossed all they're looking for is drugs."

Creston finished his flight plan entries and they all moved toward the door with Amy close behind Rainey. They stepped into the cool, evening breezes flowing in from the Pacific. The sky was clear, but in the distance west of the airport, gray-streaked clouds billowed as they headed inland. Rainey tried to look nonchalant, but was stiff with worry. A ground attendant directed them to the reception room and customer lounge.

Two customs agents were having coffee and talking with the receptionist, a middle aged woman with red hair, dark lipstick, and wearing a blouse suggestively unbuttoned, revealing an ample bosom. The dark haired agent leaned over, speaking softly as he looked down on her, enjoying the tease. Rainey headed to the counter where a coffee urn had been placed and heard one of the agents mention smugglers, then drugs and a shoot out. The rest of their words faded as he took two cups and fixed coffee for himself and Creston. Rainey returned with the coffee knowing they were watching him. Rainey sipped the coffee, his back to the agents. As the room became silent he watched Creston's eyes move, following the agent approaching them.

"Good evening, I'm agent Smith with the U.S. Customs department. Did you folks have a nice flight in today?"

Rainey turned and instinctively stepped back as if his space had been compromised. Agent Smith was a non-assuming man of average height and build, sandy blonde hair, and tanned to a surfer-like appearance.

"It was good except for the storm a few miles off shore. We had to alter our course and fly around it but no problems," Creston answered.

"I'd like to take a look at your manifest and then inspect your plane. I presume you don't have a problem with any of this."

"No sir, no problem at all. Help yourself," Creston said handing his log book to agent Smith.

"Agent Garcia over there will inspect the plane," he said. Agent Garcia was still leaning over the receptionist, obviously flirting and not watching his counter part. The receptionist smiled, leaned toward agent Garcia and pulled her blouse closed.

"Guam is a long trip. I see here it was two of you who left here but three people coming back. Who's the lady?" Agent Smith asked.

Creston hesitated to reply. Rainey, fearing the answer was not quick enough, spoke up. "Her name is Jean Smith. We met her in Guam, I mean we were in Guam and she was there and we met her at the airport." Rainey inwardly kicked himself for fear of sounding less than natural. He calmed himself, expecting more questions.

"So how did she wind up on your plane, and why?"

Creston looked at Rainey. "I think it's one of those lover's spats," Rainey said.

Creston raised his eyebrows to the answer. Agent Smith said nothing.

"We were in Guam and had rented a seaplane to go out and do some island hopping and fly fishing. We had to cut our trip short because a business matter came up back home." He hesitated, trying to read the deadpan face of agent Smith but there was no reaction. "New Orleans is home, that's where we're headed. Anyway, when we got back to Guam we were getting ready to take off and Hannibal, he's the man we rented the seaplane from; Hannibal asks us if we can help out a lady in distress. We didn't…"

"I know Hannibal," Agent Smith interrupted, "he does some good work out there in the islands for the natives, especially the children."

Rainey had a sinking feeling, as if he had been caught cheating in school by a nun. But in too deep to stop he said, "Yeah, he is a good man. Anyway, he tells us some guy gets in a fight with this lady, Jean Smith, did I say her name already? So anyway, this guy gets in a fight with her and leaves her there, took off with her bags and all she had was her passport. And my friend here being a soft touch and a gentleman agrees to bring her back to the states. We can take her as far as New Orleans. From there she can get in touch with her family and make arrangements to get to Florida. She's from Florida, so we're trying to help a lady out."

"I changed our plans a little," Creston added. "With the storm approaching and the business thing back home I decided to get the plane serviced and refueled so we can get out of here today. We can be back to New Orleans in a little less than five hours, which is still before midnight back there." Creston stopped talking fearing he was beginning to ramble as if he was trying too hard to be carefree and convincing.

"Where's her passport and also your I D's?" the agent asked.

Rainey and Creston handed over their driver's licenses and Amy's passport. Agent Smith walked back to the receptionist desk, scrutinizing the credentials while placing a call on his radio and leaving a message. Agent Garcia returned from the plane and the two agents talked for several minutes while Rainey and Creston finished their coffee and sweated out the wait. Agent Smith took a call on his radio. He nodded, spoke but too quietly for Rainey to hear and nodded again. After several long minutes the two agents walked back to the waiting travelers.

"The plane is clean and Hannibal confirmed your story. He said you two were trying to help a lady." Agent Smith returned the passport and driver's licenses to Rainey and smiled. "You might want to lay off the coffee."

"Yeah, well it's a long flight, been awake a long time, and we're kinda in a hurry and …"

"Hey. It's a custom's agent joke. I'm kidding with you. Have a nice flight home. I hope this lady gets her things back." He and agent Garcia retuned to the receptionist and their flirting.

CHAPTER FORTY NINE

The next evening Rainey sat on the sofa in Leslie's apartment unable to find the right words. His heart raced and then sank as he struggled, about to speak when she interrupted him.

"Don't you dare ask if it was yours. You can say almost anything but..."

"I'm sorry I wasn't here for you. And, I'm sorry I stood you up. I was confused and upset, and I didn't want a confrontation. I didn't think, after so much time had passed, you wanted to have a serious talk."

"I never said it was serious," she said. "I wanted to talk, but I guess it would have wound up being serious. And it hadn't been as long as you think. We spent the night together less than three months before. I needed you and pushed you into it. It didn't seem painful at the time as I remember it."

"It was never painful until you left." He regretted his words as soon as he said them. "But I understand. It's ok. What happened?"

"Rainey, it was a miscarriage. It happens all the time, unfortunately. I was scared to tell you I was pregnant, plus a little embarrassed I was so careless. Then I was afraid to tell you about the miscarriage, thinking you'd be upset about me getting pregnant to begin with and not telling you."

"It was a while ago," he said. "But are you ok?"

"I'm fine," she said. "Are you ok?"

Rainey had been staring at the floor. "I never thought about having a child, I mean, not in a long time. I guess I figured it wasn't meant to be; maybe I had gotten too old. I feel like I've missed a big part of life." He looked away for a minute. "It doesn't feel good. I can't imagine how you must have felt. I'm sorry."

"Rainey," she said looking into his eyes, "I'd be lying if I didn't tell you I was excited about having a baby, having your baby, so yes I was disappointed when I lost it. I'm getting older and it's harder for some women to carry a baby when they get older. I'm thirty seven years old and the clock is ticking, as they say. You being here and your words are enough. Thank you." Placing her hands on her hips she said, "Now, what the *hell* is going on."

"What are you talking about?" he said.

"You know *damned* good and well what I'm talking about. What was with the little charade you and Creston pulled at Christmas? You would never act so rude and disrespectful." Leslie moved to the sofa and sat next to Rainey. "And then you tell me you're going to Florida but wind up on Guam. Start talking."

"Creston and I have a trip we have to make in the morning. We'll be gone for a couple of days. When I get back I'll have lots to tell you. I need to go home and get some rest. I'm meeting him at the lakefront airport at seven."

"I don't suppose I can talk you into staying here tonight. You can sleep on the couch," she said. "No, I can see it's not a good idea."

"It's a great idea. And I want to stay, but I have one more thing to finish and it's too important. Not more important than you, I've learned that and more, but it's got to get done," he said.

"I can see it's important so go and do whatever it is you need to do, but I want you to tell me the rest of the story, and soon."

Rainey nodded then said, "One more thing, have you spoken with my mother? I tried calling her but all I got was the answer phone. It's not like her to be gone and not tell me."

"Maybe she gets it from you. She had no idea where you were, so don't be too surprised. But no, I don't know where she is. Maybe she went over to the casino in Biloxi for a couple of days. Your mom has friends and they've gone there before." She smirked, drawing out her last point. "And, she thinks you're down in Florida doing whatever and keeping it to yourself."

"Yeah, maybe so. I can't blame her, but I still worry about her."

"You always worry," Leslie said.

"Not like I used to. The island taught me a few things, and I've changed. Some things are worth hanging on to, worth fighting for, and some things you let go. The real trick is knowing the difference between the two. Life's a work in progress."

Rainey knew well what he was missing as he walked away. On the drive to his apartment, thinking of Leslie, he regretted his decision to not stay. Settling into bed he tried to call his mother one more time. It puzzled him, but he slept well and thought no more about it.

The rented jet was smaller than the others Creston had leased, but it was fast, and they would be in the Bahamas in a little over three hours. In less than five hours they would have delivered Amy to the private island and the care and love of Mama Mary. Rainey stood on the tarmac, a chill of morning air blanketing him while he thought of Amy's island, and wondered if he would ever see it again. Maybe one day. Maybe.

Rainey entered the jet, crouched over because of limited headroom, and immediately had a flashback of the underground hospital. Shaking it off, he found Amy already on board. Natalie sat next to her, talking. Amy rose from her seat as if Natalie were not talking, approached Rainey and stood close enough to him they touched, her shoulder against his chest, and his hand on the small of her back. He wrapped his arms around her in the gentle manner Amy had become accustomed to and kissed her on the cheek. But unlike all the other times, Amy raised her arms and put them around Rainey. He hugged her a little tighter knowing a milestone had been reached. Amy sat down and fastened her seatbelt.

"Good morning," he said.

"Yeah, and good morning to you," Natalie responded. "Well?" she asked.

"What?"

"Don't what me, mister. You were with Leslie last night. And yes, it is none of my business, but so what."

"We had a nice talk and then I went home to get ready for this trip."

"What else?" she said. "Come on, there's more."

"No, there isn't. Creston and I have to finish what we started before anything else."

"Men!" she said. "Or should I say BOYS!"

"I take it Creston has filled you in on what we're doing."

"Not all of it. He said the rest was for another time. He called me and asked me to help him with a friend who needed to spend the night at his place. I made sure she was ok and put her to bed. He and I stayed up half the night talking, and you don't need to hear about the other half."

"WOMEN!" he shouted over his shoulder walking to the cockpit.

"This jet is a little cramped," Rainey said.

"The other jet had to go back to California so I hired a pilot to take it back. But, this one is fine, and it's fast."

"You sure have a way with getting your hands on planes, and quickly."

"Yeah, well the people here are trying to accommodate. They were before because I've been flying out of here for years, but especially so, now. They're afraid I'm going to sue them over the rogue mechanic sabotaging planes. I'll let them sweat a little, then let it go since the insurance will take care of most of it. In my other life I might have gone after them in court and made a big deal of it, but there are other things more important. A good friend of mine, retired lawyer, told me a long time ago to stay out of court if at all possible. It's a good idea to listen to him."

"What about Natalie? How much did you tell her?"

"She's a good woman. She doesn't ask many questions and has a good heart. Maybe a little rough around the edges, but one on one she's more refined, especially if she trusts you. A bad marriage and ungrateful patients have made her put up a wall around herself. You two will get along fine. And she certainly seems to like Leslie. Maybe I'll tell her the story when we get back."

"So, what's with you two? I would think she isn't your type, although I'm not sure what your type is anymore."

Creston thought about what Rainey had said. "You and I have both changed these last few months. And maybe me more than you, but where I've changed, such as caring about life and not as much about money, you have grown. You'll worry less and each day will be a blessing to you. And a blessing to me for which I give you credit. But I still have to work on it. Your hurdles throughout the rest of your life will be shorter ones." He looked at Rainey. "Come on; let's get this thing in the air."

Natalie stood behind Rainey. He turned and said, "Are you going with us?"

"Not this trip. I have to work, and whatever it is you're doing obviously has to be done alone. Besides, Amy's not much of a talker and I talk too much. I might be wearing her out. Go figure, me talking too much." She looked at Amy and then back at Rainey. "Take care of her. I can't wait to hear this story, and while you're at it, take care of him, too, he looks up to you." Moving into the cockpit, she whispered to Creston and then was out the door, walking toward his car.

Rainey was anxious and jittery as they took off. Let's get through this with no accidents and then we're home free, he thought. He exhaled strongly as Creston banked east.

"One more thing," Rainey said into the headset, "we don't have to fly into the Bermuda Triangle, do we?"

Creston shook his head. "No, we don't have to fly over the triangle, but if you feel like pushing our luck we can divert the plane a little and clip the edge before heading to the Bahamas."

"We've been diverted enough. Maybe next time." Rainey got up, walked back to Amy and sat next to her.

"Am I going to die?"

Caught off guard with her question he took Amy's hand. "No, you are not going to die." He studied her eyes and said, "Why would you think you're going to die?"

"Mommy and daddy died. They went away." She stopped, searching for words. "We go away."

Rainey was chilled with Amy's words. Of course she didn't understand, not after a lifetime of seclusion.

"Amy, you're going to another island. It has a real house and a lady to help you. She'll take care of you like your mother used to. And Creston and I will come visit you often." Her English had been getting better, but Rainey knew he sometimes spoke too fast, or with incomplete thoughts. Amy was literal. Anything inferred and not completely spoken was not understood by Amy.

"I hope we've not bitten off more than we can chew," Rainey said after settling back into the co-pilot seat. I'm having second thoughts about what we're doing."

"About what we're doing or how we're doing it?" Creston asked.

"I think she needs more help than we thought."

"If you've taught me anything, you've taught me the power of prayer, so don't quit praying. We'll get her settled in and make sure she has what she needs. We'll fly in a therapist to help Jean Smith," Creston said. "So stop worrying already."

Creston lined up for a landing at Lynden Pindling International Airport on Grand Bahamas Island and started the descent over the multi-hued, blue and green waters of the Caribbean. Rainey was struck by the similarity of the Bahamian waters to the waters of Amy's island.

Creston had picked the Bahamas because it was close to the mainland of the United States, and clearing customs was never as difficult as some of the other islands. There were no expected "tips" required by the officials. The Bahamian people were friendly and appreciated the American tourist. He was confident they wouldn't encounter any problems.

Creston, directed by the ground crew, taxied to the designated spot on the tarmac. Rainey sat with Amy, unbuckled her seat belt and then held her hand while waiting for Creston to exit in front of them. Amy looked out the window and Rainey hoped she understood she was close to home.

It was late morning as they stepped from the plane. The sky was clear except for a few scattered clouds. A breeze waltzed across the island.

In thirty minutes they had taken their luggage and cleared customs, pleased the agents were so friendly, and grateful there were no lengthy questions. A small seaplane waited to fly them to the remote island several hundred miles from Grand Bahama. Creston looked out of place as a passenger but quietly settled into his seat and waited; exhibiting the patience he had learned on the island.

The water landing was as smooth as in the Albatross. Rainey was starting to like seaplanes even if they were slow. It was much more relaxed, and water landings made it worth the extra time.

The pilot guided the seaplane to the dock, and in ten minutes Rainey had the plane secured to the davits and safe for disembarking. Creston and the pilot got out but Amy made no movement to leave the plane. She looked at Rainey, and he realized she wasn't moving until he helped her. He offered his hand and Amy grasped it tighter than usual, giving him a sense she knew she was somewhere special, somewhere she would remain for a while. Rainey sensed maybe she was starting to understand. He clasped her hand and led her down the board walk. It ended at a path in the sand which would take them to the house nestled amongst the Caribbean pine trees, bushes of Yellow Elder, sea oats, and several different palms.

The house was a two story island home made of pinkish, almost white coquina shell and coral sand with a roof of blue shingles. Bahamian shutters painted bright blue were open above the windows, but were easily dropped to protect the windows should a fierce storm or hurricane approach.

"It's thirty five hundred square feet inside with two thousand square feet of screened verandah on both sides and the back of the house," Creston said. "Has four bedrooms, three baths, a full kitchen, pool, Jacuzzi, and it's totally self contained. Fresh water and electricity of course. It used to belong to a big investment banker out of New York, but he made one bad investment too many. A real estate management company handles it. They've tried selling it several times but ten million is a little too steep, so they rent it." Creston looked at Rainey. "Don't ask but if I decide to buy the island I can use some of the rent as a partial payment. We have to see how this is going to work out first. I have the money even though this was never on my list of things to buy before I die. Maybe it should have been, but we'll take it a month at a time." Creston opened the front door.

Rainey was speechless as he stepped inside and viewed the great room. It was sunk almost two feet. He walked down three steps to the floor and moved to the center of the room. The others followed and looked around. The walls were paneled in a light colored wood and the ceiling matched the walls. Four ceiling fans turned slow enough to see each blade but still move the cool air of a central air conditioning system. The dining room was adjacent to the kitchen and the bedrooms were down a hall, one side of which was a wall of glass with a view over the pool and hot tub. Beyond the pool a path had been cut through fifty feet of sea oats, Cascarilla shrubs, Yellow Elder, and small palms, all wafting in the gentle Caribbean breeze. Clear, shallow water lapped at the white sand beach but turned turquoise farther out, and then became the deep, azure Caribbean.

Rainey looked at Creston. "Ten million looks like a bargain."

"It might be a bargain, but I can get it for less. You have to have a reason to be here, or more money than God, to pay that much for a few weeks a year. We have a reason so I'm still negotiating with the realtor and waiting to see what else comes up. I'm keeping my options open."

"So this is our special lady I heard about."

Rainey recognized Mama Mary's voice and turned. Her presence relieved him and he was a step closer to keeping his promise. Amy stood her ground as Mama Mary approached. Rainey knew it would take her best effort to win Amy's trust.

Mary took Amy's hands and Amy didn't resist. She dropped her eyes to the joined hands, curious at the contrast in skin color.

"My goodness child, you got some catchin up to do," Mama Mary said.

Rainey moved closer and took Amy by the arm, careful not to break apart the hands of the two women. "Amy, this is Mama Mary. She is going to take care of you for a while. She will help you get used to the island and the new home."

Mary remained looking into Amy's eyes but spoke to Rainey. "Well, you're not exactly correct."

"What's not correct? Creston said he arranged for you to take care of her."

"We talked about it some, and I thought about it real hard. But it juss never felt like it shoulda felt. So I figured out someone else instead of me."

"I'm going to stay with her."

Rainey and Creston both turned as Rainey's mother entered from the rear bedroom. "I was in the back getting her bedroom ready." Rainey stared as his mother approached.

"Florida, huh? How many times did I tell you not to lie to your mother?"

"Mom, what are you doing here? I thought you were in Biloxi with your friends. Why didn't you tell Leslie where you were? And what about New Orleans? You love New Orleans. Why would you be here?"

"It was Mary's idea. She explained what had to be done. I listened, and the more I heard the more excited I became. It gave me a purpose. I was needed, and then I knew it was right. Amy needs patience and understanding, someone to take care of her. None of us has been told the whole story, but I heard enough to realize she needs someone, and I feel it should be me. Mary agrees. And I'm sure Amy is practically a sister so it even makes more sense."

"She's right. This ain't for me," Mama Mary said. "But I think it is right for Joan. I need to get back to New Orleans where I'm supposed to be. But I'm sure I'll be back. And you two will be back often."

"I'll probably see more of you here than I did at home," Joan said pointing at Rainey.

Rainey collapsed onto a large sofa, his head falling back and his eyes staring at the rotating blades of the ceiling fans. His mind raced, processing the last few minutes. The plan he and Creston had crafted was already dramatically changed. He sat up, looked out the wall of glass, and was calmed by the view of the Caribbean.

"One thing's for sure; if my mother's taking care of Amy then she'll be fine."

"Let's all get settled in and then start preparing dinner," Creston said. "Rainey and I made sure there was plenty of food in the house. The seaplane is coming back in two days so we have enough time to get settled and explain how we got here. Mama, you can come back with us." Creston turned. "Miss Joan, I think the master bedroom is where Amy should be, but don't be surprised if she sleeps on the floor."

"Mary and I have already started in there trying to give it a woman's touch. I'll be in the bedroom next to her. This will work out fine. And we've already fixed dinner, one of Rainey's favorites." Joan looked at her son. "Lower Coast Chicken," she teased.

"I thought my nose was playing tricks on me," Rainey said. He had grown up eating the chicken cooked with bell peppers, onion, celery, and garlic. It was fixed in a pot on the stove, made with rich, savory gravy and served over rice. Joan had gotten the recipe from a cousin who grew up on the west bank of the Mississippi River in an area known as Lower Coast Algiers, a suburb of New Orleans.

Rainey walked into the kitchen and a rich fragrance of seasonings and chicken stimulated his sense of smell and made his mouth water.

The view from the circular table in the dining room was vast and non ending, as if another dimension lay off in the distance. Amy sat quietly between Joan and Rainey as they all ate and talked. Rainey had given thanks for the food, and thanks for their successful trip.

Creston, usually quiet during a prayer, added his thanks and a distinct amen.

The meal was savored more for the gathering of friends than the food. Rainey enjoyed it more than his first meal after being rescued near Kwajalein. Amy used her fingers to pick at the chicken, like she had with the first fish she brought to Rainey and Creston. She was relaxed, but remained silent.

Rainey and Creston finished their meal, excused themselves from the table and went outside to the pool. The descending sun accelerated as it neared the horizon and Rainey flashed back to Amy's island and the similar sunsets he had watched. Soon this island would be in darkness. A day at a time had meaning to him as never before. Tomorrow's new opportunities excited him.

"Tell me where you keep going," Creston said gazing out at the multi-hued water.

"We've done the right thing, but I think it's man's nature to question his actions, his motives, to make sure he hasn't made a mistake. I'm questioning myself." Rainey turned toward Creston and said, "You've never said anything about the cost of all this. It must be a small fortune."

"Yes, but I've learned from you life is not ruled by money. But it helps to be rich." Creston shook his head. "I guess I sounded a little snobbish, but I've been worse many times."

"Don't compliment yourself," Rainey said. "Where do we go from here? With all the secrecy this is a little anti-climactic."

"There's much to do but not here. When we get back to New Orleans, you'll see."

They turned when they heard the sliding glass door open. Mama Mary walked up to them. "Just as I thought," she said. "You two ain't never gonna change. But you," she said looking at Rainey, "you better hurry up or he's gonna have a baby before you."

"What baby," Creston exclaimed. "You don't see a baby for either one of us. Hell, we aren't even married…"

"Didn't stop him," she said. "Or didn't he tell you."

"Wait a minute!" Rainey looked at Mama. "He doesn't know about the miscarriage, but even if he did, he's right, we aren't married."

"Miscarriage, what miscarriage?"

Rainey looked at Mama. "What are you trying to tell us?"

"You two needs to settle down, and I don't need to see nothin to know what I know. And, since you two don't plan on settlin down, I think you need to at least get married so y'all will slow down."

"And I suppose you see this in the stars or whatever," Creston said sounding more sarcastic than intended.

"You two is good men. I don't have to see it for it to be true."

"Hey, wait a minute," Rainey said. You always see so much but what about the map I showed you. I asked you where would you start and you got this look on your face and then pointed to a square on the map. But it wasn't the right spot. It wasn't even close."

"So?" she said.

"So! So how do you explain it?"

"You asked me where I would start so I picked a square on the map. It was as good a spot as any. And you wouldn't a been happy if I'd refused."

"You didn't see anything?" Rainey asked.

"I seen you finishing what you had to do and comin home." She looked at Rainey. "Nothin else mattered includin where I put my *finger*."

Rainey walked up to Mama Mary and hugged her. Through the glass door he watched his mother sitting with Amy, talking while holding her hand. There was still much to do but for now all was perfect.

CHAPTER FIFTY

The last evening together had been wrapped around a comfortable meal of seafood gumbo prepared by Mama Mary. It was her family recipe and Rainey savored it as if it had come from Brother Lee's restaurant in the French Quarter. Rainey and Creston told their story of finding Amy, how she lived, and how long they thought she had been alone. They included the connection to World War II, and the part they believed the Japanese had played in Amy's existence. They said Amy was born after the Japanese had abandoned the island, but intentionally left out who her parents were. Following dinner Rainey talked privately with his mother in her bedroom.

"There's a journal in the bottom drawer of the dresser. Don't read it until we're gone. You'll be amazed, I can promise you. But you must never tell anyone what you've read. No one else has read it. All of us must keep it secret, at least until we've had time to think this through."

"Rainey, I'm sure you haven't intentionally done anything wrong. I don't understand all this secrecy, but if it's what you want, then I trust you."

"You've been there for me so many times and here you are again, taking care of me," Rainey said.

Amy and Joan had settled in and a bond was forming. Rainey checked for the third time to make sure he was not leaving anything behind. By the third time he realized he wasn't looking for anything. He was nervous about leaving, and feeling the urge to stay.

The seaplane had arrived with provisions Creston had ordered. They had been unloaded and stored in the house. There was food enough to last at least a month and maybe a week more. They all gathered on the dock, hesitating to board the plane, delaying the departure. The pilot waited patiently.

"Amy," Rainey said, "we have to leave. My mom will stay with you, and Creston and I will be back soon."

"Amy is…I am sad."

"It's ok to be sad, honey," Mama Mary said. "The most important thing in life is family, but when family leaves it can make you sad. All of us here is your family. Miss Joan will stay with you until we come back. And when we come back, you'll come a runnin down this here dock to meet us, and you won't be sad."

"Miss Joan, I have something else to leave with you," Creston said. He reached into his grip and pulled out a black bag slightly larger than a lunch sack. "This is a satellite phone. You can make a call from here to anywhere in the world. There's a manual in the bag and it explains how to make calls, charge the batteries and most everything you need to use the phone." He handed her a piece of paper. "These are phone numbers to get in touch with us including the numbers to our mobile phones, mine and Rainey's. If you need anything you call one of us. We'll make sure you get it as soon as possible. I have an agreement with the owner of the seaplane. He'll bring you whatever it is you need. His number is on the paper, too, and you can call him direct."

Joan held on to Rainey's hand and watched as the others walked to the seaplane, not ready for him to leave. She needed another minute alone with him. Rainey smiled at his mother as they embraced.

"We're not supposed to come back for a couple of months, but I don't think Creston will last that long. We'll be back in a few weeks." He bowed his head. "I'm a little embarrassed I didn't think of you first to help Amy. You're perfect for her, and she needs you. I should have seen this, but I was so caught up I missed the obvious."

Joan placed her hand on Rainey's cheek. "Quit worrying about everybody else and start taking care of yourself. I'll be fine here with Amy and she's what matters the most. Get on the plane. You have unfinished business in New Orleans."

Rainey kissed his mother on her cheek like he had all his life, reached for Amy and kissed her on the cheek. "Read the journal tonight," he yelled over his shoulder as he walked down the dock to the seaplane.

The jet landed at the lakefront airport with an hour of daylight remaining. Rainey helped Mama Mary down the steps to the ground. A huge burden had been lifted from his shoulders and dissolved like sugar in hot tea, gone completely. Occasionally a feeling of euphoria would grasp him, and Rainey savored the feeling, as if he was walking with God.

Big O was waiting at the airport with a large van. They would all go to dinner at Sal's in Buck Town, an area of New Orleans on Lake Pontchartrain dating back before the turn of the century. They would eat boiled crabs, shrimp and crawfish and drink cold beer.

The van was parked outside the fence which protected the flight line service company from spectators who came out to watch the private planes take off and land, hopeful of catching a glimpse of a celebrity. Rainey walked through the gate where Leslie and Natalie were waiting. Because he had remained distant so many times Rainey expected Leslie to reject him. He approached her, pulled her close and kissed her lips.

The others watched, surprised as much as Leslie. Rainey held the embrace for a minute, released Leslie but held onto her hand. Mama Mary had taken the front seat with Big O, Creston and Natalie were seated in the rear leaving the middle for Rainey and Leslie. Big O drove the van over the Seabrook Bridge and into the setting sun as they headed toward Buck Town. Rainey's phone rang.

"Mom, is everything all right?" He looked at Creston and shrugged, wondering why his mother would be calling so soon. It had been six hours since they had left the island. He held the phone up with the speaker on for the others to hear.

"Rainey, you knew who her mother was and you didn't tell me? Do you have any idea how important this is?"

"Mom, calm down, and yes, Creston and I realize how important it is. But it's not more important than Amy. She's the reason we went back. Not because of who her mother was. Besides us, no one else knows, at least not yet. And it needs to stay quiet until we think it through."

"Well, you certainly could have told me. What are you going to do about this? I mean, people will want to know. Not to mention making you two famous, maybe get on TV, and no telling what else."

"Mom, this is not about us, and we don't want to be famous. Think about it for a minute. What do you think will happen to Amy if the world finds out? It wouldn't be fair to her. The world would destroy her, and she's been through enough."

There was silence for a few seconds. "How did you get so wise? You're not old enough to be this wise."

"So true," Creston added.

"Mom, if we're lucky we learn as we go. You'll take care of her and teach her the things she needs to know. When she's ready, Amy can make the decision to tell the world or not. There's no hurry. We are NOT playing Russian roulette with her life."

Leslie and Natalie were confused but did not ask any questions. Mama Mary sat with a smile on her face, proud of Rainey and Creston.

"Mom, say goodbye. I'll see you soon. Take care of Amy, and one more thing, see if you can get her to start talking.

"I'll get her talking. Getting her to stop will be the challenge," Joan said. "Goodbye, y'all come see us soon."

"We'll explain all of this to you tonight, after dinner, but we're all sworn to secrecy. No exceptions," Rainey said.

CHAPTER FIFTY ONE

Rainey stayed with Leslie and shared her bed. They lay together and Rainey remembered back to their first night. This night was better. They knew each other so Rainey dropped his guard and melded with Leslie, consumed in passion pure and honest. He had longed for this and Leslie gave back as much as she received. Each kiss was an exchange of souls, and with each touch a memory sourced through them. She did not disappoint him, nor he, her.

Over coffee and day-old croissants as buttery and fresh as if they had come straight from the oven Rainey told Leslie the whole truth. He talked for several hours and the story of Amy was revealed.

"I think if it was anyone else but you I wouldn't believe any of this."

"I worry if we've done the right thing, keeping Amy hidden," Rainey said.

"You can always introduce her to the world, but once you do there is no going back. After listening to the story I think it's best to wait."

"My mom will be great with her, but it's not enough. Creston's checking with several therapists. He'll talk with them and make a choice as to who he thinks will be the best for Amy."

"You've done a remarkably good thing." She took his hand, pulled him back into the bedroom and made love to him one more time.

"Rainey, I don't want to lose you again. I made a mistake, and I've told you this before. But I can't be convenient until you decide what you want. It's presumptuous of me, but I needed to tell you."

"Leslie, we were married in the church. You know how important it was for me. Our divorce was a civil matter. I never considered an annulment." Rainey stared at Leslie. "In the eyes of the church we're still married, which is more important to me than anything else."

"Rainey, are you sure? I need you to be sure."

"Leslie, there was a void in me when you left. I want to be whole again, and that can only happen with you."

CHAPTER FIFTY TWO

It had been three months since Rainey and Creston had brought Amy to the Bahamas. There had been several trips back bringing supplies and items Joan needed to help with Amy's progress. Creston had made two trips with Dr. Bill Naquin for him to observe Amy while pretending to be on a fishing trip. Dr. Naquin concluded the therapy would start later, and declared Amy to be in good hands.

Rainey sat with Amy and his mom in the great room. It was mid-morning and they sipped mint flavored iced tea as the ceiling fans turned.

"I want to thank you for all you and Creston have done," Amy said. "Mom has taught me so much. She sat with me, never leaving, helped me with my speaking, got me reading again." She looked at Joan. "She helped me read the journal. We cried together."

Rainey fought his own emotions as he listened to Amy. "I need to thank you, too. If it wasn't for you, well Creston and I might not have survived. You brought us fish and showed us how to live on the island. You gave us hope and the courage to leave. We might still be there if it weren't for you."

Amy squeezed Rainey's hands. "Why are you by yourself?" she said releasing his hands. "Where is Creston?"

"He's back on Grand Bahama Island. Come on," he said, "get your things. We're taking the seaplane back to Grand Bahama for the day. We'll do some shopping; eat at a nice restaurant, like the one in Hawaii. Maybe even have the crème brulee. We'll make a day of it. Leslie and Natalie are with him and they want to spend some *girl time* with you. They see you as their big sister. I hope you can handle the attention. Mom, you can spend the afternoon at the spa, or whatever you want. You've earned it."

June in New Orleans can be overbearing with humidity and temperatures both in the nineties. But it can also be mild. This June day was the latter. Café du Monde was quiet, but most early morning Sundays in the French Quarter were. Rainey sat at a table in the far corner of the patio closest to Decatur Street, his back toward a concrete wall preventing a view of the Mississippi river. He sipped café au lait and watched Jackson Square. Creston walked through the open gates of the large wrought-iron fence surrounding the square and crossed Decatur Street at the light. He entered the patio through the black-iron fence surrounding the outside serving area of the café. Creston pulled a chair out, brushed powdered sugar from the black, vinyl covered seat and placed a box on the small table as he sat.

"What's in the box?" Rainey asked.

"Open it and see."

Rainey picked up the box and opened it. Inside was the compass Big O had given Creston. He looked up.

"Dr. Banyan sent it to me. When the first mate pulled us from our raft he took it from my hand and put it in his pocket. I guess he forgot about it, and by the time he realized he still had the compass we'd already left the island. He included a nice note wishing us well." Creston turned and looked toward the Mississippi River. "I was thinking…"

"Stop! I've seen that look before," Rainey said. "I don't have another adventure in me. I'm back with Leslie. Dr. Bill said Amy will be ready to move to New Orleans soon." Rainey looked sternly at Creston. "It's time we grew up."

Creston returned Rainey's stare. "Bullshit!"

They stared at each other until Creston broke the silence. "As I said, I've been thinking…maybe we should go find Elvis."

"You are such a pain in the ass."

Rainey shook his head, wondering what Creston had in mind this time.

THE END

From the Author

I lived on Kwajalein in the Marshall Islands from December, 1961 until May, 1964. In 1963, at the age of 13, I took a class field trip, by plane, to the island of Roi-Namur which was two islands, Roi and Namur. The small islands had been joined together with a short roadway built by the navy construction battalion. The plane ride took about thirty minutes. We spent the day exploring the island, visiting the World War II Japanese bunkers, and experiencing history. Our guide took us to a specific location on Namur and instructed us to enter by stepping down, cautioning us to watch our heads. The area was dark, damp and musky. We had been taken to the "underground Japanese hospital". It was overgrown with island flora and virtually untouched since the war. In a corner of the space was an old bed frame, rusted from years of exposure. A cabinet was against a wall and inside the drawer was a piece of X-RAY film. It had a profound affect on me.

This is a complete work of fiction. Many of the places are real, some are not. There are historical facts I have respectfully taken liberties with. For example, Fred Noonan did move to New Orleans as a seaman, but he did not live next door to Rainey's mother.

I cannot explain how, forty plus years later, I wove this story around the memory of a field trip but I am forever grateful.

Copy and paste into your browser:

http://www.flickr.com/photos/movementarian/401927601/

As of April, 2014 the above picture was still on the web. I recommend an internet search of Japanese bunkers in the Pacific for the history buff.

ABOUT THE AUTHOR

Houston Neal Gray was born on Coronado Island in San Diego, California. The product of a career navy family he has lived on the west coast, east coast, north, south, and an island in the Pacific (Kwajalein, Marshall Islands). New Orleans is where he has spent the majority of his life and considers it home. The passion, food, and people of New Orleans inspire him and he can't imagine ever leaving. He and his wife, Jo Ann, live in a house that looks out over  the Mississippi River that offers great sunrises and equally great wine moment moonrises.